# Custodial Rites

## A Novel by Larry Carr

Barkwood Press Paperback Edition, 2014

# Also By Larry Carr

In the Den

Apotheosis

Endure

# Chapter One

The gun tasted like a handful of nickels in his mouth: hard, metallic, foreign.

He pulled it out and pointed it at the side of his head, pressing the barrel to his temple, wrinkling the skin around it. Then he placed it under his chin, jamming it up into the soft underbelly of his jawline. Finally, he grasped it with both hands and held the barrel against his chest; the bullet would only need to shatter his fragile breastbone before it exploded his broken heart, the source of his pain, for good.

He didn't know which way was best, and decided it didn't matter. So long as it worked, and he'd heard that a .357 Magnum, which was the gun he'd bought nine days ago from the Arms & Ammo Hut in Boonsboro, could put a bullet through an engine block. He didn't know if that was true or not, but the guy who'd sold it to him had assured him that it was one of the most powerful handguns ever made. The guy actually had tried to talk him into purchasing something smaller, less violent, easier to control, like a Berretta or a Les Baer 9mm, but Marty had insisted on the Magnum.

It was heavy, and he knew from reading about it on the Internet that it possessed a violent kick when fired. He figured that putting the barrel in his mouth was probably the safest bet. At least that's what it had said on the Internet. There were all sorts of interesting tips on there for suicide, such as: if you planned on slitting your wrists, the proper way to do it was not across the arm but long ways, straight up the length of the vein. That would bleed you out a lot more quickly and effectively.

But Marty didn't want to slit his wrists; the sight of blood made him ill. More than that, he wanted it to be over with as quickly as possible, a snap decision to end a lifetime gone too far. He didn't want to wait minutes to bleed out, or swallow a bunch of pills and gently slip into a strange dark void. He didn't want to leap off a bridge or out a twenty-story window, either; regret cropped up too fast, and he couldn't imagine having second thoughts while the end rushed on him.

A gun was the most definitive way to do it. It was brutal and unforgiving, the eradication of your very state of being, and Marty had come to hate himself to the point that only the most violent of deaths would satisfy him. Taking pills and drifting off to a never-ending slumber? That wasn't death. That was a high gone too far.

Marty was here, cloistered in the chaotic, disheveled isolation of his apartment, drunk on red wine and toying with a gun, preparing to fire it only once, because life had become too much for him to handle. He could no longer go to bed another night knowing that in the morning he would wake up and still be himself.

He hated himself because he was small, because he was weak, because he was an ineffectual piss ant with nothing to offer. He hated himself because he was a failure, because he was a joke, because he was alone.

He put the gun down at his side and reached for the nearly-empty bottle of wine he'd been chugging like a homeless louse. He lifted it to his lips and gulped a couple more mouthfuls, adding to his despair and delirium. He set the bottle back down, grabbed the gun again. There was nothing more to do.

He'd written a note to memorialize the occasion, a rather cryptic one line that read: ***Nothing left but this.*** It was a second draft. The first draft had been much longer, going into painstaking detail, listing reasons and opinions, attempting to explain and justify his decision. But he concluded that no one wants to hear a bit player drone on at the end of his cameo, and he ripped that copy to shreds. The second copy, the short and sweet one, was on the nightstand, signed in his scratchy, drunken hand. Next to it was a letter specifying his wishes for burial and his estate.

He had masturbated, twice, figuring he should enjoy one last pathetic go around with himself before he tolled the bell. He had thought about getting a prostitute, a sassy redhead or pert brunette who would gladly do whatever he wanted, but he had no clue how to go about something like that. So instead he jacked-off to a porn film that Mandy had bought for them, along with a variety of toys and novelties in an effort to spice up their routine. That should have been his first hint.

The porn video was still in the DVD player. He thought about removing it for the sake of decorum, but ultimately decided against it, figuring it made no difference. As far as he was concerned, the more pitiful and wretched he looked the better. A collection of shameful adult videos and magazines, the small skyline of empty Valium and Vicodin bottles on his dresser, the messy house, with booze bottles in the trash, beer cans scattered about, dirty dishes in the sink and clothes on the floor ... and his dead body, just lying there, stinking, decomposing, the back of his head split open, dried clumps of blood caked on the carpet and smeared on the wall – that was the scene he wanted them to find.

That was how he wanted the world to remember him.

He put the gun back in his mouth and pressed the barrel to the roof. Then he pulled it out and pressed it firm against his chest. After all, it was his heart that ached. It was his heart that had him here, at the end of things.

In his last thoughts, he wondered what the people in his life might think when they heard the news. His father had never been around much, and Marty had to think he'd shed only a few tears, if that. He had moved on long ago, after leaving Marty and Marty's mom behind to be with another woman, whom he had another family with. He lived in northern Michigan now, on the Upper Peninsula.

His mother had died of pancreatic cancer four years ago, and Marty missed her dearly. There was no way he would've even considered something like this if she was still alive. But she wasn't. He had watched her suffer for nine months, wasting away to nothing, skin and bones and barely a mind. She was the only person who had ever loved him, and now that she was gone, he felt utterly alone.

He had no siblings, just a smattering of uncles, aunts, and cousins that he didn't even consider family. After his mother's death, Marty had had very little contact with them; truthfully, he would have had trouble picking most of them out of a lineup.

His aunts and uncles and cousins would show up to pay their last respects, he believed, along with a few of his friends, and they would stand around talking with each other, exchanging pleasantries, making idle chitchat with a dead body in the room.

Funerals are such a morbid scene, thought Marty, more than ready to catalyze one. Morbid and perfectly honestly.

Everyone dies alone.

He thought about some of his friends and what they would say. Really, he only had one true friend, Charlie, and Marty couldn't help but feel a twinge of guilt when he thought about how this might affect him. Charlie was a gentle soul who undoubtedly would have a hard time accepting such an act.

Ha! An act! Marty had to laugh at the idea.

This was certainly no act.

Finally, he thought about Mandy. She had betrayed him in the most callous manner, then had coldheartedly cut him out of her life as if he was the one who'd done something wrong. He tried to remember the good times, but seeing how things had ended, Marty had no choice but to reconsider the merit of those good times, believing that of the two of them, only he was happy. Given what had happened, he had to think that Mandy had been faking it all along, simply putting up with him, biding her time until she met someone else, someone better. It was hard to remember her as anything but a liar and a slut, and Marty hated himself all the more for loving her.

He decided, somberly, that that should be his final thought in this world: Mandy and love gone wrong.

And he pulled the trigger.


Around the same time, across town:

It had been a long night for Ally and all she wanted to do was go home, take a hot shower, climb under the covers, and go to sleep. The hot shower was a necessity given her morally unsanitary line of work. She trolled the bar at a place called Teasers, a mid-level strip joint outside Hagerstown, Maryland, and though she refused to work the stage, the ridiculously skimpy outfit that bartenders were required to wear – booty shorts so short and tight she might as well have been wearing underwear and a lacy halter top that did more to show her breasts than conceal them – subjected her to the same moist, glassy-eyed stares and none-too-subtle comments that the dancers received.

She had promised herself that she would quit at least twenty times, usually after there was a fight or altercation of some kind. She was nearly hit with a rocks glass a couple weeks ago when a skinny punk fired his bourbon and coke at a former high-school jock that kept making snide comments. The glass had whizzed past Ally's ear, hitting the wall just behind her, spraying her with ice and tiny shards of glass.

Dado and Chauncey, Teasers' crack security staff, two men large enough to carry a small car up a flight of stairs, escorted the skinny punk and the belligerent washed-up jock from the club in a casually brutal manner that had become all too common to Ally.

But it wasn't violence that had Ally thinking about quitting yet again as she made the five-mile drive home at three-fifteen in the morning, past all the darkened houses and desolate storefronts that populated downtown Hagerstown at this hour. It was that one drunkard, that one slobbering, slurring, greedy-eyed fool, and even though his face changed from night to night – he could be old or young, white or black, harmless or shameless – the message was always the same. Tonight it had been Carl Something, a sad sack semi-regular who always started his night at the stage but invariably ended up at the bar, nursing beers and trying to engage Ally with witty and charming banter that usually was neither witty nor charming. Carl had asked her, in his desperate, drunken state, as he had a few times before, why she never got up there and danced, telling her, muttering lasciviously, that she had the body for it; in fact, she was the prettiest damn girl in the whole place, and if she got on stage and took it all off, she'd be sure to make buckets of money. Why he himself would gladly pay the hundred dollar fee for a twenty minute soiree with her beyond the velvet ropes. He said this as if it was some sort of incentive, as if Ally might right then and there start peeling off what little clothes she had on.

As usual, she beat back her thoughts, bit down on what she

wanted to say, and forced a winsome smile, her facial muscles setting naturally. And she told him, just like she told all the others, "Thank you, but dancing isn't my thing." Then, before he could go on, before he could make another inappropriate pitch, she politely excused herself, saying she had to check something at the register.

Being courted to go on stage was nothing new to Ally; she possessed a distinct cuteness that was as impossible to ignore as an air raid siren in a phone booth. Her mother was full-blooded Colombian, a beautiful woman herself, while her father was bi-racial, of Caucasian, specifically French, and African American descent. The mix was a bit unorthodox, but the end result was a thing of beauty. Ally had flawless light brown skin, the biggest, darkest brown eyes you could imagine, and a sweet, wholesome, angelic face framed by a wild, frenzied mess of crow-black hair.

She was a small girl, standing five-foot-three and tipping the scales at a hundred and ten pounds. But she possessed all the curves a woman's supposed to have, even if hers were a little less ample in certain areas. Up until a couple months ago, she practiced yoga, took two spin classes at the local YMCA, and swam a hundred laps three times a week. Though recently she had abandoned her once rigorous workout regimen – all the parties and late nights robbing her of her desire to hit the gym and stay in shape – she was still young enough and active enough to hold onto her figure. In fact, it was probably easier to find a needle in a haystack than an ounce of fat on her sylphlike frame. She attributed this to good genes and a high metabolism, though the nervous energy she expended spinning circles on the nose candy certainly helped.

Taking everything into account – her body, her grace and flexibility, her boundless energy, her sweet, girl-next-door face, with that cute, charming smile of hers – it was no wonder everyone wanted to see her on stage. She'd been asked, cajoled, even bribed to flaunt her exceedingly attractive wares since day one, by Dado and Chauncey, by Albert Holt, Teasers' disreputable owner, by the other dancers, and, most recurrently, by the customers, the majority of whom couldn't help but imagine what she looked like naked, seeing how good she looked scantily clad.

But Ally refused to strip in front of a group of drunk, slavering men, all of them shouting and laughing, eagerly waving dollar bills like wicked little kids waving sparklers on the Fourth of July. Not that it was much of a stretch from what she was doing now, which she justified by telling herself that her outfit, while unquestionably prurient, actually left more to the imagination than the average bikini. Plus – and this was a major issue – dancers were not just encouraged but expected to push the bounds of decency in the private rooms, exchanging sexual pleasures for cash. They also were often asked to give special performances downstairs, where their escapades were taped and posted on one of Holt's many adult websites. Ally was not about to agree to those terms. She was hardly a saint, but she wasn't a prostitute.

There were lines.

She put on her turn signal and pulled into the A&P Mart, the last twenty-four hour convenience store on her way home. She needed cereal and milk, and she wanted her favorite oatmeal raison cookies and, despite recent revelations, cigarettes.

Like her job, Ally knew she needed to quit smoking, too. She'd had only two so far tonight, and had planned on bumming a few from one of the dancers so she wouldn't have to stop and buy a pack for herself. But she'd forgotten to do that. She knew she shouldn't give in to her craving, but she also knew that she'd want one whenever she got home. After a long night at the bar, dealing with all the juvenile bullshit and drama, it normally took her an hour or so, a couple cigarettes and a couple glasses of wine, to wind down.

Eddie, an amiable thirty-something, corpulent and baby-cheeked, with soft hanging jowls and a swiftly receding hairline, was manning the counter as usual. He was the midnight guy at the out-of-the-way convenience mart, which Ally couldn't believe remained open all night seeing how she rarely ever saw anyone else in there. Not that she was going to complain; it was only two blocks from her house, and she stopped there all the time, so much so that she and Eddie had become casual friends.

"There she is," Eddie said when she walked in. "My favorite customer."

"Yeah, yeah, yeah," replied Ally. "I'm your only customer."

"The only one I've had in the last hour. And definitely the best looking."

Ally smiled politely and said, "Why thank you." Then she grabbed a basket from the stack and ventured into the first aisle.

"Just getting off work?" Eddie asked her as she opened one of the many coolers that stretched along the far wall.

"You know it." She reached in for a quart of milk. "On my way home."

"Can I assume it was another exciting night at Hagerstown's premiere gentleman's club?"

"The usual. Naked girls, perverts, and horny drunks."

"Hey. Careful now. I happen to be a perverted horny drunk myself," Eddie told her in a playful, self-mocking way.

"All men are," said Ally. "I wouldn't know what to do with one who wasn't."

"True. True. But don't try and pretend you women are any better. You're just as bad as we are. You're just more ... clever and delicate about it."

Ally laughed. "Yeah, you're right," she admitted, talking loud enough for her voice to carry the length of the store. It didn't matter, they were the only two people there. She found her cookies and put two packs in her basket, then moved down to the cereal. "But it's more attractive on us."

"No doubt there," Eddie agreed. "Speaking of attractive, how come you never wear your uniform in here."

Ally poked her head around the corner and gave him a look. "That's for the club only," she told him. "No free shows."

As soon as her shift ended and the last patron was ushered out, Ally went in back and changed into jeans and either a sweatshirt or t-shirt, depending on the weather. She never walked around in the flimsy little number she was required to wear behind the bar. Never.

"Foiled again," said Eddie, snapping his fingers theatrically. "I have no manner of luck. You know, I'm going to have to come to that club of yours some time and see you work." He always said that, but never followed through.

"Trust me, with all the stark naked women there, strutting

around and pushing their boobs in your face, you wouldn't even notice me."

"No chance. You're the bartender, and I love my beer."

"Even more than naked women?"

"Depends. Naked women I actually have a shot to sleep with? No. Naked women who are only interested in stealing my money? Well ... no."

Ally laughed again. "Right," she said. "Just what I thought." She grabbed a box of Honey Nut Cheerios and a package of strawberry Pop Tarts, an impulse buy, and made her way up front.

She began taking items out of the basket and setting on them on the counter, and Eddie began swiping them over the scanner, the register beeping and flashing the prices on the screen.

Ally said, "Oh, give me a pack of Marlboro Lights, too," as she opened her purse. She pulled out her wallet, which was fat with creased and crinkled bills of all denominations, fingered through it until she found a twenty, and waited for a total.

"That'll be nineteen-eighty-nine," said Eddie.

"Get out. That's the year I was born."

"Really? Well, there's a sign. Maybe it's gonna be your lucky day."

"You never know," said Ally, hoping he was right. She could use a little luck. She handed him the twenty and put her wallet away.

A half second later, luck burst through the door.

Unfortunately, it was the bad kind.

His name was Adam Dubinsky, and he was as far down on his luck as one could get before going six feet under. Drugs, mostly crack cocaine and oxycodone, had turned his once average but functioning brain into a sopping mash of tapioca pudding that had neither the ability nor the desire to apply thought to anything other than the procurement of his next high. It had been three days since he'd seen his dealer, a man called Bobbo, and his cravings had become unmanageable. Bobbo had shut off Adam's line of credit at two hundred dollars and told him that he would not, under any circumstances, sell him another pill or rock unless he received cash in exchange.

A trip to his parents' home had proven fruitless; they had changed the locks about six months ago, having had enough of their sweet son robbing them blind while they were at work or out with friends. He had an addiction, and they begged him to get help, pleaded with him to go to rehab, but he always declined. He'd been crashing with friends and living on the streets for over a year now, and he was as desperate as he'd ever been. Currently he was squatting in an abandoned schoolhouse about eight blocks away from the A&P, sleeping on old sofa cushions he'd taken out of a nearby dumpster and living off whatever food, clothing, and necessities he could scam from Goodwill and the City Mission. Earlier in the day he'd hit the jackpot, stealing a gun, a DVD player, and some power tools from his great aunt's garage. He'd already pawned the DVD player and tools for ninety bucks, but the pawn shop, he knew, wouldn't take a gun, leaving him short on funds for a score.

That's when he got an incredibly stupid idea, even by his standards: he would use the gun to rob the A&P Mart on Donner Avenue. It was an out of the way place that was almost always empty between two and six in the morning, and there was no video surveillance or security to worry about, just one bored clerk at the register. He knew that because he had a friend who used to work there, and his friend would always say that it was the perfect place to hold-up. Adam speculated he could probably net about a hundred dollars, if not more, for a minute's work.

He had never committed a crime against the public before; against himself and his family he'd committed countless acts of illegality, but those were different, safe by comparison, as he knew he was never in any real danger of suffering consequences. His mother and father refused to press charges against him, refused to even call the cops, even when he pushed his mother down and stole her diamond earrings. A crime against society, however, was a different matter. Charges were pressed automatically, especially in cases of armed robbery, and if caught, jail time undoubtedly would follow. Adam, a five-foot-six, hundred-and-forty pound white kid from the cushy

13

suburbs, knew he would not fare well in prison. He also knew that if he didn't get a hit of something soon he was going to go insane.

Of the two, the high was a more pressing concern.

And so wearing gloves, dark clothes, and two bandanas, one over his head and one on his face, so that only his worn, desperate eyes were visible, Adam Dubinsky burst in the A&P Mart brandishing his late uncle's Saturday Night Special, a gun that had been in the family for forty-five years and hadn't been fired in more than thirty.

"This is a robbery!" he shouted at the top of his lungs, startling both Ally and Eddie, causing them to jump back. "Put your hands up! Now!"

Ally's hands flew in the air, and she let out a quick, high-pitched chirp of fear that tapered to a shrill, fearful whine. Eddie's hands went up, too, and the portly cashier cringed so hard that his face seemed to disappear, becoming one pudgy smear of pale, wrinkled flesh. There was a button for a silent alarm under the counter, but he was at an awkward angle and reaching for it would draw attention. The robber, at least to Eddie, who'd been held up three times in the last nineteen months, looked nervous and terrified; the gun was shaking in his hand like a tambourine, and his eyes kept darting back and forth, frantically shifting from Ally to Eddie, Eddie to Ally, the shaking gun in his hand following a half-second behind.

"It's cool, man" said Eddie, trying to stay calm, not wanting to give this guy an excuse to lose his obviously tenuous grip on reality. "No trouble here. We'll open the register and give you whatever you want."

"Right," said Adam. "The register. Open the register. Do it now!"

Eddie went to the register, slowly, his hands held up in front of him in a conciliatory pose. He very deliberately punched two keys, the drawer sprung open, and he began to pick out the money. Ally, meanwhile, had her hands raised high and her chin pinned to her chest. She did not want to meet the assailant's eyes or give the impression that she was any sort of threat; she didn't want to see his face or for him to see hers, and under her breath she kept saying, "Please God, don't let me die," over and over.

"Come on! Hurry up!" Adam cried out, his panic-stricken voice shuddering weakly, giving his words a strange, fragile echo. He whipped his head around to make sure no one had pulled into the lot or happened to be wandering by. When he turned back around, he saw the young woman with her hands still in the air, her head down.

"Your purse," he said to her, motioning with the gun. "Give me your purse."

Without looking up, she grabbed it off the counter, but instead of just handing it to him, for some reason she reached inside for her wallet, figuring that's what he wanted. When she did that, Adam, terrified that she might be going for a weapon, freaked out. He reacted suddenly, aggressively lunging at her, snatching at the purse, trying to yank it out of her hands, yelling, "Give it to me! Give it to me!"

Ally was not looking at him when he did this, fear keeping her eyes on the ground, driving reason and logic out of her mind and leaving only instinct. And her instinct was to hold onto her purse. Adam, driven by adrenaline, anxiety, and pure, unmitigated terror, pulled her into him with a violent tug.

"Hey!" Eddie cried out, sensing Ally might be in danger. "Stop!"

Adam gave the purse one more yank, and this time Ally let go. Not expecting that, Adam lost his balance and fell to the ground, and when he hit with a thud, his finger squeezed the trigger and a shot went off.

"Nooooooo!"

The voice, an explosion of sound that rattled the windows, came out of thin air, just as something darted in front of Ally, taking the bullet that would have taken her to the grave. She saw a flash, heard the gun go off, then she felt herself falling, felt something heavy land on top of her. It was a young man, and when he rolled over she saw that he was bleeding from the chest.

Adam was back on his feet again, smoking gun in hand. He was clutching Ally's purse to his chest, but his eyes were fixed on the young man bleeding on the floor. "Where'd he come from?" he said, stunned, shaken with fear. "I never ... He wasn't

... He ... " Adam realized then, for the first time, that he had shot the young man and his simple little convenience store robbery had just escalated to a possible Murder One. He looked at Eddie, whose mouth was hanging like a broken gutter, shoved the gun in his face, and demanded the rest of the money.

"Here! Take it!" said Eddie, pushing it across the counter.

"We have to call an ambulance," Ally shouted.

The young man was shaking, and there was so much blood. Pain wrenched his face, giving him a dreadful, almost inhuman look, and his chest heaved as he labored to take in breath.

Adam gave him a final look, and then ran out of the store. He wouldn't stop running until he made it back to the schoolhouse.

"Call 911," Ally cried out. She took off her coat and used it to put pressure on the wound, trying to stop the bleeding. "We need to get him to a hospital. Now!"

Eddie picked up the phone and dialed the number, asking for the police and an ambulance, saying it was an emergency, there had been a robbery and a shooting at the A&P Mart on Donner Avenue.

"Don't you die on me," Ally said to the young man as she continued to put pressure on the wound. He was gulping at the air like a fish out of water, and every breath he took was followed by a horrible gurgling sound. He coughed once, then again, spitting up a freshet of blood, which poured over his lips and down his chin, the dark red color a stark contrast to the pallor of his cheeks. His forehead was moist with sweat, and there was an emptiness in his eyes that Ally had never seen before. It brought her to tears, but she continued to plead.

"Come on. You can make it," she told him, even as she felt the life draining out of him. "The ambulance is going to be here any minute. They're going to get you to a hospital."

The young man opened his mouth to speak, but no words came out, just another spurt of dark red blood. His eyes were begging for help, begging for life, which made Ally cry all the more. There were tears running down her cheeks, and there was blood on her hands, on her jeans, on her shirt.

She was relentless, though, refusing to give up. She continued to press down on his chest, which helped to stem the bleeding, and she kept talking to him, imploring him to hold on, telling him that the ambulance was going to be there any moment, that the wound wasn't that bad, that he'd be up and around in no time. It was all lies, but what else was she supposed to say?

In the distance, sirens broke through, softly at first, then gradually increasing in volume. Eddie rushed to the window and looked out. "They're coming," he said. "I can see the lights."

"See?" Ally told the young man who'd saved her life, the white knight who'd come out of nowhere to take a bullet for her. "They're coming. They're almost here."

He gazed up at her with fading eyes, looking every bit like a grisly prop from a bad haunted house. His complexion was the color of cream cheese, his lips were bluish and swollen, and his face was covered with a patina of blood, sweat, and tears.

His eyes drooped, then fell under the weight of impending death. Ally shook him, cried for him to wake up, shouted at him to hold on just a little longer. He somehow managed to force his eyes open once more, and he fixed her with a hopeless, vacant stare that seemed to pass through her. Summoning all his fortitude, he mouthed barely audible words: "Don't worry. It's … okay."

He coughed again, spitting up more blood. Agony contorted his features into a macabre mask. Then, unable to keep them open any longer, his eyes fell shut. His body stopped shaking and went limp.

"No!" cried Ally, bordering on hysteria. She shook him. She slapped his face. "Wake up! You're not going to die on me! You hear me? You're not going to die!"

Red and blue lights flashed against the windows and illuminated the inside of the store as two police cars and an ambulance pulled into the lot, sirens blaring.

"They're here! They're here!" Eddie cried out, and rushed to the door to meet them.

By the time the cops and EMTs got inside, the young man Ally was desperately tending to was no longer breathing.

# Chapter Two

## Ally and Vaughn

They first hooked up at the strip club, at one of the many after-hours parties Holt was famous for throwing, bringing together strippers, employees, and his best customers and friends, generously providing for them an open bar and any sort of drug they may want. It was the first party Ally had ever attended at Teasers, and the always brash and confident Vaughn swept the young and impressionable, not to mention incredibly drunk, bartender right off her feet. She was four years younger than him, but like most girls her age who went to North, she knew him well. She'd had a crush on him for years, and his good looks and confidence breezed right up her skirt.

That had been eight months ago. Eight swiftly-moving, mostly-blurry months, fueled by a disorienting diet of cocaine, booze, and sex.

At the start, Ally was a recreational user only, a part-time powder gypsy who liked the numb elation that quality cocaine provided. Dating Vaughn, it didn't take long for her recreation to acquire a steadier, more aggressive beat. A line here and there to boost a wine buzz slowly evolved into a habit, one she found herself indulging more frequently. The other night she'd polished off a sixteenth by herself, coupling it with two bottles of cheap red wine, working up a buzz that kept her dizzy and smiling into the wee hours of the morning. She didn't wake the next day until late-afternoon.

It was a delirious descent into a neon-bright abyss where there were few rules and plenty of company. Teasers loose, freewheeling atmosphere and never-ending lineup of young, attractive, self-indulgent individuals lent itself to a party hard mentality, and Ally, enabled and enticed by Vaughn, slid headlong down the rabbit hole. She rarely went to the gym anymore, exchanging yoga, laps in the pool, and her spin classes for cigarettes and daytime television; the only exercise she got now was working at the bar and having sex, and the sex wasn't nearly as energetic or satisfying as it once had been. The bloom wasn't off the rose, but the petals had started to wilt.

The end, like always, came abruptly.

It was a cold, rainy Wednesday morning. Just another square block on a calendar that marked a desultory path, except ...

Ally didn't know what she was expecting to see on the third go-round that she hadn't on the first two, but she wanted verification. And so once again she dropped her shorts, sat, and worked her hand between her legs.

She started to pee, just little dribbles at first, but soon there was a stream, and it splashed off the stick and sprayed her hand. When she was done, she spread her legs and removed the stick, and then she just sat there, waiting, staring hopelessly at the little oval section that would reveal her fate, watching as once more a little Plus sign slowly took shape and color, starting as a ghost, becoming reality.

Third time's a charm, she thought, and hung her head.

Pregnant? How could she be pregnant? Sure, Vaughn never wore a condom, saying that he hated them, that he couldn't feel anything, and that sometimes by the time he got it on the mood was over, which meant he was limp. But she took the pill religiously, and almost always made him come on her, not in her. Getting pregnant was not part of the plan. She was too young, too irresponsible, her situation too unstable. She didn't want kids, not now, and not with Vaughn. He already had two children he didn't see or take care of, and the mothers, well, word was that soon after he learned they were pregnant, he discarded them like gum that had lost its flavor. Ally wasn't sure if that was true or not – Vaughn had always denied it – but she couldn't help but notice that he wasn't exactly the fatherly type. He was a backroom player, a guy who most likely would dump her and move on to the next young piece of trim as soon as it was convenient. Ally wasn't in love with him, but she liked him. Regardless, she didn't want to have a kid.

She sat there on the toilet, panties around her ankles,

positive pee-stick in hand, the little Plus sign mocking her, and started to cry. She knew what she had to do. The choice was easy. She couldn't have it. If she had it, she would lose Vaughn, she would lose her job, she would lose everything she had. Not that what she had was anything special. Still, what she had was hers, and it was better than nothing. Besides, she wasn't ready for her youth to be over. Not yet. Not now, with everything in disarray.

She wrapped the stick baring her guilt in toilet paper and stuffed it at the bottom of the trash, along with the box for the pregnancy test. Then she pulled up her panties, threw on some shorts, and took out the trash, getting rid of the evidence. She wouldn't even tell Vaughn, she decided. She would just go and get it done at the Center, and the few days it took her to recover, she would tell him that she was sick. He wouldn't come around if he thought she was sick. Then it would be over, done with, and she could start to get her life together. Quit doing drugs, find a better job.

This was a wakeup call, she told herself as the first seedlings of doubt broke through the surface. It was a sign that she needed to change.

And change is just what she'd do.


Vaughn was tall and lanky, with dark brown skin, closely-shaved hair, and a trim goatee. He had a network of tattoos going up each arm that he took a considerable amount of pride in, and he often wore sleeveless shirts to show them off. He used to be an athlete back in high school, a damn good one, and probably could have earned a Division II scholarship to play either basketball or baseball. But even back then he had an unhealthy penchant for booze and pot and girls, enjoying his fruits to excess. He took full advantage of being a one-time high school legend and playground hotshot, and seemed to have no problem living off the fumes of a reputation that had long ago started to fade.

These days he worked for Albert Holt, the owner of Teasers and Ally's boss, running errands, collecting debts, dealing dope. It was in this capacity that he found himself at Oliver Cantrell's apartment on the south end of town, over by the outlets, along with Oliver, Oliver's friend, Alex, and a leggy stripper named Simone, who, just a month ago, had given Vaughn a spirited blowjob at the club.

"How much?" Oliver asked. A baggie of cocaine lay on the table before him, with half an ounce of Holt's primo stuff inside. Simone was practically salivating.

"Fifteen," said Vaughn. "You know that."

Oliver, like always, scoffed theatrically. "Come on, man," he said, throwing his hands up like he was being robbed. "How long we been friends, V? What? Eight years now? Ten? You really gonna do me like this?"

"Why we gotta go through this every time?" replied Vaughn, shaking his head. "It's the best deal you're gonna get. You know that. You don't want it, go buy that twice cut and stepped on shit Mackey is selling."

Oliver was tall and skinny and strange, a strung out suburban punk who looked lily white but acted – or at least tried to act – New Jack Black. He was in a robe and slippers, and wore a headband high on his forehead, making his dirty blonde hair stick up like banded stalks of dead corn. "Twelve," he said, negotiating for the hell of it, just having fun.

Vaughn didn't bother to answer. He just gave a look.

"Okay. Fourteen," Oliver tried. "That's all I got. I swear."

"Bullshit," said Vaughn. "You're a rich motherfucker, Ollie. Everyone knows it."

Oliver betrayed himself with a smile, and then chuckled guiltily. "All right, all right," he said, and looked at his friend Alex, who was as stiff and silent as a storefront mannequin. "Get him the money, brother. No use playing games. Vaughn's a hard screw."

Alex stood and left the room.

"Every time we have to do it," said Vaughn. "Why?"

"Just bustin' your chops is all. It's good fun."

"Not for me it's not."

"Come on," said Oliver. "You love me. I'm your best customer."

Vaughn shook his head. "Biggest pain in my ass, that's what you are."

"And that's why you love me. Admit it. You fruit."

"When's that trust fund gonna run out? That's what I want to know."

"Never," said Oliver, smiling a crooked, goofy smile. "I can live this way for the next seventy years." He grabbed a cigarette and lit up. "What about you?" he said, smoke bustling up around him. "How long you gonna be in this game?"

"Til the end," said Vaughn. "Gonna out last you."

"Scarface!" Oliver cried out, jumping to his feet. Then, acting out one of the last scenes of the iconic movie, he pretended to be holding a shotgun and shouted, "'Say hello to my little friend!'" in a nearly pitch perfect Tony Montana accent. Then he started shooting, going, "Boom! Boom! Boom!"

Vaughn started laughing. Simone, too. Vaughn said, "You are one crazy-ass white boy, Ollie. You know that?"

Oliver dropped back on the couch, took his cigarette from the ashtray. "It's all part of the grand scheme," he said. "Can't fuck with the grand scheme. God's crystal ball. I'm just playing my part, man."

It was then that Alex returned with a wad of cash. He gave it to Vaughn, who then looked at Oliver and said, "Do I need to count it?"

Oliver picked up the baggie of cocaine and said, "Do I need to weigh this?"

"You can if you want," said Vaughn.

"Ditto, motherfucker. D-I-T-T-O."

Vaughn didn't count the money, and Oliver didn't weigh the coke; they'd each wait until the other was gone before doing something so crass as to admit they didn't trust one another. They were friends.

"You wanna bump before you go, V?" Oliver said, pulling out a small, oft-cut mirror from under the couch.

Vaughn declined. "Gotta meet Holt. Got business to discuss."

"Business, business, business," said Oliver in a playfully mocking tone. "I just handled all my business. Now it's time for fiesta."

"Must be nice."

"Damn right. You need a better agent. Get a better deal."

"We can't all be spoiled rich kids, Ollie. No one would be on this end of things. It'd be all demand, no supply."

"All part of the grand plan," said Oliver. "God works in mysterious ways."

Vaughn put out a fist, and Oliver bumped it with one of his own. "Be careful with all that," Vaughn said to him, nodding at the baggie filled with fine yellowish-white powder. "Don't do it all in one place."

Oliver snorted sarcastically. "Get out of my house," he said.

Vaughn smiled and shook his head. "Never gonna change."

"Not until the curtain falls for good."

Vaughn turned to Alex. "See you, man," he said to him. Then he turned to Simone. "Simone," he said to her, giving her a nod and a smile.

She smiled back. "See ya, Vaughn. Tell Ally I said hello."

"You got it." He made his way to the door.

"Yo!" Oliver called out to him before he could leave. Vaughn stopped and turned around. "What you doing for the game tomorrow night?"

"What game?"

"Caps and Pens, man. Hockey. The only sport."

"Man, I don't watch hockey. What's wrong with you?"

"One of these days," said Oliver, "I'm gonna turn you into a fan. You watch."

"Later," said Vaughn, going for the door.

"Later," said Oliver. "I'll be talking to you."


Albert Holt was the guy who called the shots, and Vaughn was the guy who took them. Holt had been in the drug trade for the better part of a decade now, and he had made more money than he could say. In addition to Teasers, which served as his base of operations, he owned a car wash, a convenience store, three storage facilities, and a used car lot. Though all of them were legitimate businesses, he essentially used them to help expand his burgeoning criminal empire.

His latest venture was pornography, and he was discovering it to be quite lucrative. He had two websites, and the girls who danced at the club, most all of them hooked on something, be it coke, crack, heroin or oxy, always were in need of extra cash.

They gave handjobs and blowjobs in the private rooms upstairs so getting them to do a little more downstairs wasn't a tough sell. He could get them for five hundred dollars a cut, turn around and make five to six times that amount. He had transformed the basement of the club into a rather nice studio, complete with state of the art cameras, editing equipment, and at least five different sets. They were shooting a double-team scene with a fresh-faced college dropout named Melinda when Vaughn knocked on the door.

"Don't stop. Keep going, keep going," said Holt, waving them on. "I'll get it."

He opened the door, and Vaughn got an eyeful of young Miss Melinda getting shafted from both ends. She was moaning and cringing, and didn't seem to be enjoying herself at all. Vaughn felt compelled to watch.

"Hot, ain't she?" Holt said. "She came in last week, half strung out on Oxy. I tried her out myself. What a minx. Mmmmm. Look at that ass."

Vaughn was looking. "Nice," he said.

"You want a go after the boys are done. She don't care."

"No," said Vaughn. "Not my style."

"What about Princess over there?" Holt pointed out a tall, lanky brunette currently doing a line of cocaine over in the corner with a couple of the girls from upstairs. "Just came in yesterday. Fresh as a daisy."

"You hit it?" Vaughn asked, his interest piqued.

"Yeah. What of it?"

Vaughn eyed her for a couple seconds. Her hair was jet black and straight, and there was a slight olive tint to her skin. Then she turned, slightly, angling toward him, and he saw that she had some Asian in her. He asked Holt about it.

"She's half-Chinese, I think," said the crass, ambitious pornographer. "Look at her. Tight as a turtle's ass."

Vaughn was looking, and he liked what he saw.

"She hasn't even made her debut yet," Holt went on. "Just one audition with me. You want, I can tell her that you're going to be her co-star and have you two go over a scene. Whadda you think? Call it a perk for work well done."

"I think Ally would kill me."

"And how would she know?"

Vaughn shrugged as deviant thoughts whirled in his head, putting rock candy in his pocket. "And she hasn't been made yet? You know, with all this." He gestured to the set in general, where Melinda was getting it good.

"No. And the great thing is, you can fuck her however you want, no strings. That's part of the deal I make; they've got to be willing to do anything. *Anything.* And these girls, they don't care. Hell, they *want* it."

"Right," said Vaughn. "Let me think about it."

"Don't think too long," said Holt. "I'm going to use her soon. Be a waste not to."

Vaughn nodded distractedly, his eyes lingering on the exotic brunette, his mind wondering what it would be like to have his way with her. She met his eyes for a moment and smiled sweetly before looking away.

"I have to talk to you about Mills," Vaughn said, laboring to get back on point.

"What about him?"

"You really want me to break his hands?"

"Both of them," said Holt, most of his attention on the action being filmed, Melinda bent in submission, two men buried deep inside her. "You don't have to do it yourself. Take the Breaker with you. That's what I pay him for. Among other things."

Currently, Holt was paying the Breaker to break up Melinda, and judging by the sounds coming from her, he was doing a bang-up job.

"Mills is a decent guy."

"Hey, I like him, too. Bastard cracks me up. But he owes me nine grand. You want to square his debt? Otherwise."

"No. Don't like him that much."

Holt smiled devilishly. "That's what I thought." Then he said, "So, what about Erica?"

"Who?"

"China doll over there. Room three is open. Call it a perk for the unpleasantness of having to hurt poor Mills."

"I don't know," said Vaughn. "I don't think ... "

But Holt was already waving the young lady over. "She's clean," he told his friend, draping an arm over his shoulder. "We have to test them. So have some fun, will ya. You're getting too serious these days."

"I don't want it to get back to Ally. She's the jealous type."

"Look at you. A kept man."

"Hardly. I'm just saying."

"It won't. Trust me. Does it ever?"

"That's not the point."

"This girl will let you do things to her that I'm sure Ally won't. And you'll be doing me a favor. I want to know she can handle things."

Vaughn was going to protest, but he didn't get the chance. Erica was already there.

"Erica," said Holt, "this here is DJ. DJ, meet Erica."

"Hi" said Erica, in a drunk, cutesy voice.

"Hey," said Vaughn, acting cool.

"DJ most likely is going to be your co-star when you make your debut. You don't have a problem working with black guys, do you?"

Erica shook her head. "No. I don't think so."

"You're not afraid or nervous?"

"Of course not," she said. "All the same to me."

"All right then. Room three's open. DJ knows where it is. I want you two to get familiar with one another, okay? Build chemistry."

"Sure," said Erica. "Like a dress rehearsal."

"More like an undressed rehearsal," said Holt, and Erica blushed and giggled.

The dissolute kingpin reached into his pocket, pulled out a small packet of cocaine, handed it to Vaughn. "Here," he said to him. "To get the wheels greased."

"Right," said Vaughn. "Thanks."

Erica grabbed his hand. "Come on," she told him, smiling coquettishly. "Let's go rehearse."

Vaughn gave Ally a fleeting thought – he had told her that he would be home early and they could have dinner, watch a movie, hangout, just the two of them – and then she flew right out of his head. She returned again, for another fleeting moment, when his phone chimed out her personal ring tone, but by that time he was already enjoying his co-star, putting her

26

through the paces.

When he finally did get home, well after midnight, Ally was in bed.

He took a shower and slid under the covers next to her, doing his best not to wake her, figuring she'd be pissed at him for missing date night and not returning her calls. But Ally was awake; she'd heard him come in, and she'd heard him in the shower, and she'd felt him crawl into bed next to her. She didn't stir, though, didn't give him any reason to suspect she might be awake. Instead, she lay perfectly still, pretending to sleep until he fell asleep. Then she got up and went out to the couch.

The fight had to happen because Ally was fed up. She was fed up with his lies, with his cheating ways, with his jealousy whenever she so much as smiled at another guy or spent more than five minutes talking to a customer that made moony eyes at her.

She'd heard from a friend that Vaughn had been at the club last night and he'd come out of one of the rooms downstairs with a young, leggy, fucked-up brunette hanging all over him. Ally had never been to Holt's porno palace, but she, like everyone else at the club, knew what happened down there. According to her friend, one of the dancers at the club, the giggly brunette had said to Vaughn, "Can't wait to put that on film."

Ally's friend, Angela, assured Ally that it was Vaughn, and that later, when she asked Erica about it, the young lady had been more than forthright with details; though Angela did specify that Erica had told her that the guy's name who she'd been with and was supposed to do a porn scene with was DJ.

Vaughn, of course, followed the guy handbook and denied everything.

"DJ?" he barked, his voice rising up to match Ally's. "My name ain't DJ. And what? I'm gonna do porn now? Obviously Angela's wrong."

"She swore it was you."

"That bitch is lying. Obviously. What the hell would I want to fuck one of Holt's small time porn sluts for? Are you crazy? You think I want a disease."

"So you weren't there last night?"

"Yeah, I was there. I went to see Holt. We talked business. And then I left."

"Where were you the rest of the night? You said you'd be home at nine. You didn't come in until two-thirty."

"I was at Ollie's. Then I went to the club."

"That took eight hours?"

"I had other business to take care of. I know it's not a regular job, but I do work."

"Whatever. You couldn't call me and let me know what was going on? I called you like five times. I never heard back from you."

"I was busy."

"I made dinner."

"Made dinner?!" Vaughn scoffed in a mocking sort of way, snorting and shaking his head. Then he started to laugh.

"What?" Ally cried out, indignant. "I made chicken primavera. For us."

"You know, we're not married here," he said, taking an ill-advised stand. "You're not a housewife. We have a good time, but I'm not a kept man. Know that."

"Then don't come here to sleep at night. Don't come here looking to get laid whenever you want."

"Like it's all me. Who's the one calling when they want coke? And my cock? You. You don't want me around, stop fucking calling me."

"I will. Because I don't want you around anymore."

"Whatever. You'll be calling me in two days."

"Fuck you."

"Yeah. You want it already, don't you? I can see it on you."

Ally had reached the point of infuriation, and she reared back and slapped Vaughn across the face, hard, causing him to turn away.

"Fuck!" he said, stunned. He rubbed his cheek.

"Get out!" Ally demanded. "Now!"

Vaughn recovered quickly. "You want to slap me?!" he said, anger rising in his eyes. "All right then." He made a move for her, and she swung at him again. This time he blocked the blow, grabbed hold of her wrist, twisted her arm behind her back.

"Vaughn!" she shrieked. "Owww!"

He pushed her down on the couch, face first, still holding her arm behind her back. "You want to slap my face?!" he barked at her. "Maybe I'll slap your ass." And then he pulled back with his free hand and smacked her butt, hard, the slap sounding out like a fastball slapping a catcher's mitt.

"Vaughn! Stop! You're hurting me!" Ally cried out.

But Vaughn did it again, even harder, and again. Ally tried to turn her body away from him, but the vice-like hold he had on her arm wouldn't let her. He smacked her once more, and she started to squirm and wail.

"I thought you liked it when I smacked your ass!" he said, and smacked her again. "Yeah. You like that, don't you?" Another slap rang out. And another.

He was taunting her now, adding insult to abuse, and Ally screamed for him to stop. Finally he let go of her, and she rolled over, weeping, cradling her injured arm.

"Don't you ever slap me again," he said to her, pointing a threatening finger in her face. "Ever! You hear me, bitch?! That's it!"

Ally was bawling. The smacks hadn't hurt, but they had stung, and her arm felt like it was broken or disjointed.

"I'm outta here," said Vaughn, and grabbed his coat. "I don't need this shit. Plenty of girls out there to have."

"Don't come back," Ally shouted at him between sobbing breaths.

"I'll fucking come back if I want," he told her. "You don't tell me nothing."

"You come back, I'm calling the police."

Vaughn stopped, turned around, stomped over to her, grabbed her roughly by the hair and yanked her head back. Again Ally shrieked, this time in fear. She threw her hands in front of her face, terrified that he was going to strike her. "You call the police, that's the last fucking call you'll ever make!" he said to her.

Ally shrank away from him, and started crying harder.

"You hear me?! I don't play shit like that. Calling the police?! Fuck that!"

He let go of her hair with a jerk, and she slid off the edge of the couch to the floor, curling into a ball and sobbing.

He stormed out then, slamming the door behind him, leaving Ally to her tears and misery. She stayed on the floor for another ten minutes or so, until her crying jag subsided and she was able to breathe normally.

Then, ignoring the life growing inside her, she lit a cigarette with shaking hands and took a deep drag, hoping it would soothe her.

It did not. She stamped it out after only two hits and went to throw up.


## Marty and Charlie

Martin Thurston Loomis was a nice guy, and like a lot of nice guys, he had a permanent spot near the back of the line, with the other nice guys and those souls who were terminally unlucky. He was a good man, for the most part: smart, kind, thoughtful, generous. But like a lot of good people, the sting of loss and betrayal devastated and confused him.

It was, without question, one of those truly terrible days, the kind you usually hear about in country western songs or bleak foreign films. The kind of day that made other people think that, by comparison, things weren't really that bad.

It had happened nearly six months ago. Marty was a Computer Tech 4 at NTRL, which stood for National Technology Research Laboratories. He ran tests on newly adapted data systems and recorded any programming or binary errors. Then, if need be, he fixed those errors and reprogrammed the system. Marty was, by all accounts, a model employee: he never missed work, he showed up on time, he did his job effectively and efficiently, and he was quiet, respectful of others, and pleasant.

Unfortunately, technology is an ever-adapting animal, one that morphs and evolves at a rate that is near impossible to keep up with, and when the time came for the bosses at NTRL to make the hard budget decisions, easygoing Marty Loomis found himself in his direct supervisor's office, nodding along vacantly, listening to him spout off company lines like, "Times are hard," and "Unfortunately cutbacks are unavoidable," while the sick feeling in his stomach grew into a force.

Mr. Reginald Higby finished the meeting by telling Marty that he was a model employee, a real credit to the company, and if there was any way they could keep him, they would. Perhaps if he had been fucking Mr. Higby, like Jillian Banks, one of only two people in the tech department to keep their job, things would have been different. As it stood, Marty was not fucking Mr. Higby, and he found himself driving home in a daze, wondering what he was going to tell his fiancée.

Turns out he didn't have to tell her anything.

Marty returned home that day, sulking in failure, to find his fiancée, his sweet darling girl, bent over the sofa they often cuddled and watched movies on, being rammed from behind with appalling vigor by some large guy with long, black, ponytailed hair. Her naked ass was in the air, her face buried in the cushions of the sofa, and Marty, not thinking that his sweetheart would ever cheat on him, not with a Cro-Magnon like this, not in their house, on their sofa, quickly concluded that she must be getting raped and leapt to action.

He charged, jumped on the man's back like a drunken lunatic in a bar brawl, clamped a forearm around his neck, and started winging punches. The reckless force of his momentum caused the man to lose his balance, and the two of them spilled over the edge of the couch. Marty crashed on top the coffee table, the ponytail man landed on him with his full weight, and Marty felt his shoulder pop. When he tried to leverage himself up to continue fighting, his arm gave out and he fell back to the floor, crying out in pain.

"Marty?" shouted Mandy, startled and embarrassed. Then, when she noticed Berto, the man who'd been fucking her with her absolute consent and toe-curling approval, going after her injured, gentle-natured fiancé with rancor in his eyes, she cried out, "Berto! No! Stop!"

But it was too late.

Berto didn't care that Marty was smaller than him, or that Marty had dislocated his shoulder in the fall and could no longer protect himself; just like he didn't care that he'd gotten caught screwing Marty's fiancée like she was a ten dollar whore on special. He didn't much care about anything, and he reared back and hammered poor, defenseless Marty with a heavy right hand, putting stars in his eyes and sending him sprawling. Another right hand followed, striking Marty on the side of the head like a wrecking ball.

Barely-conscious, Marty thought he heard Mandy yell for Berto to stop, though the sound of her voice was muffled and seemed to be coming from far away. He tried to lift his head to see what was happening, but everything was lost in a blur of faded colors and odd shapes. He thought he heard protesting: Mandy yelling, struggling, screaming for Berto to get off of her. Then he heard her cry out, "No! Stop! Don't!"

Anger and terror burned through Marty's brain as he fought to get up. Thoughts of rising to his feet, saving his girlfriend, and thrashing the ponytail bastard to within an inch of death ping-ponged in his head like lotto balls; unfortunately, the message never got to his body, which lay broken on the floor. The room spun around him in a dizzying array of vague, unintelligible sights, like some horrible carnival ride, and the only movement he could effect was aimlessly reaching out one hand.

Then, shockingly, almost unbelievably, the primal animal sounds that Marty had heard when he first came through the door resumed: the grunting and heavy breathing, skin slapping skin in violent thrusts, Mandy shrieking and wailing like a backseat virgin. And though she may have started out fighting Berto, eventually pleasure took her in its grip, as it had before Marty had busted in on them, and she forgot all about her gentle sweetheart lying on the floor, helpless, broken, bleeding, and she started crying out, "Yes! Yes! Yes!" as Berto laid into her with his full bulk.

By the time Marty fully regained himself, Berto was gone and Mandy was kneeling beside him, cradling him in her arms like a baby sparrow with a wounded wing, crying, asking him if he was okay. He had a dislocated shoulder, a broken jaw that needed wired shut, two broken ribs, and a concussion. She drove him to the hospital and stayed by his side while the doctors patched him up, and when they questioned her about how Marty had sustained such serious injuries, she lied and told them that he'd fallen down the stairs. Marty, too embarrassed to admit the truth, agreed.

He was released early the next day, and when they got home Mandy admitted to the full measure of the affair, which had been going on for more than two months. And she told him, bluntly and mercilessly, like some sort of relationship assassin, that she didn't love him like he loved her, that she had never loved him like he loved her, and that while he was a nice guy and all, and a great friend, for her there was no spark, there hadn't been a spark in some time, and she didn't want to marry him. She moved out the next day, leaving Marty a shamed and ruined young man.

Being dumped devastated Marty Loomis, especially in the manner in which it had occurred. He had thought he had his life mapped out: a good job, a woman he loved who loved him; and all indications were a house and family would soon follow, perhaps even a dog, a white picket fence, a sensible minivan, and a welcome mat with the family name on it. All of that had been inevitable in Marty's mind, a scene easy to see on the horizon. Mandy, too, had claimed to want those things. Of course, hindsight being what it is, Marty had to think her involvement may have been a bit disingenuous.

He felt completely lost and alone after the split. Most of their friends were Mandy's friends, and despite her cruelty and infidelity, they stuck by her and turned their backs on him. In addition to that, he had no job to occupy his time, no hobbies to help take his mind off things, leaving him with nothing better to do than stew in contempt and misery. It wasn't long before he tumbled headlong into a haze of despair and animus, passing his thoughts high on painkillers and, when they ran out, stinking drunk on beer or wine. Eventually his life settled into a rather pathetic routine of daytime television, increasingly-graphic Internet pornography, and drinking in his robe and slippers.

He wanted to rebound, but he wasn't sure how to do it. He adored the fairer sex and desperately wanted to meet another young woman, someone cute and funny and sweet, someone who would love him unconditionally and never leave him, like in the movies. The problem was that Marty, though attractive and unquestionably nice, didn't possess the confidence or charisma needed to make that happen, especially after being crushed like an empty tin can. In the case of love, meeting his fiancée had been his one glorious moment of catching lightning in a bottle; all previous and subsequent attempts had left him looking like he'd stuck a fork in a light socket.

He had begun to think that he'd never meet another eligible young woman again, not one who actually liked him, which added to his despair.

This was where having a smooth, self-assured, good-looking friend would have helped matters along. Unfortunately for Marty, his only true friend in the world was Charles Maurice Bates, a young man who might best be described as the polar opposite of smooth, self-assured, and good-looking.

Charlie was Marty's first best friend. They were the same age, and had grown up right next door to each other. They used to play together every day back then. In the summertime they often camped out in the sparse woods behind their houses, and by lantern light they told ghost stories and talked about what they would do when they were older. They'd ogled with supreme fascination and burgeoning erections they didn't understand and embarrassingly sought to conceal their first pair of breasts in that tent, compliments of a stolen magazine from Charlie's father's prime collection. They had their first beer out there, too, sharing a lukewarm Pabst Blue Ribbon, also from Charlie's father's collection.

They had drifted apart after high school, attending different colleges, making new friends, traveling different paths. Marty got engaged, while Charlie, who never married or moved out of his parents' home, settled into a sad, monotonous life of solitude that threatened to never end. They remained friends, and Charlie was slated to be in Marty's wedding party, but ostensibly their friendship had become more of a casual acquaintanceship. Then came Marty's day from hell and ensuing slide into the abyss. From there, it didn't take long for the two old friends to reconnect.

Charlie Bates was a portly fellow with a pale pink complexion, a lopsided face and smile, big teeth, and yellowish-red hair that looked like something you might expect to find atop a puppet's head. He was terminally shy around the opposite sex, and often times, when nervous, ended up having to excuse himself because he could not stop hiccupping. Like Marty, his sexual conquests could be written down, in detail, on the back of a business card, with room to spare for a small grocery list.

Women were a mystery to Charlie, on par with Stonehenge, centrifugal force, the Pythagorean Theorem, most instruction manuals, and the popularity of all-u-can-eat buffets. In fact, Charlie had only two notches on his bedpost, and neither was anything to brag about. The first one, the girl who took his virginity and eventually broke his heart, was his high school girlfriend and senior prom date, Alyssa Krebbs. She was giggly and drunk that night, and immediately afterwards turned over and vomited on the floor. They dated exclusively over the summer before their freshman years, making love and making promises to stay together forever. That lasted until Alyssa got a taste of freedom and college guys, which she was only too happy to indulge, often, and by the time Thanksgiving break rolled around, Charlie once again was single.

His second and currently last conquest was a sloppy-drunk girl at a party who kept calling him Steve. She took him upstairs, dropped her skivvies, and Charlie made gentle love to her for three minutes and eleven seconds.

After an awkward goodbye, he never saw her again.

Other than that, his sexual experiences amounted to a few vigorous handjobs from a chubby girl named Tanya Billings, and ejaculating in his pants during a private dance the one and only time he went to a strip club.

It was neck and neck between them when it came to who was worse with women. They were two lame mounts rounding the first leg of a race they couldn't win, having no choice but to eat the dirt and dust kicked up by all stampeding thoroughbreds out in front.

It was in the spirit of camaraderie and commiseration that they got together on a Thursday night to share in their female-deprived misery with the aid of booze and video games. It was all they could think to do.

Marty was in a particularly bitter mood, having earlier in the day heard that his ex, Mandy, was now running around with Brent Vesko, a townie who had gone to school with Marty and Charlie. Brent had always been on the wild side; he threw the best parties in high school, taking advantage of his parents' home every time they went out of town for the weekend, hosting bashes that featured plenty of sex, drugs, and booze. Marty and Charlie knew about Brent's parties from the grapevine only, having never been invited to one. They were never part of the cool gang.

Charlie took a swig from his beer and sat down next to his friend. "Women," he snorted derisively. "Whatcha gonna do?"

"I knew she was dating," said Marty. "She left me for another man."

"I suppose. Still, it has to sting."

"Yeah. So what did you hear?"

Against his better judgment, Marty had beseeched Charlie to find out what he could from his cousin Lisa, who ran in similar circles as Brent Vesko and, on occasion, Mandy.

Curiosity has a way of making people gluttons for punishment, and Marty was no different. It pained him to think of his ex dialing it up with other men, but some sick, demented part of him wanted to know the details.

Misery is like anything else – once you get a taste, you want more.

Charlie's face wrenched up. "You sure you want to hear about this," he said in a way that implied he thought it was a bad idea. "What's done is done, right? Spilt milk and such."

"Come on, Charlie, just tell me what she said. I won't be able to sleep tonight either way."

Charlie, a good friend, felt squeezed between a rock and a hard place. He took a drink to stall for time, but that lasted all of four seconds. Marty kept staring at him, saying nothing, waiting him out. Finally, Charlie gave in.

If the situation had been reversed, if it was his ex who was out there running around, Charlie imagined that he'd want to know about it, despite the heartache it inevitably would cause. He issued a sigh born of reluctance, and with a glum look began. "It's true," he said. "Her and Brent are officially an item. Lisa said it started a couple weeks ago and they've been together ever since."

A crestfallen look gripped Marty's baby-cheeked face, warping it into a sour, unfriendly mask. He took a drink from his beer and tried not to sulk. "Brent Vesko," he said, as if he needed to hear it aloud, in his own voice, before he could process it. "That guy was always such an asshole."

"I know," agreed Charlie. "Lisa hates him, too. She said he cheats on all his girlfriends. She said he gave Missy Crender herpes."

"Are you kidding me?"

Charlie shrugged. "That's what she said. I don't know. She also said that he's into dope pretty bad. Coke and pills."

"Unreal. First she leaves me for some Neanderthal, and now she's dating Brent Vesko. I mean, am I such a loser that I can't compete with these guys? Violent dickheads and coke junkies, that's who she'd rather be with?" He conveniently ignored the part about him having become a pill junkie himself, though that habit had gone pretty much unsatisfied for the last few weeks, adding to his frustration and anger.

"Listen, man, they're all the same," replied Charlie, his voice stiff with resentment. "They want you until they want something else, and most of the time they don't even know what they want. Relationships aren't meant to work. I know from experience. One day everything's peachy, the next it's a pile of shit." He tilted back his beer and took a long drink. "It's always the same," he added bitterly.

"I guess," said Marty, trying to seem okay with it but failing. "I mean, it's not like I thought we were gonna get back together." Actually, that's exactly what he had been thinking, and hoping, too, ever since he'd heard that Mandy's first dalliance, the one with the Neanderthal, had ended.

"Brent Vesko," he said again, and shook his head.

"I say screw 'em all," declared Charlie, his tone now edged with defiance, the kind of defiance that rises out of failure and disgust. He guzzled down the rest of his beer and crumpled the can. "No relationships. They don't work. Love is bullshit anyway, right? It's all pheromones and chemistry. Ask anyone." He stood and threw the can in the garbage, then walked over to the fridge to get another. "We should just look to have casual sex," he went on, speaking as someone who'd never been able to persuade causal sex before, unless you counted the drunk girl at the party who thought his name was Steve. He was anxious for another go around, preferably with a girl who knew his name; though if she didn't, that certainly wouldn't be a deal breaker.

"Keep it simple. Be players, like Brent." He pulled out two cans and held one up for Marty's approval. Marty, though he still had more than half a beer left, nodded, and Charlie returned to the table. He slid a beer across to his friend, then popped his open. "I saw Debbie Derek the other day," he said, and a lewd smile crept across his face, bunching up those portly cheeks of his. "Remember Debbie Derek?"

Marty shook his head.

"Barb Derek's little sister? Remember Barbie Derek?"

"Of course," said Marty. Everyone remembered Barbie Doll Derek. She was one of the hottest girls to ever live in Hagerstown. "Her little sister has to be young."

"Well, she's younger than us. Twenty-two, maybe. She's even hotter than Barbie, if you can believe it. I'm telling you, this girl is smoking."

Marty grunted as a means of reply. He was still thinking about Mandy.

"See, that's what we need," said Charlie, going on. "Young women who are looking to have a good time. And these girls today, they're crazy. They run around with no panties and no morals. Sex is nothing to them. They get a couple drinks in them and start giving out blowjobs like candy mints."

That was pure speculation on Charlie's part, cultivated from extensive research on the Internet and the glossy pages of men's magazines. He'd yet to experience it for himself, unfortunately. But one of these days ...

Marty said, "Didn't Brent used to date Barbie Derek?"

Charlie nodded. "Yeah. In high school. Then, while she was in college, they'd hook up from time to time. I think she's married now, to some cop in DC."

"Unbelievable. What does Brent Vesko have that we don't?"

"Well, I hear he's hung like a horse," replied Charlie, not thinking.

The look that warped the edges of Marty's already-sullen face would have brought a tear to a sociopath's eye. Charlie's face colored bright red. "Sorry," he said. "I didn't mean to ... "

Marty waved off his friend's apprehension, though it was clear he didn't appreciate it. "Don't worry. It's not a problem," he said, doing his best to sound unaffected.

"Most girls say size doesn't matter anyway," Charlie went on, sliding clumsily into damage control. "It's ... you know, how you move and ... well, where you put it ..."

"It's all right," Marty said again, a bit sharper this time, letting Charlie know that he had no desire to discuss the matter further. "Anyway, like you said, it's all spilt milk."

"What about you? You want to try that Internet dating thing? I'm game if you are. I was checking it out the other day. There's some hot young talent out there."

Going on an Internet dating site was one of Charlie's hopeful suggestions, and Marty had agreed, halfheartedly, to think about it. The whole thing smacked of desperation to him, and he really didn't want to go that route just yet, believing it to be the last ditch effort of the truly hopeless. Then again, he had seen all there was to see of Internet pornography over the last couple months and his hand had started to cramp up on him. He was really hoping to find someone else to touch his dick for a change.

"I don't know," he said. "I think maybe we should try to go to a bar this weekend. Out of town, of course. I don't want to run into Mandy."

"Okay," said Charlie, who didn't particularly like bars. He liked young women, though, and bars certainly seemed to get packed with them on weekends. "I heard The Cottage in Chambersburg is a good place. That should be out of the way enough."

Marty nodded and said, "Sounds like a plan

The Cottage was a groovy little boozebox in the heart of Chambersburg that catered to a young, attractive crowd rich on themselves and looking to cash in. The music was handled by a jukebox that boasted mostly classic rock, and though there was no dance floor, that never stopped young women, high on the sanguine confidence of wine and sweet-tart shooters, from finding enough room to shake what they had. The bar itself stretched the length of the main room and was tended by a tall blonde girl who wore the kind of tight, low-cut, revealing outfits that counted for tips.

It was nine when the boys got there, and the tables were nearly filled. Charlie saw a couple seats at one end of the bar and cut a path, with Marty tailing reluctantly behind. Marty was as comfortable at a bar as a banjo-strumming redneck at a country club; it wasn't that he looked or even felt out of place, he just couldn't see the point. Sure, there was the social aspect, but Marty was not good at being social. Neither was Charlie, but unlike Marty, Charlie's ineptness came paired with cockeyed optimism, which never let him run short of that most dangerous of commodities: Hope.

"Yuengling," said Charlie, after gaining the bartender's attention.

"For you?" she asked Marty.

"The same," he said.

She grabbed a couple bottles out of the cooler, twisted off their tops, slapped them down. "Five-fifty," she said, and snatched up the twenty Charlie proffered. She made his change and was off before he could summon the courage to ask her a question or toss out a friendly comment.

Looking over the bar, at all the people clamoring and moving about, Charlie said, "Pretty cool place. That redhead down there is hot. The one in the green shirt."

Out of a sense of fellowship, Marty threw the young lady a glance. One thing was certain: Charlie had good taste. The redhead was a looker, with one of those soft, angelic faces that was the very definition of feminine. Marty had to think that the four guys standing around her and her friend, a pudgy brunette who presently was cackling like an excited hyena, thought so, too.

"Yeah," he said.

"How about the girl in the striped shirt?"

This would go on for a while, Marty knew: Charlie scoping out the place, pointing out the women he found particularly attractive, making comments about their looks and who they reminded him of. The girl in the striped shirt, according to him, resembled someone named Kristi Vantori.

"Who's that?" Marty inquired.

"You don't know Kristi Vantori?" Charlie was appalled. "She's a lingerie and swimsuit model. She's all over the Internet. You have to Google her."

"I'll do that."

"Obviously the girl down there isn't as hot, but she's got the same ... you know, look."

"Kristi Vantori is a brunette?"

"Jet black hair. Gorgeous. And what a body." A comment about Miss Vantori's perky breasts was on the tip of Charlie's tongue, but the bartender swung down their way and he quickly swallowed it up.

"You guys all right down here?" she asked them. She caught Charlie gawking at her in a strange, guilty sort of way and she narrowed her eyes on him.

"Umm ... We're good," he told her, smiling goofily. "This is our first time here," he added. "Is it normally like this?"

"Like what?" asked the bartender.

"Crowded?"

The tall, lanky young woman gave the place a quick look. "This ain't crowded," she said, and was gone again.

"She's hot," said Charlie, ogling her as she walked away.

Marty said, "Yeah," and took a drink.

It went on this way for three rounds; the two friends talking back and forth with each other and no one else while conspicuously scouting out beautiful women and not doing anything about it. They talked about movies and actresses and sports, and reminisced about high school and childhood and some of the good times they'd shared. There was a good bit of laughing, not necessarily because something was funny, but because it had happened so long ago and they both had been there.

Charlie tried to engage the bartender in conversation but was unable to hold her attention for more than two sentences, which actually was better than he usually did. Finally, as beer three was dwindling down, Marty, somewhat buzzed and frustrated, said, "What are we doing here, man?"

"We're out," said Charlie. "What do you mean?"

"I mean we could have sat at home and did this. Talk to each other and drink beer. And we could have played video games."

"The scenery's better here. There're girls."

"They might as well be posters on a wall. All we do is look at them."

"Hey, it's not so easy. I don't know anyone here. Do you?"

Charlie's sad, defeatist tone prompted Marty to heave a sigh. "I just mean that maybe we should *try* to talk to them," he said. "Take a chance."

"What? Walk up to them out of the blue? I can't ... "

"I'm just saying that I don't feel like we're doing anything."

"It's my fault," said Charlie. "We're in the corner here. There're no girls around us."

They were sitting by themselves, over near the bathrooms. The closest people to them were a couple of older guys who were really drunk and really loud, slurring and chortling and slapping each other on the back. Other than that, every-so-often a girl would pass by them on the way to the restroom, usually with another girl or two. Not easy to strike up a conversation under those conditions.

Neither Charlie nor Marty had the chops to approach women cold, no matter where they were. They needed to know a girl before they were able to summon the courage to talk to her, and seeing that they really didn't know anyone in Chambersburg, they were out of luck. Marty was feeling particularly annoyed.

"I just want to ... I don't know, talk to someone," he said. "No offense."

"Hey, me too," said Charlie. "I'm just not very good at it."

"Yeah, I know. Me either. Especially in a bar. I'm just tired of ... I mean, I'm not saying I need to meet some girl and take her home and have sex with her. It would just be nice to meet someone, talk with them, joke, flirt, something like that."

"I know," said Charlie. "I agree."

"I haven't had sex in almost seven months."

"I haven't had sex in fourteen." Actually, for Charlie Bates it had been twenty-three months and eleven days since he'd had sex, nearly two years, and he was beginning to worry that he might never have it again. He often, in moments of quiet, drunken reflection, apologized to his penis.

"Why can't we meet a couple of nice young women? I don't even care if they're pretty. I'd just like to hang out with them."

"That's why we really should do the … " Charlie paused and gave a quick look around, making sure no one in earshot was listening, " … Internet dating thing. It's not just for losers anymore."

"Yeah. I think that's their slogan now."

Charlie laughed heartily.

Marty grumbled something under his breath, words that weren't at all clear. Then he said, "I always hear women complain there are no good guys out there. Well, we're good guys. And here we are."

"I know. They'd rather date assholes."

"I don't even care. My ex has already been with three different guys since we've split up, if not more, and I haven't even kissed another woman." Marty tilted back his beer, draining it, and then slammed the open bottle on the bar with enough force to draw a few glances from some nearby patrons. "I'm sick of doing nothing," he said.

"You want to go someplace else?"

"No. I want to talk to someone." Marty looked around the bar, searching for a couple of young women in the same boat as he and Charlie, lonely souls out on the town together, sharing in a drab, shallow, uneventful evening because there wasn't anything better to do. But most of the girls at The Cottage were part of a group, and all those groups, big and small, had guys in them.

"You want another one?" the bartender asked Marty.

"No," he said. "I'm done." As she walked away, Marty turned to Charlie and said, "I think I want to go home now."

Always loyal, Charlie nodded in agreement and quickly downed the rest of his beer. They had walked into the bar with hopefulness and desire, with a sense of anticipation that perhaps something great, or, at the very least, interesting awaited them. Two hours later they walked out with the spiritless, shoe-scraping stride of the perpetual loser, a pathetic zombie gait that no one bothered to notice. And when they were gone, all that remained of them was the brief blast of cold air that rushed in when they opened the door to leave. And then that was gone, too.

"It's going to be okay," Charlie said as Marty's car sat idling in Charlie's parents' driveway. "It'll work out. You know that."

"No, I don't. And neither do you."

Marty was right, and that was the problem. He wanted to believe that things were going to be okay, that eventually the storm would pass and his ship would right itself, but it had been months since Mandy had eviscerated him and he actually felt worse now than he had that day. Things will work out? That was just something to say to keep you hanging on in the hope that time and good luck eventually would be on your side. But Marty had begun not to trust time, or luck, or life, or hope, suspecting, given his recent heartbreak and crashing descent, that sometimes those trains were on different tracks.

"Yeah, I guess I don't," Charlie admitted somewhat dejectedly. He was one of those guys who liked to tell you the glass was half full when really he believed it was half empty. "But maybe it will be."

"And maybe it won't."

"And maybe it won't."

Marty issued an exasperated sigh that seemed to go on and on. Then he said, "I just want to go home and pass out."

"I understand. Be careful driving."

"Why? I've only had three beers. Besides, what difference does it make? I don't have a job. I don't have anywhere I need to be. Bring on the DUI. Maybe they'll shoot me if I act like I have a gun or resist arrest."

"Don't say that," Charlie chastised him.

"No difference either way."

Charlie nodded somberly as the reality of Marty's pessimistic words and attitude hung in the air between them. "So, we still on for tomorrow?" he inquired.

Marty gave a sardonic snort. There would be another tomorrow – that had become the great joke of his life, and the bane of his existence. Tomorrow would dawn and he would still be himself. "I don't know," he said. "Call me."

Charlie opened the door and got out. Despair such as Marty's was like the flu, and Charlie could feel the effects of it seeping into his bones, into his brain, making him ill. Of the two, his was the life more pitiable. He was about to walk into the house where he'd lived the entirety of his life and sleep in the same bed he'd slept in when he was in junior high and high school. If that wasn't bad enough, he knew that first he would peel a couple sheets of paper towels from the roll in the kitchen so that he had something to masturbate into before he crawled under the covers and went to sleep, with his parents just down the hall.

Marty, meanwhile, made it halfway home before a flickering neon sign caught his attention and made him turn into the parking lot of a club he had passed often – every time he drove home from Charlie's place – but had never stopped at. It was a place called Teasers, a Hagerstown landmark and the last ditch for many a weary, rejected party rat not quite ready to call it a night.

He parked, but left the engine running, not sure whether he wanted to go in or not. There'd probably be at least a ten dollar cover, he figured, and beers would run him anywhere from four to six dollars apiece. But he wasn't yet ready to go home, and the thought of live naked women strutting around, shaking their asses, spreading their legs, pushing up their breasts, held a certain appeal. Interactive porn. And there was almost no chance he would run into Mandy.

On the contrary, if he went right home, all he'd do is chug back a couple more beers and dig deeper into his craterous hole of depression, wallowing in self-hatred before finally jerking off and going to bed.

Six in one, half dozen in the other.

His mind made up, however tentatively, he cut the ignition and climbed out of the car. A few minutes later, after showing the massive bouncer his ID and paying the obscene twelve dollar cover charge, Marty Loomis shambled through the dimly lit club, past the main stage, where a short but energetic blonde was bouncing around to a hip-hop song, and up to the bar. The far end was open, and he took the stool on the corner, where he had a good view of the stage.

The bartender, a cute little minx in a tight, skimpy outfit, approached. She pasted on a fake smile and spoke in the friendly, well-practiced tones of servers everywhere. "What can I get you, hon?"

"Yuengling," Marty replied.

She returned with an ice cold bottle of the lager and set it down in front of him. "Five-fifty," she told him.

Marty snorted a laugh, and pulled out a ten. Unemployed and paying six bucks for a beer, on top of twelve to get through the door. A den of sin built on fools and cowards, money exchanged hand over fist.

The bartender swiped his cash, made change at the register, and returned. "Need anything else, let me know," she told him. "Name's Ally."

"Marty," said Marty. "And I'm fine for now."

She left, heading back to the crowd of young, well-dressed men at the other end of the bar, men who were clamoring for her attention and tipping well, and Marty settled in and looked around.

The club was incredibly loud and garish, with lots of lights, mirrors, and shiny baubles. Reflections of different color flashed here and there with alarming rapidity, giving the place a rave-like atmosphere. There was a smaller stage off to one side, currently being worked by a busty brunette, much to the gaping-eyed wonder of a couple older men in suits and loosened ties. On the main stage the lively blonde was hanging upside down from the pole, her fake tits perfectly in place. Seats around the main stage were packed with young men, a few of whom were beckoning the tart young blonde with cash money, calling her over, making her earn her take.

A few strays sat at the tables on the main floor, away from the stage. A man and woman – a couple, presumably – watched intently as a brunette danced seductively for them. She was paying more attention to the woman – sitting in her lap, going cheek to cheek with her, twirling a hand through her hair – which, judging by the width of his smile, seemed to delight the man to no end.

The woman appeared to be enjoying herself, too.

Over in a darkened corner, two girls wearing mere threads of lingerie sat in a booth with a couple of guys, just talking.

Marty had heard rumors about this place, and had, in his own imagination, worked up a picture that closely resembled the truth. He came to the quick conclusion that he would drink his one beer and leave, never going to the stage or asking for a private dance. He couldn't really afford that sort of fun, anyway; he could barely afford the beer.

Besides, he wasn't really in the mood to have a good time.

A young woman with short brown hair, very cute, came up beside him and leaned over the bar. "Hello," she chirped pleasantly, giving him a smile. Then she raised a hand and motioned for the bartender.

Ally made her way down, and the cute brown-haired girl said to her, "Danny said Vicki isn't coming back and you have to work all night. Sorry."

Ally showed her frustration with a groan. "Unbelievable. You know that if I pulled this shit they'd fire me."

"Vicki is one of Holt's favorites."

"She's one of his downstairs girls."

"Yeah. That, too."

"So I get screwed."

"Better to get screwed up here than down there," said the short-haired brunette, and smiled playfully.

Ally rolled her eyes. "Whatever. Three more hours. I can use the money."

"There you go." The brunette then turned to Marty, who'd been politely feigning indifference to their conversation, listening intently to every word but pretending not to care. "How are you, sweetie?" she asked him.

"I'm okay," he replied. "You?"

"Just ducky. Can I interest you in a private dance?"

He looked at her. She was unquestionably cute, and he wouldn't have objected to seeing her naked, only ... "I have eight dollars to my name."

"Eight?"

"That's it."

"Oh well," she said, "guess that's my cue to hit the stage." And she turned and sauntered off, her cute little ass jiggling sexily.

"See ya," Ally called after her. She then looked at Marty. "Hate to tell you this," she said to him, "but this is the wrong place to be with only eight dollars in your pocket. There's an ATM over there, in case you need it. And we do take credit cards here at the bar. Not for private dances, though. Just so you know."

"Thanks. But this'll probably be my last beer."

"One beer? You paid a twelve dollar cover to have one beer and you only have eight dollars in your pocket?"

Marty shrugged feebly. "I know. Stupid thing to do. But I wasn't ready to go home yet, and I figured this would be one place I wouldn't have to worry about running into my ex."

Ally gave him a thin-lipped smile. "I get it," she said. Before coming to work, she'd called her ex – she was already calling Vaughn her ex – and told him that if he wanted his stuff, he better get it tonight, while she was at work. She told him she was having the locks changed tomorrow. The appointment was already set.

"Me and my boyfriend just broke up," she went on, empathizing. The guys at the other end of the bar certainly had more than eight dollars among them – they were throwing around cash like confetti, with over fifty dollars finding its way into Ally's tip jar – but she found herself wanting to talk to the poor, lonely, broken-hearted sap trying not to cry in his beer. "We were together almost a year."

"I was engaged to mine," said Marty. "Caught her screwing someone else."

"Really? Like *literally* caught them? Caught them in the act?"

Marty nodded somberly. "Came home early from work, after being fired, and got an eyeful of her bent over the couch, some Neanderthal having his way."

"Oh my God. You got fired *and* caught your fiancée cheating on you the same day?"

"Yep." He raised his beer in a mock salute, then tilted it back and took a drink. "Worst day of my life. And it hasn't gotten any better since."

"I can't imagine," said Ally, her sweetheart face set with a look of solemn commiseration. That certainly constituted a bad day. Then she thought of her recent travails – the pregnancy, the rumors about Vaughn and another woman, their fight – and she felt compelled to befriend this downhearted young man. "How long has it been?" she asked him.

"Happened last year, October 26th. It was a Friday."

Ally quickly did the math in her head. Then, in a voice that came out much more incredulous than she had intended, "That was six months ago."

"I was in love with her," Marty replied, quite defensively. "We were getting married."

"I'm sorry. I didn't mean it like that." Then, in the interest of sharing, she told him that she was having her locks changed tomorrow.

"Why? Is he violent?"

Ally thought about Vaughn wrenching her arm behind her back and smacking her ass while she screamed and cried for him to stop. Her wrist was still sore, and the openhanded smacks he'd hit her with had left her butt cheeks red and swollen.

"No," she said. "I just don't trust him."

Marty shook his head miserably. "Can't trust anyone these days."

"I wouldn't say that."

"I would. Soon as you do, things fall apart."

Ally discovered, somewhat to her surprise, that she was nodding in agreement. She stopped abruptly and said, "Come on. We're too young to be bitter. Right?"

Marty sounded out a cynical laugh. "Maybe. I don't know. Truthfully, I don't even think I care anymore. I keep thinking it's going to get better, it has to get better, but it never does."

Once again, Ally caught herself nodding along. "Breaking up is never easy," she said, and she thought about the unintended life growing in her belly. A sudden flood of emotion overcame her, shackling her with a look of vulnerability.

Marty, meanwhile, glanced around at all the glitz and glamour that Teasers had to offer; he looked at the mirrors, the brass fixtures, the gleaming, plastic, alcohol-induced smiles; and he looked at the leggy, dark-skinned girl slinking around on stage with graceless sex-appeal, bending and leaning over in ways that accentuated her feminine wiles. "I guess this is an appropriate place to get down to the naked truth of things," he said offhandedly.

Ally's brow furrowed. "Here?" she said. "No one's naked here. Just because they don't have clothes on doesn't mean they're naked. Everyone here is hiding something. Take it from me, this place is as far from the truth as it gets."

Marty nodded in agreement, the thoughtful, contemplative way in which Ally had voiced her opinion convincing him she must be right.

"So, what are you hiding?" he asked her. "Unless that's too personal."

She gave him a look and said, "Afraid so." She wasn't even ready to admit it to herself, let alone a stranger.

A soft, soulful groan escaped Marty. "Why can't it be easy?" he said. Then, before Ally could retort, "*Easier*, anyway. It never seems to get any easier."

Ally concurred. "The more you know, the more you experience, the less you understand. That's just how life works."

"Tell me about it."

It was then that Vaughn strolled into the place with an entourage of friends, and the night got a whole lot harder for Ally.

# Chapter Three

He wasn't sure how he woke up, if there was a noise that shook him or he felt some sort of pain. Unlike falling asleep, which just happens, the moment of waking often has a catalyst, a sharp sound or sensation that rudely pulls you from the depths of unconsciousness. The alarm goes off, or your asshole neighbor starts cutting grass at seven in the morning, or the person next to you stirs or screams in their sleep.

When he first realized he was awake, noise was at a minimum. The room was dark, except for an ambient glow from the monitors surrounding his bed, and he was alone. It was what he felt that brought him to the murky light of sentience, and what he felt was sore all over. There was a deep, painful, burning sensation in his chest, unlike anything he had ever felt before, and the steady thumping in his head, like a couple of two-by-fours being clunked together inside his skull, was no picnic either.

His eyes fluttered open, blinking their way to sight, and he saw that he was in a hospital room, alone, attached to all sorts of strange machines. There were pads on his chest, an IV needle in his arm, and the monitors looking down at him, judging him, flashed numbers and made soft little beeping sounds.

He attempted to lift his head and look around, but pain stopped him. A sharp ache jabbed down the length of his spine, all the way to the middle of his back, and he cringed and went, "Ugghhh!"

One of the monitors at his bedside made a loud *Blip* sound, and the number in the upper right corner jumped from 58 to 66, then, after another *Blip*, to 77. A readout on a different monitor had his blood pressure at 114 over 71.

He lifted his head again, slowly this time, gingerly, and was able to take in more of his surroundings: the main door was closed, the bed next to him was empty, and the television mounted on the wall was blank.

None of this made sense, and he fought for some shred of memory or familiarity, something that might hint at who he was, where he was, what had happened to him. The last thing he remembered was ...

There had been a blinding white light, all-encompassing, and it had consumed him and everything around him. He remembered someone yelling at him, or singing to him. And there was a clear, overwhelming sense of fear; fear of the known and the unknown at the same time. Fear of what lay ahead.

He looked at the IV needle sticking out of the fleshy underside of his wrist and tracked the attached tube until it disappeared somewhere behind him, most likely into another machine. Next he turned his curiosity to the three white pads on his chest; two of them were the same, but the third was different. It was perfectly square, held by strands of white tape, and unlike the other two, there was no tube leading from it to a monitor.

It was a bandage.

Something oily and yellowish-red in color had seeped through the surface of the gauze, and when he poked at the edges of it with an experimental finger, he was visited by a sharp pain. Again he cringed and went, "Ugghhh." He thought about removing it and having a look, but something told him not to.

Instead, he put his mind back to work, fighting to recall the events that had led him here, to a hospital. Yet again he found his memories lacking definition and fluency. He could sense the residue of truth hanging in the air menacingly, much like the eerie afterthoughts of a bad dream, but the details remained lost somewhere in the murky beyond. You bust through the subconscious mind to the conscious mind, but some things get stuck in the divide between.

It was then that he became aware of another presence in the room, and despite the pain it caused him, he whipped his head around. There stood a young man of a tall and lanky build, with a neat thatch of curly brown hair, small, round eyes, and an angular mouth. He looked vaguely birdlike, and when he came forward, it was with the high-lifting gait of a wren walking on land.

The man in the hospital bed wondered if the birdlike man had been there all along, and he concluded that he must have been, seeing that neither the main door nor the one to the bathroom had been opened. He didn't remember seeing him there initially, but he was terribly groggy and out of his element, leading him to surmise that he must have missed him the first time around. Oddly enough, the birdlike man, dressed in an old-fashion wool suit, was the first thing the man in bed recognized. He couldn't place his name or face, but he knew that he knew him from somewhere.

"Whit? Is that you?" the birdlike man said in an inquisitive tone of voice. He looked bemused and hopeful.

The man in the hospital bed recognized the voice, the familiar twinge of a posh British accent, and said, "Edmund?"

"It is you," Edmund gasped, his small, round eyes opening wide. He heaved a deep sigh of relief and said, "Thank God."

"Where am I?"

"You're in hospital. You had an accident."

"An accident? But ... How?"

Edmund shrugged guiltily. "We're still trying to figure that out, sir."

## Whitman

The White Room.

They called it the White Room because it was pure white, a blinding blizzard sort of white that consumed everything, creating an aura of ethereal nothingness that made you feel somewhat disoriented and ill-at-ease. The floor and ceiling were white, the walls and fixtures were white, the massive, courthouse-style judge's bench with three separate seating sections was white. There were no windows, and the only door was white. If you had never been inside the room before, if you didn't know exactly where the door was, you had no choice but to feel your way around the walls until you found it.

Whitman knew where the door was. He had been to the White Room too many times to remember. It was where he was called to answer to his duties, where the Elders summoned him to make his reports and either congratulate him on a job well done, or, as had increasingly become the case, admonish him for his failures.

It would be another unpleasant affair, he knew, considering his district's most recent numbers, which, as always, he planned to blame on contemporary social and economic conditions that were, professionally speaking, untenable, the moral decay of civilization, and the nefarious influence of all things technological.

Whitman, like most elderly individuals, had a habitual distrust of progress, especially where technology was concerned. "We never had all these problems back in the good ol' days," he would expound from time to time, whenever he was feeling particularly dispirited. If you asked him, he'd tell you that the Internet, cell phones, and video games were responsible for most of the insanity in the world. Movies, modern music, and reality television played their part as well.

The whole damn world was going mad and it sure as hell wasn't his fault. He had as much control as a bumblebee in a windstorm. And that's what he'd tell them, too, when they sat up there on their bench and looked down their noses at him, judging him with their condescension and sanctimony.

Not that any of it made a spit of difference in the grand scheme of things. They had a job, and he had a job, and down the line it went. When the numbers weren't good, and they hadn't been good for some time now, meetings had to be called, mandates had to be handed down, thinly-veiled threats had to be made.

The Grand Scheme? Whitman sighed miserably. He was too old for this bull. His hair was as white as everything else in this damn room, and the network of lines on his weathered old face had been there so long they might as well have been etched in stone. He was tired, frustrated, and utterly annoyed. He would've quit, but that wasn't an option; he had a contract, and breaking the terms of that contract would bring down on him consequences he was not prepared to deal with.

He had no one to blame but himself. Two-hundred and thirty-six years toiling away on the Custodial staff; it was a record length of service, and the depressing part was that a promotion was not imminent. Most Custodians served between a hundred and a hundred and fifty years. A few had served over two hundred. But no one had ever gone as long as Whitman. Those he had entered the ranks with had long since graduated and moved on to greener pastures; some had become Elders, former Custodians who had earned an increase in status and power, becoming members of the Lower Echelon of Angels, the highest honor a human could hope to attain; others held sentry posts in the spirit realm, making sure the borders between worlds were protected. Not Whitman, though. As far as he'd made it was District Director, which meant he oversaw a small garrison of Custodians and liaised with the Elders come census time.

Two-hundred and thirty-six years and the light at the end of the tunnel seemed just as far away as it had on day one.

The door to the White Room opened silently on its hinges, as it always did, letting in the slightest reflection of color from outside, what looked like some pastel shade of yellow or pink; though minor, it immediately distorted the severe tone of the room, imbuing the unremitting whiteness with a gentle warmth, giving it a sense of scope and realism, which was promptly extinguished a moment later when the door was shut again, the majestic thump of it swinging back in place echoing in the large, desolate room like a single knock of knuckles on a thin plank of wood.

Whitman turned to watch the Elders, three stoic, austere gentlemen dressed in stately white robes and white headdresses, stride into the room like Supreme Court Justices. Not one of them so much as glanced his way or paid him any mind at all as they made their way to the bench. Whitman, meanwhile, watched them the entire time, using a wary, sidelong gaze to mark their every move. In their flawlessly-pleated white robes, which tied off at the neck and swept the floor at their feet, they looked like three disembodied heads bobbing along in a snowstorm. The affect was oddly comical, but Whitman didn't dare laugh. He had enough problems as things stood.

The men moved crisply in single-file fashion, their posture perfect and strong, and they climbed the three stairs to the bench from which they would look down at Whitman. The first one up moved to the section on Whitman's right, the second one took the middle segment, while the last one took the seat on Whitman's left. They removed their hands, along with the thick white folders they routinely consulted during these interviews, from somewhere within the folds of their smocks. They did this with unnerving synchronization, as if only one of them was real and the other two mirror images. All three looked up at him at the same time, showing their ancient faces.

Whitman recognized all three.

The one in the middle was Tyrus. His time on the panel predated Whitman's time in the organization, which meant that whatever Whitman thought he knew, there was a good chance that Tyrus knew it better. He was tough but fair, and his generally pessimistic views on life and humanity were analogous with Whitman's. Alain was the one on the right, and though Whitman had sat before him in the past, at least three different times, he really didn't know much about him. From what he could tell, Alain was bitter, tight-lipped, and, if Whitman's assessments of facial expressions could be trusted, eternally skeptical. When he did speak, he did so in a persnickety way, as if it were a bother. Whitman wasn't sure if he liked Alain or not, and decided it made no difference.

Last and most certainly least, in Whitman's humble opinion, was the man on the left, William. Whitman knew William quite well. The two of them had started with the organization at same time, in the same district, and it was widely believed that both would ascend the company ladder at record speed. Whitman was the best, and William was right behind him. Back then they were friendly rivals and confidants; they worked together, they pushed each other to get better, they sought each other's opinions and advice, and they helped each other out. Then one day Whitman made a fateful decision that was not looked upon kindly by the Elders; he was promptly busted down, and William was promoted. Now William sat on the bench as an Elder, and Whitman had no choice but to answer to him. It wasn't that he was mad at William, though admittedly he could do without all the smug looks and cynical criticisms his one-time-friend seemed to relish handling him with; he was mad at himself for going against the grain and failing miserably, leaving the Elders no choice but to reprimand him. Had he not screwed up, twice, he could've been on the bench; he could've been presiding over these meetings, influencing protocol, making crucial decisions. Or, better yet, he could've been a sentry in the Spirit Realm. That's where the real war was being fought.

But no, he had to go and buck the system, had to try to make a difference because he believed it was the right thing to do. And so he was stuck in the trenches, stuck fighting the same old war he'd been fighting for what seemed like forever now, watching the casualties rise like the body count in a seventies' slasher flick.

"Whitman," said Tyrus, welcoming him. "How are you?"

"Good, sir. And yourself?"

"Wonderful. Thank you. Every day is a blessing."

"Glad to hear it, sir." Whitman turned to Alain next. "Alain," he said to him, giving a nod. He then did the same for William, though his voice betrayed a tinge of bitterness when he greeted his old friend.

"Whitman," replied Alain without inflection.

William said, "Good to see you again, Whit." His voice, conversely, hinted at conceit, and the mordant, I'm-better-than-you grin he showed surely was meant as an affront.

"It's been how long since we've seen you last?" Tyrus inquired, even though he knew the time down to the minute.

"Three years, sir," replied Whitman. "Give or take a day." He smiled, endeavoring to show a carefree demeanor.

"That sounds right." Tyrus flipped open his folder and, using a finger as a guide, scanned down his notes.

Alain and William opened their folders, too.

Whitman didn't have a folder. He was expected to know everything about his territory    and be able to extemporize thoroughly and intelligently thereupon any relatable subject broached.

"Not a very productive period for you, it seems," said Tyrus, getting right to business in his customary dignified manner. He had a dry voice, and made a point of properly enunciating every word. "You dropped from fifty-two percent to just over fifty. Is there a specific cause for this?"

"Other than the constantly evolving, or should I say *de*volving, vagaries of society?" replied Whitman.

"Yes. That's what you blamed it on last time, if I remember correctly."

Whitman hesitated, embarrassment and uncertainty coloring his face. He had hoped the panel wouldn't remember that line from last time. It left him with a couple ripe old chestnuts in his hip pocket that he no longer had the confidence to use.

"Well?" said Tyrus. "Aside from the vagaries of society, was there anything else that contributed to this decline?"

"Um. Economic uncertainty," Whitman ventured. He hadn't used that one last time, not that he could remember.

"Yes. Of course." Tyrus turned to Alain. "We've been hearing that one a lot lately."

Alain, his face rumpled like an old pillow, nodded petulantly. "Yes," he said. "That seems to be the case. Very popular rationalization these days." He looked at Whitman. "And this is a contributing factor why exactly?"

"Well ... You see, there's a lot of hardship going around," Whitman labored to explain. "Money's tight. People are scared. And when people get scared, they tend to ... well, act out." Then, going off the cuff, which was not a strong suit of his, he added, "Probably why numbers are down all over."

William, like a lion in the bush, pounced. "The national average is fifty-four percent," he pointed out. "*Fifty-four* percent. That puts you nearly four points below average. You can't afford to fall any lower."

"I think what my colleague here is trying to say," Tyrus was quick to cut in, "is that we cannot allow things to slip away. It's a critical time for us. We have to focus our attention on what's most important. We simply cannot slip below fifty percent."

"Yes, sir. I understand," said Whitman, knowing the most common punishment for District Directors who slipped below the fifty percent mark was a six-month probation period followed by a demotion of rank should the district's numbers not rebound. He did not want to think about that, however; the idea terrified him.

"If you understand that, why no change?" William inquired. "Look, I know how you feel, Whit, but perhaps the time has come to change your approach. Times are changing, and we have to change with them. As difficult and depressing as it is to accept, some people are beyond salvation."

"I suppose I don't believe that," Whitman replied. "No one is beyond salvation."

"Unfortunately that's not true," William shot back. "Quite a few are. And we've got the numbers to prove it. Don't be naïve, old friend. We can't afford it. Not now."

Whitman felt his heart accelerate and his cheeks flush with rage, and he noticed, after a deep breath, that his hands were clenched into fists. Anger was not tolerated in the White Room, not so much as a harsh word could be spoken, especially from subordinates, and so the mark of antipathy on Whitman's weathered old face, coupled with the rigid tension in his muscles, led Tyrus to speak up quickly. "Easy now, Whit," he said. "Remember where you are. And who you are."

It wasn't spoken harshly, but there was little doubt in Whitman's mind that he'd just been rebuked. He took another deep breath, and he held the air in his lungs for a few seconds before letting it out.

"I'm just saying," he began, his voice tempered, respectful, "that it's not so simple. There are variables. Life is unpredictable."

"We understand that. Just like you need to understand that we need as many victories as we can get."

"Yes, I know. And me and my group have been working extra hard lately. Tightening the screws, as they say."

"Yes. *Your group*," said Alain in a clearly distasteful way, as if uttering some terrible perversion.

Tyrus, always the diplomat, said, "We understand you don't have the most productive team to work with. But you're supposed to be one of our best leaders." He flipped a page in his folder and read over a couple lines. "You have ninety-four Custodians under your charge, accounting for 49,738 souls. Of those ninety-four, only thirty-eight are over fifty percent, four are at fifty percent, and fifty-two are under fifty percent. Clay, at fifty-six percent, is your most accomplished. He is a fine example. Emilia at fifty-four percent and Alina at fifty-three are the only other members of your team over the national average. Then there's Edmund Van Roy."

Whitman cringed. He knew they were going to bring up Edmund. They always brought up Edmund.

"Mister Van Roy is at forty-two percent, which is one of the lowest averages we've ever seen. I think it's fair to say that he wouldn't even be here if we weren't so shorthanded. Forty-two percent?"

"Intolerable," sneered Alain.

"We placed Edmund with you because we thought you would be able to help him. You used to be a great motivator, a great teacher, Whitman. His numbers were forty-three percent at his last post. They've actually gone down under your tutelage."

"True. Edmund has experienced some growing pains," Whitman said, choosing his words carefully. "But I believe recently he's gained some perspective, and now has a better understanding of his influence. He's coming around. Really. I see good things in his future. We just have to be patient."

"You can't be serious," said William. "I like the boy, Whit, he's a good kid, but he's bordering on incompetent. I think the time has come for him to babysit Ducks for a spell."

"I disagree," replied Whitman. He turned to Tyrus, speaking directly to him. "We need to continue to teach him the nuances of the job and give him time to learn and gain more experience. Besides, if I give him nothing but Ducks, the others will complain. They're overworked as it is."

"Every district is overworked," said William.

"Yes. But we've got a higher caseload per associate than any other group in the area." That was one statistic Whitman had in his favor, and he was not afraid to toss it out there when needed. "You took three Custodians from us last year, three of our best, too, and haven't replaced them yet. We're doing the best we can."

"I know," said Tyrus. "And we understand. But these reports, Whit, they're not good. And Edmund hasn't progressed like we hoped."

"He's still young. Some need more time than others."

"He's been with us long enough," said William. "Numbers are numbers. We can't carry him forever. Perhaps he'd be better suited elsewhere."

"His numbers will go up. Trust me."

"Yes, I'm sure they will," said Tyrus. "Because we're putting him under your direct tutelage for the next year."

Whitman looked at Alain, which was a lot like looking at a brick wall, and then he looked at William, who wore, quite plainly, an expression of righteous superiority. Finally, he turned to Tyrus. "In what capacity, sir?" he asked.

"You will take over the bulk of his current caseload and he will observe you, learn from you, and assist you as needed. Also, as we noted earlier, we believe it would be in his best interest to babysit a couple hundred Ducks. If you want, you can give him a few Fences, too, so he can continue to cut his teeth."

Whitman's brow bunched up like a frightened caterpillar. "You want me to start working the streets again on a daily basis?"

"What a terrible inconvenience," said William mockingly.

Whitman heard him, but refused to look his way. He was too consumed with the prospect of going back to the frontlines.

"We want you to be Edmund's direct mentor," Tyrus explained. "We want him to shadow you, watch your every move, learn from you."

"And, quite frankly, we want to see if you still have what it takes," grumbled Alain, not one to mince words or beat around bushes.

Whitman's stunned expression remained in place. "Me?" he said.

"Recently questions have been raised in concern of your leadership abilities."

Whitman's head automatically snapped in William's direction.

"Don't look at me," said William.

"From an impartial monitor," said Tyrus. "And we would be remiss, given the steady dip in your numbers and this person's concerns, if we didn't investigate."

"But I haven't worked the streets in decades."

"Like I said before, it's a critical time for us. We need as many capable men and women on the street as possible. And your group is shorthanded."

"Given the state of your district," Alain sneered, "I'm surprised you haven't volunteered to do this already."

Whitman's brow remained bunched.

"You're not the only District Director we're asking to do this," said Tyrus. "Others are being called to task."

This did little to soothe Whitman's despair.

"Don't fret. It's only for a year," Alain said to him. "It'll fly right by."

Whitman stared senselessly into the white abyss, his mind reeling.

"And if the group's numbers go up," added Tyrus, "and they very well should, especially Edmund's, then you can resume your regular post." He made no mention as to how high they expected the numbers to go, or what would happen if the numbers stayed the same or, God forbid, went down. Whitman was not about to ask.

"Time has come that we all pull together as a team," William recited, a smirk hiding just below the surface. The others may not have seen it, but Whitman did. He wanted just one chance to wipe that smirk off William's face for good, preferably with his bare knuckles.

"So, any questions?" said Tyrus.

Whitman issued a plaintive sigh. "This starts immediately, I presume?"

"You're to inform Edmund and the rest of your Garrison of the change tomorrow. The sooner you get moving on this, the better."

"Of course," said Alain, "you will be required to continue your normal duties as District Director as well. I'm sure you can handle it."

"Of course," replied Whitman, unable to keep himself from sagging in defeat, much like a prize fighter returning to his stool after taking a terrible beating.

"Well, that sums up our end," said Tyrus, closing his folder. "Do you have any questions, concerns, or requests for us?"

Whitman had a list of topics he wanted to broach, but he was finding it difficult to keep hold of a thought other than his impending return to the streets. He had expected to be reprimanded, and rightly so; he had expected the council to put on a grave show as they went over his many mistakes, his few successes, his paltry numbers; and, in the end, as they wrapped things up, he expected them to make a point of telling him that he had to do a better job, that things had to improve, to which he would put on his most sincere face and promise them that next time would be different. That's how it was supposed to go. That's how it had been going for the last twenty years.

Not this time, though.

After an awkward valediction, Whitman stammering his words, unable to look the Elders in the eye, he skulked out of the White Room with his head cast down, his tail between his legs, and a nauseous feeling in the pit of his stomach.

"I don't understand," Edmund said in the thick British accent he'd yet to lose, and most likely never would. He still said things like 'bugger' and 'wanker' and 'bloody hell', which made him a target for the others, all American, who rather enjoyed mimicking his haughty-sounding intonation. The baffled expression on his face, a near permanent look for him, dug in a little deeper. "I'm being ... *reassigned?*"

"You're now the General Account Representative for this district," said Whitman, spouting off the title he'd created to spare Edmund's feelings. "It's because our branch's numbers are so low. They want me back on the street as a full time Custodian."

Edmund nodded somberly, a rumpled, hangdog look adding a dash of melancholy to his normally bemused mien. "Okay," he said. "I guess I understand. But I'm getting better, right? I mean, this isn't a demotion or anything?"

He was such a sweet kid, and he really was trying his best, which made it all the more difficult for Whitman to be as forthright with him as necessary. Also, Edmund didn't possess the type of character that handled criticism well, only the continual pats on the back and reassuring clichés like, 'Don't worry, we'll get 'em next time,' and 'Nothing you could do about that one; that's how things go sometimes,' weren't working. Edmund's numbers had started out historically low and had been going downhill ever since. The time had come to be more direct with him.

"Not in the least," said Whitman, lying through his teeth, unable to unload on such a gentle, well-meaning young man. "We all need help from time to time. I'll be reshuffling everyone's caseload, not just yours."

This seemed to brighten Edmund's mood. "Oh. Okay then," he said, his hangdog look morphing into an awkward smile. "Brilliant. Let me know what I can do to help."

"We'll have an official meeting Monday morning. We'll go over everything then."

"Sounds like a plan to me, boss. So, I suppose your meeting didn't go too well, what with them making you reshuffle and everything."

"No. Not good at all," said Whitman. Then, breaking out the company line, "But it's a critical time. We all have to pull together as a team."

"You can count on me, boss. I'll do whatever's asked."

Whitman nodded, knowing that to be true.

Edmund was as loyal, faithful, and loveable as the family mutt … and quite nearly as dumb. If you asked him to do something for you, you could bet your bottom dollar he'd do it, without question or complaint. His problem, unfortunately, was competence.

"We'll talk about it Monday," said Whitman, not interested in delving into the details. It had been a long day, and all he really wanted was a drink.

"Right, boss. I understand. And there's some work I need to do."

"Good. That's what I like to hear."

Edmund said his goodbye, got up and left, and Whitman opened his bottom drawer and pulled out a plain bottle of something orangish in color. He retrieved a glass from the same drawer, dumped in three fingers worth of the fine honey wine that was his drink of choice, and slammed it back in one smooth motion. He poured himself three more fingers and screwed the cap back on the bottle, though he did not put it away. Then, in a theatrical sort of way, though there was no one in the room but him, he heaved a sigh and leaned back in his seat.

It was going to be a long weekend, of that much he was certain. He was going to have to take a few clients – if you could call the mix of infants, handicapped, and at-death's-door geriatrics he had in mind clients – off each of his other reps and give them to Edmund. There'd be a lot of bellyaching going on over that, he knew, all the others in the group moaning and complaining, saying it wasn't fair, that they were already overworked and underappreciated. But he didn't have a choice in the matter. If he had a choice in the matter, he sure as hell wouldn't be taking over the bulk of Edmund's client ledger, and that's what he'd tell them.

He took another drink, then put a call out to Emilia. "Em?" he said, seemingly to the air. "You available?"

A few seconds went by before her ghostly reply came back. "I suppose. Though Friday night is usually a busy night for us. Caged animals set free. Why?"

"I need to talk."

"I figured you might be calling, given your meeting with the boys upstairs. I think I can find some time. The usual spot?"

"I'll meet you there in five." Whitman grabbed another glass, grabbed the bottle, and went on his way.


The usual spot was a long abandoned railroad trestle, a hundred and twenty feet high, overlooking a whole lot of nothing about six miles outside of Hagerstown. This was his special place, his sanctuary; it's where he went when he needed to get away and clear his head. Recently, after keeping it private for many years, he'd invited his favorite and most trusted employee, Emilia, to join him, and now, on occasion, they'd meet there, share a drink or two, and have a chat about whatever was on their minds. This little ritual of theirs had become a more frequent occurrence as of late. It seemed that most of Whitman's nerves, the ones that made up the Mercurial spiritual psychology of him, had reached that oh so tender exposed phase, where any little contact caused great and terrible pain.

He arrived at the trestle first and took a seat on the western side, on one of the old iron railway bridge's many platforms. From his lofty perch, which jutted out a few feet from the dense, looming structure of the bridge, Whitman was able to survey miles of tranquil darkness – a motionless black sky above him, a canopy of gently rustling pines below, each canvas stippled here and there by rogue patches of twinkling lights.

Emilia showed up a few minutes later and, taking a seat next to him, dangling her legs over the chasm below, said, "We keep meeting like this and the others are going to talk."

She was short, dark-skinned, slightly-overweight, with a spherical puff of black and lightly-graying hair that sat atop her head like the ash on a cigar. Her big brown eyes, set deep, filled with the wisdom of too many mistakes seen, regarded Whitman with a mixture of mirth and empathy, and she shook her head back and forth and said, "My, my, my, don't you look a mess."

He filled the extra glass with honey wine and handed it to her. She took a deep, satisfying sip, and afterwards went, "Ahhhh," like they were filming a commercial. Then, looking out over the peaceful expanse, which stretched on from dark to interminable blackness, she added, "Nice night."

"Relatively speaking," replied Whitman offhandedly.

"That bad? Well, it couldn't have been a surprise. You knew the numbers going in."

"True. But you know the higher-ups; they always have a surprise for you."

"What kind of surprise?"

Whitman took another sip of honey wine, sighed again – a dismal utterance that over the last decade or so had become as much a part of who he was as his face, his frown, his mane of white hair – and then started in on the whole ugly story, telling Emilia about the Council's decision to reorganize the group and send him back to the frontlines, where he was expected to not only train Edmund but headman a charge to raise the group's overall numbers to a more respectable level. As he progressed through his account, his stoic demeanor gradually gave way, succumbing to the duress of infuriating details and the warming effect of the honey wine. By the end, his words were slanted with virulence and his overall demeanor had edged into the cold waters of bitterness.

Emilia couldn't help but smile. Being a friend, she took no satisfaction in Whitman's distress, though she couldn't deny that it was quite entertaining when he lost his cool; it was the equivalent of watching someone of debonair comportment accidentally go face first through a spider web.

When she knew he was finished, she said to him, "So, you have to hit the streets again?" She tweaked her smile, turning it into a mordant, thin-lipped grin that certainly was made at Whitman's expense.

"Yeah, yeah, yeah," he said, looking away. "You're probably enjoying this."

"I am," she replied. "Truly. I've been saying it for years, Whit. Upper management needs more tangible contact with the real world. I think a lot of you have forgotten what it's like out there. Everyone should have to do this. All of you, from the top down. Your superiors, and their superiors, too."

"The Elders? On the street? Ha! Like that will ever happen."

"Not saying it will, but it should. I'm talking about really getting out there. Like this. Taking on a full territory, handling a diverse cross-section of clients on a day-to-day basis. How long has it been for you, if you can even remember?"

Whitman scoured the windswept halls of his swiftly-depreciating memory. It had been a long time since he'd been a grunt working the streets, at it every day and all hours of the night, busting his hump in the epic battle between good and evil. He had a vague recollection of the start of Rock and Roll, of Elvis and Chuck Berry, of hoop skirts and drive-ins and what now were regarded as classic cars. A lot had changed since then, and he wondered if he could still hack the madness.

The world was a crazy place filled with crazy people and an endless assortment of crazy things to do. In Whitman's opinion, the whole damn experiment had been an exercise in lunacy from the very start. But what made it worse now was that the world was smaller, the population greater, and the envelope had been pushed open so far that it had begun to rip at the edges. It wouldn't be long, Whitman believed, before the whole damn thing went up in flames like a backwoods shithouse. Of course, he'd been saying that for forty years now, if not longer, right around the time Charles Manson had hit the scene. His old friend Max had been saying it since the roaring twenties and prohibition.

"It's been a while," he said as he stared out at the night, wishing everything could be so beautiful and serene.

"Yeah, well, it's a different ballgame these days. You'll see."

Emilia Castley was a real straight shooter, an Annie Oakley of truth who had no patience for ulterior motives and saw no point in mixing words. She had been on the job for a hundred and twenty years now, approximately half the amount of time as Whitman, and not much surprised or shocked her anymore.

She was his favorite employee because of her candor and her honesty, because she believed in what she did and truly sought to make a difference, and because she had been around the block umpteen times and remained dedicated and optimistic. Most importantly, at least in Whitman's opinion, was that she had been accepted in the ranks back when the criteria was a lot more strict, which meant she had earned her post as a Custodian fair and square; she wasn't a legacy or part of the ill-conceived open matriculation program circa 1981 that allowed any fool who survived Purgatory a spot on the team. It used to be you weren't even looked at unless you earned direct admission into Heaven or defeated the trials of Purgatory before the length of your sentence. But over the last hundred and fifty years or so, with the population boom and more and more souls going to Hell or serving longer sentences in limbo, the requirements for Custodianship had to be relaxed. Most Garrisons were terribly shorthanded, and it was continually getting worse. Back when Whitman had first started, Custodians had no more than forty or fifty charges to deal with, and often all or most of them were part of the same family unit, which allowed for more opportunities to affect positive change. These days, however, most Custodians were responsible for four or five hundred souls. It was no wonder they were losing the war.

"It's the same ballgame as ever," Whitman said to her. "And I'm no fool in the dark. Sure, I may have lost touch over the last twenty or thirty years, but I was on the street plenty in my day, more years than you or anyone else in the Garrison, and I remember what it's like. The rampant drug use, the sex, the greed, the unconscionable violence. People doing whatever they want whenever they want and to hell with the consequences."

"The consequences, and Hell, catch up to them eventually," said Emilia.

"Yes they do. That's the sad truth."

"But today it's the lack of guilt that's the real killer. The total disregard for anything approaching expiation. Nobody does anything wrong anymore, don't ya know. Everyone's busy trying to be accommodating. You'll see."

"The job has never been easy. Times change. People stay the same."

"Perhaps. But times *have* changed, significantly, and now you have to deal with those same people, flawed and foolish, in myriad ways. Drugs and alcohol have always been a problem, but now you've got doctors prescribing powerful psychotropic drugs to nine and ten year old kids, and everyone wonders why these same kids go on murder rampages a few years later. Or lust. Lust has been around since the dawn of this world, but now all people have to do is plug in a computer and surf on line. People having sex, all sorts of sex, disturbing, violent, aberrant sex, pops right up like nothing. Remember spin the bottle?"

"Of course," said Whitman. "Popularized in the Fifties, I believe."

"Well, they still play it today, but now the stakes include fellatio and intercourse."

"Dear God," Whitman gasped.

"Kissing just doesn't register anymore. It's too vanilla. Why just the other day one of my good girls, at least I thought she was one of my good girls – goes to church every week with her folks, studies hard, is nice to her friends and little brother, volunteers at the local animal shelter – anyway, she goes to this party and ends up drinking some wine, smoking a joint, and giving some guy a hummer in the bathroom. A hummer is slang for fellatio. You'll have to familiarize yourself with all the slang used now. It's like a different language. Anyway, this girl, sixteen years old, honor roll student, and there she is in some basement bathroom performing oral sex on a twenty-year-old goofball. You'd think she'd have more sense than that. I was appalled."

Whitman cringed, understanding that the witnessing of such horrid scenes most likely lay in his future. Then, trying to console his friend, he said, "She's young. Inexperienced. Everyone makes mistakes."

"That's just it, though. To her it wasn't a mistake. Sure, she was a little embarrassed at first, but by lunch the next day she was laughing about it with her friends. Hell, the guy Tweeted about it."

"Tweeted?" Another word that had yet to make it into Whitman's lexicon.

"Social Networking," explained Emilia, rolling her eyes. "What they call Progress. You'll see soon enough."

"Can't say I'm looking forward to that."

"Of course not. I know I wasn't raised like this. My mother's probably spun in her grave all the way to China by now. I'll tell ya, Whit, I never thought I'd see this sort of casual debauchery and hedonism."

They were silent for a while, two earnest, compassionate, genuinely-concerned Custodians staring off into the lonely scope of night, sharing a bit of honey wine and ruminating on the dissolute state of modern society. Finally Whitman said, "So, if you had a chance to do it all over again?"

"What?" said Emilia. "Life?"

"No. Heavens no." Whitman chuckled at the absurdity of the idea. "I meant accepting your current position."

"Oh. That?" Emilia took a few moments with her thoughts. It was an unexpected question, one she had never been asked and had never thought to consider. Finally she shrugged and said, "It's no picnic, that's for sure. But if I can help just a few people along, then it's worth it."

# Chapter Four

"I'm what?" gasped Whitman, appalled.

"Alive, sir," replied Edmund timidly.

"Alive? I know I'm … Wait." He looked around the room with ever-widening eyes; he looked at the hospital monitors surrounding his bed and the TV hanging on the wall, and with his fingers he felt the blanket covering his body. "You mean … *Alive?*"

Edmund's head started bobbing up and down. The terrified, ill-at-ease look on his face remained perfectly in shape and made him look as if he had stomach cramps.

"I can't be alive, Edmund. It's impossible."

"Right, sir. I know. It's a bit of a conundrum."

Whitman ran a hand over his face and through his hair. He lifted the blanket covering the lower half of his body and discovered that he had legs and knees and feet. He had always had legs and knees and feet, ever since he could remember, but he hadn't had flesh and blood human ones in over two centuries. He wiggled his toes and they responded.

"From what we've been able to ascertain," said Edmund, the pallor of his complexion giving him a corpselike appearance under the dim fluorescent lights, "you died."

"I know I died," replied Whitman petulantly. "I died of scarlet fever. Two hundred and forty-nine years ago! On July the 14th. It was raining."

"Yes, well, apparently you … died again, sir."

"I can't *die* again, Edmund. I'm dead. I'm a spiritual being for … " Whitman bit down hard on his words, stopping himself from blaspheming. 'Christ's sake!' had been on the tip of his tongue, and he could hardly believe the words had popped in his head let alone nearly passed his lips. He took a deep breath and started again. "How exactly did this happen?" he inquired with restrained frustration.

Edmund shrugged helplessly. "We're not sure."

"What do you mean you're not sure?"

"Well ... Apparently there was an ... *incident.*"

"What sort of incident?"

Edmund gave his boss, whom he knew as a tall, austere man with flawless white hair and steel blue eyes, certainly not the foppish twenty-something with wild, tumbling locks and sketchy hygiene before him, a dubious look. "You ... Well, far as we can tell, you became *human* again, somehow ... and, well ... died."

As far as explanations went, it wasn't very convincing, and it did nothing to mitigate Whitman's puzzlement or ire. "I can't *become* human again, Edmund. I passed on. Do you understand what I'm saying?"

"Right, sir. Certainly. And don't fret, Emilia's looking into it. She'll get to the bottom of things. Now, do you remember *anything* that might help us?"

"Obviously not!" Whitman snapped. He looked around in utter disbelief. "This is real?" he said, still struggling to wrap his mind around the idea. "I'm ... *human?*"

"Yes, sir. Quite."

"But ... It's ... Wait. Did you say that I died?"

"You did, sir. Yes. But the paramedics were able to revive you. Thank goodness, too. Who knows what may have happened if they were unsuccessful. And you have no memory of what you were doing last?"

Whitman tried to think back, but there was an entire patch of time missing from his memory bank. He knew who he was, where he came from, what he did for a job ... and then he remembered waking up in a hospital

"You had taken over most of my accounts," Edmund explained. "Remember? You were in the field again, much to your chagrin."

Whitman nodded absently. He had a solid recollection of the meeting in the White Room with the Elders; they had castigated him, as usual, and demanded he go back to work. He was put on probation, so to speak, forced to return to hard labor. He remembered sitting on the trestle and talking with Emilia afterwards, and he remembered how she had laughed at him and told him it was a good thing.

He wondered if she would still think it was a good thing.

"Do you remember who you were watching at the time?" Edmund inquired. "That's the key, we believe. We assume something must've happened on the job. That's what we've come up with thus far."

"Really? That's what you've come up with thus far?" There was sarcasm in Whitman's voice, brimming with animus. "With all the resources at your disposal? Not exactly conclusive, is it?"

Edmund shook his head glumly. "Sorry, sir. Best we've got."

"What about you? You were supposed to be observing me, weren't you? Where were you when this happened?"

"Not entirely sure, sir. We're not certain of the timeline. And if you remember, I still have a few accounts of my own."

Whitman grumbled, and then crawled back into the dense, murky swamp of his brain. He remembered ... And then there was ... And then he ... And after that he ... woke up.

Wait. There was a moment of ...

Just then the main door swung open and a tall man in a spotless white frock, carrying a clipboard and a small Styrofoam cup of coffee, entered. He wore an unpleasant expression, and when he looked at Whitman, it was with the stern, condemnatory glare of a federal judge. He was followed by a waiflike nurse, a frail shadow of a girl who seemed to disappear into the wall.

"You're awake?" the doctor said, a note of surprise in his voice. His face, however, remained an implacable mask of superiority. "When did you wake?"

Whitman stared at the man as if he had never seen a man before. His eyes then traveled to the nurse, who shrank from his attention.

"Can you hear me?" asked the doctor, coming forward.

Whitman looked to Edmund for help.

"Don't look at me," replied the puzzled Brit. "I don't know what to tell you. There's nothing like this in the manual. I checked."

"He can see me?" said Whitman, horrified.

"Who are you talking to?" asked the doctor, his gaze traveling to where Whitman's was aimed. He saw nothing but two empty hospital chairs and a bare coat rack. "Hey!" he said, snapping his fingers. "Over here."

"You better answer him," said Edmund nervously.

Whitman turned to the doctor and gave him a look like there was a large spider crawling up over his shoulder. "I ... don't ... know," he managed.

"You don't know who you're talking to?"

Whitman turned to Edmund again, desperate. "Is this real?" he said. "It can't be real. I'm dreaming, right? Only I don't dream. I don't sleep."

"Who are you talking to?" the doctor repeated. "Of course this is real."

"Remember, he can't see me," said Edmund, whispering for some reason.

Whitman looked at the doctor and smiled wanly. "No one," he said. "Nothing. I uh ... I think I'm just ... Well, I'm not sure what's going on. I'm feeling a little ... a little ... "

"Wonky?" Edmund suggested, trying to helpful.

"Wonky," Whitman finished before he thought about it. And then he turned and scowled at Edmund for his choice of words.

"Wonky?" said the doctor skeptically. "That's a new one."

"Sorry. I'm ... confused, I think."

"Right. Very good, sir," said Edmund. "Play dumb. And whatever you do, don't tell him who you are. Who you *really* are. They'll lock you up in an asylum."

Whitman swung around on Edmund and burned a stare into him. "Find out what the hell is going on here," he said to him, forgetting his visitors.

"Nurse," said the doctor, turning to her, "I think he may be delusional. Let's get twenty milligrams of Rioxipam in him, to help calm him down. Then we'll need to do a full workup – CT Scan, X-rays, EKG. We'll need blood work, too."

The nurse nodded obediently, and ducked out of the room.

"I assure you I am not in an agitated state," said Whitman, regaining some composure. "And I certainly don't need drugs. I'm merely confused."

"That's understandable, I suppose. Including surgery, you were unconscious for nearly twenty-four hours. We didn't think you were going to make it." The doctor moved around the bed, checking the monitors standing guard on Whitman. "And there's the trauma of being shot, of course."

That news came as quite a shock to Whitman. "Shot?!"he cried out. "By a gun?"

The doctor fixed him with an incredulous stare. "Yes. What else? You don't remember any of this?"

Whitman once again looked at Edmund, who had recoiled into the corner over by the bathroom, as far from Whitman and the doctor as he could manage. The novice Guardian Angel shrugged and said, "Well, at least we know what happened to you."

"Find out what's going on!" Whitman demanded in a harsh whisper. "Now!"

The doctor stared at his young patient with some confusion. "Excuse me?" he said.

"Not you," said Whitman, still not quite grasping the entirety of the situation.

Over in the corner, Edmund said, "Don't worry, sir. Edmund Van Roy is on the case. Rest assured." Then, like that, he was gone and Whitman was alone with the doctor, who asked him, quite seriously, if he was hallucinating.

"You know, I can't really say," Whitman replied somewhat feebly, his uncertainty and unease as evident as a smear of black paint on a white wall. "I have to think I am. Either that or I'm having the worst nightmare of my life."


Emilia was staring at the spitting image of her boss, Whitman, whom she'd known for more than eighty-four years now. Only it wasn't him. It looked like him, from head to toe, but his eyes, though they were the same movie star shade of blue, lacked a certain depth and wisdom. And when he spoke, there were subtle differences in his pitch, his cadence, his enunciation ... not to mention the words he used and the context he put them in. He was from the modern world, of that they were sure, and after more than twenty hours of diligent investigation, they believed that they finally knew his identity.

"Does the name Martin Loomis mean anything to you?"

Emilia asked him.

The man's weathered old face – Whitman's face – bunched up with serious thought. Then, suddenly, as if the sound of his own name woke something in his conscious mind, he started to nod. "Yes," he said. Martin Loomis. That's me."

"We just figured it out," said Emilia.

Martin had showed up in the Spirit World right about the time Whitman was dying on the floor of the A&P Mart in Hagerstown. Somehow, in a yet inexplicable cosmic glitch, they had switched bodies in the mystical void that bordered both the real world and the spirit world: Whitman became corporeal, taking the human form of Martin Loomis, while Martin Loomis, having committed suicide, somehow ended up in Whitman's spiritual body. Their minds, however, were still their own.

"Do you know what happened to you?"

Memories flooded back to Martin at once. His whole life flashed before his eyes in exquisite bedlam, every joyous and painful moment falling down on him at once, including the end. He remembered vividly the gun against his chest and his finger on the trigger. And he remembered nothing more.

"Am I ... *dead?*" he asked, horrified by the thought.

"Yes," said Emilia plainly. "You're dead. Believe it or not, death is often a consequence of someone shooting himself."

Her scorn flew past Marty, who was more preoccupied with his hands. He'd yet to see his face, but he could tell by his bent, wrinkled, age-spot dappled hands that he was not the young man he remembered himself to be. "How long have I been dead?" he inquired.

"About a day," Emilia told him.

"A day? But ... " Martin paused, looked around. He was in a conference room with white walls, a white door, a white table. This white room was not like the White Room the Elders used for their meetings, but it was still disconcertingly colorless, especially for someone fresh from a world of vibrant color.

"Am I in heaven?" he asked, associating white with heaven. Also, it was comfortably cool in this strange place, about sixty-five degrees or so. He imagined that hell would be much hotter, and vaguely reddish.

"No!" Emilia replied. "Sorry to tell you, but when you hold a gun to your chest and pull the trigger, you don't get to go to heaven."

Martin's face, showing all the wrinkles and lines of your average octogenarian, sagged with regret. "You saw that?" he said.

"We just pieced it together, actually."

"So where am I? This isn't hell, is it?"

"No, it's not hell. And where you are doesn't matter."

"It matters to me," said Martin sadly.

"Well maybe you should've thought of that before you shot yourself."

The harshness of her tone struck a nerve this time, and tears began to well in Martin's eyes, which, to Emilia, were Whitman's eyes. She never thought she'd see those steel blue eyes shed a tear; then again, she never thought something like this was possible, and she'd been living behind the curtain for a long, long time.

"I wasn't ... " Martin began, his voice catching in his throat.

"Save it," said Emilia. "It has nothing to do with our current problem. Though I would like to know why a nice young man such as yourself would go and do something so stupid as to shoot himself? How did you think that was going to turn out?"

"I just ... wanted it to be ... over," said Martin, stammering with emotion.

"Oh, stow it!" Emilia snapped back at him. "Over a girl. Don't you know any better?"

"She was cheating on me. I walked in on her."

"Well what did you expect? Where'd you meet her?"

Marty hesitated. "At a bar," he said.

He remembered it well. Amanda was wearing skin-tight jeans and a low cut top, and she was arguing with some guy who looked like he'd stepped straight out of a department store catalogue. He left her there after she slapped him and threw a drink in his face. Amanda and Marty's cousin, Lisa, were good friends, and over the course of the night introductions were made, drinks were drunk, and the rest, as they say, is history ... right up to the point where a .45 caliber bullet mashed Martin Loomis's heart to bits.

"Exactly. At a bar," said Emilia. "And how long before you

were sleeping together?"

"Three dates."

"Three dates." She said this in the manner of a skilled litigator, in a way that said she'd proven her case and had no further points to make.

Truthfully, Martin and Amanda had had sex on their second date. The night they met, they fooled around in the back of his car, his hand clumsily and ineffectively wriggling around down her pants, her hand wriggling around down his with significantly more aplomb, bringing him to a jerking, grimacing climax in only a few minutes. Little did Marty know that only four hours earlier she and the catalogue-guy had had sex on the floor of her apartment. That was Amanda.

"So what? Who cares?" he piped, not interested in being questioned or condescended. "What's that got to do with anything?"

"I care," said Emilia. "You should, too."

"That's really not the point here."

This new voice came from the other end of the room, and both Emilia and Martin looked that way. Clay, the top field associate in the group and acting District Director with Whitman unaccounted for, strolled inside wearing his usual arrogant grin.

Martin didn't know him, but he certainly knew Martin. Martin Loomis had been one of his clients, and despite the young man's tragic and untimely demise, Clay didn't feel the least bit responsible. Much like the Elders, Clay believed that while everyone deserved a chance, some people were beyond salvation. It was up to the Custodian in charge to decide how much time and energy to expend on each client, and Clay was of the opinion that time was too valuable to waste on lost causes.

Martin, a gentle soul in desperate pain, could've used Clay's guidance in the waning days of his life. Instead he was left to the whims and whispers of the wicked.

"Who are you?" Martin asked him. "Are you angels?"

"No. We're Custodians," replied Emilia, which was, in the pantheon of heavenly beings, their official title. It always struck her as oddly appropriate that though they were celestial spirits of power and prominence, they were referred to as Custodians.

Like she used to tell Whitman: "What else do we do other than clean up messes."

"You mean like janitors?" said Marty, his confusion growing. "You don't look like janitors. Or are you guys like janitors in heaven?"

"You're not in heaven," said Emilia again. "Give it a rest."

"Now, now," said Clay, coming to Marty's defense. It was the first time in a while he'd done that. "The boy's been through enough already." He looked at the young man whom he used to quietly counsel, now wearing the aged body of his currently deposed boss, and said, "How are you feeling? Are you all right to talk."

Marty thought about the question and nodded. "Sure. I suppose. I certainly have a few questions for you."

"We'll answer any queries you might have in time," replied Clay. "But what we're looking for right now is answers."

"Answers you should already have," Emilia mumbled under her breath. Usually she wasn't so tactful when it came to Clay, but he was Acting Director in Whitman's absence and she didn't want to give him a reason. He was the type that didn't need one.

"I'm sorry?" he said to her, cupping a hand to his ear. He had heard her say something, but he wasn't sure what.

"Nothing," she said, smartly.

"Right." His eyes, narrow with suspicion, held her in their gaze for an extended period. Then, in a tone of pure upper-crust conceit, he said, "Emilia, don't you have something else you could be doing? We are short-staffed, after all, and as Acting Director these interviews are part of my duties."

"Of course," she said in her best replication of civility. And she turned on a heel and went on her way.

When she was gone, Clay took the seat next to Marty, settled in, and said to him, "Now, we know what happened to you last night. Dreadful turn of events. But we have some questions as to why."

"Why what?" said Marty.

"Why you committed suicide."

"Oh. That?"

"Yes. There was a girl involved, correct?"

Clay actually remembered the worst day of Marty's life quite well. He remembered the pain that poured out of his young client like hot acid. He remembered the unyielding heartbreak and despair. He had stayed loyal to Marty through the initial phase of the breakup, and those had been some dark days. But he lost interest when it became clear that Marty was drowning in denial and self-pity. The boy wouldn't listen to good advice, and he refused to dust himself off and give life another spin. You can't save someone who doesn't want to be saved, Clay believed.

"Yeah. There was a girl," Marty said, remembering Amanda and her heartless betrayal. Usually the thought of her caused emotion to bubble up inside him, eventually spilling over and making a mess. But presently he felt only a dull, hollow ache, and he wondered if maybe he had made a terrible mistake. "We were engaged," he went on dispassionately. "She was the love of my life."

"Go on."

Marty nodded, ready to continue, ready to admit to the epic downfall that eventually ended his life. But strangely any thoughts he had of Amanda fell from his head like worthless confetti. They were replaced by a palpable sensation of fear and curiosity as he looked around the room, taking in the blinding nothingness of white that surrounded him. "Where am I?" he asked, concern weighing on his words. "Seriously. I'd really like to know. Just ... well, because. You know, if I'm in hell, I just want to know, so I can ... I don't know, make my peace with it. The woman, she said this isn't heaven. But it doesn't feel like hell. Is it the other one?"

"The other one?" Clay asked.

"Yeah. The one in the middle." Marty knew there was another place souls supposedly went when they died, he just couldn't recall the name.

"You mean purgatory?" said Clay.

"Yeah. That's it. Purgatory. Is this purgatory?"

"No. You're not in any of those places. Yet. At the moment, you're in a spiritual weigh station. A holding cell of sorts."

Marty's mouth dropped open, giving him the haggard appearance of an awe-struck drunk. "Where you weigh my life?" he said. "To determine where I go?"

"Sort of," said Clay, lying.

"Oh man." Sudden panic swept up Marty Loomis and he began to defend his life with urgent supplication. "I used to give to charity," he said, desperately. "Honestly. All the time. March of Dimes, the Red Cross. Whatever I could manage. When I was working, that is. And once, in college, I helped build a house for that Habitat place. You know the one. I mean, I didn't get to church that often, but I prayed. Sometimes."

Truthfully, Marty hadn't been to mass in more than eighteen years, and any prayers he might have said recently revolved around selfish desires.

Despite the careless, carnal way in which he lived his life, Marty had never considered himself an atheist; he called himself, when people asked about his religious beliefs, agnostic, though he wasn't entirely sure what that meant. To him, God did not exist, not in any tangible way, and the only time he ever thought to recognize the possibility of His existence was when he really, really wanted something or when he felt he'd been wronged and needed someone to blame.

Like most people, he never judged his selfish, indulgent behavior as immoral. He had never killed anyone – other than himself, that is; and that, to him, was his prerogative, a clear cut example of freewill – and he'd never raped or purposefully injured anyone. He hadn't cheated on either of his two girlfriends, for what that was worth, and he'd never gotten into a fight or screamed at someone for no good reason. He was kind to animals, and children, and waitresses. He brought up all of these points in one long, run-on sentence that made Clay's head start to spin.

"Sure, I told a few lies in my day," he blathered on, gesturing wildly with his hands. "Little white ones, though. *Tactful* lies. 'Yeah, that casserole was great, mom,' or, 'No, your butt doesn't look fat in those jeans.' Little things like that. But I never told a lie to hurt anyone. Honest. And I never tried to ... "

"Whoa, whoa, whoa," Clay interrupted, holding up his hands as a signal for Marty to stop. "Easy now. That's not what this is about."

"Oh," said Marty, seeming both relieved and wary. "What is it about then?"

"I want to talk about your life the last couple weeks. Your friends. People you know. People you may have met. What it was like at the very end."

That was information Clay should already have had, only he had forsaken Marty in his darkest days, deeming him to be 'spiritually unredeemable.' Whitman and Emilia would have termed his actions reprehensible, but Clay called it responsible time management, and with his numbers where they were, well above everyone else's in the Garrison, the Elders would have backed him up.

"Start with your ex-girlfriend, if you don't mind. And go from there."

It wasn't a nightmare, unfortunately.

Whitman had been dead for nearly two minutes before the EMTs brought him back to life. He had lost a lot of blood, and none of the doctors in the Emergency Room thought he would make it. But against all odds he recovered, remarkably so.

His gunshot wound had healed nicely, despite the damage it had done to his heart, and though it took him nearly a full day to regain consciousness, his vitals held strong throughout. After he stabilized, it became a question of *when* he would wake up, not *if*, and though he remained in Intensive Care, the prognosis was good.

His test results baffled the doctors, who contrived to attribute the anomalies to shock and the fact that he'd been dead for almost two minutes. They had never seen a CT scan that showed so much brain activity before. His blood work also came back out of the ordinary, with abnormally high levels of both white and red blood cells, and close to triple the normal amount of platelets. They already were planning to use him as a case study, hoping to get published in the New England Journal of Medicine.

The problem they were having was that they didn't have anything to compare their results to. In addition to being a celestial being trapped inside the constraining human carapace of a recent suicide victim, Whitman was a John Doe, so there was no patient history on him. Whitman himself had never been to a hospital before. Once, long ago, he'd gone to see the doctor the next town over about a pesky ache in his side; he was given a truss and a foul elixir made from opiates for the pain. There was no paperwork to fill out, and payment was made in bread and eggs.

Whitman wasn't about to admit to that. Like Edmund had told him, the doctors wouldn't believe his story, and if he tried to tell it, good money said that he'd find himself wrapped in a canvas jacket and locked inside a padded room.

Instead, he listened to Edmund's advice – actually, it was Emilia's advice through Edmund – and pleaded amnesia like a daytime soap diva, claiming, quite convincingly, his current state of fear and bewilderment aiding his effort, that he had no idea who he was or what had happened. He told the doctors that he didn't remember anything about himself, not even his name. Seeing he'd been brought in without identification, it left those tending to him without much to go on. The best the police could do was make inquiries and check for missing persons. As yet their investigation hadn't yielded any leads.

Presently, Whitman, who had originally died almost two hundred and fifty years ago, at the ripe old age of seventy-four, which was quite old back then, was trying to comprehend the strange reflection staring back at him in the mirror.

He knew himself to have a blaze of snowy white hair, a bent nose, a scar over his left eye, and more wrinkles than a beach towel at the bottom of a laundry basket. But now when he looked at himself, he saw a young, decent looking fellow with a full head of brown hair, dark brown eyes, and nice teeth. He was taller than before, nearly six feet, and thin. There was no scar over his eye, his face was wrinkle-free, his nose arrow straight.

He had no idea how he'd gotten into this strange human skin, but he wanted out as soon as possible. His celestial body might have been old and gray and withered, well past its prime, but it didn't feel pain, fall to exhaustion, or suffer injury. There was no such thing as hunger or thirst, though he had been known to enjoy a drink of honey wine on occasion, to take the edge off. But he never had to worry about relieving himself. Since waking in this dreadful new world, he'd already had to go to the bathroom twice; the first time, initially unaware then dubiously unsure what to make of the uncomfortable sensation pushing down on his bladder, he nearly wet himself.

Pain, too, had been reprised, much to his chagrin. His chest, where he'd been shot, produced a dull ache that was as continuous as it was irritating, and every time he moved the wrong way or coughed it sent a sharp pang through him. Whitman didn't remember getting shot so he couldn't say how badly it had hurt; but he had to think the pain of a bullet paled in comparison to the pain he felt when the nurse, a bleak, severe-looking woman built like an old ringer washing machine, yanked the cathedra tube from his scrotum. His whole world had went white and he'd yelped like a scalded dog. He then had chastised her with a string of mostly benign words, 'heartless masochist' being the worst of them, to which she returned him an evil little smirk that said she took a small measure of pleasure in his agony, and would again should occasion arise.

Whitman also had given into his appetite for the first time in centuries, satisfying the rumble in his belly with a full meal. Chicken tasted different to him now, though he mused that it had been so long since he'd had chicken he could barely remember what it tasted like. The french fries had been a treat, the pudding a revelation. He couldn't wait for breakfast; he'd filled out his menu card earlier, ticking off scrambled eggs, bacon, hash browns, and toast. For drinks he ordered coffee and orange juice.

Eventually fatigue, another biological inconvenience he hadn't been burdened with in a couple centuries, got the better of him and he pulled himself away from the bathroom mirror, away from his strange, alien face, and drowsily shuffled off to bed. The drugs they had him on, a potent mix of sedatives and pain killers, laid him down and gently escorted him to the blurry world of narcotic bliss, numbing his pain and dissolving his will. His eyelids sagged, his normally crisp thoughts jumbled together and fell apart. Then, without realizing it, he fell headlong into dream world.

Edmund leaned over a snoring Whitman and whispered, "Sir? Hello? Are you sleeping?"

Whitman snuffled and snorted, and turned his head.

"Sir?" Edmund tried again. "Can you hear me?"

Subconsciously, Whitman became aware of someone or something hovering over him and his eyes blinked opened. "Yaiiii!" he cried out when he saw Edmund's pale, gaunt face only two inches from his.

Edmund shrieked, and stumbled away.

"Are you trying to give me a heart attack," said Whitman. "Dear God. I was just shot in the chest. What's wrong with you?"

"Sorry, sir," said Edmund. "You were sleeping."

"Yes. I know. I sleep now. And eat. And *urinate*."

Edmund's nose wrinkled in disgust. "Really? How distasteful."

"Tell me about it. And with this food they're feeding me, I'm sure it's only a matter of time before I have to ... well, you know."

Edmund cringed. "Please, sir," he said. "Decorum."

"Right. Sorry. What time is it?"

"Eleven in the morning. Are you just getting up?"

Whitman levied himself to an upright position in bed and looked around. "No," he said. "I had breakfast, and they did more tests. I guess I must've dozed off."

"How very strange."

"You have no idea. So, what's going on? Any information?"

"You mean on your situation?"

"No, Edmund. On the current socioeconomic state of Mozambique."

Sarcasm tended to sail over the Brit's head, but there was no confusing Whitman's tone. "Sorry, sir," he said. "I'm a little frazzled."

"Oh really? *You're* a little frazzled. You don't say."

"Sorry. I didn't mean to ... "

"Don't worry about it," piped Whitman, waving him off. "Just get me out of here."

Guilt made a mess of Edmund's oddly-attractive face. "Well, sir," he said.

"Well what?"

Despite his unease, Edmund forced himself to maintain eye contact with his boss and mentor, who currently looked like an unemployed skateboarder. "Well, sir," he said, "there seems to be a bit of a problem."

"What sort of problem?"

"We're not sure, really. But we're working on it."

"What about the Elders? What did they say?"

"Still haven't got word to them yet, sir. We're trying."

Whitman's face darkened three shades of red, prompting Edmund to take a good long look at the tops of his shoes.

"You haven't gotten word to them yet? What do you mean you haven't gotten word to them yet?! That's the most important thing I need you to do. They're the ones that'll have the answer."

"Yes, sir."

"I'm human, Edmund. Human! I don't want to be human. It's like going down a few rungs on the evolutionary ladder."

"Yes, sir," Edmund said again.

"I want to see Emilia."

"Actually, Clay is running things now. Emilia is not happy about that, I can tell you."

"Clay?! Why that pompous little ... " Instead of blurting out the colorful words he wanted to say, Whitman growled petulantly, like an angry old bear.

"He was second in command, sir," Edmund explained. "Only made sense."

"I don't care. I want to see Emilia. Now."

"Right. I'll tell her. I'll be back in two shakes."

As it turned out, two shakes equaled eighteen minutes and change, and Whitman discovered that he did not like being a slave to time. He had learned to deal with the concept of eternity, but waiting around a few minutes got up his dander.

On seeing him, Emilia burst into a smile. "Dear me," she said, placing a dainty hand on her chest. "I never would have thought this possible."

"I want out of here," Whitman said to her right off. "Now."

"Of course you do. We're working on it."

"How are you working on it? Has anyone talked to the Elders yet?"

"No. Haven't been able to reach them. Clay said he was going to try again, but I don't trust him, Whit. He's a little too pleased with all this."

"Of course he's pleased. He's been after my job for years. I know he's the one who told the Elders that I lack leadership skills."

"I'll try again when I get back, but they usually don't take my calls."

"You have to tell them this is an emergency. They have to know."

"Of course."

"I'm human."

"Well, technically you're liminal," Emilia corrected him. "However it happened, you seem to be able to experience *both* worlds. Though it seems as though you're stuck in this one."

"Well lucky me. Liminal, you say?"

"That's what they call it. You're a hybrid of sorts."

"Yeah? Well, I don't much care what they call it, I want out of here. Immediately. Do we know what happened yet?"

"Not entirely. We're still piecing together the facts. But we do know *who* you are."

Whitman's young, innocent-looking face hardened. "I'm Whitman!" he cried out, his voice trembling with belligerence. "Jeremiah Benjamin Whitman! That's who I am."

"We know whose *body* you have," replied Emilia calmly, maintaining composure.

Some of the blood drained from Whitman's cheeks. His eyes lost their menacing glare. "Whose?" he said.

"A gentleman by the name of Martin Thurston Loomis," she told him. "He was a recent suicide victim."

Whitman slapped a hand to his forehead and groaned. The strings of fate had gotten twisted somehow, and he was, against all odds and the very nature of physics, human again. Human! He hadn't been human since before there was a president. Now here he was, in a hospital in modern day Hagerstown, Maryland, as alive as the day he came out of the womb and his grandmother – not some stuffy doctor, because back when he was born they didn't live in a town with a doctor – slapped his keester and he let out an infant yowl.

"Sir?" The worried look on Emilia's face didn't change when Whitman looked at her. It actually found another depth.

"Yes?" he said, distractedly.

"Are you okay? You seemed to go off there."

He stared at her for a while, silently, his eyes wide and woeful. Then he said, "Suicide? How very tragic."

"Yes, sir. One of Clay's. A dreadful situation really."

Emilia recognized the audible scoff Whitman gave at the mention of Loomis being one of Clay's clients and it made her smile in spite of everything. "I know," she said. "And I agree."

Whitman's personal worries faded some as the thought of their side losing another soul weighed on him. They were losing more and more, but to what end he did not know. What was the point? Where was it going? Everyone in the ranks liked to talk about the Grand Scheme, as if all the variables of life were destined to perfectly align at some point, but as far as Whitman could tell none of it made sense. He was of the opinion that most of life was a coin flip, only there was no logical way to make heads or tails of it.

"Okay then," he said, quickly coming to terms, which was something he'd learned to get comfortable with over the years. Custodians had little choice but to develop a short memory as dwelling on losses assured further losses. "What's next?"

"We continue to work on getting you back, of course."

"The Elders. You have to get in touch with the Elders. They'll know what to do."

"We're doing all we can, Whit. It's not easy. We don't have any answers. Not to mention, we have to put up with Clay now, power-hungry little slug. He's already working on reassigning client lists and changing territories, if you can believe that."

Whitman's primary focus once again jumped tracks. "What?" he exclaimed, his voice booming. "On who's authority? I'm still the boss, dammit! This is a temporary situation. You tell that son-of-a-bitch that if he ever ... " The look of shock on Emilia's face ground Whitman's invective to a halt. "What?" he said.

"You," she told him. "Cursing and raising your voice. It's something to behold."

Whitman moaned miserably. "I know. I'm sorry," he said. "This whole thing has me flustered. But you tell Clay not to get comfortable in *my* chair, and not to change anything. This is still my district."

"Like he'll listen to me."

"Get word to the Elders. To Tyrus."

"I'm trying."

"Trying isn't good enough."

Emilia softened her look. Her big brown eyes poured out sympathy. "I understand, Whit. You're frustrated. I would be, too. But we're working on it. Believe me, we want you back. In the meantime, you need to remain strong and not lose focus."

"I'm falling free here, Em. I feel helpless."

"I know," said Emilia. "And we're going to get this fixed. Soon. Trust me."

Whitman nodded as if agreeing, but the pained look on his young face told a different story. "I will," he said, unconvincingly.

"Now as far as you're concerned, we think it's best you don't admit anything. Not yet. Not until we know more. And whatever you do, don't mention the name Martin Loomis. With any luck, this'll all be over in a few hours."

"I understand. And I pray you're right. Just make sure to get word to the Elders. To Tyrus. Make sure to ask for him specifically."

"I will. I promise."

Whitman threw his head back and let out an agonizing groan. "This is unbelievable," he said. "How in the world did this happen?!" It was a rhetorical question that Emilia had no plans to answer, not that he gave her any time. Right away he followed up by saying, practically pleading, "Please, Em, I don't know how much more of this I can take."

Emilia's puckered plum of a face took on a matronly air; it was a look she used quite often, and it suited her well. Under different circumstances, Whitman might have assumed he was being condescended. Things being what they were, however, the look actually provided him with a measure of comfort.

"I just want this to be over," he said. "Soon."

"I know," she told him.

A brief pause followed, long enough for Emilia to take the initiative. "So," she said, her manner a cross between curiosity and reluctance, "what's it feel like?"

"What does what feel like?" said Whitman.

"Being alive again."

The old Custodian shook his head dolefully. "Unfathomable. I have to urinate now. Can you believe that? And I get tired. The drugs they're giving me spin my head all directions so I can hardly think."

"Sounds horrible."

"It is." Then: "On the plus side, though, the food here is *fantastic*. Have you ever had pudding before? It's so creamy and delicious."

"Once," said Emilia. "A long time ago."

Whitman's face took on a demented sort of cheer. "I ordered two cups for lunch. One chocolate, one vanilla. I'm going to mix them. They told me they don't usually allow that, but they'd make an exception for me."

"Nice," said Emilia, smiling pleasantly. "Enjoy."

# Chapter Five

Charlie had gotten quite used to his friend's absentee behavior since the fateful day that turned his life inside out. Marty had become somewhat of a recluse since then, living on unemployment checks, booze, pills, cigarettes, and a deep despair that seemed to never relent. It was nothing for him to load up on supplies and lock himself in his apartment for a week straight, never leaving, never so much as opening a window to let the sun in. When he did go out, it was usually at night. He'd put on sneakers, put on a hat, and walk around town for hours, his head cast down, his feet scraping along the pavement in a sad zombie shuffle.

He'd go days without taking calls, too, Charlie had learned; though he'd usually shoot a text back saying something to the affect that he was okay, just not in the mood to talk.

All part of the new Martin Loomis.

Marty was a great guy, always had been a great guy, but he was a gentle soul who didn't do well with rejection or failure. He had never recovered from what Mandy had done to him, and Charlie privately wondered if he ever would. Charlie missed the witty, fun-loving, intelligent best friend he used to have; the Marty Loomis he now knew was morose and bitter, never more than a step away from depression, and Charlie's heart went out to him. That's why he could no longer wait for a call or text. He was worried. He hadn't heard from his friend since Saturday night and he had a bad feeling that something was wrong.

Charlie never mentioned anything, but he had noticed a disturbing increase in Marty's drinking the last couple months. He'd visit and there'd be three or four empty wine bottles near the trash and dozens of empty beer cans lying about. And then there were the pills. Charlie had given Marty an old bottle of

Vicodin a few weeks ago after Marty claimed that he was still in pain and the doctor wouldn't write him another script. Charlie, taking his friend on his word, thinking only of helping him, handed over the bottle without fuss. A couple weeks later, an edgy, irritable Marty came by and asked him if he had any more. Charlie didn't, and Marty promptly left in a rush.

Thinking back, Charlie wished he would've handled things differently. But how? Eighteen Vicodins certainly hadn't pushed him over the edge. Mandy had done that, quite coldheartedly, and ever since Marty had been falling free. Charlie wanted to stop that fall, he just didn't know how. He thought about having an intervention, but he didn't want to embarrass him. Besides, Marty didn't have any family to call on, and since his split with Mandy, he didn't have many friends either. That being the case, Charlie thought perhaps a personal heart-to-heart might be a better idea.

Marty's car was out front when he arrived, setting in its normal spot. It hadn't been washed in months, and dirt and grime had started to take over. Paint had begun to peel and chip around the dent in the front quarter panel, that dent the result of a late night craving for chicken nuggets, a sturdy drive-thru guide rail, and one too many glasses of red wine. The guide rail had won, but Marty had gotten his nuggets.

There was a flyer for a Chinese restaurant on the windshield, and Charlie picked it off before he entered the building. He climbed the stairs to the second floor and walked down to Apartment 23B, where Marty had been living for the last three months ... after he had to move from the three bedroom condo he and Mandy had shared because he couldn't afford the rent anymore. Another loss on the ledger, thought Charlie, who still lived at home. He had suggested that they get a place together, a real swinging bachelor pad for two young, single guys on the make, but Marty had told him that he needed his privacy. Charlie now wished he would've pushed the idea more.

He put his fist to the door, knocking three times, and waited. He listened for sounds coming from within, any sounds, but didn't hear anything. He reached out and knocked again, louder this time, and even called out, "Marty? You in there?"

Again there was no response.

The worry that had been pestering Charlie Bates for the last few days jumped up a couple notches, making him feel as though he could use a drink.

He tried again. "Marty?" he said, his knuckles beating against the thick plank of wood that was Marty's door. "You in there, man? I was up the street, at the Bid Barn, figured I pop in on you. Got a Chinese menu from your car windshield. Maybe we can get some egg rolls and a couple six packs."

Silence was the return Charlie received, deep and eerie, like the silence beneath still waters. He glanced down the length of the hallway, and then knocked one last time. When there was no answer, he reluctantly turned away and started off. On the walk down to his car, he tried Marty's phone again. It went straight to voicemail, and though he felt like a nagging hen, he left another message.

"Hey, buddy, it's just me. Was passing by, saw your car so I stopped. But I guess you're not home. Maybe you're out on one of your walks. Anyway. Look, I'm getting a little worried here. Haven't heard from you in a few days. Just give me a call, or send me a text, let me know you're okay. Okay? All right then. I guess I'll talk to you later. Take care of yourself. Good bye."

He hung up. Before getting in his car, he glanced up at Marty's window, hoping to catch some sign of life. The window was shut, the blinds closed. There was no sign of Marty Loomis.

Charlie Bates got in his car and drove home.

The club was a discordant blast of hip-hop noise and exuberant voices. Limber young women, both morally and physically, traded away little pieces of themselves a song at a time, never to get them back. Ally, meanwhile, was lost in her own world.

Most of the crowd was surrounding the main stage, where three of Teasers' finest were working on each other, getting quite creative with whip cream, a banana, and their tongues. The few patrons not enjoying the Banana Split showcase were scattered about in the dark recesses of the club, whispering, consorting, making deals.

The bar was empty save an older gentleman and the lovely-limbed dancer currently picking his pocket. That suited Ally just fine; her nerves were frayed like the chords of an old rope and she wasn't sure how long she could trust them to hold.

She was still with child, and though the idea of becoming a mother scared the hell out of her, part of her had begun to toy with the idea, wondering what it would be like to be pregnant and give birth, musing on whether she would rather have a boy or a girl, and dreamily picking out names. She liked Landon for a boy, Melina for a girl.

When she first found out that she was pregnant, the decision to have an abortion had been an easy one, reached quickly and decisively. There was no dithering or nagging ambivalence, no pro-and-con list to make and weigh. She viewed herself as too young and unsettled to take on such responsibility, and Vaughn, she knew, wouldn't be any help. He was a deadbeat dad twice over, which, given his selfish personality and criminal lifestyle, was probably a good thing for his kids' sakes. Ally had to think a child was better served absent a male role model in their life than having someone like Vaughn; he was an immoral man and a negative influence on everybody he met.

Yet he was the father of the baby growing inside her.

So certain was she that she was going to get an abortion she hadn't stopped smoking or drinking yet, figuring there was no point. She had stopped snorting cocaine, smoking pot, and taking pills, but that had more to do with her wanting to escape that life. Cigarettes and red wine, however, remained a part of her routine, a routine that had been piling wasted night atop wasted night in what was quickly becoming a wasted life.

One day at a time: that's how it happens, how everything in life happens, good and bad.

She used to roll her eyes and shrug off the slurred, self-pitying comments of the older, sad-sack patrons who'd sit at her bar and cry into their beers about life and how it had passed them by when they weren't looking: "One minute I was twenty, had the world by the balls and my whole life in front of me. Next thing I know, I'm forty-six, broke, alone, nothing better to do than go to a strip club on a Wednesday night." They'd show her pictures of their kids and moan about not being a part of their lives anymore, about missing soccer games and class recitals, about them growing up so fast; then they'd slurp down their drinks and stumble into the back, beyond the sag of the velvet ropes, with whatever girl was their favorite. Ally couldn't help but recall that some of the pictures she'd been shown were of girls not much younger than the girls on the pole. Talk about disturbing.

Ally had started to worry that she might be on the same track. The pattern was the same, there was little debating that. Bad decisions have a way of quickly adding up; they take you down paths unwise, and by the time you realize you're not where you need to be, where you want to be, years have gone by and you're not sure where to turn.

Ally didn't want that to be her; she didn't want to be one of those hot young party girls who wakes up one day not so young and not so hot, with the party she thought would go on forever long ago over. She didn't want to be another beleaguered single mom working a job she didn't enjoy, a job that didn't offer anything close to a career or respectability, relying on handouts and unfortunate give-and-take courtesies, having no choice but to lower her standards across the board, from the men she dated to the clothes she wore. The bars and stores and streets were littered with those kinds of women, and they all looked the same, talked the same, acted the same. Some of them were in the club right now, spinning on stage, showing their tits and shaking their asses. One day soon they'd be too old for such displays, and with nowhere else to go they'd inevitably stumble down the path of washed-out, worn-out women who used to have something to offer.

Despite all that, a kid just wasn't in the picture. Not right now. Not if she was serious about turning her life around and making something of herself. And she was. The incident at the A&P Mart had been a revelation. She wanted more than a low-class, demeaning job slinging drinks at a strip joint, wearing a uniform that was nothing more than spandex lingerie. Holt, the owner of the club, her boss, dealt drugs and used the downstairs to shoot cheap pornographic videos. A lot of the dancers, some of them friends of hers – not exactly trusted best friend types, but friends nonetheless – starred in these demeaning graphic shorts. She had gone from being a weekend party girl to working in a sex den with a drug dealer for a boyfriend and wannabe porn stars for friends.

What kind of life would that be for a child?

What kind of life was that for her?

"Hey there, baby girl."

Ally didn't have to turn around to know the voice that had mouthed those words belonged to her ex, Vaughn. The deep intonation, seasoned with arrogance, coupled with the cute little pet name he called her in moments of intimacy, 'baby girl', which now came with a completely new connotation, added up to him and him alone.

She didn't want to see him, didn't want to deal with him and his juvenile bullshit, but she knew that as long as she worked at the club it was going to happen. He was there three or four nights a week, if not more, and he wasn't the type to avoid her. If anything, he was the type to confront her head-on, like the other night, the night John Doe had been there, when he and his friends mocked and taunted her mercilessly, treating her like the dirt on the bottom of their shoes.

"What do you want, Vaughn?" she said without turning around.

He appeared in her sightline a moment later, taking one of the open stools in front of her. "A bottle of Heineken to start."

Upon first hearing his voice, Ally figured she was in for another long, torturous night of running herself ragged and having to put up with insults and innuendo. But there was something in the tenor of his voice that told her he was not there to bother her or be obnoxious. She saw it in his face too, a shade of genuineness that was rather easy to recognize because it wasn't often there.

She went to the cooler, grabbed a cold one, set it in front of him. "You want me to start you a tab?"

"Yeah," he said, and took a drink.

"You here to see Holt?" she asked him.

"Gotta talk to him about something, yeah. Here to see you, too."

"Me? Why me?"

"Heard you had a little trouble the other night. Wanted to make sure you're okay."

"I'm fine," said Ally, though she did let out a bit of sigh. "Little shaken up is all. How'd you hear about that?"

"It was going around. Ollie told me. Then Holt. So why didn't you call me?"

A little embarrassed, Ally shrugged and looked away. "We're not together anymore," she said. "Didn't want to bother you."

"So it's like that?" said Vaughn, not sounding hurt, but offended.

Her expression hardened. "You remember the last two times I saw you? The one time you twisted my arm behind my back and kept hitting me ... "

"Slapping you," said Vaughn, as if that made a difference.

"Whatever. Slapping me. It still hurt. A lot. And the other time, you and your friends came in here and treated me like shit, telling me to *fetch* you beers and saying that if I show you my tits you'll give me a good tip."

Vaughn nodded, accepting the blame, understanding that he'd probably taken it a little too far. "Look. I'm sorry about that," he said. "But when you hit me ... " He stopped, shook his head. "I don't know, I guess I just saw red."

Ally nodded, which was the best she could manage. She certainly wasn't about to apologize for slapping him, and she wasn't about to accept his rather lame apology either, not after the other night.

"Anyway," he went on, "I just wanted to see how you were and if you needed anything. And to tell you that I'm checking into it."

"Checking into what?"

"The shooting. What else?"

"The police are checking into it. I'm sure they can handle it."

"The police round here can't find their ass with both hands. The kind of people they have to talk to, the junkies and dealers, the scumbags, those people won't talk to them. But they'll talk to me. And I'll make sure they tell the truth."

Ally wasn't sure what to say to that. Part of her was impressed that Vaughn would take it upon himself to try and help her, and she had to admit that the police didn't seem to be making any headway. As yet they had no suspects. Still, she didn't want to be sucked back into his world, like all the other times.

This most recent fight had not been the only one they had, though it had been the only one that had turned violent. Physically violent, anyway; Vaughn did not shy away from verbal abuse or raising his voice. But then he'd apologize and do something nice, and Ally would find herself forgiving him, and on they went. This time was different, though. This time she didn't want him back.

"Don't do anything stupid, Vaughn," she told him. "You don't need to get in trouble. Besides, I'm fine."

"Not the point. The point is shit like this can't be tolerated. Not here. So I'm going to find the fucker who did this and make him pay. Street-style. You got my word on it. No one fucks with my girl."

"I'm not your girl anymore."

"Really? Just like that?"

Ally's eyes narrowed. "No. Not just like that. I don't want the drama anymore. Okay? Or the bullshit."

"So that's it then? Because I was thinking maybe I could come over tonight, bring a little wine, some of the good stuff, and we could go over what you remember." He let loose one of his charming smiles, the kind that used to turn Ally to mush. "We could play it out, you know? I can be the cop, you the witness."

Ally felt a smile coming on, just the twitch of one, but she fought it off. "No," she said. "I don't think that would be a good idea."

Vaughn's brow bunched, giving him a surprised, confused look. "Really?" he said. "Well, guess you wanna be like that then. Okay. I get it."

"I just don't think I'm ready to forgive you yet."

Vaughn nodded as if just now he began to understand. "Okay," he said. "I get it. You want me to jump through hoops? All right. Go on, play your games, baby girl. Just so you know that two can play at that."

"It's not a game, Vaughn. I want to change my life. No more coke. No more parties."

"Oh? Want to be a good girl now? Wipe the slate. And how long you suppose that'll last?"

"For good," said Ally, but even as she said it, she wasn't sure.

She'd already been thinking about getting some coke, maybe having one of the other girls get it for her, or going straight to Holt herself. Not much, just enough to take the edge off. With everything going on, she had found it tough going cold turkey.

"All right," said Vaughn, nodding. "For good. Hope you do it, girl." There was something insincere in his voice, though, something that said he didn't think she could, or would. Nor did he want her to. After all, he was a dealer.

"Thank you," she told him.

"I'm still looking into the shooting. That won't change none. Call it my way of making amends. Besides, I don't like junkies getting away with shit on my streets. Next time, who knows, maybe this asshole shoots me."

"Who shoots you?" Holt came up behind Vaughn and laid a hand on his shoulder. "Not me," he said. "I wouldn't shoot you."

"That's right," said Vaughn, turning to face his boss. "You like knives."

"I like to see the expression on their face when I turn the blade." The small town business thug took a seat next to his number one dealer. "I'll have a Courvoisier, straight up," he told Ally. Then, as she went to pour it, "You two kids work out your differences? I hope so. Makes me believe in love."

"We're talking," said Vaughn, and with Ally's back turned, he gave his boss a smile that said he had it in the bag.

Holt busted out a laugh, and again clapped a hand on Vaughn's back. "I know how it goes," he said. "Women." He laughed again, and Vaughn laughed with him.

Ally returned and put Holt's drink down in front of him. After he thanked her for it and took a sip, he said to her, "So, heard you had a bit of a scare the other night."

"I'm fine," she told him. "Just a little shaken up."

"We're conducting our own investigation. Vaughn tell you?"

"Yeah." She glanced at her ex, at the chiseled, tough-guy look on his face, and felt that old familiar twinge again. "He mentioned it."

"What about the guy who was shot? He live?"

"Yeah. I called the hospital. He woke up late last night. They said he's going to be okay."

"Don't you worry none," said Vaughn. "We're gonna find the

asshole who did this. I promise. No one fucks with my people."

"That's right," agreed Holt. "No one!"

Ally reiterated to her boss what she'd just told her ex: "Thanks, but I don't want you getting in any trouble. Seriously. Let the police handle it."

"The fuzz? Ha! They're fucking useless. And trust me, they're not going to give me any trouble, not with what I know about them."

Ally really didn't want their help, but she didn't want to protest, either; both Holt and Vaughn had a way of taking offense when none need be taken. She tried to come up with a lie, something to discourage them from their little investigation without making it seem like she was refusing their offer, but before she could think of one Holt was up off his stool and ready to get on with things.

Drink in hand, he tapped Vaughn on the arm and said, "Okay then, let's go. We have things to discuss. Bring your beer."

Vaughn grabbed his Heineken and slid off his stool. Before following after his boss, he turned to Ally and said, "We'll talk later, okay?"

Not knowing what to say to that – or, perhaps more accurately, not strong enough to say what she wanted to say, which was that she really didn't want to talk to him later, or at all – she nodded and told him okay.


The reason people go to rehab is that detox is not a joke. They say that the only withdrawal symptoms that can kill you are the ones you get from alcohol. Adam didn't have a problem with booze; his substance of choice was heroin, and, when he couldn't procure any of that, oxycodone. Booze was a last resort, and the one he currently was depending on to help see him through the ever-darkening forest of his life.

It had been more than two days since the shooting and though there had been no eyewitness description matching him to the crime and the police had yet to officially name a suspect, Adam believed he needed to keep a low profile. He was a stray dog, and enough people knew him to be desperate and down on his luck.

He had learned from a copy of the Hagerstown Sun he'd taken from the bench outside the liquor store that the man he'd shot, listed only as John Doe, had not died as a result of his wound and was expected to make a full recovery. It wasn't murder they'd get him for, but attempted murder and armed robbery. Hardly a consolation prize, but it provided Adam some relief; he was not a violent man, and the thought that he may have killed someone bothered him quite a bit.

He had been holed up at the school since the incident, only coming out in the early morning hours, between seven and noon, to snatch up small caches of food, necessities, and booze. He had made two hundred and sixty-four dollars on the score, most of that cash coming from Ally's purse, though it had cost him two hundred to settle his bill with Bobbo. Then came the bad news, the kick to the teeth he never saw coming: Bobbo, the only dealer in Hagerstown still willing to sell to Adam, was out of product. And he would be out until Thursday, or so he said.

Adam was devastated. He was a dirt-junkie on the edge of madness, in desperate need. He asked if anyone else had anything, and Bobbo shrugged and said he didn't know. "All I know is that I don't, and I won't for another seventy-two hours." Then, because Adam had paid his tab, and because Bobbo had a bit of a soft spot for him, he gave him a handful Vicodins to help tide him over.

A poor substitute, Adam knew, but anything was better than nothing. If only he knew how to control himself. Those seven pills lasted him all of twelve hours, and once they were gone, his hunger for something more grew intense. He wanted heroin, needed heroin, just a hit or two, just enough to keep the demons at bay. The liquor wasn't doing the trick, and even if he could wait until Thursday, he no longer had the money for a decent score. Not to mention, time alone, in a state of perpetual depression, had given rise to paranoia. The more he thought about it, the more he feared going to see his dealer. No doubt Bobbo would turn him in to curry favor with the cops, if it came to that. It was alarming how the two sides had learned to coexist with one another.

Adam considered going home, but quickly nixed that idea, knowing his parents were through protecting him. The last time he'd gone to their house they told him that if he didn't leave immediately they would call the police. He wasn't sure if they were bluffing or not, but he wasn't about to take a chance. The last thing he wanted, or needed, was a date with cops. No, he was on his own on this one.

Eventually it would all blow over, he told himself. Time would pass, other crimes would be committed and take precedence, and he'd be free to restart his life. It wasn't a stretch to think that he'd get away with it; they didn't have a weapon, they didn't have his description, and there was no reason to suspect him.

Another violent tremor roiled through him and he felt his stomach seize up. A moment later, he was hanging over the edge of the window sill, retching and vomiting into the weeds below. He had been vomiting off and on now for the last two days, and the pain and sickness was getting worse. A film of sweat lay on him like a second skin, and no matter how many aspirins he took, there was no relief from the pounding in his head, the ache in his bones, the nausea in his gut.

He would have to go out again, soon, to get more booze and aspirin. Luckily for him, the school, though closed for three years, still had running water, which allowed him to wash up and even brush his teeth. You couldn't tell by looking at him: his hair was greasy, his skin moist and grimy, and his breath smelled like rotting death in the summer. He'd lost a tooth the other day; it had come loose when he was eating jerky and later fell out during one of his vomiting fits.

He was a mess, and there were no signs that he was getting any better.

He'd heard that symptoms of withdrawal lasted anywhere from two to five days, and he hoped that his would end soon. The cravings would always be with him, he knew, a constant devil on his shoulder, whispering seductively in his ear. At the moment, the fear of prison had him beating that devil back.

He slunk off the window sill and fell back inside the school room where he slept and lived like a bum. He left the window open; the breeze and cold air felt good on his skin, which was burning up and shivering cold at the same time.

He wanted it all to be over, for the sickness to be gone, for the man he had shot to live, for the police to call off the investigation, for his life to go back to normal. And, of course, he wanted another high. Just one more, whispered the devil on his shoulder, the voice a siren's song. And Adam thought about dropping in on Ricky Dee or Lester, two guys who had told him to never come back again, to see if he could mend fences and maybe pick up something with his twenty-three dollars and change.

No! It wouldn't be enough, he told himself. It was better to have a supply of booze and food than a paltry amount of smack.

And then another thought popped in his head, in that familiar and haunting junkie voice: *You still got the gun. It's buried in the woods around back, but you know where it is and you could dig it up and use it one more time. Hit another out of the way place, bank a couple hundred dollars, and come Thursday you can get what you need. And you can always hide here. No one ever comes here. Think about it; it's the perfect crime. You already got away with it once. The second time will be even easier.*

It was an interesting thought, Adam believed. He still had the gun, and he already had gotten away with one robbery. Why not try another? Then he could ...

His thought process was stopped short by another sudden spasm. His entire body cinched up on him, every muscle tensing to the point of snapping, and he hurriedly pulled himself up and over the window sill and let loose with another blast of sickness. The discharge was runny and vile, the color of brown mustard, with little smears of blood-red here and there. It stank like decaying flesh, and he hacked and spit and coughed, trying to clear his mouth of the horrid aftertaste. He then fell back inside and curled into a fetal position, his body trembling. There were tears in his eyes and sweat on his brow, and he squeezed into himself for warmth and comfort that was not there.

"I'm ... going to ... die here," he muttered to himself, his words brittle and broken, coming out on dry puffs of air. And then, mercifully, his brain shut down and he passed out.

# Chapter Six

Emilia was nervous and scared, and really not sure what to say. She had all but demanded this meeting, and now it was happening.

She had only met the Elders once before, on her day of Inauguration, and all she had said to them was, "I understand, and I accept." She had made that statement with seven other individuals slated to become Custodians. The Elders had never spoken to her personally, and they knew her only by her name and the numbers she turned in ... and only then when they had her folder in front of them.

She had never been to the White Room before. She had heard stories, of course, most of them from Whitman, who spoke about it with a mixture of reverence, cynicism, and disdain. He called it, whenever he had a bit too much honey wine influencing him, the Chapel of the Chaste, and on those rare occasions it was not uncommon for him to refer to the Elders as the Hoary Horde. "You know, white is the combination of all primary colors," Emilia remembered Whitman telling her once, and she had responded by telling him that black was the absence of all color. The conversation had stopped there, but now, sitting in the White Room, the pure, blinding whiteness of it burning her eyes, she was reminded of it, as she was reminded of her friend, Whitman, who was lost and in bad need of help.

Clay was with her. He was officially running Whitman's territory now, and he was working diligently to improve the numbers while Whitman was predisposed, hoping to prove to the Elders that he deserved the post full time. He had personal success stories ready to list, and he was prepared to make a vow on behalf of his abilities and commitment to the position.

He also was prepared to cite examples of Whitman's checkered history, which included multiple infractions of insubordination. He had been rehearsing all morning.

He turned to Emilia and said, "Let me do all the talking, okay?"

"I'll talk when I have something to say," she replied testily. It was easy to tell she did not like Clay. She thought him to be arrogant, pragmatic, and a major league kiss-ass.

"These are the Elders," he told her. "They don't suffer fools."

"Then perhaps you should let *me* do all the talking."

"Very funny," Clay sniped, not the least bit amused. "Remember, until Whitman comes back, *if* he comes back, that is, I'm running the show, and maybe I won't be so inclined to go easy on you like he does."

"What's that supposed to mean?"

"You forget, I've seen the files. I know how he protects you, gives you more than your share of Ducks. I'll tell you now, so there's no mistaking, when I take over there's going to be a change in how things are run."

"He doesn't protect me, you fool," Emilia shot back. "My clients are my clients. Most of those *Ducks* have been with me for years. I was there for the battles, when they were young and sin was constantly on their minds." She stabbed a finger against her chest. "Me. I was there. Who do you think *made* them Ducks? And who says you're taking over anything?"

Clay smiled deviously. "Only a matter of time."

Emilia's eyes glared like black coal. "We'll see about that." Then, under her breath, she mouthed the word, "Jackass."

That was when the door to the White Room swung open and the Elders walked in, one after the other, in perfect single-file. As all Custodians were aware, any word uttered in the White Room, no matter from whom or at what volume, made its way to the Elders' ears, so long as they were in the room. Clay himself had barely heard it, but Alain, Tyrus and William had, and the disapproving scowls they cast on Emilia as they settled at the bench made her shrink three sizes. All of a sudden she wanted to be anywhere else.

"So," said Tyrus, taking the lead as usual, "there seems to be a quarrel of some sort here. Please explain."

He didn't give the directive to either of them specifically, but it was known that he wanted to hear from Clay first, seeing that Clay was the higher-ranking of the two. Emilia was not about to give him the upper hand, though, not if she had anything to say about it, and, of course, she did. And so while Clay postured himself up and cleared his throat for speaking, Emilia let loose.

"The problem, sir, is that Clay is more focused on taking over Whitman's territory than on getting him back. It's reprehensible."

"Sir," Clay cried out defensively. "Are you actually ... "

"And don't even get me started on this whole *corporeal* thing," Emilia went on, talking over Clay, who looked like an unprepared junior lawyer being verbally mauled at a deposition hearing. "It's been two days and Whitman is still stuck down there. And it doesn't seem like anyone cares. Who has the answers? When are we going to get him back? This is serious business."

"Yes, it is," snapped Alain, having had enough. "As is your attitude."

The sting of disapproval caused Emilia to recoil. She couldn't say she agreed with the Elders, but they were in charge, and they were to be respected. They had been where she was now, and without their endorsement she could not move up the line. Even worse, they could, if they had reason enough, bust her back down to Purgatory, which was a fate far worse than what Whitman presently was facing. One time around that block was enough for a hundred lifetimes.

"This is not Whitman's freewheeling office," Alain went on as Emilia cringed and Clay beamed like the morning sun. "There are rules here. This room, along with its members, shall be respected."

"Yes, sir," said Emilia softly.

"I think perhaps you've gone too long without proper supervision. Whitman's a decent enough man, but he's lax and permissive, which probably explains why his numbers are so low. Such liberties won't be tolerated here."

Emilia nodded, and again said, "Yes, sir."

It was then that Clay spoke up, his voice a happy whine. "I told you, sir. There's very little supervision. Nobody's held accountable. It's chaos."

Emilia fought back the urge she had to smack Clay with the back of her hand, and then, realizing where she was and who she was with, she banished the thought from her head. Not quite fast enough, though, because when she looked up she saw that Tyrus was staring at her with disappointment. She again shrank back in her chair.

"It's an entirely loose, easy-going culture that needs remedied before it's too late," Clay was saying, laying it on extra thick. "We're at a critical juncture, as you know, and what we need is structure and discipline. You asked me to keep an eye on him and I have. He's a good man, sure. He's honest, and kind, and genuine. But he's not a manager. He's not a leader. He can't see the big picture. I think the time has come to make a change."

Alain and William were nodding along, which spurred in Emilia a sudden need to come to her good friend's defense. "Jeremiah Whitman is the finest Custodian I know," she declared, her tone quiet and respectful, yet strung tight with conviction. "He taught me everything I know, and I trust him completely."

"No one here is questioning his character," replied Tyrus. "Whitman's a square fellow, no doubt. But he's had problems before, and your group is underperforming."

"But that's not his fault."

"No, not entirely," said William. "But he has to shoulder some of the blame. He is the leader. Wouldn't you agree?"

Emilia didn't want to agree, but the point was valid and lying was not tolerated in the White Room. "I suppose," she said, the words a struggle for her. "But it's not from lack of effort or care. And it's not incompetence, either."

Next to her, Clay scoffed.

She turned on him swiftly, set him with a fierce look, and said, "Is there something you'd like to share?"

Clay shrugged innocently, acting as if he had no idea what Emilia was talking about. This wasn't an outright lie on his part, but it was an obvious display of impertinence, which was something else not tolerated in the White Room.

Tyrus did the honors: "Clay Winters, this is not a place for scorn or pretense. We do not appreciate it."

Clay's face went as white as the walls. He nodded obediently and said, "Sorry, sir. No offense meant."

"You have something to say, say it. Otherwise sit in silence and pay respect."

"Yes, sir."

Emilia showed no outward response at all, but inside her heart sang a joyous song. It was about time someone put Clay in his place; she only wished that she could've been the one who'd done it.

After a couple moments of awkward silence, Alain said, "Now that that's finished, what do you say we get to the point of this meeting? We're all very busy."

Everyone seemed to agree, and Tyrus said, "Where do we presently stand?"

Clay took the lead. "We know what happened to him, sir, but we're still not sure *how* it happened. We're still piecing that together."

"We were hoping you might have some answers for us," added Emilia.

But Alain said that they hadn't the foggiest idea why or how this had happened, and Tyrus noted that they were still waiting on word from on high concerning their next move. "This one has everyone scratching their heads," he said. "Even the Angels. As far as things go, this is unprecedented."

"So there's no easy way to switch things back?" Emilia asked.

"Not that we know of," replied William. "If there was, don't you think we would have done it by now?"

"And there's the question of fate to consider," Alain put in. "Quite fickle, fate. Don't want to go messing around with it when we're not sure what the consequences might be. That's how you get in trouble."

"How do you know that what happened to him wasn't fate?" Emilia posited.

"That's preposterous," piped Alain. "Fate does not govern Custodians."

"An absurd notion," echoed William.

Feeling bold, Clay jumped on the pile, snidely saying, "That's not how fate works."

"And how would you know?" Emilia shot back at him. "No

one knows how fate works." She was this close to turning on the Elders and telling them that not even they understood fate's intricate clockwork, but she wisely stopped herself.

It was at this point that Tyrus put a fist to his mouth and cleared his throat, which was his way of conveying that he had something to say and everyone else needed to stop talking and start listening, which they did. "We are working diligently on getting him back," he said, specifically to Emilia. "But we need to make sure that bringing him back doesn't jeopardize anyone involved, including Whitman himself. This is an unprecedented event. Custodians have the ability to become corporeal, as you know, but barely and only for short periods of time. And never has one *switched* bodies before."

Emilia nodded submissively and said that she understood. She then added that she would do whatever was needed to help.

Tyrus thanked her for her kind offer, and said they'd let her know.

It was then that William spoke up. "You know," he said, quite pompously, "your boss and good friend really has no one to blame here but himself. You may be aware that he's done this sort of thing before: going rogue, interfering with life and making decisions he has no right to make, decisions that ultimately affect others. It's the chief reason why he's still toiling away in the Custodial ranks."

"To my understanding, his interference produced positive results," Emilia was quick to point out.

"We don't know that. Not conclusively. There are way too many variables to consider. We have no way of gauging the affects, either positive or negative, that his rebellious actions have had."

Emilia had never been one to buy into the whole butterfly effect, especially now, in these times, when everyone was so self-involved and emotional when it came to their own lives yet robotic and insensitive when it came to the lives of others.

'Ineffable' was the word the Elders liked to toss around. Clay, too. They bandied it about like a badminton shuttlecock, using it, quite liberally, to explain away all sorts of misdeeds and misnomers. Death and disease, murder and mayhem, all the madness of man stuffed into the frayed and sweaty sock of ineffability. If it had all been decided, Emilia often wondered, if Christ's victory had been complete, then what was the point? She had always said that, despite what was preached by the Elders and those supposedly in the know, and Whitman, more than anyone else she'd met since her earthly demise, agreed with her.

Ineffability? The idea was absurd. Why did they need Custodians then? Why were there demons running amok? Why did they need Sentries in the Spirit World? If fate had already been aligned, what was the point of making sure it remained aligned?

Freewill, they claimed, *they* being the Hoary Horde and, supposedly, the Angels above them, amounted to one decision: it was the decision to forsake your own wants and desires in favor of His. His will, not yours, was the choice you had to make.

But the more that Emilia witnessed, the more incongruous this seemed to be, and though she usually kept that opinion to herself for fear of how it would be received, she concluded that now was not the time for prudence.

"He was trying to help people," she said to the court in general. "Isn't that what we're supposed to do? Ideally?"

"No!" said Alain, and his voice, brusque and heavy, echoed off the plain white walls and reverberated back on itself. "We're not to interfere or make contact. That's Rule One! We're to observe and, when appropriate, gently nudge them in the right direction. We're never to change their decisions."

"We're to keep them on the right path," said Tyrus, his voice, as always, commanding attention. "*Their* path. Unfortunately, some paths wind through darkness and despair, while others end suddenly. Some lead over cliffs. Some go in circles. It's not perfect, but that's how it has to be."

"That's one of the problems your boss has always had," said William. "He often forgets we're not here to fix people's lives. We're here to observe and whisper guidance. If they don't listen, then they don't listen."

"You're right," said Emilia, conceding. Not that she agreed, she just understood that arguing the point would get her nowhere. "But that doesn't change the fact that he's stuck there and needs our help to get back."

"And as soon as we figure out how to get him back, safely, we will," said Tyrus.

"Until then," Alain was quick to add, "it's paramount that he stay put and have as little interaction with people as possible. We can't have him running around, compromising himself or fate, while we're trying to figure this mess out. That said, we believe the hospital is the best place for him. Not much chance for him to change things in a place like that. And the longer he can claim to have amnesia the better."

William couldn't help but smile at the thought. Clay, too. Emilia noticed both their grins and wanted so badly to wipe them from their faces. Instead, she repressed her desires and agreed with Alain's opinion.

"I'll tell him, sir," she said.

"No. Tell Edmund to break the news to him," William instructed her. "He'll be Whitman's Custodian for the time being."

The thought of that nearly made Emilia swallow her tongue. "Edmund?" she said, having to work to keep her voice at an even keel. "Do you really think he's the best person for the job? I would be glad to ... "

"No. You're too close to him," said Alain, not giving her a chance to volunteer for the post. "And considering how shorthanded we are right now, we can't afford to spare you. Besides, Edmund and Whitman have a good working relationship, and we believe it'll be a good test for Edmund. And if Whitman does as he's told and stays in the hospital, I can't imagine he'll be a difficult client to watch."

Emilia nodded dutifully, and said she would pass along their instructions.

She spoke with sincerity and aplomb, but Tyrus could tell that she was unsure of the decision. "Trust us, child," he said to her, his stoic manner and calm tone of voice a soothing tonic. "We want Whit back as much as you do, but we're not going to rush it. We'll figure out the best way to handle this. Then, and only then, will we act. The last thing we want to do is make a mistake. Like all situations, there's more to this than meets the eye." Then he said, "Was there anything else?"

Emilia was this close to asking when they thought they might have the situation taken care of, but she was unable to loosen the words. They stayed in her head, and her mouth stayed shut, and Clay jumped on the opportunity to speak his mind.

"My good sirs," he began with pretentious reverence. "I was wondering if I could speak to you privately for a moment. Under the circumstances, there are matters of some import that I would like to discuss with you."

Emilia cringed at the thought of what those matters might be, and again she thought to speak her mind, to say that this was her meeting too and that anything Clay had to say he could say in front of her. But her courage failed her again, and though this time she managed to unhinge her jaw and open her mouth, just like before no words came out. She just sat there, mute and still, her eyes locked in a dead stare, mesmerized by the blinding white maw of the White Room.

"Emilia?" said Tyrus, addressing her in that gentle, commanding voice of his.

She looked at him, and her eyes gained focus. "Yes?" she said.

"Was there anything else?"

She considered the offer, and ignored all the questions and qualms piled up in her head. "No. I don't think so."

"Fine," said Tyrus.

"You are dismissed, Emilia," said Alain. "Your opinions have been noted, and I can assure you that your visit will not soon be forgotten."

There was something in his stately voice that made Emilia wince. Looking back on it, she realized that she had put on quite the spectacle, raising her voice and casting aspersions, calling Clay a fool, and she now felt the need to apologize ... and, hopefully, mitigate some of the damage she may have done.

She stood, nodded to the three Elders on the bench, and then spoke to them with the sort of deference and humility they expected.

"I'm sorry if I was out of line," she said. "Whitman's a good friend, and the finest Custodian I know. I want him back."

"As do we," said Tyrus, while William and Alain sat silent and stone-faced.

"Thank you for the opportunity to be heard," she went on. "I know you're very busy. And I know you'll do what's best."

"Thank you," said Tyrus sincerely.

"Yes. Thank you," said Alain, somewhat less sincerely.

William merely nodded his head.

Emilia then walked in the direction where she believed the door to be, and after a moment or two of straining her eyes, searching for it, she found a seam and pushed. The door opened at her hand, and the glow of soft color broke into the world of white and flooded her eyes with dimension and depth. Without so much as a glance back, she walked out, closing the door behind her.

Her first ever visit to the White Room officially ended when the door clunked shut, but Emilia was of the opinion that her visit essentially had ended before it had begun. It was a disingenuous meeting meant to appease and mislead her. She had accomplished nothing, and now Clay was in there, meeting with the Elders alone, most likely discussing and deciding the fate of Jeremiah Whitman.

It seemed, at least to her, that the Elders weren't all that eager or interested in fixing things; she got the feeling they had their own agenda, and that rescuing Whitman wasn't on it. She wondered if it ever had been, and she wondered whether or not they cared one way or the other. That scared her.

God works in mysterious ways, the old quote went, and there was very little debating that. Emilia had always wondered about those ways, but this was the first time she had ever thought to doubt them.


There was a talk show on television. A rotund woman was yelling at her boyfriend and his new lover, a homely but slim young woman, a stripper with blonde hair and a leopard-print tattoo on her lower leg. The rotund girl was calling them names and gesturing wildly, and the crowd was cheering and applauding. The two women charged like a couple of rams ready to butt heads; they threw wild, looping, openhanded slaps and pulled on each other's hair while a large man, apparently a security guard of some sort, partially held them back. The crowd went wild, especially when the skinny tramp's top was pulled down and her breasts popped out. Meanwhile, the young man they were fighting over, a goofy looking fellow by the name of Jasper, stood there and smiled expressively.

Whitman was appalled, but found himself unable to look away. "Dear God," he said. "This is insane."

Custodians knew about the ills of television and movies, video games and music, but they rarely concerned themselves with any of it. Given their few numbers in comparison to the populace, they had little choice but to manage their time more appropriately. It was then presumed that most people could not get themselves into serious spiritual turmoil while watching television or listening to music. Sure, there were unpleasant words and images that might tempt untoward behavior, but the general consensus was that if someone was at home at two o'clock on a Wednesday, just sitting in front of the tube with a soda and some corn chips, their soul was not in imminent danger. Custodians tended not to involve themselves unless major consequences hung in the balance. Sex, abortion, marriage, infidelity, parenthood, alcohol, drugs, violence, greed – those were the situations that decided someone's course in life, and perhaps their eternal fate, not what television program they chose to watch or music they listened to. That was immaterial.

Or was it?

Whitman could hardly believe what he was seeing. These people were plum out of their gourds, yelling and swearing and throwing blows. He was reminded of something his mentor, Francis Villeux, the man who had trained him to be a Custodian, had once said: God made us in His likeness, and the devil, in his hatred and jealousy, does everything he can to turn us into animals.

No wonder they were losing the war.

The program broke for commercial and Whitman promptly changed the channel. After a brief search, he settled on a police procedural, the sight of a man lying on top of a coroner's table, pale gray and all cut up, grabbing his attention. The actor playing the coroner stuck a hand in the dead man's chest cavity and removed a reddish-brown blob. Revolted, Whitman turned his head and groaned.

"How can this possibly entertain people?" he wondered aloud. Despite that, he continued to watch, cringing from time to time yet unable to look away for more than a few seconds. It was strangely intriguing.

"It's obviously the husband's lover who did it," he said to the television, after gaining a feel for the theme of the episode. "Any moron could figure that out."

"Did what, sir?" It was Edmund. He had appeared out of thin air like some ghost haunting an old mansion, and his strange, stork-like presence startled Whitman.

"Dear God, Edmund, be aware, you'll give a man a heart attack."

"Sorry, sir. Not used to being seen. Or heard."

Whitman gave his damaged heart a moment to get back on beat, then he turned off the television and said, "All right then. No harm. To business. Please tell me that you found a way to rectify the situation."

"Welllll ... " The way Edmund stretched out that one word told Whitman all he needed to know. But that didn't stop him from fixing his young apprentice with a severe look, one that said an actual verbal response was expected.

Edmund seemed to understand that, and swallowed hard. "No," he said, finally.

Whitman was not pleased. "Come on, man," he said with a jolt. "What's the problem?! I'm losing my marbles here."

"It seems we have a cosmic glitch on our hands, sir. Quite inconvenient."

"A cosmic glitch?!" Whitman's tone possessed the sting of a backhand slap.

"Ineffable, sir," replied Edmund, doing his best to hold himself together. "Emilia's word, not mine. Ineffable. Good word, I think. Appropriate."

Whitman let loose a heavy-hearted groan. If there was one thing that he'd learned over the years, it was that you could not fight ineffability ... mostly because there was no way to understand what the hell it was. "What about the Elders?" he said. "What did they say? They have to know something."

Guilt made a mess of Edmund's face. He went, "Ummmm." He

followed that up by not saying anything else.

"What's the hold up?!" Whitman cried out. He was on the verge of so many different emotions he could barely tell them apart. "One of their top supervisors is yanked out of the spirit world and they're out to lunch."

"Well ... Umm ... "

Unlike Whitman, Edmund was a world-class bush beater. Any words that might be inconvenient or unwelcome and you could expect him to drag them out like an opera solo. A lot of times he sounded like a toddler just learning to talk, uttering odd sounds and mismatched syllables in the place of actual words ... though doing so in his posh British accent made him sound smarter somehow. Whitman was quite familiar with this characteristic and in no mood to put up with it.

"Dammit, Edmund! Just tell me."

Whitman's outburst only served to exacerbate Edmund's timidity. The poor boy's mouth dropped and his face went mime-white. The only sound that came out of him was a protracted, high-pitched croak that brought to mind an ailing goat. Whitman, realizing what he'd done, issued a sigh of regret.

"Edmund," he said soothingly, "I'm sorry. I didn't mean to yell. It's just this situation. And this damn body I'm in. I've got to urinate. And I feel pain. I get sleepy, and hungry. I even sweat. Can you imagine?"

"No, sir," said Edmund. "It's all right. I understand."

"Thank you. I know you're doing your best."

"Yes, sir. You have my word."

Whitman gave his young apprentice a nod of respect and told him that he was proud of him. "Emilia said you've been working hard. I appreciate that."

"I am, sir. Truly. I'm knuckling down, doing my best."

"Good. That's what I like to hear. Now, about the Elders?"

Edmund lifted himself up some, and this time when he spoke it was with an air of confidence. "Emilia met with them earlier and they're looking into it. We're just waiting to hear back from them."

"Did they say anything else?"

"They made mention that this is unprecedented, sir."

"No kidding."

"And also ineffable. Ineffable and unprecedented."

"Of course. Lucky me. How long ago did you make contact?"

Edmund gave his boss a blank stare.

"Well?" said Whitman.

"Ummmm. You mean in human time, sir?"

"Yes. Human time. Approximately."

"An hour ago? Maybe two. Hard to say."

"And they haven't gotten back to you yet?"

"No. But they're very busy. You know that."

Bullshit, thought Whitman, though he was careful not to say the word. Unfortunately for him, Edmund didn't have to hear words to get a tag on what someone was thinking. Custodians weren't able to read minds, not verbatim, but they were able to glean a general feel as to what sort of mood someone was in. They could tell if a person was upset, or angry, or about to do or say something exceedingly stupid.

"Sir?" said the novice Custodian. "You disagree?"

Whitman fixed his young, ghostly friend with a blunt look. "Excuse me?"

"Wellllll," said Edmund, squirming some in his spiritual skin, "it's just that I thought I ... " He stopped abruptly, the stone-cold look of condemnation just beginning to shade his boss's young alien face bringing him to a screeching halt.

"Don't you pull that Custodian crap on me, young man," Whitman scolded him. "I'm still your boss. You hear?"

"Yes, sir. Of course, sir. Old habit."

"Well practice it elsewhere. Not on me. I'm not impressed. In the meantime."

"Yes," said Edmund, nodding, glad to be off the hook. "In the meantime, sir, I've come to give you some details about an incident we think may have been the catalyst for all this. We're hoping it'll jog your memory."

"That's progress," said Whitman. "Why didn't you lead with that?"

"Sorry, sir. Lot on my mind. Are you familiar with the name Adam Dubinsky?"

Whitman let the name sink in, and even repeated it a couple times, hoping that saying it in his own tongue would help him remember. It didn't, and a somber look overcame him. "No," he said. "I don't recognize it."

"He was one of mine. Or one of yours, I suppose. There was an incident the other night. A shooting at a convenience mart."

Whitman listened to every word of the account, but no bells rung, no memories swam to the surface. At the end, he sighed and admitted he couldn't remember any of it.

"No worries," Edmund told him, trying to be supportive. "I'm sure it'll come back to you in time. Right now we need to get you up to date on Martin Loomis. Just in case."

"Just in case of what?" Whitman asked.

Edmund shied away. He put a fist up to his mouth and cleared his throat, somewhat less regally than Tyrus. "Just to be on the safe side," he said, unable to look his boss in the eye.

Whitman was not one to be misled, and he stared at his young, skittish protégé until the tension in the room became unbearable. Edmund, as usual, cracked like an egg, and Whitman promptly scrambled him.


Whitman's face, currently the young, rosy-pink face of Marty Loomis, wilted like a dead flower, adding age to it that didn't tally well. He was trying to remember what he'd been doing before the incident in the hope that it would help him put things back in order, or, more appropriately, give the Elders a better idea of how to put things back in order, but his mind wouldn't let him get there. The last thing he had any recollection of was a tall, gangly man with a tattoo on his arm. From there, his mind kept shooting him back to the White Room and the meeting he'd had with his superiors.

Edmund had told him that he'd been shot during a store robbery, but Whitman had no recollection of that at all.

"That's quite all right, sir," Edmund told him. "I'm sure you'll remember soon enough."

Whitman nodded, and dug back in. But it wasn't long before he got lost in the swirling shades of gray that now occupied most of his thoughts, camouflaged beautifully by the rest of the natural world, which had become, in Whitman's eyes, one big gray canvas. He fought for focus, and the vision of a small brick building, crumbling on one side, popped in his head; he saw an empty playground, a basketball hoop, swings gently twisting in the wind, and a faceless man in boots.

Then, like before, that vision flashed and turned blinding white, and once again he found himself standing before Tyrus, Alain and William, defending his beliefs and his team, kowtowing to men he'd lost a little bit of respect for over the years, not that he'd ever say that aloud. He was a company man, after all.

He heaved a somber sigh and slouched in his bed. "It's all so frustrating," he wailed. "I'm just a fool caught between."

Silence took hold then, sinking in deep and fast. Whitman fell into sullen musings, feeling sorry for himself, feeling powerless and forsaken, feeling lost and alone. He was terrified he would never remember what had happened, thus there'd be no reversing this cosmic glitch and he'd be stuck wearing another man's mortal body for years to come.

Then what, he wondered. How was he supposed to live in this chaotic world with so many knuckleheads and jabaronies running around, acting stupid, talking stupid, doing stupid things? He could not abide.

He liked human beings, for the most part, so long as he didn't have to interact with them. They were a tough lot to like, to be honest. Sure, they had their moments, but those moments had become few and far between, sort of like quick commercial breaks in a movie that offered nothing but gratuitous sex, violence and greed.

Sin had always run rampant in the world. Greed, Vanity, Wrath, Lust, Pride – they were as prevalent in Whitman's day, the late seventeen hundreds, as they were today. But it was different now. Sin wasn't sin anymore; it was merely a choice made, one benign, casual decision amongst many. And if there were no tangible consequences, then there was nothing to worry about. Even when there were consequences, there existed all sorts of clever ways around them. Sin was an empty word now, a hollow echo from the mouths of preachers and street-corner prophets.

The sound of Edmund clearing his throat broke into the outer edges of Whitman's consciousness but failed to stir him. He was stuck in his own head, like a fly caught in a web, becoming more and more tangled. Edmund tried again, and this time added a firmly stated, "Sir?" with it.

It worked. Whitman woke from his trance and his eyes regained their light. He put them on his friend.

"Maybe we should concentrate on the facts of Martin Loomis's life, sir. It could be a couple more days before the Elders put things right."

Whitman scoffed. "I don't know what's taking so long. They have the power to fix this. I know they do. Cosmic glitch, my ass! They're experimenting, I'll bet. Playing God. That's what they're doing."

"The grand scheme, sir," said Edmund dutifully.

"Malarkey! The grand scheme? Freewill? It's all one big stew. It's fluid, Edmund. I've been privy to all sorts, and life is fluid."

"Perhaps. I don't know."

"No one knows. That's the point. *Ineffability.* One big mess on the floor, that's what it is. And now here I am, smack in the middle of it."

"Right, sir," said Edmund. He then gulped down a breath of empty air and said something he really didn't want to: "Doesn't change matters, though."

The look he got in return brimmed with animus, though it lacked a certain something. If it had come from the steel blue depths of Whitman's eyes, eyes that had seen the dirt and desperation of more than a dozen generations, Edmund very well may have faded from sight. But not so in the genial, puppy-dog brown of Martin Loomis's eyes.

Whitman said, "I don't trust them, Edmund. Something's wrong, and they're not telling us what. It's suspicious."

"I wouldn't say that, sir. They don't want to bugger things up is all. Lives hang in the balance. They want to make sure they get it right."

"Malarkey! This is a test. Or it's payback. Punishment for interfering."

Guilt returned to the wan countenance of Edmund Van Roy and he quickly looked away. Emilia had mentioned something to that affect, and Alina, one of the other Custodians in the Garrison, had agreed it was a possibility. Whitman had been reprimanded for meddling before, and it was no secret that the team had been underperforming for a while now and the Elders were not pleased. This could be a message, a punishment of sorts, and if that was the case, there was no telling how long it might last.

But Edmund was not about to bend to pessimism. What his boss needed now was positivity, and perhaps a bit of humor. Unfortunately, humor and positivity were two things Edmund didn't possess a talent for, unless you counted his freakish ability to manage them accidentally or ironically.

"I think they're just trying to figure things out, sir," he said with a dash of British spunk. "And when they do, well, they'll snap their fingers and you'll be back in a jiff. Remember, they are quite old. They don't get around so well anymore." He then grinned to let his boss know that he was joking.

Whitman made no reply; much to Edmund's chagrin, he didn't even break a smile. There was too much on his mind, and he worried that if he couldn't remember what had happened, and why it had happened, he might be stuck in the real world for a long, long time. And that was simply unacceptable.

"Look. Give it a day or two," Edmund advised him. "You suffered a traumatic event. You just need time. And the Elders, well, I'm sure they'll figure things out soon enough. The important thing is to stay positive."

"*Time*," said Whitman irritably. "Time heals all, right? Everything in its time."

Edmund, who wasn't very adept at picking up on cynicism, happily agreed. "Precisely, sir. Everything in its time."

His point missed, Whitman sighed. He then tried another angle. "You realize the police are coming by to question me about the robbery. They want to fingerprint me, too. I don't know what I'm supposed to tell them. The amnesia story isn't going to hold water forever. And if I admit who I am, or they find out."

"Yes, sir, I know. It's quite the conundrum."

Whitman snorted, and shook his head. "Thanks for clearing that up for me. What does Emilia say? And why isn't she here?"

Edmund's face floundered under the weight of another guilty look.

"Edmund?!" Whitman barked at him.

"She was told not to come, sir," Edmund admitted.

"By whom? Not Clay?"

"No, sir. The Elders. They think she's too close to you, that it might cloud her judgment."

"That's bull! She's a pro, and I trust her."

"I know, sir, and I plan to keep her apprised. Consider me a liaison between the two of you. I can pass messages back and forth."

That eased Whitman's mind some, but not much. "So the plan," he said, "is to stay put and keep playing dumb? That's the best you can come up with?"

"They said it's important that you have as little effect on the world as possible. You know how the Elders feel about fate."

"I know. They're obsessed with it. But what if the police find out? Then what?"

"Well ... " Befuddled, Edmund paused to scour the mostly empty neural passageways of his brain. Not finding anything particularly creative up there, he chose to go with a vague cliché, one that he'd been waiting to use for some time now. "I suppose we'll cross that bridge when we come to it," he said, and smiled hopefully.

"Great," replied Whitman. "So long as you have a plan."

This time Edmund picked up on the sarcasm, and his nose wrinkled. "Sorry, sir," he said. "We're doing our best."

Whitman drew out a heavy-hearted sigh. "No, I'm sorry," he said. "It's just that I don't want to be here anymore. Sure, the food is great, and they serve you right in bed, which is quite pleasant. But I can't stand not doing anything all day. I don't know how people do it. And the drugs. And that blasted thing." He gestured to the television hanging on the wall. "Whoever invented that should be shot. Repeatedly."

"Perhaps," said Edmund. "Though there are some interesting documentaries on Ancient Aliens. It always amuses me how wrong they ... "

A polite knock on the door interrupted them. Whitman turned, expecting to see a doctor or a nurse, or the pear-shaped woman who delivered his food. He had an appointment to meet with a psychologist later, a Dr. Thomason, to test his awareness, mental acuity, and overall psychological state of mind. He was not looking forward to that at all.

Instead, he was greeted by an unquestionably attractive young woman.

"Look. You're up," Ally said to him as she came inside, closing the door behind her. "They told me you woke up. I had to come and see for myself."

Whitman's jaw dropped and hung like a broken gutter. He went, "Uhhh."

"You probably don't remember me, do you?" she said to him as she approached, her steps soft and gradual, as if he was sleeping and she didn't want to wake him.

Whitman, his mouth still hanging open, shook his head. "I don't think so," he managed.

"They said you have selective amnesia."

Whitman turned to Edmund for assistance, but that was as reasonable as looking at a brick wall for a reflection. Edmund shrugged and said, "I have no clue who she is, sir. She's not one of mine."

Whitman turned back to the girl. "Um ... Who are you?" he said to her. "I mean, what's your name?"

"Alison," she told him. "Ally for short." She was at his bedside now, staring down at him, her immaculate face aglow with warmth and kindness. Whitman was instantly enamored. "They said you don't remember who you are," she said to him as he mindlessly gawked at her. "And you didn't have any ID on you."

Whitman gulped, and looked at Edmund again.

"You want I should go, sir?"

"No!" Whitman cried out. Then, realizing he'd said that a bit loud, and, at least as far as Ally could tell, to no one in particular, he turned to her and quickly added, "Sorry. I'm having some trouble ... thinking."

"Good recovery, sir," chirped Edmund, always positive.

An awkward pause followed. The look on Whitman's face could best be described as optimistically demented, whereas Ally appeared skeptical.

"How's your chest?" she asked him. "Where you were shot?"

"Not bad." Whitman glanced down at the gauze pad covering his left pectoral. "It doesn't hurt, but they keep giving me drugs."

"Hospitals have the best stuff."

"Makes it hard to concentrate, though. Lots of ... *buzzing* in my head. And my thoughts tend to ... " he gestured as if shooing a fly away from his ear, "... scat off before I can make proper sense of them."

Ally smiled politely, and Whitman's heart skipped ahead three beats. She moved around to the other side of the bed and laid her jacket and purse down on one of the chairs. "What do the doctor's say?"

"Um ... Prognosis is good. Full recovery. Good as new in a few days. Soon as I get my wits back, that is."

"Really? That's incredible. I'm so happy for you."

"Thank you. It is good news, considering." He was staring at her, half his brain entranced by her stunning looks, the other half busy trying to place her face. All humans looked alike to him, but this one, well, she was a ten-count knockout. In the hesitant tones of someone trying not to offend, he said, "I'm sorry, but how is it that we know each other?"

She gave him another smile, this one softer, almost bashful. "Well, we don't. Not really. I was there the night you were shot. You died in my arms."

What Whitman tried to say was, "Oh my, that's something," but somewhere between his brain and his mouth the message became garbled. What came out was a series of incoherent syllables, none of them related to any known word in the English language, aside from those occasionally spoken by infants.

Ally looked perplexed. "Thankfully it was only temporary," she added.

"Right," he said. "Temporary. Because ... Well, here I am. Clearly not dead."

"Yes," she said, and smiled. "Clearly. Thankfully."

"Sorry. I'm just a little ... well, you know how it is. Sort of ... well ... " He smiled feebly, knocked on the side of his head like he was knocking on a door, and finished with, "Whoopy," which isn't a word at all and did nothing to explain how he felt. Whitman, a self-purported master communicator, felt like a tongue-tied schoolboy alone with his cheerleader crush. Red-faced and numb, he looked away from her, and for the first time noticed that Edmund was no longer there; the bastard had snuck off when he wasn't looking, leaving him to flounder on his own.

"It's all right," Ally said to him. "I understand. You've been through a lot."

"Yes, I have," he said, thinking more about the part where he was human again, not about getting shot and lying in a coma for nearly a day. "You have no idea."

"So, you don't remember anything about that night?"

He shook his head. "No. Sorry. I just ... I guess maybe I left those memories in the coma." As soon as he said the words he felt completely stupid, but Ally seemed to accept the notion, and even nodded in agreement.

"I can understand that," she said.

"It's very frustrating."

"Well, you saved my life," she told him. "It was amazing. That bullet was meant for me and you jumped right in front of it. It was the most incredible thing I ever saw. It was so ... *courageous*. So selfless."

Whitman wanted to rejoin with something witty and clever, or merely gracious, but the synapses in his brain were shooting off like fireworks, rendering him dumb. What he came up with was, "It was nothing."

"Nothing?" replied Ally. She wasn't angry, but disappointed, and it showed. "I could be dead, and you call that nothing."

"I uh ... No. No, of course not. I didn't mean it ... you know, like that," Whitman labored to explain, his face finding another shade of red. "I just meant, you know, it just happened. I reacted. I really don't remember."

Ally nodded, accepting his stammering explanation. She was at his bedside now, and she reached down, took his hand in hers, and squeezed. Whitman, who hadn't been touched in two hundred odd years, not in an intimate way, not in any way that he could feel, was struck hard and fast by a primal stirring as old as mankind.

"Take it from me," said Ally, clutching his hand, "it was definitely *something*."

There was a gleam in her eyes, more than admiration, more than gratitude, and it worked to put Whitman on edge. Far as he could tell, it bordered on worship, at the very least affection, and that, coupled with the touch of her hand, caused him to start ... growing.

Ally didn't seem to notice. "You saved my life," she was saying, and Whitman, anxious to keep her eyes above his waist so she wouldn't see what was happening to him down there, started nodding like a fool. "I might be dead right now if not for you."

He was helpless. It kept getting bigger and bigger, bulging in his lap. He quickly fixed his blanket to keep his mortifying secret hidden.

"Are you all right?" Ally asked him. "You don't look so good."

He didn't look good. He looked as though he either might have or was in the middle of having a stroke. There was a patina of sweat on his brow, his cheeks were the violent color of cheap cherry wine, and the smile on his face looked like something you might expect to see on a ventriloquist's dummy.

"Uhhh ... Sure," he muttered. "Right as rhubarb."

"Rhubarb?" She hadn't been expecting to hear that.

"Ummm ... Yes. Rhubarb. It's a vegetable." Then, feeling the need to go on, he added, "Some people make pies out of it."

She gave him another sweet smile. "Okay. You know I came to see you yesterday? But you hadn't woken up yet."

He opened his mouth to reply, but only a wisp of pudding-scented air came out. He just couldn't think, not with her right there, looking so beautiful, her warm, soft hand holding his. Not with an erection lurking under the covers, desperate to be free.

"Are you sure you're all right?" she asked him.

He nodded desperately.

"You seem, I don't know, confused."

"It's the drugs," he managed. "I'm not used to them."

"Do you want me to go?"

"No. You can stay. Please."

She let go of his hand, doing so in such a way that hinted she was surprised and maybe even a little embarrassed to find herself still holding it. That provided Whitman a modicum of relief. Thoughts began to form in his head again, and a few of them actually seemed to make sense. He optimistically tried one out: "The police are supposed to come and talk to me about what happened."

"They already questioned me," said Ally. "Twice. You know, they still haven't caught the guy who did it."

"I don't think I'll be any good to them. I don't remember anything."

"It happened so fast. I stopped in to get a few things, and right when I was ready to leave, this guy came in with a gun and started yelling."

"You didn't see him?"

"He was wearing a mask." She paused. "The funny thing is, I don't remember you being there. Neither does Eddie."

"Oh? Who's Eddie?"

"He was the cashier. Neither of us remembers you being there. Not until you jumped in front of the gun."

Whitman shrugged, trying to hide his guilt. "Well," he said, "I was."

"Thank God, or else I might be in that bed right now. Or a casket."

It was then that Nurse Manion came waddling into the room, her pear-shaped form less than flattered by the pale blue nurse's uniform she wore. The dowdy old girl looked at Ally first, then at Whitman; she tried a smile, which didn't fit her at all, and said, "Good afternoon. How are you feeling today?"

Whitman cleared his throat. "Good," he said. "Better."

"Any memories yet?"

"Not yet. Alison and I were just talking about that night."

Nurse Manion looked at Ally. "You were with him the night he was shot?"

"Yeah. He saved my life. Jumped in front of the robber and took the bullet."

"Oh? You're a hero," Nurse Manion said to Whitman. "Saved a beautiful young woman's life, but you can't remember who you are."

"Just my luck, I suppose."

"Well, we're going to work on that for you. Dr. Thomason will be in sometime today. He's the hospital's psychotherapist. And then, depending on what he says, the police may stop in and ask you a few questions."

"For joy," Whitman deadpanned.

"You want to find out who you are, don't you?" said Nurse Manion critically.

Whitman already knew exactly who he was; he didn't want anyone else finding out.

"Of course," he said. "It's just ... frustrating."

"I understand. Don't you worry, though, Dr. Thomason is good at what he does."

"You know, I should probably go now," said Ally, taking this as her cue to leave. "Sounds like you're going to be busy."

"Oh. Okay," said Whitman. He didn't want her to go, but he didn't think he should just blurt that out. He felt foolish enough already.

She scooped up her purse and jacket. "I have to work tonight," she said. "So."

"You can come back tomorrow, if you like."

She nodded. "Sure. I think I can make it."

"I'd really like to talk to you some more. It might help me to remember."

"Okay," she said. "I'll try to stop by tomorrow."

She sidled up to his bedside again, leaned over, and kissed him on the cheek. "That's for what you did," she told him. "Thank you."

"You're welcome," he replied, all the blood in his body rushing to his groin. And just when that problem had started to go away.

"I'll see you tomorrow," she said to him as Nurse Manion diligently went about her duties. She was checking the monitors, making sure all the numbers were in line, making sure the IV tube was working properly.

Whitman didn't seem to notice. "Good," he said to Ally. "I'll see you tomorrow." And he didn't take his eyes off her until she was gone.

Nurse Manion showed him a smile. "Pretty girl."

Whitman nodded dreamily.


Dr. Felix Thomason was a short, stumpy, middle-aged man with a pale, mottled complexion, big eyes, and red, red lips, like the kind you see on lipstick commercials and drag queens. His hair was threadlike, parted down the middle and feathered in a long forgotten style. He was dressed in a frumpy corduroy suit, dark blue in color, a red and blue check tie, and brown loafers. He carried a black briefcase at his side.

He strolled into Whitman's room and greeted him with a diffident smile and limp handshake. "Hello," he said, "I'm Dr. Thomason. How are you feeling today?"

"I'm fine," said Whitman, lying. He actually was feeling a bit thick at the moment. The drugs they had him on were swamping his brain, making it hard for him to think. The doctors and nurses had assured him that the drugs were necessary, but Whitman wasn't sure why; the gunshot wound to his chest had nearly healed completely, much to the surprise of his doctors, and he wasn't in any physical pain. Far as he could tell, they were giving him drugs out of a sense of protocol.

"You lost your memory," said Dr. Thomason, setting his briefcase down on the table next to Whitman's bed.

"Yes, sir."

"You have no recollection of anything since you woke up from your coma? Not your name, where you're from, what happened that night?"

"No, sir."

Thomason stared at Whitman, his big eyes the color of old mahogany. "The shooting was three nights ago and no one has reported you missing. We can probably assume you live alone. No wife or children."

Whitman remained silent. He concentrated, the best he could, on showing a blank face. He knew that everything he said and did would be analyzed and scrutinized – his words, his tone, his gestures and expressions – and he didn't want to betray any secrets or unintentionally give away hints to the truth. Not that anyone would believe the truth; he could hardly believe it himself.

"It's a good bet you're unemployed," the doctor went on. "Or else your boss or coworkers would have reported you absent."

Feeling the need to give some sort of response, Whitman shrugged. Then, building on that momentum, he said, "I was dead for two minutes. Did they tell you that?"

Dr. Thomason nodded glumly. "Oh yes, I'm aware." He went

to his briefcase and snapped open the clasps. He lifted the top, pulled out a folder, a tablet, and a small digital recording device. He closed the briefcase and placed those items on top of it. He then dragged one of the chairs in the room to Whitman's bedside and took a seat, sighing as he settled in, as if he'd just finished some daunting physical task. His mottled complexion had colored, giving him a nice raspberry finish.

"I'll be recording this session," he said as he reached for the recording device on top of his briefcase. He pressed a button and a green light flashed on. "So I can listen to it again later. In case I need to."

"Okay," said Whitman warily. He didn't trust technology, and he didn't like the idea of his words being recorded. "But is that really necessary?" he asked. "Can't you just remember what I say? You're a doctor, after all. You fellows are supposed to be smart."

Thomason gave a friendly chuckle. "True. Unfortunately my memory's not so good. The tape and notes I take allow me to go over everything again. I find that it helps me to be more thorough in my diagnosis. More objective, too."

Whitman gave the device a dirty look. The remnants of that look remained when he turned his eyes back to the good doctor.

"Is there a reason why you wouldn't want this interview taped?" inquired Thomason. His voice may have been light, his expression almost comically innocent, but the question carried a measure of shrewdness.

"No. No reason," Whitman replied, fighting to keep trepidation from his tone. "If that's what you do, that's what you do."

"Good. We can get started then." Thomason reached for his tablet and took a pen from his shirt pocket. "So," he said, clicking his pen to point, "why don't you start by telling me what you do remember."

Whitman stared at him for a few seconds, blankly, densely, as if he didn't understand the question. Then he said, "About what, exactly."

"In general terms. How about the last thing you remember."

"Ah. That's easy," said Whitman. "Pudding. Vanilla. It was divine."

Thomason's glance meandered over to the near-empty tray of food on the bedside table opposite him. There were two empty pudding cups on it, one lightly smeared with the somewhat unsettling dark brown of chocolate, the other with the obviously fake pale yellow of vanilla.

"That pudding," he said, pointing to the tray with his pen.

Whitman looked. "Yes. That. It was sublime."

Thomason let out a delicate sigh, barely audible; the sigh was as much a part of who he was as his pudgy, disheveled appearance and unassuming deportment. As part of it, his shoulders sagged and his paunch plunged further over his waistline. "I meant *before* the incident at the convenience store. Do you remember anything about the night in question?"

Whitman pretended to think, which he believed had a lot to do with looking meaningfully up at the ceiling and going, "Hmmm." He did this for a few seconds before finally saying, "No. Nothing."

"Do you have any memories of your life? This could include a car or a house. It could be your parents or a friend."

Once again, Whitman pondered for a moment, somewhat less conspicuously this time. He then started shaking his head. "No. Sorry."

Dr. Thomason looked mildly disappointed. "This is peculiar," he said, almost to himself.

"How so?" inquired Whitman.

"Well, complete memory loss is abnormal for someone who was in a coma for such a short period of time. And your CT scan didn't show any brain damage. Quite the opposite, really. It showed an extraordinary amount of activity, especially in the frontal lobe. Using that as a determining factor, I wouldn't expect you to have memory loss, and certainly not complete memory loss. Are you experiencing any other symptoms?"

"Such as?"

"Oh, I don't know. Numbness? Headaches? Problems with your motor skills? Confusion? Hallucinations? Hearing voices?"

Whitman started shaking his head on 'problems with your motor skills' and continued right through the 'hearing voices' part. "No. None at all," he said in summation.

"Dr. Ingello said something about you experiencing hallucinations. He said you saw and were speaking to someone or something not in the room."

Whitman feigned ignorance, as if he had no clue what Thomason was talking about. "I have no idea," he said, looking improbably bemused. "All I know is that the drugs they have me on, they spin my brain around. I'm not used to them."

"Well, I suppose that could cause confusion."

"Can you tell the doctors to stop making me take them. They won't listen to me."

"I can make a recommendation, but I'm afraid they're the experts when it comes to matters of the body."

"But I'm not in any pain, and they keep giving me pain killers."

"I'll make note of that in my report," said the corpulent psychotherapist, and he scrawled something on his tablet. "Right now I'm more concerned with these hallucinations."

"I'm not having any," said Whitman.

"Really?" Thomason replied skeptically.

"I'm serious, Doc. No hallucinations. I just can't remember anything."

Thomason made another notation on his tablet, his pen scratching away at the paper in a hand that was impossible for anyone but himself to read. Then he looked up at Whitman, narrowed his eyes on him, and said, "Tell me about the girl."

"What girl?"

"The girl whose life you saved. I believe her name is Alison."

"Oh. Her?" On Whitman's face rested a shy, guilty sort of look, one that intimated he had something to hide. But really it was just the memory of the girl and the feelings she had stirred up inside him, feelings of an untoward and embarrassing nature, that made him look so suspicious. "I don't really know her," he said.

"No? I was told she was here today, and that you two talked about the incident."

Whitman nodded agreeably. "Right. Of course. She was here. She wanted to thank me for saving her life."

"But you don't remember her?"

"I don't remember my own name. How am I supposed to

remember her?"

"It's odd what we remember sometimes. I had an early-onset Alzheimer's patient who couldn't remember or even recognize his son or wife, but he could remember, in detail, this woman he once met when he was a young man in the service. The mind is a puzzle that can't be figured out."

"Then exactly what is it you're doing here?" Whitman replied with stinging, deadpan accuracy.

This blunt, unexpected comment caused Doctor Thomason to fluster; the crests of his cheeks reddened, his nose twitched, and he blinked very quickly three times. "Umm ... " he said while tapping his pen on his briefcase. "Well ... "

It was obvious that Thomason, like most shrinks – most cops and lawyers, too – wasn't as comfortable answering questions as he was asking them. But he was nothing if not keen, and he drew himself and gave it a go. "There are indicators, of course," he began, uncertainty in his voice. "And what I do is take those indicators and form a theory. It's very complicated, the human mind."

Terribly frustrating as well, thought Whitman, who was finding it difficult to understand and control the undeniably human thoughts that kept popping into his head. Many of those thoughts centered on Ally, which proved to be very distracting.

"I wish I could help you, Doc," he said, "but I really don't remember anything."

"Yes, yes, you've said. And that's quite all right. Your memories will return to you shortly, I'm sure. Right now I'd like to do a little test."

"What kind of test?"

"Well, they call it a Rorschach Test. Ever heard of it?"

Whitman shook his head. "No. Does it hurt?"

Thomason let out a soft-hearted chuckle. "No, no," he said. "It's totally painless." He reached for the folder on his briefcase and opened it. "You know what ink blots are?"

Whitman had heard of them – a splotch of black ink on a plain white page meant to have an odd, vaguely-subliminal form. He had never seen one before, though.

"Yes," he said. "Why?"

Thomason held up the first ink blot photo for Whitman to

see and said, "Tell me the first thing that pops into your head."

"Pudding," replied Whitman automatically, paying no mind to the photo.

The good doctor's brow bunched up with confusion and he turned the picture around to give it a look. "Pudding?" he said dubiously.

It was a theme that would recur often over the length of the test.


"Well," said Doctor Ingello, "what do you think? Is it real, or is he faking it?"

Dr. Thomason gave an ambivalent shrug, which changed the myriad wrinkles and creases of his shirt. "Perhaps," he said.

"Perhaps?" sneered Ingello, an unforgiving man who had the bedside manner of a constipated wolverine. "The janitor could have told me that. We called you in so that we'd know, not just suspect it."

"The brain is a complicated entity," said Thomason. "You just can't ... "

"Just give me your best determination," said Ingello, cutting him short.

Being on the spot gave Thomason an uneasy feeling, as if he was in danger of being slapped. He stood perfectly still, attempting to hide his nervousness with a world-class empty stare. He looked very much like a figure in a small town wax museum ... aside from the sweat beading on his brow.

"Well, I'd wager there's a chance he's hiding something," he said without conviction.

"I suspected so," replied Ingello meditatively.

"That's only my best guess, of course. I can't be sure. Not yet."

"There's absolutely no structural damage to his brain, Thomason. Nothing to suggest he's suffered irreparable harm."

"True. Nevertheless, he seems ... out of sorts. Remember, he did die for nearly two minutes, and then he spent twenty hours in a coma. He *could* be suffering memory loss. The human brain has a way of protecting us, shielding us from the truth when it's too painful. Denial is a powerful psychological condition."

"It's also often an excuse," said Ingello. "No one knows who this guy is. No one who fits his description has been reported missing. There's a crime, a shooting, and no one remembers seeing him there. Something's fishy."

"I suppose that's one way to look at it."

"Well that's certainly the way I'm looking at it. The logical way. I'll give him one more day, then I'm turning him over to the psych ward. Let them have a crack at him. A few hours in there and I bet he starts remembering things."

"What about his gunshot wound?"

"What wound? It's nearly healed. Never saw a wound that bad heal so quickly. Another point of suspicion in my eyes. Something's wrong about this guy."

"He did mention that he'd like to be taken off the pain killers," Thomason said. "He told me that he's not experiencing any more pain and that the pills make him loopy. In truth, they could be hindering his ability to remember."

Ingello gave the suggestion, and the reasoning behind it, brief consideration. He then began to nod. "Perhaps," he said. "I'll consider it."

"I'll give you a call after I do my follow up," said Thomason. "I'm interested in going over his answers to the Rorschach Test again. He seems unnaturally fascinated by the pudding you serve here."

"Really? Pudding?"

Thomason shrugged again. His shirt rumpled some more. "And the girl, she's of interest, too. I can't say how, though."

"What girl?"

"The girl whose life he saved. She visited him today."

That information seemed to intrigue Ingello. "Really?" he said. "Hmmm."

"I got the feeling he might've been hiding something. When I asked about her, he seemed to get ... *uncomfortable*. He mentioned something about her coming by tomorrow to see him again. At the very least, maybe she can help him remember."

"I've got the police coming tomorrow morning to take his picture," Ingello noted. "Perhaps if they circulate an actual photograph of him they'll get a hit. If not, well, we'll ship him off

135

to Wellesley, let the state take care of him. You just know he doesn't have any damn insurance. We'll end up eating the whole bill. You watch."

Dr. Thomason nodded obediently. He was not worried in the least about the financial implications of the case, though he was not about to admit that to Dr. Ingello. Instead, he said, "Was there anything else, sir?"

Ingello stared at him for a moment. "No," he said, shortly. "Thank you, Thomason." He then turned and walked away.

In three years on the job, Dr. Ingello, Chief of Medicine at Hagerstown General, had yet to refer to Dr. Thomason as Doctor. He called him by his last name only, when he called him anything. It was a fact that never failed to escape Thomason's attention, and never failed to leave him feeling inferior.

The portly headshrinker skulked away dejectedly, his scuffed loafers scraping the cold linoleum floor like dull sandpaper.

# Chapter Seven

The alleys of life are easy to navigate when you've grown up walking them. Though only twenty-seven, Vaughn had been walking the alleys of Hagerstown for more than twenty years. As a kid, he had a father he never knew, a mother who didn't care, and an older brother, Russell, who made delinquency look cool.

Of his family, only Russell showed him any love, though it was the kind of love a young, impressionable kid like Vaughn most likely would have been better off without. Russell got his kid brother drunk for the first time at age eight; got him stoned for the first time at age ten; got him laid for the first time, by a sixteen year old girl named Carla, at age eleven. Russell took his kid brother around town, took him on deals, had him hold and deliver drugs because a minor couldn't get in serious trouble. Then, two days after Vaughn's fifteenth birthday, Russell died in a single car accident.

Vaughn never really got over his brother's death. It dropped him in a hole he'd yet to climb free from, not that he ever tried. Sports should have been his way out, but Vaughn had more talent than heart. All he ever bothered to give was the bare minimum, which was more than enough in high school, where he was a man amongst boys. But in college the bare minimum was not enough, and it wasn't long before his lack of effort and bad attitude got him kicked off the team. Not that he cared. He preferred living a reckless life. He liked pot, and booze, and loose women. And in Hagerstown he was a star. Everyone knew who he was, from the mucks who dealt for him to the cops who turned a blind eye, from the junkies he occasionally had to rough up to all the young, stupid, hungry girls who'd grown up idolizing him. Everyone knew Vaughn, and he took advantage of that to piece together his own investigation into the shooting at the A&P.

Two phone calls and a visit to his old buddy Oliver's house

was all it took before Vaughn found himself at the home of a guy he knew well enough. Robert Cider didn't sell for Vaughn or Holt, but he sold. Unlike Vaughn, who'd ascended to what might be referred to as upper management in the corporate world, Robert, or Bobbo as he was known around town, was a street dog. He lived in a small drug den on the north side of town, only three streets removed from where Vaughn had grown up. Vaughn's mother still lived over that way, along with his aunt and some guy they both were fucking.

So it was. So it would always be.

Bobbo was a big man of Honduran descent, with milk brown skin, unnaturally kind eyes, and curly black hair. He was the same age as Vaughn, but they'd gone to different schools, kept different acquaintances, lived different lives. Their paths crossed from time to time, but they weren't friends. Bobbo mainly pushed heroin and meth, while Vaughn, pedaling for Holt, concentrated on moving rock, powder coke, pot and pills. They almost got into a fight once, about four years ago, over some girl that didn't matter but for a fuck. Words were exchanged, threats were made, but cooler heads prevailed. They since had made nice.

Just in case, though, Vaughn brought Chauncey for backup. Not that he needed it, but in this neighborhood, under these circumstances, backup was never a bad idea, especially when you were knocking on someone like Bobbo's door. No telling what kind of fools frequented such a place. That's why Vaughn was there – he was in search of a fool.

Someone Vaughn didn't know answered the door, a skinny white kid, no older than eighteen, with long, stringy hair and dead eyes. He looked at Vaughn, then his gaze drifted to Chauncey, sort of like how smaller objects are naturally drawn into the orbit of larger ones. Those dead eyes of his gaped, and his jaw dropped a little.

"We're here to see Bobbo," Vaughn said, and when the kid didn't reply, he added, "You speak English."

Bobbo's voice rang out from inside. "Who the hell is it, Brandon?"

"It's Vaughn," Vaughn called out as Brandon stood there mindlessly scratching a hand in his hair.

Bobbo appeared from around the corner and pushed Brandon out of the way. "Go get me a beer," he told him. He looked at Vaughn, moved aside to let him in. "You want a beer? Nice and cold."

"Yeah. Beer sounds good," said Vaughn.

"Big man?"

Chauncey nodded, and in his deep bass voice said, "Yeah."

"Make that three!" Bobbo bellowed. He then led his guests into the living room.

The house was small, but seriously decked out. There was a seventy-inch flat screen TV in the living room, two leather sofas, both with attached recliners, a rack of blue ray movies and video games along one wall, and three different video game systems setting on the floor. In one corner there was a table with two laptops on it, one of those fancy notepads, and various cell phones. Techno gadgets were pawned all the time to buy drugs, and Bobbo had his share of junkie clients.

The whole place reeked of pot and cigarettes, and under that, barely perceptible, lay the fusty, unsanitary odor of neglect. The place hadn't been properly cleaned in years, since the last owners had moved out, and the smell of hundreds of wasted nights clung to the walls and hung in the air, polluting every breath taken.

As soon as Bobbo sat down, he added to the putrescent bouquet by lighting up a smoke, Vaughn did the same. Brandon returned with their beers. Bobbo cracked his and leaned back in his recliner.

"So, what's the dealio?" he said. "You in need?"

"In need of information," Vaughn replied, and took a draw from his cigarette.

"Information?"

Vaughn cast a wary eye on Brandon. He was here to talk about criminal things, possibly violent criminal things, and Brandon looked the type to sing given a choice. Skinny kid, quiet, nervous, all strung out – those were the ones that turned Narc as soon as the offer was made. One day they're pawning their mother's wedding ring, the next they're pawning you off to the police.

"I'd rather do this in private," Vaughn said, and Bobbo got his meaning.

The thick-cut Honduran looked at his friend and said, "Yo, Brandon, why don't you go take Julio for a walk. He needs his exercise."

Brandon looked disappointed, like a kid being told he couldn't be part of the game.

"Julio?" Chauncey asked.

"The dog," said Bobbo. "He's out back."

Brandon stood up, his scrawny frame unfurling like an empty suit, and sluggishly made his way to the kitchen.

"Get me a pack of smokes while you're out," Bobbo told him. He looked at Vaughn. "You need anything."

Vaughn shook his head, and Chauncey said that he was fine.

"Newports. And a pack of blunts, too. Vanilla."

"Got it," Brandon called back, his voice a listless rattle. The sound of a door opening and closing followed, and a few seconds later a large dog started woofing.

"All right. Clear as a bell," said Bobbo, relaxing. "So, you want information?"

"This here is a sensitive issue," Vaughn said, making sure to get that point across from the start. "Understand?"

Bobbo smiled knowingly. "Of course. I get it. Keep my mouth shut."

"You help, and maybe there's something in it for you."

"Like?"

"Like better supply. Better cut of product. More money."

"Hard to argue with money," replied Bobbo casually. "Those dead presidents don't talk." Then he laughed.

Vaughn and Chauncey joined in, because that's what you did when someone you were looking to get something from made a joke. When the laughter died down, Vaughn spoke up. "The robbery at the A&P Mart the other night," he said. "Hear about it?"

Bobbo nodded his cement block of a head. "Sure. Some guy got capped."

"That's right. He's gonna live."

"I read that. They don't know who he is."

"John Fucking Doe, that's who he is. Anyway, he wasn't the only one there that night. You know my girl Ally?"

Bobbo nodded his head again, thoughtfully this time. "Yeah. Works at Teasers, right? I seen her around. Cute."

"Yeah. She is. Damn cute."

"You hitting that?"

Vaughn sort of shrugged off the comment, but then he said, "You know how it is. She's a nice girl. I want to make sure this don't mess with her head. That bullet almost got her."

Bobbo was starting to get the drift. Vaughn wanted to know who'd done the robbery so that he could exact a little vengeance of his own. And there was no better place to start nosing around than the local smack and meth dealer. Quickie robbery jobs were nothing new to the kind of junkies Bobbo dealt with.

"Police haven't found the guy yet, have they?" he said.

"Nope. No leads, neither."

"Let me guess, you want to beat them to it?"

Vaughn nodded slowly, determinedly. "Damn right. Make sure it don't happen again. Fucking junkies."

"Easy now. That's my bread and butter," replied Bobbo, and sounded out a laugh.

Chauncey laughed with him, but Vaughn held firm. "I figured you might've heard something about it," he said. "I know you hear a lot."

Bobbo said that he did. Bobbo said that he heard all kinds of things.

"Police come talk to you?" Vaughn asked him.

Bobbo gave a sarcastic snort, and shook his head. "Fuck no. Those boys don't come down here but to fuck with me."

"Clueless bastards. They're never gonna solve it."

"No shit. Unless they catch a guy with a gun in his hand, they don't know what's what."

"That's why we're looking into it."

"You know," said Bobbo, in the manner of someone suddenly remembering something that might just be important, "I did get a strange visit that night."

"Strange how?" asked Vaughn.

"One of my junkies, never has any money, always trying to pedal stolen phones, VCR movies, old jewelry, bullshit like that. Once he came here with a fucking bowling ball. What the hell I want with a bowling ball? I was half-tempted to tell him I'd give

141

him a nickel if he'd let me drop the ball on his foot."

Chauncey laughed at the thought.

Vaughn merely smiled, and that smile disappeared quickly. "Who is it?" he asked, all business. "You got a name?"

Bobbo's lips pursed, and most of his mocha brown face winced with skepticism. "I give you a name," he said, calculatingly, "that puts me in it. And this guy, he's a ... Well, I wouldn't call him a friend, but I like him well enough."

"How about two bricks for your trouble?" said Vaughn, understanding that they'd just reached the negotiation point.

Bobbo shook his head. "I don't care for that shit," he said. "I sell it, don't do it. But if you were to drop off some of that fine Colombian gold dust, the uncut shit you boys keep over there at the club, that would be appreciated."

"How much?" asked Vaughn.

"A few ounces should do the trick. I'm goin' to Atlantic City this weekend. Me and this crazy chick from Pink Palace. Destiny."

Vaughn said that he knew her. "Didn't she used to date Tony Denko? The cop?"

"Yeah. Now she's not. And I plan on corrupting her."

"Nice," said Vaughn. "Though she may end up corrupting you."

Bobbo laughed, and said that would be fine by him.

Chauncey said, "I love Pink Palace. Is Destiny the short one with the tattoo of a butterfly on her ass?"

"That's her," said Bobbo. "Fly, ain't she?"

"Yeah."

"Consider it done," said Vaughn. "All for a good cause."

A smile broke wide across Bobbo's ham hock of a face. He said, "You know, I like it when things work out even."

"Now," said Vaughn, "about this visit."

Bobbo wasn't one to give without getting first, but he knew he had the cards. Information was power, and he had it all. No doubt Vaughn was going to do something with the name he was about to get, and there was a strong chance that that something would include blood and broken bones. So if Vaughn tried to welsh on the deal, all Bobbo would have to do is make a phone call. Not that he thought it would ever come to that – Vaughn had a reputation of being a standup guy when it came to deals – and not that he would ever make that call. But he had that card, and Vaughn knew it.

"You know a local junkie named Adam?" Bobbo said, and watched for their reactions. Chauncey's expression didn't change; Vaughn's, meanwhile, tightened up some. "Skinny kid," Bobbo went on. "White suburban smackhead. Another lab rat in the sewers. Some people call him Scarecrow."

"Yeah," said Vaughn. "I think I know who you mean."

"Not saying it was him, mind you, but I'd ask him about it, if you can find him. The night of the robbery, he came by here, late, with cash. He rarely has cash. Paid off his tab, a couple hundred worth, and wanted to buy more. I was out, though. Gave him a handful of Vikes to tide him over. Haven't seen him since."

"Got a last name?" Vaughn asked.

"I think it's Dubinsky, but I'm not sure. He seemed in a bad way that night. Then again, he's pretty much always in a bad way. Not the kind you'd expect to pull a robbery. Certainly not the type to shoot a gun. I found it strange is all, him showing up with money. And then that robbery on the same night."

Vaughn was nodding along. Chauncey, too.

"Don't have a clue where you might find him," Bobbo continued. He lit up another cigarette; the last one had burned out in the ashtray. Vaughn swigged back the rest of his beer. "His folks are from town, but they kicked him out long ago. Try the shelter maybe. Or the scrap den over on Wildon."

Vaughn stood. Chauncey followed his lead. Though he was quite comfortable in his recliner, beer in one hand, cigarette in the other, Bobbo stood with them.

"Thanks," Vaughn said. "That should get us started."

"Any time," replied Bobbo. "Gotta help when we can on this side of things."

"You know it," said Chauncey.

"We'll be back in an hour with your payment," Vaughn said. "That work for you?"

Bobbo said that it did.

"Two ounces now, and if it pans out, two more later."

Bobbo put down his beer and reached out a hand. He and

Vaughn shook.

"Sounds fair."

Chauncey and Bobbo shook hands next, and then they all made their way to the door.

"Adam Dubinsky," said Vaughn, setting the name to memory. "Scarecrow."


Meanwhile, across town, the guy some people called Scarecrow currently was the half-living embodiment of death puked up and warmed over. The inside of his mouth tasted of bile and blood, his flesh was clammy and hot, and a dull, consistent ache persecuted every muscle and joint in his body. He worked himself to a sitting position against the wall and grabbed a jug of water. It was warm, but he didn't care; he drank it down as if he'd just spent three days in the desert. When he finished, he realized, for the first time in a while, that he was hungry. He still had two cans of ravioli left, and he popped the top on one of them. A plastic spoon served him well enough, and he scooped the can clean, going as far as scraping the sauce off the sides and the bottom. Then he lit himself a cigarette. He only had three left. Three cigarettes, one can of ravioli, a half a bag of chips, four or five shots worth of cheap vodka, and little else. At least he didn't have to worry about running out of water.

It was nighttime now, and the darkness outside had edged it's way inside the school, casting everything in shades of black and gray. The water may never have been turned off, but the electricity had been. Adam wouldn't have taken the chance of turning on a light anyway. This was the perfect hiding place because no one suspected it.

He reached in his pocket and pulled out his wallet. He had only nineteen dollars to his name, which was enough for a bottle of liquor, a bottle of aspirin, some cheap food, like a couple more cans of raviolis, and, if he had enough, another pack of cigarettes.

He couldn't go out looking like he did, though.

That in mind, he made his way to the bathroom, shuffling down the hallway like a lonely zombie, occasionally using the lockers for balance. He took a piss, then he washed his face and hands with the soap he'd found in a janitor's closet. He did his best to wash his greasy hair, vigorously scratching his wet hands through it, and then slicked it back off his forehead. He brushed his teeth with warm water and his finger, and rinsed his mouth out a couple times. He used his tongue to experimentally poke at the space left by the molar he'd lost the other day and found that it was still quite sore.

He checked his pockets again and found a couple quarters and a couple dimes. So, nineteen dollars and seventy cents was the grand total. That's when he remembered his plan about holding up another convenience store. The gun was out back, buried under one of the many evergreen bushes that surrounded the schoolyard, along with the two bandanas he'd used to cover his face. He thought about what place would be best to hit: the Gas 'n' Go on Widmark, the 7/11 on Cherry Wood, or maybe the Super Go on Washington. All of them were at least a mile away, and the Gas 'n' Go and 7/11 were heavily patronized and located in well-lit plazas. Super Go was probably his best bet.

He looked at himself in the mirror, staring deep into eyes he didn't recognize anymore, eyes that didn't show or really see anything, and tried to remember what it was like to care about something, anything, other than getting high.

Perhaps the gun would be put to better use at the side of my head, he thought to himself. Death, he believed, would most likely save him a lot of heartache and trouble. For his parents, too, who were at the end of their rope.

But Adam wasn't quite there yet. Truth was, he was afraid to die. He may not have been inside a church in more than five years, may not have prayed or read the bible in that time, may not have lived his life with any semblance of religion or morality, but somewhere in the dark corners of his mind, in the places that had been blighted by his struggles and addiction, there was a part of him that believed in and was terrified by Hell.

Perhaps because he felt that his present life might just be a precursor.

For that reason and that reason alone, he left the gun and bandanas buried under the evergreen bush and used the nineteen dollars and seventy cents in his pocket to buy a bottle of cheap vodka, a pack of cheap smokes, aspirins, and four cans of raviolis, which were on a two-for-one special. He also took a bold chance, shoplifting a bottle of Nyquil, figuring if all else failed it could help ease the aches and pains.

The clerk behind the counter gave him a sideways look while he was checking out and Adam thought that perhaps he was going to have some trouble. But ultimately nothing besides the retail transaction happened.

Adam bought his things and was left with exactly ninety-six cents. He used fifty of those cents to buy a paper from the machine out front. The remaining forty-six cents went in his pocket, because it was better than nothing.

Next time I come here, he thought as he shambled away with his meager yet life-sustaining supplies, I'll have a gun with me. There was little doubt in his mind that eventually it would come to that.


The police were interested in Whitman's story *and* his identity. Blood, fingerprint, and DNA samples hadn't produced any matches in the system, and at sixty-four hours into the investigation they had an astounding lack of evidence and zero suspects. Per a request from the doctors, they had agreed to give John Doe some time to rest and recover his bearings, but time was ticking and their patience had run thin. They didn't necessarily think he was guilty of anything, but the fact that *he* didn't know who he was and *they* didn't know who he was made them suspicious. They were anxious to hear what he had to say.

The older detective, Detective Milner, was short and soft around the middle, with a receding hairline and a pug nose. He didn't look like a cop; he looked more like a scientist or accountant, someone who slouched at a desk forty hours a week and used his brain more than his body. He certainly didn't look like someone who fought crime for a living. His partner, Detective Rainer, was much younger; he had a stern jaw and close-cropped hair, and looked at least capable of running down an assailant without cramping up or tripping over his own feet.

Both wore white button-down shirts and sloppily knotted ties, and both sported a gun on their belt.

Milner did most of the talking. Rainer more or less just stood there and sneered menacingly. Whitman idly wondered which one was the good cop and which one was the bad cop, and decided that Rainer had to be the good cop due to his youth and superior physicality. Edmund, who had quickly prepped him for the interview, hadn't explained the concept very well.

"And you don't remember what you were doing there?" said Milner skeptically. Everything he said came with a skeptical slant, which led Whitman to think that either Milner didn't trust him or that this was the first time he had ever questioned a witness and he wasn't very comfortable doing it.

"No. Sorry."

"And you don't remember where you were before you went to the A&P?"

This was the third time they had broached the subject and Whitman was beginning to feel confounded. "You know," he said, quite earnestly, "the doctor who was in here earlier, Dr. Thomason, the psychotherapist, he had a device that records conversations. It might behoove you to get one of those."

The detectives exchanged a look that seemed to carry a lot of meaning. When Milner turned back to Whitman, his brow had flattened and there was a hostile glare in his eyes. "You think that's funny?" he said to him sharply.

"It might keep you from repeating yourselves," replied Whitman, utterly oblivious.

"This is getting us nowhere," grumbled Rainer. His eyes also were set in a glare, but that was more of a natural look for him. "He's not going to tell us anything."

"Because I don't remember anything. Honest."

"That's fine," said Milner. "Completely understandable." Then, leaning closer to Whitman, and dropping his voice a notch, he added, "Just so you know, Dr. Ingello wants to put you in the psych ward until you *do* remember what happened. He says there's no physiological reason you should have memory loss. That makes me skeptical."

And there it was, thought Whitman. Mystery solved. Milner was skeptical. He imagined that most cops probably were, given some of the fools and losers they had to deal with on a regular basis. Whitman could relate.

"I'm sorry," he said. "But I don't know who I am."

That was a lie, of course, one that Whitman was doing a fine job telling. He knew exactly who he was, two-fold: on one side, he was Jeremiah Whitman, a revolutionary era shopkeeper and farmer who over the last two-hundred and twenty odd years had been a Custodian in the celestial ranks; on the other side, the bizzaro side, he was some sort of manifestation of Martin Loomis, who currently was some sort of manifestation of Whitman in the spirit world. How they had switched bodies was the question.

Of course he couldn't say any of that or they'd lock him up and throw away the key. Then again, it seemed they were planning on locking him up anyway. Still, the kind of truth he was carrying was not for everyday digestion. The two badges before him, they certainly wouldn't understand, and Whitman couldn't fault them for that.

"You know," he said, "I was dead for a couple minutes."

"Yes, we know," said Rainer. "You told us."

"I don't remember anything."

"You told us that, too."

Whitman sighed and sat back.

"You may have died, but you're very much alive right now and all your test results came back normal," Milner pointed out. "According to Dr. Ingello, your mind is tiptop."

Not knowing what to say, Whitman nodded guiltily.

"Which makes us suspicious. Suspicious of who you are and what you were doing in that store."

"I don't know what to tell you," Whitman said. "Honestly, I'd like to help you, I would, I have no quarrels with the police, but I don't know anything. I remember waking up here, in the hospital, and that's it. If I knew who I was, I'd tell you. Why wouldn't I?"

"Because maybe you have something to hide?" said Milner.

"I don't have anything to hide. I don't know anything."

Milner shook his head. He looked disgusted. "What about the girl?" he asked, changing gears. "You remember the girl?"

"You mean Ally?"

"Yes. Ally. The girl whose life you saved. Do you remember her?"

Whitman shrugged. "She visited yesterday. She's supposed to come by today."

"You don't remember her from before?" That suspicious slant, as steep as a Yosemite rock face, had returned to Milner's voice. It was so obvious that Whitman wondered if it was meant to be facetious.

"Nooo," he said, hesitantly. "Why?"

"You don't remember seeing her at a strip club a few nights before the shooting?"

"A strip club?" replied Whitman with genuine surprise. "Heavens no. What do you take me for, a deviant?"

"She remembers you."

"From a strip club?"

"She said you came in for a beer but left right away."

Shock and horror occupied the pale, youthful face that currently belonged to Jeremiah Whitman. He couldn't believe that Ally, the sweet, beautiful young woman who had come to visit him, worked in a strip club. She seemed to him like a teacher or a nurse, or one of those pretty girls that work the counter at upscale boutiques spraying perfume samples and rubbing on hand creams. She certainly didn't seem like a stripper. He felt tricked or betrayed in some way.

"So, were you there?" said Milner. "Or don't you remember that either?"

Whitman heard the question, but his mind was stuck on Ally. "She's a stripper?" he said,   disappointment dragging his voice down.

"No. She's a bartender."

"Though I'm sure she's no stranger to getting naked," added Rainer snidely.

"Hey!" Whitman snapped. "That's not a nice thing to say about a lady."

"A lady?" The young detective shook with a laugh. "That's a new one."

"It's not nice," Whitman persisted. "You're being rude and crude. Didn't your mother teach you any manners?"

"Why do you care what we say about her if you don't know

who she is?" said Milner, quick to pounce.

"Maybe because she came to visit me here and was nice to me. Or maybe because everyone, no matter who they are, deserves respect and kindness. Remember, there but for the grace of God."

The two detectives exchanged another look, this one weighted with disbelief. Rainer rolled his eyes.

"So you're telling us you don't know who she is?" Milner said, still working that point.

"Yesterday is the first time I remember seeing her," Whitman replied. A flash caught his eye then, and when he glanced that way he saw Edmund standing in the corner, cringing. The prim, ghostly Brit wore a look that said he wished he had a white flag to wave.

"You realize they won't release you until you remember who you are?" Milner told Whitman. "Now, I don't know if you've ever been to a psych ward before – "

"I'd wager he has," Rainer cut in, smirking.

" – but I guarantee you that you won't like the accommodations. The food stinks, they keep you heavily-drugged most of the time, and you have to go to countless therapy sessions. You understand what I'm saying to you?"

"Yes, I get it," Whitman huffed, finally showing some frustration. "But it doesn't change anything. I'm telling you the truth."

"You don't remember," said Rainer cynically.

Whitman looked him square in the eye. "No. I don't remember." Then, going on the offensive, figuring he had nothing to lose, he made a speech. "What I would like to know is why you're so suspicious of me? What did I do that makes you doubt my story? I saved a young woman's life. That's a good thing, right? That's one in the win column. I'm sorry I don't remember doing it, but perhaps that might have something to do with the fact that I was shot. I died. I spent a day in a coma. Now, I cannot tell you whether or not my brain suffered any permanent damage, just like I cannot give you a medical reason as to why I'm unable to remember anything. But that's the truth, like it or not."

Building on that momentum, he continued: "Trust me when I

tell you that I don't like being here." That was a gross understatement, one that crossed dimensional lines. "And I certainly don't want to go to an asylum. All I want is for this to be over with so I can go home. *Believe* me, that's *all* I want. I want to go home. So as soon as I remember something, anything, I'll tell you."

"Okay," said Milner, nodding along. He still had his doubts, though. Something about the situation didn't feel right to him, and he was determined to uncover the truth. "While you're plumbing the depths of your barren mind, we'll be circulating your picture."

On cue, Detective Rainer removed a small digital camera from his pocket. He fiddled with it for a moment, looking over the buttons, pressing a couple of them experimentally. It came on, and the screen began to show video of what the lens was aimed at – currently Whitman's bare feet. He handed it to his partner and said, "Is this right?"

Milner took it, checked the screen. "Yeah," he said. Then he pointed it at Whitman. "Say cheese," he told him.

Whitman said, "Cheese."

Milner took three shots, made sure all three were stored in the camera's log, and handed it back to Rainer. "We're going to pass these shots around town, give 'em to the newspapers and local news. I'm sure we'll find someone who knows you." He said that last part almost as a threat. "Only a matter of time."

"Fine," piped Whitman, standing his ground. But he was having a hard time maintaining his cool under such duress, especially with Edmund standing watch in the corner. "I'd like to know myself."

"Sure," said Milner. "We'll be in touch. Soon."

He and his partner left then, walked right out the door without looking back.

"Whoa. They certainly were a scary lot," said Edmund, coming forward.

Whitman stared at him. "Tell me you have a solution."

The dismal, apologetic look the Custodian gave made words unnecessary. He nervously jumped right into explanation mode. "Emilia's on it," he said. "She's supposed to talk to Alain today. We're waiting to hear how that goes."

"So ... Nothing yet?"

Edmund's head began to wobble back and forth. "No. Nothing definitive."

"They're going to put me in an asylum, Edmund. You heard them. I don't think they're playing around."

"No. Doesn't seem so, sir."

"Not to mention what's going to happen if they put my picture – Martin Loomis's picture, I mean – on the news. I can't imagine that will have positive results."

"No, sir. Probably just the opposite."

Whitman gave his Custodian a pointed look. "Yes. Thank you."

Edmund put a fist to his mouth and cleared his throat in a mannerly way. Then he said, "Perhaps this would be a good time to talk about Plan B, sir."

"Yes," said Whitman, nodding. "That's a good idea. Let's hear what you got."

The shape and color of Edmund's face changed drastically. It came to resemble a face you might expect to find on someone who has just realized they are standing naked in a roomful of people.

"Edmund?" Whitman said inquisitively.

"Yes, sir?"

"Plan B?"

"Umm ... Well ... " It was rather clear that Edmund didn't have a Plan B to fall back on, at least not one worth mentioning. "I was kind of hoping that you'd know what that was, sir," he said. "I've always been more of a Plan A kind of guy myself."

"Right," said Whitman, biting down hard on his tongue. "Let's put our heads together and see what we can come up with, shall we?"

"You got it, sir. As they say, two heads are better than one."

And you, my dear Edmund, thought Whitman, are undoubtedly the exception that proves that rule.

# Chapter Eight

Martin Loomis, trapped in the celestial body of a sexagenarian celestial being, sulked in his little white holding room like a jilted lover. His memories had come back, and the thought of them laid bare brought him great sadness.

He had clarity now, perfect and crystal clear. He knew things, understood things, and the somber images of his last moments of life, moments littered with the debris of wine and porn and sorrow, haunted him terribly. It was decidedly worse than the memory of Amanda's betrayal, which had been playing in his head on a constant loop since it had happened. It had been on his mind that night. It had been the last thought that flickered in the haze before his finger squeezed the trigger and a bullet physically did to his heart what she had done to it metaphysically.

Was it worth it, he wondered. He didn't feel the same torturous pain anymore. He didn't feel anything, really. And now he was stuck in some sort of spiritual waiting room, his eternal fate yet to be decided.

He got up and started pacing back and forth. There was no door to this room, nor bars to hold him captive. As far as he could tell, there were no walls and no windows, no floor or ceiling either. But yet he could not escape. There was nowhere to go. When they first left him alone, he had tried to sneak off. He started walking, and kept walking, and walking, and walking, but he never seemed to get anywhere. No matter how far he walked, no matter which direction he walked, he always ended up in the same place. Wherever he was, there was no way to escape.

"Hello?" he called out. His voice echoed like a whisper in a dream, going nowhere. "Hello?" he tried again. "Anyone?"

He was starting to get frustrated. They had asked him all sorts of questions and he had answered them in grim and honest detail. And some of them had been personal questions, too, of the embarrassing variety. The funny thing was, though he was embarrassed, he never thought to lie. They asked, and he told them the truth, though on quite a few occasions he felt the need to look away.

Then they had told him to sit tight, they'd be right back. That had been ...

Marty couldn't tell how long it actually had been, but it seemed like a really long time. They had promised to answer some of his questions – 'quid pro quo,' they had called it – but he was beginning to wonder if that offer was genuine. These religious types – Marty had them pegged for religious types on account of how they spoke and conducted themselves so properly, in addition to the point that he knew he was dead – threw around obscure Latin phrases all the time. For all he knew, he might've agreed to take part in some sort of baptismal ceremony.

It could be worse, he reasoned. He could be in Hell right now. There could be some red-faced demon sticking a pitchfork up his ...

"Hello?" he called out again, his voice ringing, going on and on in the great white emptiness around him. He felt like he was in a snowstorm in Antarctica, only it wasn't cold, and there were no penguins.

All of it was ridiculously absurd. It was Amanda's fault. She had betrayed him. She was such a ... Such a ... Such a ...

The word was on the tip of his tongue but he couldn't seem to say it. It started with a B, and there was one that started with an S, too, and another one that started with a C. And he had a vitriolic rant cluttered with F-bombs and Bs and Cs and Ss ready to roll, but the words wouldn't come out.

"Hello?!" he shouted. "Anyone?!"

Finally, he got a response.

"Gees, Louise! What's all the fuss about?"

It was the same woman as last time, the sweet though somewhat brusque black woman with a wild puff of graying hair. What was her name again, Marty wondered. Amy? No. Emily? No. Emilia. That was it.

"Hello," he said to her in a desperate sort of way. "Emilia, right? I've been waiting."

"I know. And we've been working."

"Sorry. I didn't mean to interrupt."

"Yes you did. That's what all the yelling was about."

The tart impatience of her tone put Marty on the defensive. "You said you were coming right back," he told her, somewhat accusatorily. "You promised you would answer my questions. Quid Pro Quo, remember?"

"*When* we had the time," Emilia replied, really emphasizing that first word.

Marty's posture went slack. He let out a whiny groan. "Come on," he said. "I'm dying here. I have to know what's going on. Please."

Emilia issued a sigh, one yielded in submission. She felt bad for Marty, and seeing that he looked exactly like her boss and good friend, Whitman, she found it difficult to ignore his pleas, even though they were terribly juvenile and selfish. "Okay," she said to him. "I'll answer one question. Only one."

"One?" Marty whined. "How about three?"

"Two," she countered, showing two fingers. "Then I must be going."

Marty figured he had about a hundred thousand questions in need of asking right about now, but he didn't want to push it. Two was sufficient. Now he just needed the right two, and the right context.

He put his mind to work, and the seconds began to tick away.

After twenty or so, Emilia's impetuousness got the better of her. "Marty?" she said to him. "Any time now."

"Right," he said, nodding hurriedly. "I got it. Ready?"

She made no reply, other than to give him a look that said he really needed to get on with it. He did just that.

"What is this place?" he asked her. "I know you said it's something like a spiritual waiting room. But a waiting room to what? Heaven? Hell? Purgatory?"

"Right now you're behind the scenes in the spirit world, somewhere between Heaven and earth," said Emilia.

"Heaven?" Marty gasped, his face, which was Whitman's face, a handsome face trodden with years of age and wisdom, lighting up. "So I'm going to Heaven? That's awesome."

"Easy there," said Emilia. "You're not going anywhere right now. And you're certainly not on your way to Heaven."

Marty was instantly crestfallen. "But ... " he said. Then he said it again. "But ... "

"We don't know what's going to happen to you yet," Emilia told him, her tongue sharpening some, letting him know that the situation at hand was far from pleasant, and far from over. "There are bigger issues at play. A cosmic shift, you might say. Variables beyond understanding. We have to put things straight before your fate can be decided."

Marty nodded obediently, and put his mind back to work. He had one more question left, and he really didn't want to waste it. With a thought toward self-preservation he drew himself up and said, "Is there anything I can do to help?"

Emilia looked at him, her eyes cast with doubt. "Help?" she said.

"Well, it's just that I'd really rather not go to hell, you know? Fire. Brimstone. Doesn't sound all that fun."

"It's not," she told him. "Purgatory's no picnic, either. Something you probably should've thought of before you shot yourself. Don'tcha think?"

"True," said Marty glumly. "You're right. Hindsight is twenty-twenty."

Emilia nearly swallowed her tongue. "Hindsight? Are you serious? Tell me, young man, just what sort of vision leads you to think that putting a gun to your chest and pulling the trigger won't end badly?"

Marty stared at her, and shrugged helplessly. "I don't know," he said. "I guess I never really thought all that much about it. Never really thought any of this was ... " he had a quick look around, taking in the sterile, antiseptic environs of wherever the hell he was, " ... you know, real."

Emilia gave a resentful shake of her head. "Always the same," she said. "World's gotten too filled up, that's the problem. Can't see the truth of things when there's so much garbage around."

"Precisely," said Marty, not quite grasping that he was being talked down to. "It's tough out there."

A surly smile curled up on Emilia's face. "I'll tell you what," she said to her guest. "You want in my good graces, show me some patience. Sit here, keep quiet, and let us mind our business. If we need you, we'll let you know. In the meantime, you may want to think about saying a few prayers. Better late than never. Know what I mean."

Marty nodded thoughtfully, and right before his eyes Emilia disappeared. He blinked once, then again. He looked around for her, but saw only shapeless, formless, colorless white. She was gone, vanished like a snowflake in a snowstorm, and all that remained was silence, and a creeping dread that told him this was not going to end well.

Such is life, he thought, borrowing an expression from his mother. It was the first time he'd thought of her since this had happened, and he wondered if she was around here somewhere. He wondered if maybe he could get word to her, use her as a character witness on his behalf. It was worth a shot. As for now, he decided that Emilia's advice was worth heeding, and he got down on his knees and started to pray.


Who was John Doe?

Of all the thoughts and questions pestering Ally's brain – quitting her job, going back to school, being pregnant, her current broken relationship with Vaughn – it was by far the most intriguing and mystifying. Not only did she not know, no one did.

She remembered him from the club a couple nights prior to the shooting at the A&P Mart, remembered talking to him briefly about relationships and thinking that he was honest and kind and down on his luck. She had felt a kinship for him then, empathy borne out of the misery that love gone bad tends to cause. He had lost his fiancée, and she was fresh from her split with Vaughn. She thought he was cute in a moppish sort of way, but couldn't say she was interested in him; she was much too concerned with the present troubles of her own life to start thinking about getting involved with someone new, especially someone still hung up on another woman.

She fought to remember his name, but couldn't. She'd even asked around the club, hoping to find someone who remembered him from the other night. No one did. It was hardly her fault for forgetting, she told herself. That was the night Vaughn had come in with his friends and treated her with cruelty and malicious indifference, ordering her to "fetch" him a beer and telling her that if she wanted a good tip she was going to need to work for it. He'd made other inappropriate comments that night, trying to embarrass her and show her who was boss. Then, at the end of the night, after goading and belittling her for more than two hours, he left her a seventy cent tip on an eighty dollar tab.

She had wanted to throw it back in his face, but instead she found the strength to take the two quarters and two dimes, thank him kindly for it, and walk away. Sometime during that painful little episode, the nice young man in the corner had skulked off without saying goodbye, leaving a five dollar tip behind and nothing else.

Then, three nights later, he saved her life.

She wondered, idly but with some concern, if maybe the guy had been stalking her. She had never had a stalker before, though she was no stranger to unwanted attention from men. And the club seemed to draw the type. Rarely a week went by without one of the dancers making a request for the bouncers to throw out a particular customer because he wouldn't leave her alone, or because he had gotten a little handsy, or because he was creepy and weird. Ninety percent of the guys who parted the doors at Teasers were creepy and weird, thought Ally. It was only the ones who didn't tip well that were singled out.

But John Doe hadn't come off like a stalker. And even if he was a stalker, Ally figured the fact that he'd saved her life more than made up for it. She felt she owed him another visit; if seeing her and talking to her could help him remember who he was, a trip to the hospital was the least she could do. And maybe she'd get some answers, too.

On the way there she stopped off at her favorite eatery, Elwood's Meat and Cheese Shack, and got a couple cheeseburgers, an order of fries, and a slice of their famous cheesecake. One of the cheeseburgers was for her, the rest of the food was for John Doe, though she did steal a few of his fries, unable to stop herself. She figured bringing him some outside food would be a nice gesture, not knowing that Whitman was thoroughly enjoying the bland, unimaginative hospital grub being served to him. All things considered, it was a significant step up from the cuisine of the late eighteenth century.

At the hospital, she went straight to his room on the second floor, only he wasn't there. The bed was empty and made up, and the place had the feel of a hotel room that had just been flipped. She flagged down one of the nurses on duty and asked her where John Doe was, but all the young woman would tell her was that he had been transferred to the fifth floor. Ally went there immediately to see if she could get some answers and discovered that they were holding him in a secure room.

"What does that mean exactly?" she asked the woman at the reception desk.

"Well, it means they don't want anyone visiting him right now."

"I don't understand. I saw him yesterday. Is something wrong? Is he okay?"

"Oh yes, he's fine. Medically speaking. The cops were here, though, and they said he wasn't allowed anymore visitors."

"The cops? Did they say why?"

The woman shook her head. Her burnt red hair didn't move at all. "No. Sorry. They were talking to Dr. Ingello about it. He's the Chief of Medicine here. I'd say to ask him, but he's a very busy man." She leaned forward, lowered her voice to a whisper, and added, "And kind of an asshole."

"But he's okay? John Doe? There were no complications or setbacks?"

"Not that I know of. The one nurse said that his wound is almost completely healed. And they're not giving him anymore pain medication. They're hoping maybe that'll help with his memory loss."

Ally nodded. "Good. That's good. I just ... " She stopped, reached into her oversized purse, and pulled out a brown paper bag, the bottom of which was stained with grease. The smell that came with it was intoxicating. "I got him this," she said. "A cheeseburger from Elwood's. It's a cheeseburger, fries, and a slice of their homemade cheesecake. Could I just go in and give it to him?"

"Sorry," said the woman. "We're not allowed to let anyone

in."

"I'd let security escort me, if that helps."

The woman shook her head primly.

"Okay. Can you take it to him for me?"

The woman looked at the bag, then at Ally.

"Please. I'm the girl who would have gotten shot the other night if he hadn't jumped in front of the bullet. I thought ... well, I just wanted to get him ... something."

The woman nodded, and reached for the bag. "I'll take it," she said.

"Thank you."

"You're welcome. And what's your name, dear? So I can tell him who it's from."

"Ally."

"Ally. All right, Ally, I'll get it to him."

Ally nodded as if satisfied, but she was reluctant to leave. She turned to start away, then stopped, turned back, and said, "I was wondering, could I call him if I wanted?"

Again the woman shook her head. "No. Sorry. His phone privileges have been revoked, too. No communication."

That sounded rather ominous to Ally, but she didn't know what to do about it. Hospitals weren't in the habit of giving out information to non-relatives, and it was a good bet that with the cops involved, giving orders, doing their thing, the situation had taken an unexpected turn. Ally didn't want to seem nosy or obnoxious, but she couldn't pull herself away just yet.

"He's not in trouble, is he?" she asked, wanting to know.

The woman shrugged. "Honestly, I don't know. All I know is that the police don't want him having any visitors right now, and Dr. Ingello agreed."

"Is this ... *normal?*"

"Let me tell you, dear, almost nothing around here is normal," replied the woman, saying it like a line she had used before and would again. "And I really don't know any more about it. I'm sorry."

Ally had more questions, but it was rather obvious to her that the woman behind the counter, though respectful and courteous, had said all she had to say and wanted the conversation to be over. It was in her tone and written on her face, and Ally felt she should respect that.

"I understand," she said. "Thank you for your help, and thank you for taking him the food. Have a nice day."

"You too, dear. And don't worry, I'm sure everything'll be okay."

Ally nodded politely, but she wasn't sure if she believed that. Something was wrong, she could feel it, though there seemed to be nothing she could do about it. As she walked away, she wondered if maybe she should try to call the detectives she'd talked to after the shooting and see what they had to say about John Doe; she still had their cards, and they had told her she should call if she remembered anything else or had any questions. This was probably not what they had in mind, she speculated, but that was hardly her concern. She felt connected to John Doe and wanted to know what was happening with him, good or bad.

Maybe there was something she could do to help.


Whitman had always been a man of action. At least, Jeremiah Whitman had always been a man of action. In the seventeen-hundreds, a man had little choice but to be a man of action. You had to break your back just to survive.

Those instincts had been drained out of him over the last couple centuries, like air slowly leaking out of a pierced tire. A man of action, a hardnosed man who lived right, who said what needed said and did what needed done, reduced to a ghost whispering advice into the ears of an increasingly-deaf population.

You weren't supposed to judge, and you weren't allowed to make your presence known. You weren't permitted to make things happen, or unfairly influence events to help your cause. You just had to be there to observe and guide with soft words, while the other side walked free, setting traps and instigating mayhem. It was unfair, and went a long way in explaining why the tide had changed. Whitman and his crew were fighting a losing battle, and every passing day it seemed to get worse.

Despite stringent rules and regulations, Whitman had had his share of controversy. He had, on two separate occasions, gently steered fate the way he wanted it to go, which was considered an egregious violation of policy. There was a young boy, ten years young, who was dying of bone cancer; that would have been back in 1850-something, before doctors even knew what cancer was, let alone how to diagnose and treat it. Whitman laid on hands, and the boy walked away, living to the ripe old age of forty-one. And there was the young mother, Candace, in the year 1955, who died giving birth to a daughter; Whitman had intervened there, too, bringing the woman back before she was all the way gone, working what the doctors referred to as a miracle.

He had paid a steep price for those sins, losing rank and having to do three years of hard penance in Purgatory. Those acts were the main reason why he wasn't an Elder yet. The Angels alone were allowed to make decisions on miracles, and they made them infrequently, outside the bounds of logical criteria. Whitman had once heard that they simply rolled the dice, though he wasn't sure he believed that. Given the sheer randomness of life, though, he sometimes wondered.

It made no difference, really. Not anymore. He had acted impulsively then and had suffered the consequences. But the truth was that he'd do it again. He had done what he'd done because he felt it was the right thing to do, and though he had made apologies afterwards, he had never felt sorry.

And now, fifty-some years later, it appeared he once again was caught in the thick of fate's tangled web. Somehow he was human again, trapped in the uncomfortable body of a young man who had taken his own life, and it seemed as though no one knew how to get him back. Or they just didn't care to.

Either way he knew he was in a bad spot. The Elders were a tough, no-nonsense crowd, and despite what Edmund had told him, this felt very much like a punishment to Whitman. The only way something like this could have happened, he surmised, was if he tried to intervene in someone's life and got caught. He must have tried to stop Marty from killing himself, or the other one, Dubinsky, from shooting Ally. Those were the only two things that made sense, only he couldn't remember.

Not that it made a difference. For whatever reason, be it fate, bad luck, a cosmic glitch, a terribly unfunny practical joke made at his expense – there were quite a few Angels known for their puckish reputation – he had been transformed, and it seemed as though he was trapped in the human body he had inherited ... at least for the foreseeable future. And his orders on high were to stay in the hospital, talk to as few people as possible, and continue to play dumb. That simply would not do.

The police were suspicious of him, for whatever ridiculous, cockeyed reason passed for common sense in law enforcement's collective brain, the doctors were planning on sending him to a psych ward if he couldn't remember who he was by lunch tomorrow, and his crew of trusty Custodians and the Elders who governed them were either clueless or complicit. The only ones he trusted were Edmund and Emilia. He trusted Emilia more, of course, based on IQ points and overall competence; but what Edmund lacked in smarts, and experience, and ingenuity, and so many other areas, he more than made up for with Labrador-like obedience and loyalty. Also, given what Whitman intended to do, he had a good mind to suspect that Emilia, a stickler for rules, even ones she didn't agree with, would not comply. Edmund, on the other hand, might protest at first, and ask a bunch of annoying questions, but ultimately he would yield and do as he was told. And Whitman had an idea he was going to need help. For one thing, he didn't have any wearable clothing. And so after convincing Edmund that what he was about to do was the right thing, the only thing, and swearing him to secrecy, he sent him on a mission to procure clothing for an escape.

Forty minutes after receiving his orders, Edmund returned triumphant.

"Here, sir," he said, dropping stolen clothes at the foot of Whitman's bed, completing a simple physical task that exhausted all his mental capabilities. Custodians were able, when necessary, to stimulate corporeal acts, though only in the most crucial and urgent situations. And they better have a damn good reason for doing it, and they damn well better not get caught. That was grounds for dismissal and a sentence to Purgatory.

Edmund, against the odds, had succeeded.

"Put them on," he told his boss. "Hurry." He nervously looked over his shoulder at the door, as if he expected someone to burst through and foil their mastermind plan before they got the chance to execute it.

Whitman stared at the clothes. There was a pair of blue jeans that looked like they'd been rolled in mud, a long-sleeve t-shirt with the image of a monster truck crushing beneath its monster tires a row of small helpless looking cars, with the caption **That's How I Roll** overhead, and a pair of brown, crusty, leather boots that smelled of feet and sweat and dirt. All of these articles were at least three sizes too large for Whitman and had, here and there, smudges of blood on them.

"I'm not wearing these," he said. "They're dreadful."

"I'm sorry, sir," Edmund replied. "They're all I could find short notice."

"They've got blood and dirt on them."

"The young man they belonged to was in a motorcycle accident." Edmund's noble British features puckered. "He wasn't wearing a helmet His face looked like, well … like maybe it was on inside out." He cringed at the thought.

"They're huge," Whitman cried out.

"He was a big chap. And it wasn't like I had time to shop. I went to four rooms before I found these. The first one was this lady, and I didn't think you'd want to go on the lam in a cocktail dress and heels. The other three were all men, but two of them were very small, and the other one, well, he was about your size, sure, but no grown man should be caught wearing colors like that. Purple and green and yellow?"

"Colors? I don't care about colors."

"They were dreadful, sir. There were stripes. You would have looked a fool."

Whitman gawked at Edmund, then he nodded to the clothes at the foot of the bed. "And I won't look a fool walking around in clothes three sizes too big?" He pointed out a violent smear of now dried crimson. "Look at that?"

"Yes," agreed Edmund, "that is nasty."

"And you want me to wear them? Be serious."

"Well you can't go running around in nothing but a hospital gown, with your backside hanging out, free for all to see."

"So instead I should go around looking like a homeless

vagrant." Whitman paused, took a whiff of the shirt, and, after jerking his head away, added, "Smelling like one, too. Now please, can't you find me something more suitable. I'll wear the green and purple. I don't care. Anything but this."

"Do you have any idea how hard it was to get those to you," replied Edmund. "I'm not exactly good at the corporeal thing, Whit. There's a great deal of concentration involved, as you know, and now I've got a splitting headache."

Whitman, though not exactly appeased, conceded, figuring he should thank God for small miracles. He then stood, grabbed the clothes, and began to dress.

Edmund, British proper to his core, turned around to give him his privacy.

Whitman quickly slipped out of the flimsy hospital gown he'd been wearing the last two days, revealing his very real penis and testicle sack, a sight that still caught him by surprise. He had always had a penis and testicles, in some form or another, but it had been centuries since he'd seen them, or even thought about them. As a Custodian, a spirit entity, he had a body, his body, the body he'd had when he was last alive. But as a spirit, there were certain aspects about his body that no longer were animate in the human sense. His genitals were one of those things, as was his digestive system – he no longer had to or bothered to eat food, though he did willingly and at times excessively drink honey wine, a vice not looked upon kindly by his superiors – his immune system – he didn't get sick or fall victim to infection or injury – and his circulatory system. Also, his physical build remained exactly the same, always, his hair and fingernails didn't grow anymore, though his hair had changed color over the years, going from a pedestrian steel gray to a more distinguished white, and his teeth, which at the time of his death were false and made of birch wood, had actually regenerated and needed no brushing or maintenance.

They took away your immoral desires, too, along with the nagging guilt, the shame, and the irrational fears of the flesh. All of it was stripped away from you in Purgatory, layer by layer, along with the sins you carried there from life.

It wasn't a bad set up, all in all. The mind and soul were all that really mattered, and they were left not just intact, but pure and strong. The appearance of your body in the spirit world was a reminder of not only who you had been, but also that at some point you were one in the same with the people you were now trying to help. It was a constant reminder that you had been human once, too, and that you owed something to those who came before you and after you. It also permitted you to act and move around in the real world, on those rare occasions when it was necessary.

Whitman's eyes lingered on his new genitals for a time, long enough for his expression to change from one of interest to uncertainty to underlying disgust. He had been looking at them a lot since waking and remained ambivalent. There was a part of him – a base, revolting, horrible little part of him, the same part that had cropped up when Ally came to visit and caused *it* to stir with a simple touch of her hand – that liked the strong, virile feeling it engendered. The other part of him, the logical, reasonable, spiritual part of him, the part of him that was the man he'd been when alive and the celestial being he'd been the last two-hundred odd years, was wary and somewhat frightened by it, as if it held some sort of mythical and dangerous power.

"Sir? Are you listening to me?"

It was Edmund. He was standing by the door, alternating between peering out the little window and glancing expectantly at his boss.

"What is it?" replied Whitman as he pulled up his pants.

"I said hurry up. We have to be ready."

Whitman buttoned his new jeans. He could have fit a small dog, an umbrella, a dictionary, and a bowl of egg salad in the extra space he had.

"Look at this," he said, pulling on the waistband to exaggerate the poor fit.

"There's a belt," replied Edmund, ignoring the fact that his boss looked like a vagabond in clothes from a secondhand Big & Tall store. "Buckle them up."

"I haven't worn dungarees in ... well, over two-hundred years." Coincidentally, not since 'dungarees' was the popular, and only, nomenclature. He looped the belt around his waist, pulled it tight, fastened it. He looked ridiculous.

"I can't believe I'm doing this," he muttered to himself, but loud enough for Edmund to hear. He wriggled into the shirt, which, after it fell on his shoulders, hung on him like a cocktail dress. "Exactly how big was this guy?" he said.

Edmund shrugged. "Big. Fat, too. And that was what was left of him."

Whitman put the boots on. He had worn snowshoes before, a couple centuries ago, and that was the image that popped in his head. He laced them up nice and tight, but they still flopped around on his feet like oversized slippers.

"Dear God," he said, taking an experimental step. "I'll break my ankle if I have to run."

"We need to be ready to go," said Edmund, ignoring him. "As soon as the guard goes on break. We'll have to sneak past the nurses, then to the stairs. No elevators."

Edmund was also in charge of reconnaissance and mapping out the best possible escape route, which he had managed to accomplish quite easily. His ghostly constitution came in handy for such a chore; all he had to do was observe the comings and goings of certain hospital employees, and eavesdrop on their private conversations.

In only three hours, he believed he had the routines of the nurses and security personnel memorized and the perfect escape plan in place.

All that was left to do was ... Escape.

That was the part that had him concerned.

"Look," he said as Whitman tucked his shirt in his pants, completing an outfit that one might expect a perspective rodeo clown to wear on a job interview. "If you're sure about this, I'm with you. A hundred percent. But you're going rogue. Clay's not going to be happy. Not to mention the Elders. You know how they are."

All good points, Whitman had to admit, but not one of them changed his mind. "They're going to ship me off to the bin," he said. "That's where they put electrodes on your head and shoot electricity into your brain. And they make you take all kinds of pills. They're famous for their pills these days. I'm standing here and I'm fine, but no one's doing anything. Clay's not doing anything. Emilia's not doing anything. The Elders. None of them.

I'm a human being, Edmund. Look at me." He held out his arms, showing a sad picture of a lost, confused young man in clothing that didn't fit. "This is ridiculous. And no one's helping. No! I'm not going to let the doctors stick me in a bin. And I'm sure as hell not going to let the police arrest me and put me in jail. As for the Elders and the Angels, it seems as though they need a fire lit. Perhaps this will spur them to act.

Edmund nodded awkwardly. It was a good speech, and very similar to the one that Whitman had made to convince him to help. "Okay, sir," he said. "Right you are."

"I can still count on you, right Edmund?"

"Of course, sir," said the Brit. "I'm your man."

"Because I don't think I can do this without your help."

"You won't have to, sir."

Whitman gave his trusted underling a smile, and told him to keep watch.

Edmund promptly disappeared, then reappeared a few seconds later. "Be ready, sir," he said. "Any moment now."

Whitman took a seat on the nearest chair, and in the shadowy silence of the night he allowed doubt to creep into his mind. He was going on the run from the police and the hospital, not to mention his friends in the spirit world; he was going against the law and against orders, and he had swayed innocent Edmund to help him. It was probably a dumb idea, he conceded, especially since his plan shaded into a gray area after the part where he escaped. What then, he wondered, thinking of the old cliché about getting out of the frying pan only to land in the fire.

He thought about going home – Martin Loomis's home – or perhaps swinging by Ally's place, wherever she might live. He would need food and shelter, necessities he hadn't worried about in a long time, and his options and means were limited.

Loomis supposedly had a trusted friend, too, according to Edmund. A guy named Charlie Bates. Perhaps he could help.

Whitman stood, and heard something crinkle in his pocket. He patted the pocket, and then slowly reached an experimental hand inside. His fingers felt ... paper, and when he pulled it out, he was shocked to see money.

"Edmund?" he said. "What's this?"

Edmund turned and looked at the money in his boss's hand.

"Oh. Right," he said, a tinge of guilt in his tone. "I forgot about that."

"You knew about it?" Whitman said to him critically.

"Well, sir ... Yes."

"You stole the man's money?"

Edmund nodded. "I thought it might come in handy, sir."

Whitman was aghast. He began to finger through the bills, counting them out.

"It's only fifty dollars or so," Edmund said as means of justification.

"Fifty-seven," Whitman corrected him.

"Okay. Fifty-seven dollars. That's really not that much when you think about it. Trust me, the guy's not going to miss it. He has more pressing concerns."

"But still. You stole. That's against the commandments. Thou shall not steal. Number six. A big one. What kind of example is that?"

"I stole his clothes, too, sir," replied Edmund. "On your orders."

Whitman's mouth opened, but no words came out.

"These are desperate times, sir," Edmund went on. "You're about to go on the run from the police looking like a migrant farm worker and you're worried about fifty-seven dollars? You might need it, sir. You'll definitely need it more than the guy I took it from. He'll be lucky if he can still count to fifty-seven."

"That's not the point. Clothes are one thing, money's something else. You shouldn't have done that."

Edmund looked crestfallen. "We'll get it back to him when we can," he said. "Until then, we have an escape to make."

Whitman had more words for his friend and partner in crime, but he decided that now probably wasn't the best time to voice them. Anyway, Edmund didn't give him a chance; the novice Custodian picked that moment, whether purposefully or not, to vanish from sight. It was an ability that Custodians used hundreds of times a day and thus never gave it a second thought; Whitman, now human and unable to evanesce, found the habit terribly annoying.

When Edmund returned about a minute later, appearing out of thin air like a warm breath on a cold night, he had news. "The guard just left for his break," he reported. "And the nurse went to the break room for coffee. We have to go. Now. We may have ten minutes to make this work."

Whitman nodded. On the young, pale-cheeked face of Martin Loomis rested a look of grim determination. He was desperate and dubious, and about to do something stupid with an altogether daft knucklehead who tended to screw up even the simplest of plans. It was a foolproof recipe for disaster.

But if he stayed at the hospital he'd be forced to spar with the cops, and the doctors, and that slightly odd fellow obsessed with ink splotches. And when they were through with him, chances were they'd strap him down and ship him to the bin, where madness was measured in little plastic cups.

He wanted to go home, back to that obscure in-between world where he had dwelled for the last two hundred and thirty years. He couldn't claim that things made perfect sense there, but he understood how they worked. He knew the patterns, the people, the vagaries. He knew where the margins were and how to work within them. And, most importantly, he knew himself there. Here, he knew nothing, he knew no one, and, despite having observed so much, he hadn't a clue how things really worked. It was an utterly irrational place ruled by feelings, emotions, and crass bodily functions.

Whitman was a man of reason; he was rooted in it like a mighty sequoia. He prided himself on his powers of logic and common sense, on his ability to view, assess, understand, and deal with any situation.

Or at least that's what he thought.

This current circumstance had him as flummoxed as a deaf person at a Kenny G concert. It reminded him of the first time he had ever seen a mosh pit; thinking a riot had broken out, he frantically intervened by pulling the fire alarm, which, to his surprise, had very little effect at all. He'd taken a hell of a reprimand for that decision. The bosses didn't like it when you altered the natural order. They referred to it as the Lion's Den for a reason.

"Sir! If you want to do this, we have to go. Now!" Edmund looked harried and slightly ill, and he was anxiously gesturing for Whitman to act.

'Want' has nothing to do with it, thought Whitman, and then he smiled at the irony. It was all about 'want' when you got down to it. That's what made life so damn frustrating.

"All right!" he said, and hitched up his jeans. "I'm coming." He made it exactly three steps, almost to the door, before he stumbled and fell the first time.

Whitman fell a third time getting off the elevator on the first floor, in front of an old, bleary-eyed janitor pushing around a mop and bucket. The second time he'd fallen was walking down the stairs, which they had used because, unlike the elevators, they didn't have to pass the nurses' station to get to them; he turned an ankle and toppled over like a blow pop, crashing down on the landing and banging his head.

After that fiasco, they decided that the elevators were probably a safer bet, especially down on the fourth floor, which was a non-secure wing.

"Whoa, whoa, whoa," said the janitor as Whitman cursed and Edmund gasped. "You okay there, son? You're gonna damage yourself."

"Just learning how to walk in these damned things," replied an embarrassed Whitman as he straightened himself up. "They're ... tricky."

"No wonder. Look at the size of them," the janitor marveled. "Why'd you go and buy boots so big?"

"Um ... I thought I'd grow into them."

"Good recovery, sir," said Edmund, always ready to supply a little positive reinforcement. The janitor, meanwhile, gave Whitman the sort of sideways look that one usually reserves for the really stupid or really drunk.

"They're comfortable, too," Whitman added after noticing the janitor's skepticism. "Lots of room for my ... toes ... to wiggle."

"Remember, sir, take one step in front of the other, like the song," said Edmund. He was playing the role of scout, leading the way, telling his grumbling, stumbling boss where to turn and when the coast was clear. "Slow and steady wins the race."

"I know that," replied Whitman peevishly. "Don't condescend

me."

"Condescend you?" said the janitor, confusion deepening the wrinkles on his face. "Who the hell's condescending you? You knock your head or something?"

Whitman realized quickly that there was no clever or even reasonable response to that question, so instead he said, "Sorry. I have to go. To work. I'm a very busy man."

"Aren't we all."

Had the janitor cared, even a little, he might have radioed security and told them about the strange young man in clothes three sizes too big for him stumbling down the hallway, cursing and mumbling to himself about going to work and needing wiggle room for his toes. But as it stood, the janitor, a bald, black man known as Curly to his friends, didn't give a rat's ass about Whitman, just like he didn't give a rat's ass about anything other than what he had to do. And so he ignored the muttering vagabond, sloshed the mop in the bucket, and got back to work, thinking only of the break he had coming in ten minutes, a break he was planning to share with a hot cup of coffee and a cigarette.

"I'd say we're just about home free, sir," Edmund reported as he peered around the corner. There were a few people scattered about in the lobby, and there was a guard at the reception desk, but no one seemed to be paying much attention.

It was nearly four in the morning, and the scene outside the giant bay windows was one of bitter darkness, broken only by the hollow glow of fluorescent lights shining down from the drive-thru canopy.

"Follow my lead, sir," said Edmund confidently.

"Hold on a second," replied Whitman, a sudden strike of trepidation keeping him in place. They were approaching the point of no return and second thoughts had begun to creep up on him. "Are we going out the main doors?"

Edmund fixed his boss with a bewildered look. "Of course, sir. Where else?"

"Shouldn't we wait for the security guard to go on rounds?"

"That one stays out front most of the night. Doesn't seem to move very much, as I'm sure you can tell by his considerable girth. The chips and cookies don't help, I'm sure. You'd think a man that works in a hospital would take better care of himself."

Whitman sighed. "Yes. Whatever," he said. "But perhaps there's a side door. A less visible exit to use." He was stalling, and he knew he was stalling. They had made it this far with relative ease, with only his difficulty walking in boots three sizes too big slowing them down. They had avoided all the nurses and security personnel, and now were only forty feet from freedom ... if you could call being alone in a world that had passed him by more than two-hundred years ago freedom.

It had to beat the bin, Whitman believed. Or jail.

"I suppose I could have a quick look," said Edmund. "But from what I've seen most of the side doors have alarms."

Whitman accepted that answer with a nod, and tried to ease his nerves. "So, what's the plan?" he said. "Just stroll right by?"

"Yes, sir," replied Edmund. "Confidence is the key, sir." Spoken, suspiciously, by someone who had none. "You have to make it seem as if you're supposed to be leaving. Remember, you're not escaping, just leaving."

"What if he stops me and asks me a question?"

Edmund's ghostly face scrunched up, and he scratched a hand in his hair. "Well," he said, uncertainty ringing in his rich British tone, "once more I say that confidence is the key. No matter what you say, say it with confidence. And don't worry, I'll be right there with you the whole time. I'm very good when it comes to on-the-spot thinking."

That wasn't so much a lie as it was an enormous personal misapprehension. Whitman let it slide, though. Time was ticking, and he was much too nervous to answer back with sarcasm or wit; besides, sarcasm and wit, much like any kind of thinking, on-the-spot or otherwise, tended to soar far over Edmund's head.

Instead, Whitman said, "How about we try a diversion. Do you think you can make something real happen? Something to draw the attention of the guard?"

Edmund opened his mouth to answer, but before he could get one word out someone from behind them said, "Boy, I'm not entirely sure what the hell's wrong with you, but you're starting to make me nervous."

It was the janitor; he was back, his mop and bucket no longer with him. He wore a look of genuine unease, like he was thinking that perhaps the strange young man in the frumpy clothes was in need of professional help. After all, the boy was sneaking around like a cartoon cat burglar, talking to himself, or an imaginary friend, about diversions and making something real happen. The boy might not be dangerous, thought Curly the janitor – he certainly didn't look dangerous, with his moppish hair and ridiculous clothes – but it was rather clear he was a good distance from normal's front door. The stupid, fearful look on his face alone was cause enough for concern.

Edmund said, "Quick, say something clever, sir."

To which Whitman replied, "What do you want me to say?"

To which Curly said, "I don't give a good whoop what you say. I'm guessing whatever it is won't make a hell of a lot of sense."

"Give him money," Edmund prompted his boss, showing off his impressive on-the-spot thinking skills. "A bribe. That's how they do it here."

With a look of utter befuddlement, Whitman reached in his pocket and pulled out cash. "Would you like ten dollars?" he said, hesitantly proffering two five dollar bills. As far as bribes went, it wasn't the smoothest.

Curly looked at the money, then at Whitman. "There's something wrong with you, ain't there?" he said to him. "You got brain damage?"

"No. I just really need to get out of here," Whitman replied, taking a stab at honesty. "They want to send me to the bin," he added. "I fear I won't do well there."

"Actually, that might not be a bad idea," said Curly. "Maybe they can help you."

"This isn't going well," Edmund cut in. "Sir, I think we need to get out of here. Now."

Whitman looked at Edmund, whom Curly couldn't see. Then he looked at Curly.

"Listen," said the janitor, making use of a kind, sympathetic tone, "I'm not sure who you are or what you're doing, but it's obvious that you're up to *something,* and in my experience that usually means no good."

"Sir, I think we should run," suggested Edmund, his voice

strung a bit tight now. He wasn't used to such fretful moments, and the last thing he wanted to do was go back to Emilia and Clay and tell them that Whitman had gotten pinched trying to escape the hospital, which went against direct orders from the Elders. There'd undoubtedly be questions, and accusations, and a disciplinary review, all of which scared the holy bajeesus out of Edmund.

"Please," Whitman said to Curly, his desperation rising, "I need to get out of here. I'm not crazy. Really. I'm fine." He stabbed the money at him, two wrinkled five dollar bills. "There's ten bucks in it if you help me?"

But it was too late. Sometime during their conversation, Whitman had unknowingly stepped out from around the corner, just enough to make himself visible to the security guard, who now was on his way over, the many keys on his belt jangling with every step he took, marking his prodigious stride. When he was close enough, he said in a voice that echoed, "Curly, there a problem here?"

"Bugger!" cried Edmund, just now noticing the security guard, now that he was right up on them. "They have us surrounded, sir."

"Excuse me," Whitman croaked, looking around frantically.

"I think this young man is lost," said Curly.

The security guard, Ernesto, looked at Whitman and said, "You a patient here, son?"

Edmund cried out, "Deny! Tell them nothing! Tell them you're a doctor. Undercover."

"An undercover doctor?" said Whitman, forgetting himself and his current circumstance. He could hardly help it; the pure absurdity of the idea provoked repeating.

"You're an *undercover doctor*?" replied Ernesto, his face lined with suspicion.

Whitman was flummoxed, and Edmund was no help. Undercover doctor? There was no way that he could conceive to justify an illogical statement like that. So instead he just stood there with a stupid look on his face and went, "Uhhh ... "

"Wait. I know you," Ernesto said, shaking a finger at him. "I saw your photo on the news. You're that guy. John Doe. The guy that got shot in that robbery the other night."

Realization dawned suddenly on Curly. "You that guy?" he said to Whitman.

The former celestial spirit now corporeal being saw an opening. "Yeah, yeah, that's me," he said. "I'm that guy. And I need to get out of here."

But the opening that Whitman thought he saw closed quickly, with a thud. Ernesto said, "I thought they had you on lockdown up on the fifth floor," and like that Whitman felt all the air go out of him.

Again he went, "Uhhh ... "

Edmund, however, had a plan. "Run!" he cried out, and his invisible spirit form dashed off in a mad sprint to the front door.

Whitman had never believed that following Edmund was a good idea, and he had years of anecdotal evidence, not to mention hard facts and statistics, to back that up. But, he quickly reasoned, when caught in the grip of sheer lunacy, perhaps the most sane and logical path was to trust the lunatic.

And so against all logic he ran.

He threw the two five dollar bills in the air as a distraction and ran like a panicky debutante escaping a bloodthirsty maniac in a bad horror movie: head and shoulders back, arms flailing as if they were attached by rubber bands, knees lifting up comically high and straight. The huge boots he was wearing hammered down on the linoleum floor like planks of wood, causing him to stumble and lurch like a 3am drunkard. A man on stilts looked to be a safer bet for balance, but somehow Whitman kept his feet and covered the lobby with surprising speed.

"Hey! Stop!" Ernesto cried out, and started after him. He was a big man, badly out of shape and not used to running. He was someone who considered walking through the cafeteria line high-energy exercise, and by the time Whitman reached the front door, Ernesto was trailing far behind and laboring for breath.

Curly, meanwhile, gave chase in a slow trot, not really looking to catch the young man who'd run off, only hoping to see which direction he went so if the police should happen to question him later he could tell them something helpful. Truthfully, he didn't want to overwork his lungs so close to his smoke break.

Ernesto, the gradual impetus of his corpulent physique propelling him, much in the same way a freight train slowly gains momentum and makes its way, pushed through the front doors and staggered out into the night. He saw the young man running towards the wooded area behind the parking garage and quickly concluded that there was no possible way he could catch him ... unless the young man should suddenly keel over or trip and break his leg. He unclipped his walkie-talkie and, fighting through the kind of deep gasping breaths that often presage a heart attack, put out a call. "Got ... a runner. John ... Doe. Wearing ... " He stopped, unable to go on, his lungs burning, his face the color of raw salmon.

Curly had just made it outside, and he took the walkie-talkie from his coworker and picked up the communication: "John Doe, the guy who was involved in that shooting the other night, he's escaped. He ran off into the woods. Call the fuzz."

There were four security guards that worked the late shift at Hagerstown General and not one of them was young enough or spry enough to give chase. Instead, they phoned the police. Then they stood around drinking coffee, smoking cigarettes, debating why this had happened, and talking, in length, about how they didn't get paid enough to go chasing after crazy people. Whitman, meanwhile, didn't stop running until he fell a fourth time, about a hundred yards into the woods, where the brush was thick and heavy and dark. His clown boots caught a hole, his ankle twisted, and he collapsed in a heap.

"Son-of-a-bitch!" he cried out as pain, a sensation he'd yet to get comfortable with, attacked his lower leg.

"Edmund!" he shouted, his winded voice echoing weakly amid the silence of the trees and bushes.

"Yes, sir," said Edmund, dutifully appearing at his side.

"Where the hell are we?"

Edmund glanced around. "In the woods, sir," he said.

Whitman glared at him. He was still huffing and puffing, trying to catch his breath. It felt as if someone had set his lungs on fire. Yet another sensation he wasn't used to. Being human, he realized, quite demonstrably, was a pain in the ...

"Where do we go from here?" he managed.

Once again, Edmund looked around. "Um ... West," he said, vaguely. Currently he was facing north.

Something shot out from behind a fallen tree, kicking up leaves and twigs, and Whitman jumped back and frantically looked around, searching the implacable darkness for whatever dangers might be out there. "What was that?" he said, eyes darting.

"Most likely a squirrel or rabbit, sir. Possibly a bear."

"A bear?" Whitman's voice carried into the woods and died in the eerie silence. A bear could eviscerate him in his current state.

"Probably a squirrel," Edmund reiterated. "Nothing to fret. They're harmless creatures, mostly. Except for the rabies."

Whitman stood perfectly still. "What was I thinking?" he said, chastising himself.

Edmund looked at his boss and shrugged. "Hard to say. When exactly, sir?"

Whitman knew he couldn't physically strike Edmund, but the desire to do so rose up inside him like a wild hunger. He was not a violent man by nature, but Edmund could tangle and strain the nerves of even the most pious Buddhist monk, and Whitman found that patience was a virtue he no longer held in large supply.

"Just get me out of here," he growled. "Now."

"Right away, sir. Follow me."

And on they went, deeper into the wood.

# Chapter Nine

It had to end. Now. It had to because that bullet had been meant for her and to keep going on like nothing had happened was tantamount to slapping fate in the face. No one had seen the man who'd jumped in front of that bullet like a deranged, overzealous secret service agent: not her, not Eddie the cashier, and not the assailant, who had seemed more surprised than any of them. Whoever he was, he had seemingly come out of thin air to save her life, and, ostensibly, the life of her child. At the very least she owed it to him – and to herself – to try and live a better life, to be a better person, to start respecting herself and the choices she made. She didn't know if what had happened was a sign that she was supposed to keep the baby or not; sometimes she thought it was, other times not. Presently, with everything in disarray, she still believed the best thing to do was to have an abortion. Either way she believed that what had happened had happened for a reason. It was a sign that she needed to make changes, because, as she'd been blatantly reminded a couple nights ago, life had a way of making them for you, whether you liked it or not.

Ally was no longer satisfied with a passive role in her own existence. Life may throw her a curveball every-so-often, but there was no excuse not to be ready for the fastballs. That in mind, she was busy at work, taking care of business and researching some options, taking the first steps in rearranging her desultory life.

It had taken hours on the phone over the last few days, but all her credit card accounts, which had to be canceled and then reinstated under new numbers, were up and running again. New cards had been reissued, with the first two coming in the mail yesterday. Her banking information also needed changed, for her protection, though in neither case had any unauthorized activity taken place. And two days ago, before work, she'd gone down to the DMV and got a new driver's license.

Now, after all that, she was busy researching schools,

planning for a better future. She had decided something she had decided many times before, only this time her decision was weighted with determination. She'd get her degree, find a job that was worth going to everyday, a job that made a difference, that wouldn't make her cringe in shame when someone she hadn't seen in a while asked her what she was doing these days and where she was working.

She had gone to nursing school after graduating high school and had liked it; and just the other day she'd read an article in the paper about the growing field of Radiation Technology. With her base of credits from nursing school, she figured she could earn a degree in a little over a year. And from what the article had said, graduates in the field had no trouble finding employment. It was a smart, practical move, and just the kind of decision she needed to start making.

Fortunately she hadn't been totally profligate in her life. She made a lot of money at the club and had managed to sock away nearly nine thousand dollars' worth. The next round of classes didn't start until mid-September, which gave her another three and a half months to save. If she cut out drugs and wasteful spending, she figured she could bank another three grand by the time classes started. That would give her about twelve grand in all, which, she believed, would be more than enough to live on for a year or so. That was *if* she could stomach working at the club without taking part in all the extracurricular activities that were so prominent there. Not to mention seeing Vaughn, who was a regular. It wouldn't be easy, she knew, but it was something she felt she had to do. And it would only be for three more months.

She went to the kitchen to refill her coffee, and then returned to her computer. She sat, one leg crooked under the other, and lit a cigarette. She scrolled from the page on Hagerstown Medical and Technical College to one listing information on student loans; she didn't think she'd need one, but she wanted to check the rates and see what kind of deal she could get. No use spending all her money up front if she didn't have to.

Two more clicks and she came to a page that detailed basic loan rates per amount borrowed; there also was an online application form that she could fill out and send in, free of charge. Then she found a link to a page that had information on certain education grants that would allow her to go back to school for free. Talk about ideal, thought Ally. Of course, she doubted whether she'd be eligible for such a program; she never seemed to be eligible for the best deals. That page came with an application, too, and she stamped out what was left of her cigarette and got to work filling it out. The deadline for the grant expired in two weeks and she didn't want to miss it.

She made it through her name and address before she was interrupted by a resounding knock at her door. It was still morning, and she wasn't expecting any visitors. That's when it hit her: it was Vaughn. He had said that he was going to stop by and check on her, see if she was okay. She had told him to call first, but he never listened to her.

She got up, walked to the door, unlatched the deadbolt, and swung it open without consideration, expecting to see her ex there. She was greeted not by Vaughn, but by Detectives Milner and Rainer, the two men heading the investigation into the shooting at the A&P Mart. Suddenly Ally felt terribly underdressed. She was in her bedclothes, which were nothing more than a tiny pair of panties barely covered by a flimsy t-shirt. Not that she wasn't used to skimpy outfits, but in her own home, in front of strangers? She closed the door a little and hid herself behind it.

"Good morning, Miss Armenti," said Detective Milner. "We were wondering if we could have a word with you."

Ally went, "Uhhh ... "

When it seemed as though she didn't recognize them, Milner said, "We're the detectives handling the shooting case. Remember?"

"Of course," Ally said, nodding. "I remember. I'm just ... I wasn't expecting you is all. Is there a problem?"

"That's what we wanted to talk to you about. May we come in?"

Ally was a young woman who'd spent most of the last year living well outside the law, thus she had developed a certain level of distrust for cops. She believed most of them to be corrupt, arrogant, pompous slugs who happily took advantage of the power of the badge, and she had seen more than her share of examples of that at the club. There was no drunk worse than a drunk cop, the girls liked to say, and Ally had to agree. She had learned to regard them with a mixture of suspicion, resentment, and fear.

Mostly she tried to avoid them at all cost.

But that was the old her, that sweet yet capricious girl who'd taken a walk on the wild side and got lost over there for a while. Besides, these guys weren't here to investigate her, to badger her and give her a hard time; they were trying to apprehend the man who had robbed the store and shot John Doe.

They were, in this case, allies.

Of course there was that whole thing about them sequestering John Doe and not allowing him any visitors or phone calls, which Ally found to be suspicious. But perhaps she could get some answers about that from them.

"Okay. Sure," she said, and stepped back, opening her home to them. "Just let me throw some clothes on first."

Both Milner and Rainer were of the opinion that Ally looked just fine the way she was, with her bare legs and bare feet and mussed hair, and they watched her, a salacious glint lighting their eyes, as she walked away, watched her bare legs scissor in and out, watched her hips snap back and forth rhythmically, hypnotically, just above the hem of her skimpy little t-shirt. They both wondered if she was naked under that shirt, and they both imagined that she was.

"You can have a seat," she called back to them. "I'll only be a minute." Ally then ducked into her room, glad to be rid of their leering eyes, which she'd felt lock onto her soon after she let them in.

She pulled on the first pair of jeans she found, changed her shirt to one that fit a little better, and went back out. The older detective, Milner, was standing in the kitchen, looking around, while the younger one, Rainer, was leaning over her computer, checking out what was on the screen. Typical cops, thought Ally, nosing around, making anything they can their business.

"That's better," she said pleasantly, subtly interrupting their not-so-subtle inspection. She had learned long ago that it wasn't wise to challenge cops, not if you didn't have to. "So, what can I help you with?"

Rainer sidled away from the computer, somewhat guiltily, while Milner left the kitchen area. He waited to see where Ally sat (first she retrieved her coffee from the desk, then she primly took a seat on the couch) before throwing his shoulders back and taking a stand. Though he was hardly an imposing figure, he made sure his full bulk was square in her sightline. Then he began.

"John Doe," he said, his voice deep but smooth. It was all he said at first, and Ally's brow bunched with confusion as she waited for more. Then, inquisitively, he said, "Have you spoken to him recently?"

Ally nodded. "Yeah. The other day. I went to visit him. We talked for about ... I don't know, ten, fifteen minutes."

"You were there yesterday, too."

Again, Ally nodded. "Yeah. They wouldn't let me see him, though. I was wondering about that. Is he in some sort of trouble?"

"Maybe," said Rainer. "When was the last time you saw him?"

"The other day," Ally replied. "I just told you that."

"You work at Teasers, right?" said Milner, cutting back in. They were coming at her in waves. "For Albert Holt."

"Yeah. So?"

"Rumor is you're Vaughn Middling's girl."

"*Was* his girl," Ally corrected him. "Not anymore."

"Okay. Was. Not that that makes much of a difference."

"This is relevant why?"

"Because we know what kind of things Holt and Vaughn are into."

"Yeah. I know, too," said Ally, matching Detective Milner's stare, not shying away from him in the least. "I probably know more than you."

"I wouldn't doubt that."

"Not exactly something to brag about," added Rainer.

"Not at all," said Ally. "Which is why Vaughn's an ex."

"But you still work at the club."

"That's right. The money's good."

"So I've been told."

Ally caught Rainer's implication, his little smirk, too, and she returned him an unpleasant look. "I don't see why my employment is an issue here," she said to him. "I'm a bartender. I don't do anything illegal."

"Run in certain circles," replied Milner.

"*Used* to run. And what's that have to do with John Doe?"

Milner and Rainer exchanged a look, and though they hadn't been partners for very long, they'd developed a tacit understanding of one another. Great minds think alike, they say. That's also true for mediocre ones, like those that gravitate to law enforcement.

Milner said, "Ever hear of Martin Loomis?"

"Martin Loomis?" Ally turned the name over a couple times, thinking. She then shook her head. "No. Why?"

"Well, we posted John Doe's picture on the news last night, and in the newspaper, too. We got a solid hit."

"So that's his name? Martin Loomis?"

"That's the information we got. After this, we're going to meet the guy who gave us the tip, see if we can confirm it."

"So he still doesn't remember?"

"Who?" Rainer asked.

"John Doe? Or Martin Loomis? Didn't you ask him if that's his name?"

Milner said, "We wanted to, only he escaped last night."

"Ran off in the middle of the night," added Rainer. "We have an APB out on him, got surveillance on his apartment, but as yet we haven't had any luck. We thought maybe he might try to contact you."

Ally's confusion moved to surprise. "Me? Why me?"

"Because he seems to show up wherever you are. When we first talked to you, you mentioned that he was at the club a couple nights before the shooting. Then he just *happened* to be at the A&P Mart, at 3am, when the place was robbed. Pretty big coincidence, don'tcha think?"

"You think he's stalking me?"

Rainer shrugged, his muscular shoulders rising and falling impressively. "Maybe. You remember anything else about him?"

Ally tried to think, but her thoughts broke apart before she could form them into questions. The idea that John Doe might be a stalker and her life might be in danger had her stunned. "He was so nice," she said. "He saved my life."

"Sometimes those are the ones you have to watch out for," said Milner. "Didn't your mother ever teach you that."

Ally gave no reply. She just sat there, blank-faced and worried, trying to wrap her head around this unexpected turn of events. She was pretty good at reading people, always had been, and she had thought that Marty – if that was his name – was a sweet, quiet, harmless young man, about as dangerous as a butter knife. Picturing him as a stalker or violent criminal seemed incongruous.

"This could just be a coincident," said Rainer, though he said it in a way that hinted he didn't believe that at all. He had a hunch that John Doe might come here, so he wanted to put doubt in Ally's head, make it so her first instinct was to call the police. Then he could get his collar. "But in my experience, coincidences usually turn out to be evidence against."

Ally nodded absently. "You think he's dangerous?"

The two detectives exchanged another look. It was Milner who said, "Given the company you keep, yeah, it's a possibility."

"I told you already, I don't have anything to do with that," said Ally, stressing her words. "I'm a bartender. The money's good. Whatever Holt and Vaughn do, that's their business. It has nothing to do with me."

"Nevertheless, you're a part of their circle, and that circle sometimes includes disreputable and dangerous individuals."

"Now, are you sure you haven't seen or talked to him since the other day?" said Rainer. "We won't be mad if you lied. We understand."

"No!" Ally insisted. "I swear. I saw him the other day, and then yesterday they wouldn't let me in. They told me he'd been sequestered."

"And before that?"

"Before what?"

"Before the hospital?"

"I told you, I remember seeing him at the club last weekend. Saturday night, I think. He came in, had a beer, and left. He might've been there half an hour. He was sad, I remember that. He was talking about his ex-fiancée. That was the first time I ever met him. What about the amnesia?"

Milner shrugged. "Most likely an act."

Ally let out a wisp of air. She was trying to process everything, though she imagined that she probably would have had better luck trying to predict the flight of a bumblebee.

"Look," said Rainer, "don't worry about it, okay? We'll get to the bottom of it. We just wanted to talk to you, see if you knew anything, see if you were okay. And we wanted to tell you to keep a look out. Do you live alone?"

"Yes."

"Keep your doors locked, just in case."

Ally shook her head in disbelief. She couldn't imagine that she might be in danger; John Doe, Martin Loomis, whoever he was, had saved her life. Why would he do that if he wanted to hurt her? She asked the detectives that very question.

Milner shrugged. "Can't say. It's probably nothing. But we wanted to talk to you, let you know what was going on."

A faraway look glazed Ally's dark eyes, while hundreds of thought-fragments buzzed around in her brain. "Right. Thank you," she said.

Milner pulled a card from his pocket. "Here," he said, handing it to her. "If you think of anything, call us. If he comes here, definitely call us."

Ally took the card without looking at it. She took the one Rainer proffered as well. She already had one of each from the night of the shooting, but she didn't think to tell them that. "Thank you," she said again. Then she said, "I don't think he knows where I live."

Rainer said, "You never know. Better safe than sorry."

Thirty seconds later the two detectives were gone and Ally was alone, which now was as much a feeling as it was a state. She locked the door behind them, latched the deadbolt, and curled up on the couch with a fresh cup of coffee and a cigarette.

Again the question 'Who is John Doe?' jumped in her head, but this time her musings went off in a different direction, quite opposite of the White Knight fantasies she'd been indulging the last couple days. Was he a criminal? A rapist? Had he been stalking her?

It certainly was possible.

But there was something about him that wouldn't let negative thoughts take hold, something sweet and innocent and real, something she had never sensed before in another person, something that told her, unequivocally, that John Doe, or Martin Loomis, was not a dangerous man. He had saved her life, selflessly taking a bullet for her; a rapist or stalker wouldn't have done that.

Then again, she thought, when it came to men she didn't exactly have the best track record. That in mind, she decided it might be best to heed the detectives' advice and error on the side of caution.

For the first time since their split, Ally missed having Vaughn in her life.

Emilia saw Alina out of the corner of her eye, winked at her, and in a flash the two of them were huddled together beneath an underpass on one of the many back roads that crisscrossed through and around Hagerstown. A moment later Jeanie arrived. She was a middle-aged woman with pale white skin and an angry bush of brown hair that curled and dangled in wayward patterns. She had goggle eyes and yellow teeth, and her nose was too small for her face. Despite that rather odd combination of features, the entirety of her was quite pretty, and back when she was younger, and alive, she had all the boys chasing her. Alina, meanwhile, still looked young and sassy, having died at the ripe age of twenty-three. She had been a spunky, small town Minnesota girl that bore a striking resemblance to Susan Dey circa the Partridge Family years until a blood vessel popped in her brain, killing her in less than two minutes. The three of them were meeting away from the watchful and all too suspicious eyes of Clay because they had just become aware of Whitman going on the lam with Edmund's help and they were worried about them. If Clay found out, he undoubtedly would go directly to the Elders and rat them out, which, essentially, was the proper thing to do. But nothing about this made sense, and the three of them were off the opinion that even if he was wrong, they believed in Whitman more than Clay.

"Anything?" Emilia inquired.

"No," said Alina. "I staked out Ally's place, thinking he might go there. She visited him the other day, and there was something about her mood afterwards."

"What do you mean?"

"She was ... *different.*"

"Different how?"

"I think she might like him."

Emilia's brow arched with surprise. "Really? You mean ... *like* him?"

"I don't know. Can't say for sure. She's pregnant, so her hormones are in a rage. And she just broke up with her boyfriend, and saw someone get shot right in front of her. Plus, she's not exactly the most focused girl. Great heart, smart as a whip, but she hasn't found her way yet. She's ... *scattered.*"

"What about you, Jeanie?" Emilia asked.

Jeanie shook her head, and her crazy hair jostled about. "Nothing. Went to Loomis's apartment, but he hasn't been there. No one's been there, actually, and the place is starting to take on an odor."

Emilia's nose crinkled. "I forgot about that," she said. "Loomis's suicide."

"The police are in for confounding discovery, to say the least."

"Why's that?"

"Because there's blood everywhere, and a gun, and a suicide note, and a pungent stench."

Emilia wasn't following. "Yeah?"

"But no *body!*" Jeanie clarified.

"Oh. Right. Because Whitman has the body."

"Yes. However that happened."

Emilia sighed. "That will be confounding."

Alina couldn't help but snicker. "Priceless," she said. "Hope I'm around to watch them try to figure that one out."

"Hopefully that won't be necessary," said Jeanie. "Hopefully Whitman will be back before the police get a warrant."

"I wouldn't count on it."

"That's why we have to find him," said Emilia. "We have to find him and tell him to turn himself in. It's the only way. Now, we need to keep tabs on Charlie Bates, Ally, and Loomis's apartment. And if someone can find Edmund that would be great."

"Still no word from the bumbling Brit?" Alina asked.

"He's in the wind. Just like Whitman."

"That damn Edmund!" said Jeanie, "I can't believe he went rogue."

"Don't blame him," said Emilia. "If I know Whit, he manipulated poor Edmund into helping him."

"Nonetheless. He could at least check in with us, tell us what's going on. They can't hide forever."

"They'll show up eventually," said Alina. "Someone will see them."

Emilia sighed. "Poor Whit," she said. "Alone out there, feeling forsaken, probably don't know who to trust or which way to turn."

"Poor Whit," said Alina. "He's got Edmund as a helper."

Emilia didn't want to laugh, but Alina's deadpan delivery drew a chuckle from her. Even Jeanie, a noted straight arrow, cracked a smile. "That's not nice," Emilia said. "It's funny, and accurate, but not nice."

"I just don't know what he was thinking," Jeanie mused. "Why would he run, especially after the Elders told him not to? And why would he go out into the world? What can he hope to accomplish?"

"Maybe he's thinking that if he disobeys orders the Elders will have no choice but to snap him up," Emilia posited.

"Maybe. But he has no money and no place to go, and he's in a body that's recently suffered significant trauma. Now's not the time to be running around, thumbing his nose at the establishment."

"Never a *good* time for that," said Emilia. "Just have to do it when the mood strikes. Besides, I wouldn't want to go to an asylum either. You ever been to one of those places? You could go mad."

"What if the cops find him first?" Jeanie contemplated. "He could end up in jail. Or what if, God forbid, he dies? What happens then? What if he's mistaken for Loomis and ends up in Purgatory? Or worse, Hell?"

"I'm sure that won't be the case," said Emilia, though the thought of potential consequences gave her pause. If the job had taught her one thing it was that life offered an endless supply of surprises, and just when you thought you'd seen it all, well, something new appeared before your eyes and threw you. There was no telling what might happen to Whitman in the real world, the world of the flesh, and some of the possibilities were downright frightening. "The main thing for now," she went on, "is that we don't let Clay know. Not until we know more."

"You want to lie to him?" said Jeanie skeptically. "We're not supposed to lie, Em. It's one of the commandments."

"No. I'm not saying we lie. We just don't *volunteer* the truth. There's a difference."

"What if Clay finds out on his own and asks us about it?"

"Play dumb," piped Alina, who had no issues with rebellious behavior. "Tell him you're too damn busy doing your job to worry about Whitman."

Jeanie's oddly-shaped face puckered. "Must you curse?"

Alina put on an expression of innocence. "What?" she said. "'Damn'? That's not cursing. Beavers build them."

Jeanie huffed, though she said nothing more of it. She liked Alina, but they had their differences, and she believed they always would. Instead, she said, "Sounds like lying to me. And I'm not lying."

"Then don't think of it as lying," said Emilia. She was angling, looking to justify what she wanted her good friend to do, which was, in fact, to lie. "Think of it as *protecting* Whitman. Protecting all of us, for that matter."

"And how's that?"

"You know Clay; he's a hardliner. He finds out, he'll go straight to the Elders, and there's no telling what they might do. Whit's already got a couple strikes against him. They could leave him down there for good."

"And we'd be stuck with Clay as a boss," said Alina, her voice hitting a sour note. "Don't know who'd be getting worse in that deal."

"You hush your mouth," said Jeanie. "I know Clay can be a bit overbearing at times, but he's one of us. He's been through the thick and thin of it."

"I actually like Clay," said Alina. "I just don't want him for a boss."

"Let's not even think about that," said Emilia. "I just want to protect Whit. Edmund, too. Don't forget about him. He'd be in just as much trouble. More. And Lord only knows how that boy survived Purgatory the first go around."

"And if *we* get caught lying for them?" Jeanie submitted.

That was a question Emilia didn't care to think about. She sighed, heavily, and with very little conviction said, "We won't. Okay?" Then she said, "Besides, we don't even know where they're at right now."

"That's right," agreed Alina. "We don't know where they are. That's not a lie."

"Not yet," said Jeanie. "Not entirely."

"We have to find them," Emilia insisted. "That's the most important thing. We have to find them and protect them."

"As much from themselves as from the Elders," said Alina, not joking in the least.


With Edmund at his side, guiding him – and, of course, annoying him by way of oddball questions and severely cockeyed points of view – Whitman was almost ready to make his move. They had found Ally's place after tramping through the woods for the better part of seven hours, making numerous wrong turns, going in circles, getting lost. Edmund wasn't much of a guide, and Whitman had trouble walking in the clunky boots his Custodial guide had stolen for him.

But now they were here.

They'd been hiding out in the sparse woods behind Ally's apartment building for the last thirty minutes, waiting for the cops to come and go. Edmund might have been a meathead and a terrible with directions, but when it came to spy work he was more than capable. Being a spirit gave him certain intrinsic abilities that helped, such as invisibility. It was hard even for someone like him to mess that up.

"We're good now," he reported. "The cops are gone."

Whitman nodded, but stood in place. "Maybe we shouldn't do this?" he said.

"You said you wanted to see her."

"Yes, I know. But, well ... what if she doesn't want to see me?"

"She came to see you twice at the hospital," Edmund reasoned.

"That's true," said Whitman. "Very sweet of her. And that sandwich she brought, the cheeseburger, dear God, Edmund, what a treat. The food here is an absolute revelation. No wonder people are so fat."

"It certainly looked good, sir. Been a long time since I had a burger."

"Those fried potatoes sticks were good, too. Chips, you'd call them. A bit salty for my taste, but scrumptious nonetheless. And the *cheesecake*. Holy Moses in Heaven, I could go to my grave right now and be a happy man."

Edmund grimaced. "I don't need to point out the flaw in that statement, do I sir?"

"Um ... Figure of speech," said Whitman. "No need to think on it."

But really it was more than that and Whitman knew it. Ever since he'd been off the drugs, his mind had been getting clearer, sharper, faster. Thoughts kept coming, one after the other, piling up on top of each other and making a mess in his normally spotless head. And most of them were not thoughts he was comfortable entertaining ... although, ironically enough, some of them, especially the ones involving Ally, were quite entertaining. He also could sense the lingering imprint of Marty Loomis's conscious mind, if not the deceased man's thoughts and memories, and it made him ill-at-ease.

Desire, Anger, Gluttony, Vanity, Doubt, Lust, Fear, Guilt – these things were real to him now, and produced tangible effects impossible to deny; he could feel them inside him like a sickness, and the shame they brought made him want to bury his head in the sand. He wondered whether Edmund could sense these peccadilloes, then chased the thought away, finding it too embarrassing to consider. He had to maintain his composure and his focus. There was work to be done.

"Soooo," said Edmund, his rankled British tone high and drawn out. "You think maybe we should go now? While the coast is clear."

Again Whitman nodded, and again he remained in place. His feet were planted as firmly as the roots of the trees around him.

Edmund said, "It'll be okay, sir. You saved her life. That denotes obligation. She owes you. Least she can do is put you up until we find a way to rectify the situation."

"I don't know why I can't go to Loomis's apartment? That's where I live. Or rather where *he* lived." Whitman looked down at the tattered threads covering his alien body. "I know I could use some better clothing."

"I told you, sir, the police are watching Loomis's place. They're very suspicious."

"Of what? Of me?"

Edmund shrugged. "I suppose."

"But why? I didn't do anything wrong."

"Cops are a funny lot," replied Edmund vaguely. He had no idea how to fully explain that statement, and little desire to try. Instead, he said, "I believe this is our best option." Then, as if icing a cake, "Trust me."

"But the police are watching this place, too. They just left."

"Yes. But they're gone now. From what I can tell, they've got Loomis's place staked out. And again, I remind you, you said that you *wanted* to see her."

Whitman considered the truth of that and started to nod. He did want to see Ally, though he wasn't sure why. He wanted to thank her for the hamburger, of course, and tell her that he had enjoyed the cheesecake, too, and that …

His thoughts waned, and he drifted away on the gossamer wings of fancy, getting lost in the image of Ally's lovely face. He really didn't need to tell her anything; the truth was that he wanted to *see* her.

"I don't want to trouble her," he said, a fantasy-smile, unbeknownst to him, stretching the corners of Martin Loomis's thin-lipped mouth.

"Are you alright, sir?" Edmund asked him. He had never seen his boss look so odd before. Sure, the boyish charm of Loomis's features might have had something to do with that, but there was more to it. Whitman was in there, somewhere, and he looked … *happy.* Dementedly happy, and perhaps drunk.

When he did not receive an immediate response, Edmund tried again. "Sir?" he said.

This time the fog in Whitman's eyes cleared. "What?"

"You floated off there for a moment, sir. I asked if you were alright."

Whitman was reminded of his last thoughts, which were of Ally and that adorable smile of hers, not to mention the snug fit of her shapely backside in those tight jeans she wore, and his cheeks colored with a violent blush. "Of course I'm all right!" he blistered, covering for his embarrassment. "I'm just thinking."

Edmund, though usually quite dull when it came to understanding the complex nuances of the human condition, had a pretty good idea about what. He was a Custodian, after all, an experienced celestial spirit guide, and the puppy-dog look currently swamping his boss's face was a popular one among young men in lust. No point in mentioning it, though. The water was deep enough already, and if Edmund had learned one thing in his life – his real life and his afterlife – it was that he had an effective way of making things worse whenever he offered unsolicited opinions or casual observations.

"I don't know what's taking so long," Whitman went on as Edmund stood quietly at his side, focusing his powers of concentration on not saying anything stupid. "The Elders have to know what's happening. They're probably up there *observing* me right now. I'm an experiment, that's what I am. Another white rat in the maze."

Edmund nodded dutifully. It was the safest response he could think to give.

"And I'll tell you another thing!" Whitman was rolling now; his neck muscles were tense and his eyes held a mad glare. "I'll bet it's that bastard William who's behind it. He's probably having a good ol' laugh at my expense. Clay, too. They're probably yucking it up like a couple of booners."

"Booners?" Edmund had never heard the word before, mostly because it hadn't been spoken in over two-hundred years ... and even then only by a select few clans from northeast Indiana.

"Nothing," Whitman said, waving him off. "I know they're behind it. That's the crux of this monkey business. It's a conspiracy, at my expense." He pointed a stern finger at his unlikely confidant. "You tell them that I know, and that I'm not happy about it. You tell them, Edmund. From me."

"Come now, sir, don't be like that. I trust the Elders. I believe they're trying to fix this." Edmund never spoke poorly of his bosses for fear they might be listening. He rarely used derogatory language against anyone, believing, as his mother had taught him long ago, that if you didn't have anything nice to say, fake it and lie.

"Whatever!" Whitman grumbled. "I'm beginning to not trust anyone."

" You don't mean that, sir. I'm sure that's just the new brain talking. You can trust me."

"Can I? I don't know anymore."

Edmund sniffed, and then quietly cleared his throat. He looked sullen and confused. "I'm in as deep as you are, sir," he said, that rich accent of his almost completely blotted out by his melancholy. "I disobeyed orders to help you."

Whitman wasn't used to feeling guilt. It was a lot heavier than he remembered. He looked at the humble, sweet-natured Custodian before him and attempted a conciliatory smile. "I'm sorry, Edmund," he told him. "I trust you. I do. I know you're putting yourself on the line for me and I appreciate it."

"Nothing you wouldn't do for me, I'm sure," Edmund graciously replied.

Whitman nodded, but he wasn't so sure about that. He remembered fighting for Edmund in the White Room, but he wondered if he had fought as hard as he could have. He wondered if Edmund deserved more respect. Now was not to time to dwell on such matters, though. There were bigger issues at hand.

"Come on," he said, and if he could have he would have laid a friendly hand on Edmund's shoulder to let him know that all was well between them. "Lead the way, buddy. Maybe she'll have some answers for us."

Edmund brightened instantly. "Right on, sir," he said. "I think it's a grand idea all around. She seems really nice, and really trustworthy ... aside from the whole working in a strip club, and being addicted to cocaine, and having lots of explicit sexual relations."

Crushing dismay changed the shape of Whitman's face, giving him a doleful, demoralized appearance. He knew about the strip club, but not the drugs. "Cocaine?" he said.

Edmund cringed and, in his head, cried out the word, "Bugger!" There he went again, popping off at the mouth. He just couldn't seem to help it.

"She's addicted to cocaine?" Whitman inquired.

Edmund's face screwed up, and he tried to shrug, which with his bony shoulders looked more like a twitch. "*Addicted* is a subjective term, don'tcha think? And if it's any consolation, she hasn't done any since finding out she's pregnant."

Dismay became surprise, and Whitman gasped. "Pregnant? But she's not married."

"Oh no, sir. She was dating a drug dealer named Vaughn, but she's not anymore. According to Alina, they had a primarily carnal relationship. Lots of sex. He also provided her with cocaine and other drugs. Alina said he's not a very nice fellow. Thankfully she's moving on. Trying to get her life straight."

"Sounds like she's got a lot of work to do."

"Perhaps. For the most part, though, she's a normal twenty-three year old woman."

"Still. I can't believe she does drugs."

"Alina really likes her, says she sees good things in Ally's future."

Whitman gave a cynical snort. "Alina's no judge of character," he said. "She's too young, too rebellious." Then, somewhat contemplatively, he added, "Though she does seem to have a good heart. Ally, that is. Alina, too, I suppose."

"She did bring you that food, sir."

Whitman, lost in reflection, nodded absently.

"And she is trying to clean up her act. Taking responsibility."

"Yes. Very admirable."

"Sometimes people get off path. You know how it is."

"I know."

"All in all, I think we can trust her."

Whitman gave another absent nod. He wanted to believe in Ally, but he had seen far too many people, good people, honest and kind people, fall off the beam and disappear into the great ocean of gray below. The world has a wicked way, and from his front row seat Whitman had watched generation after generation succumb.

Something told him that perhaps the most judicious course of action would be to hide out in the woods or at the mall until the Elders resolved things. Then again, he mused, given their deliberate manner and penchant for pointless debate, it might take them a while. If they were even trying to resolve the situation. They were not always the most forthright individuals when it came to ineffability and the grand scheme. Not to mention, they were yet unaware that he'd disobeyed orders and gone on the run; that certainly wouldn't help him garner any sympathy in the White Room.

"Sir?" said Edmund, goading him in his amiable British way.

Whitman looked at him, and his mind cleared. "Right," he said. "Let's do this."

"Don't worry, sir," Edmund told him, fighting the urge to clap a friendly hand on his back. "I'll be right at your side the whole time."

Whitman stared at the door for a long time, and the door didn't flinch.

"You have to knock on it, sir," Edmund told him.

"I know that, Edmund." There was exasperation in Whitman's voice, the product of nerves and primal fear. "I'm just ... I don't know."

"What's the worst that can happen, sir?"

That was a loaded question.

"I guess she could call the police and turn me in. That'd be pretty bad."

"They'd probably just send you to the bin."

"Or jail."

Edmund's face wrinkled with concern. "You really don't want to go to prison, sir. Trust me. Some of the things that go on there are truly disturbing." He shuddered at the thought. "I have a few clients who are behind bars. Not a good situation."

"I just want to go home," said Whitman. "Home."

"Yes, sir. We're working on it. But until then you need a place to hide."

Whitman nodded as if he knew that, yet still his hands remained at his sides. He continued to stare at the door as if it had been painted by Monet.

"Come now, sir, don't fret. We need to know if she'll help us. If not, we have to find other accommodations."

Whitman's right hand tightened into a fist, he raised that fist to shoulder level, and then he paused; and he continued to pause for a long time, his fist flexed tight and hovering in front of him like a flesh-colored sock puppet. Edmund was perched at his shoulder, watching keenly. Finally, Whitman rapped his knuckles against the thick wooden plank three times. It wasn't a loud knock, but it was loud enough, and after a few seconds he heard loose floorboards creaking under the weight of approaching footsteps. Then the footsteps stopped, and he saw a shadow move in the thin space at the bottom of the door.

"Perhaps she snuck out on us, sir," said Edmund, not noticing what Whitman already had. He peered down either side of the empty corridor. "I don't see how. I mean, we would have seen her, right?"

"She's here," said Whitman, whispering without moving his lips. Then, in his full voice he said, "Ally? I know you're in there. It's me. John Doe. Open up. Please. I need to talk to you. It's important."

On the other side of the door, Alison Armenti's breathing changed, becoming shallow and quiet. This was the second time today she'd assumed her ex had come to see her only to find a surprise waiting for her instead. The first time it had been the police; they had stopped by to inform her about John Doe's escape and to tell her to be careful and to call them if he tried to contact her. And this time it was John Doe himself, looking, as far as she could tell through the peephole, doomed and disheveled. And scared.

She didn't know what to do.

"Ally?" Whitman tried again. "Please. I'm not going to hurt you."

"No, sir!" Edmund shouted, startling his boss. "That's what psychopaths always say. They smile and say, 'Don't worry. I'm not going to hurt you.' 'You can trust me,' is another line they frequently use. And then they … well … you know."

Whitman looked angered and panicked. He then took a deep breath, turned back to the door, and did his best to adopt a calm, non-threatening demeanor. "Listen," he said. "I um ... I know that's ... well, I know that's what psychopaths usually say. Right? 'I'm not going to hurt you.' But I'm not a psychopath. I swear."

Now Edmund was waving his hands around as if they were on fire. "No! No! No!" he cried out frantically. "Psychopaths say that, too. Psychopaths never admit to being psychopaths. They always, *always* say that they're not."

"Well what do you want me to say?" Whitman snarled out of the corner of his mouth.

It seemed that Edmund was much more knowledgeable on what *not* to say as opposed to what *to* say when one was trying not to look like a psychopath. There was a fine line there, far as he could tell, and he didn't want to cross it.

"Well ... " he began. Then he didn't say anything else.

"Step away from the door. Now!"

Startled, both Whitman and Edmund snapped their heads to the left. There stood Alina, Ally's Custodian. She wore a look that said to be more embarrassed she'd have to be naked in a room full of dirty old men.

"What?" said Whitman.

"Alina?" said Edmund. "What are you doing here?"

"What am *I* doing here? Are you frickin kidding me?"

Edmund was going to say something about Alina's language, but decided now was probably not the best time to bring up a grievance.

"Listen to me, and listen close," said Alina, taking charge. "Back away from the door." With a stern finger she pointed to the other side of the hallway. "Go over there. And then tell her that you understand, given everything that's happened, if she doesn't want to let you in, but you'd really like the chance to explain yourself. Tell her if she would feel more comfortable, you'd gladly meet her somewhere for coffee. Somewhere public."

"Oh. That's good, sir," said Edmund, always one to jump on what looked like a rolling bandwagon. "Say that. Go on."

Whitman dutifully obeyed. He backed away two steps and said, practically verbatim, everything Alina had told him to say. And it was a good thing he did because inside Ally had her phone open and ready to dial. She wasn't sure how she felt about John Doe, but he was acting in such a way that told her she should be prepared to call the police. After he backed away and spouted off Alina's words, however, she relaxed. She closed one eye and peered out the peephole again.

"Ally?" said Whitman, continuing per Alina's advice. "I understand if you don't want to talk to me. Just don't call the police, okay? I've done nothing wrong. I'm just ... " He stopped, sighed. "I don't know what I am. But I could really use your help."

Against all odds, his honesty worked. He must have looked just pathetic and harmless enough because the deadbolt clicked, the knob turned, and the door opened.

Ally stood there, staring at him with a mixture of wariness and curiosity. "Are you Martin Loomis?" she said to him.

Whitman didn't know what to say to that. He looked to Alina for help.

"Tell her you're not sure. Tell her you still don't remember who you are."

Whitman said just that. Then he embellished: "All I remember is waking up in the hospital. It's like I wasn't alive before that."

"How did you find me?" Ally asked him.

"Tell her the phone book," said Alina.

"The phone book," Whitman said.

Ally studied him shrewdly, or as shrewdly as she knew how. Working behind a bar, dealing with almost nothing but jerks, morons, and blowhards on a nightly basis had taught her a little about human nature ... the worst of it, anyway. Because of that, she believed she could spot sincerity and goodness in people as plainly as she could spot arrogance or a bad toupee. John Doe was coming off as genuine. Odd, but genuine.

"If you're lying to me," she told him.

"I'm not. I swear. I don't lie. I can't. I don't know what the truth is. I would just really like a place to sit down, and maybe something to eat."

Ally nodded, slowly, and then her door opened a little wider. "If you try anything," she said as way of a warning.

Whitman looked confused. Then Alina said, "Tell her you

won't," and he did, and Ally's door opened all the way.

"Come on," she told him, waving him in. "You look like hell."

Whitman looked down at the torn, dirty rags he was wearing as he walked through the door. "I smell bad, too," he said. "And my thighs are chafing."

Over to the side, Alina groaned and shook her head.

Edmund looked at her and said, "Good work, Alina. We're in." And then he gave her a big smile and a thumbs up.


"I can't believe you didn't tell me you were bringing him here," Alina was saying. She'd been laying into Edmund for the better part of two minutes now, chastising him with harsh language and flailing hands. "You have any idea what could've happened?"

"I had to get him out of there," replied Edmund weakly. "The police are suspicious and the doctors were going to put him in an asylum."

"So you helped him escape from the hospital? Against the orders of the Elders?"

Edmund nodded guiltily. "He wanted to come here. And I thought, under the circumstances, that would be best."

"Best for whom?"

"For him. He can't go to an asylum. And the Elders aren't helping."

"That's right," said Whitman, mindful to keep his voice low so Ally wouldn't hear him. "They're not doing anything."

Alina, never shy, turned on her boss. "You!" she said. "They told you to stay put. You have me, Emilia and Jeanie worried sick. You have any idea what will happen if the Elders find out you went on the run."

"Perhaps it will give them the motivation they need to bring him back," said Edmund.

"And perhaps it will give them a reason to leave him here for good."

Edmund's expression soured, and Whitman said, "They won't do that."

"Why not? They're the Elders. They can do whatever they want, including busting the two of you back to Purgatory."

"They wouldn't do that. This was not my choice."

"It was your choice to leave the hospital when they told you not to."

"They left me there to rot. Cosmic glitch, my ass! I don't care what they say, there's no way I'm going to an asylum."

Alina had no good response for that. She and Emilia had had this discussion already and both of them had agreed that the Elders were up to something; and if not them, the Angels above them. Emilia believed that a switch should be easy enough to effect, and Alina concurred. Both had beared witness to greater acts. But as yet there was no plan to bring Whitman back.

"Fine," she grunted, giving in. "But you still should've told us. We're out looking for you and doing our jobs at the same time, while keeping Clay and everyone else in the Garrison in the dark. It hasn't been easy."

"I know," said Whitman. "And I'm sorry. But we had to act fast."

"You're not going to tell the Elders on us, are you?" Edmund inquired of Alina. The getting busted back to Purgatory line had put a terrible fright in him; going through that jungle of insanity once was more than enough for him.

"No. At least not until I talk to Em. She'll know what to do."

"Good idea," said Whitman. "Talk to Em. And whatever you do, don't let Clay find out. He'll rat as soon as he gets the chance."

"I'm not telling him anything."

"Don't tell Jeanie, either. I love her, she means well, but she won't lie."

"I'm not talking to anyone but Em. She's the only one I trust."

"Good. That's good."

"But *you* have to keep a low profile. Understand? That means no monkey business. They don't know you've gone rogue, and I'd like to keep it that way as long as possible."

Whitman agreed.

"So," Edmund said to Alina, keeping his voice low even though he didn't have to, "now that we're here, do you have a plan?"

"Ally's one of mine," she said. "I know things about her." She turned to Whitman. "Just follow my lead and say what I tell you to say and you'll be fine."

Whitman nodded obediently.

Edmund said, "So then you think we should stay here?"

"It's as good a place as any, I suppose. For now. Vaughn's one of mine, too, so no other Custodians should come nosing around. So long as it's cool with Ally."

"That's where you come in," said Whitman. "You can help her decide."

A quiet little groan seeped out of Alina. "Can't make that girl do anything," she said in a voice bordering on frustration. "Trust me."

"You can try."

Alina said that she would. Then she said, "So long as you listen to me and do as I say."

That was an easy deal for Whitman to make. "You got it," he said. "You're the boss."

Even Edmund agreed to those terms.

Presently, Ally was in the kitchen, brewing a pot of coffee and fixing a plate of snacks for her guest. Occasionally she'd call out a question to Whitman, or poke her head around the corner to make sure he wasn't up to anything. She had let him into her home because she felt bad for him, because she felt like she owed him, because he needed help. That didn't mean she trusted him. She had her phone in her pocket, with Detective Milner's number at the top of the log, just a press away. Not that she believed John Doe was dangerous.

But it was better to be safe than sorry.

"Cream and sugar?" she asked as she peeked out from the kitchen.

Whitman turned and looked at her. "No, thank you," he said. "Straight is fine."

"I have doughnuts, too. Cookies. Chocolate chip and peanut butter."

Whitman had recently discovered that he liked cookies very much. If they were half as good as the ones at the hospital, he mused, he was in for a real treat.

"Yes, please," he said, nodding eagerly.

Ally couldn't help but smile. There was something almost childlike about John Doe, something intrinsically likeable, and she found herself relaxing despite her concerns. She poured his coffee, put a few cookies on a plate, and came out.

"Here," she said, setting the plate of cookies down and handing him his coffee. She then went back to the kitchen for her cup. When she returned, Whitman was already chewing, slowly, elatedly, an odd, gleeful sort of look plastered on his face.

"These are *delicious*," he said, his mouth stuffed full, little cookie crumbs spitting out with his words. "Absolutely scrumptious."

"Great," said Ally, giving him a raised-brow glance as she sat. She picked up a cookie for herself, chocolate chip, and took a bite.

"You must be an excellent cook."

"No, I didn't bake these. I bought them at the store."

Whitman looked a little disappointed, but that disappointment only lasted until his next bite. Then his face turned into a blissful mask again.

"Enough cookie talk. We need to pay attention," said Alina sharply, speaking to both Edmund and Whitman. Then, to Edmund specifically, "I want you to stand there and not say a word. Got it. Let me handle this."

"I can talk if I want to," Edmund replied in the hurt, offended tones of a child who'd just been told he was too young to play. "I'm not a moron."

The glare Alina repaid him made him look away.

Alina then turned back to the scene in the living room. "I'm right here, Whit," she told her boss. "I'll guide you through this. Don't be nervous."

"Yeah, don't be nervous," Edmund parroted.

"I'm not nervous," replied Whitman automatically, forgetting where he was and who he was talking to. It was hardly his fault; his mind was consumed by the rapture of glorious peanut butter cookies.

"And why would you be nervous?" said Ally skeptically.

"Dammit! You just spoke out of turn," Alina piped.

Whitman looked up, confusion all over his face.

Again, Ally said to him, "Why would you be nervous?"

Whitman understood what had happened: he had

accidentally answered Alina and Edmund, who, at least in Ally's world, did not exist. It was the same thing as talking to himself, which is rarely looked upon favorably.

"Tell her in general," Alina was quick to say. "Tell her you're not nervous, in general."

"In general," Whitman repeated. "In general terms I'm not nervous. You know, about ... everything. In general. Generally speaking."

Ally shot him another skeptical glance, and Whitman busied himself with a bite of cookie.

"Tell her you think she's pretty," Edmund suggested from over Alina's shoulder. "Girls like that, sir. Very much."

"Absolutely not," cried Alina before Whitman could speak. "Sir, do not say that. She'll think you're a stalker."

Whitman, slowly chewing a mouthful of delicious cookie goodness, nodded subtly.

A brief pause ensued. Ally, the host, took it upon herself to break it. "So," she said, leaning back in her seat, "you said you wanted to explain yourself."

"Right," said Whitman. "I did." He glanced at Alina, who wisely had moved behind Ally's shoulder, giving her boss the perfect angle. He could now see her just by flicking his eyes to the right. Somewhere just to the left stood Edmund.

"Start off by thanking her again for trusting you and letting you in," Alina instructed.

Whitman obeyed, saying just that.

"Well, you're welcome," Ally told him. "But I wouldn't say that I trust you just yet. You still have some explaining to do."

"Of course. I understand."

And then fate, in all its ineffability, stepped in.

Alina had been chirping in Ally's ear to quit smoking for months, just like she'd been chirping in her ear to quit working at the strip club, and to quit doing drugs and doing Vaughn, along with all the other stupid, destructive, immoral things most humans tend to gravitate towards. The need to quit had intensified recently – as well as Alina's spiritual influence – when Ally discovered that she was pregnant.

However, she'd yet to fully give up the nasty habit.

With Alina worried about guiding Whitman through the

landmines of personal interaction – and on the backside making sure Edmund didn't do anything monumentally stupid, like accidentally push himself through the corporeal plane while trying to stimulate some sort of physical effect on Ally or Whitman – she failed to realize that Ally was lighting up until there was a cigarette dangling from her mouth.

It was actually Whitman who caught it first. "What are you doing?" he cried out with a critical bite. The pinched look on his face also said that he disapproved.

"What?" said Ally, already exhaling smoke. "I know, I should quit. But it's not easy."

"But you're pregnant!"

Alina had perceived where this line was going, but she wasn't quick enough to prevent it. She had actually started shouting before Whitman blurted out the words, but only barely, and by the time Whitman realized that she was yelling at him not to say anything, his words were already on their way.

The effect they had was immediate: Ally's face screwed up with shock, her eyes narrowed to a point, her posture stiffened. "I'm what?" she said, struck by a mixture of disbelief, anger, and shame.

Presently, Whitman was looking at Alina, who was cutting a hand back and forth in front of her neck, imploring him through the international language of pantomime to stop.

But it was too late.

"You said I'm pregnant," Ally said, a more forceful tone to her voice now. It wasn't a question, but it was clear she wanted a response.

"Did I?" said Whitman.

"I don't understand," Edmund said to Alina. "I thought she *was* pregnant."

"She is. But nobody except her knows."

"Oh. I see. So he sort of screwed the pooch there, eh?"

Alina slapped a hand on her forehead and groaned.

"What?" replied Edmund. "I didn't mean literally."

Meanwhile, Ally was staring daggers at a wincing and suddenly silent Jeremiah Whitman. "Well," she said to him. "How did you know I'm pregnant? No one but me knows that."

"How did I know that?" Whitman spoke as if he was

repeating the question back to Ally when really he was soliciting an opinion from Alina.

But for the first time since Whitman had known her, Alina was speechless. Usually you couldn't get her to shut up, but there she was, just standing there, her mouth wordlessly hanging open, a look of helpless bemusement pressed on her face.

It was then that Edmund stepped up with one of his brilliant ideas. "Tell her you're psychic, sir," he shouted out like a contestant on a game show.

Alina looked dismayed, but with nothing better to add, she remained silent. And Whitman, needing to respond, once again followed his Custodian's advice.

"I'm ... psychic," he said, a bit hesitantly.

Ally's expression didn't change much. It morphed from suspicion to incredulity with the only visible difference coming from her eyes, which narrowed ever so slightly. "You gotta be kidding me," she said.

No point waffling now, thought Whitman, and he drew himself up and made the statement with more verve. "Seriously. I'm psychic."

Ally let out a nervous chuckle. "Psychic?" she said, as if the idea was absurd. "You know, maybe you should go."

"Wait," said Whitman. "Honest. I'm psychic." He glanced at Alina, and with that glance he let her know it was time for her to earn her keep. As Ally's Custodian, he figured she should be nothing less than a fountain of information on the young woman.

"Right," said Alina, catching on. "Okay." She flipped through her mind for something personal about Ally, something real and deeply private, though not anything embarrassing or untoward. She settled on one, and said, "Tell her that in eleventh grade she wanted to go to prom with Calvin Mears but he didn't ask her."

Figuring he needed to sell it, Whitman assumed the role of a carnival huckster he'd seen ages ago, back when he was just a fresh-eyed Custodian newbie. He put one theatrical hand to his head, closed his eyes, and began to whisper to himself in strange tones.

"What are you doing?" Ally said, not buying it. "This is

ridiculous. You can't ... "

"Calvin Mears," he blurted out, interrupting her. "He was a ... You wanted to go to the prom with him, but he never asked you."

Ally's voice caught in her throat, allowing no words to get out. She just sat there, eyes agape, a neglected cigarette smoking between her fingers. "How did you ... " she began, but she never finished.

"I know, it's hard to believe," Whitman said. "I think it was the accident."

"But ... You still don't remember who you are?"

Whitman shook his head. "No. But I seem to know everything about you."

"Me?"

"Yes. That's why I came here. I wanted to talk to you again."

"Jolly good, sir," said Edmund. "I think we got her."

Alina was shaking her head in disbelief, part of that disbelief coming from the idea itself, which, impossibly, seemed to be working; the other part centered on the fact that it had been Edmund's idea.

"So you know all about me?" Ally asked Whitman.

He nodded, and said that he did. "Not everything, of course," he added, giving himself some leeway. "But a lot."

"Okay then, what's my mother's name?"

Alina jumped to duty. "Rebecca," she said.

"Rebecca."

"My father's?"

"Jackson."

"Jackson."

"Where did I ... "

"Lose her virginity," Alina blurted out, knowing exactly what Ally was going ask. Only Ally didn't ask. She paused, finding the topic a bit too personal to broach with a stranger. "Tell her in Randy Manson's basement," Alina went on, while Ally sat there, searching her mind for a less embarrassing question.

"You were going to ask me where you lost your virginity," Whitman said to her, as if actually prescient. "Correct?"

Ally's waning skepticism tumbled to shock. "How'd you know I ... "

"I told you," said Whitman, smiling a little to put her at ease, "I'm psychic."

Ally gulped down a stale breath of air. She could hardly believe what was happening.

"Oh, for the record, it happened in Randy Manson's basement," Whitman said. "You know he's a homosexual now? At least he's experimenting with it." Then, mostly to himself, though loud enough for her to hear, "Strange sort of experiment, you ask me."

Ally's astonishment had nothing to do with discovering Randy's secret, which up until now she knew nothing about. Her astonishment lay purely in the unquestionable psychic abilities of the man who had saved her life.

"This is incredible," she gasped. "I don't know what to say."

"Me either. I'm just as stunned by it as you are."

"And it's only with me?"

"I don't know. I think so. That's why I needed to see you. They were going to put me in an asylum and I couldn't allow that. I had to talk to you again."

Ally nodded as if she understood. Then she said, "It's like we're *united*. Well, like you're united to me. Like you somehow became part of me when you died in my arms."

Whitman was not one for recognizing signals. Whereas a normal man might have noticed the look of adoration glowing on Ally's face, it did little to light Whitman's imagination. He just shrugged and said, "I don't know. Perhaps."

But Alina certainly knew. It was the same look Ally had back when Vaughn first started nosing around. And Dexter Vexely before him. And there was Carter Morris, Colt Bentley, Jason Ryman, and, last but not least – or, if you prefer, first among all – William Bartley's current lover, Randy Manson.

Ally was smitten. She was staring at Whitman like he was a big, gooey slice of Death by Chocolate cake and she hadn't eaten in weeks. Whitman's focus, meanwhile, had shifted back to the plate of cookies.

"Mind if I have another one," he asked, already reaching.

"Go right ahead," said Ally sweetly.

"That's out, you know." He gestured to the cigarette pinched between her dainty fingers.

"Oh. My fault," she said, and discarded it in the ashtray. "I shouldn't be smoking anyway."

"No, you shouldn't. You have to take care of that baby. And yourself."

Ally didn't feel like getting into a debate over whether or not she should keep the baby, and she wondered, offhand, if John Doe knew she was planning on getting an abortion. She concluded that he probably didn't seeing that she didn't even know what she was going to do yet. She pushed the ashtray aside and curled her legs up. Then she ran a hand through her hair a couple times. When Whitman looked at her, his mouth busy rending to crumbs a delectable peanut butter cookie, she gave him a shy, flirtatious smile.

"I'm going to make you dinner tonight," she said to him. "Whatever you want."

"Really?" said Whitman, cookie bits spraying out of his mouth. "That's sounds great."

Ally's smile lingered, and again she ran a hand through her hair.

Behind her, Alina sighed and said, "Oh no. Here we go."

"What?" said Edmund, who was even more clueless than Whitman when it came to women and their signals. He wouldn't have recognized a come hither sign from a woman if she was naked, and smiling, and holding an actual sign that said 'Come hither.'

Alina looked to the heavens and sighed. "Lord, give me strength," she said.

"Amen," Edmund added.

# Chapter Ten

Charlie Bates was a gentle soul who didn't understand subterfuge, and who believed, unequivocally, that all cops were good people whose duty it was to serve and protect. So when he saw a picture of his friend Marty on the television with instructions underneath to contact the police with any information on the unknown man, Charlie picked up the phone and called the number given. Three hours later, Detectives Milner and Rainer showed up at Charlie's house, and he escorted them inside without a second thought, taking them to the kitchen, where Charlie's mother, Greta, had just taken some muffins out of the oven.

"Please, please, have some," she said to the two detectives, and she offered fresh coffee with them. She also put out a plate of cookies, and told them that her and her husband had been giving to the Fraternal Order of Police for twenty years now, and even had a couple of FOP stickers on the back windshield of their car.

"Thank you, ma'am," said Milner genially.

Rainer, after chewing a bite of muffin, said, "These are delicious."

"Isn't it just terrible about Marty," Greta said to them as they ate her wonderful treats. "I do hope he's okay. He used to be such a nice young man, until that girl broke his heart. Now I just don't know about him."

"Mom," Charlie whined, embarrassment flushing his cheeks. "They don't care about that."

The detectives, in fact, did care about that, but they showed nothing of it; they merely continued eating their muffins, chewing with their mouths closed.

Greta said to them, "If you need anything else, officers, you let me know." Then she backed out of the kitchen, leaving them to their business.

Milner threw out the first barbed comment. "Some set up you got here, Charlie," he said.

Charlie Bates hated being the guy that still lived with his parents, but he had been that guy for so long that he'd gotten used to it. "It's all right," he said, and then he quickly added his most used rejoinder: "It's temporary. I'm saving money for a house."

"Fantastic," said Rainer, who really couldn't have cared less. He took a sip of coffee, while his partner finished rending a bite of blueberry muffin goodness.

Charlie used the opportunity to pose a couple questions. "So," he said, "have you found him yet? Do you have any leads?" The report that John Doe – aka Martin Loomis – had left the hospital without permission had just made the news and Charlie was worried.

Milner shrugged. "That's what we're doing here," he said, vaguely. "Why don't you tell us about your friend, Charlie?"

"Okay. What do you want to know?"

"Anything you can share would be helpful," said Rainer. "Where he lives, what he does for a living, what he does for fun. Places he goes. His family, his friends. We even want to know about this girl who broke his heart."

"Amanda? What's she got to do with anything?"

Rainer sneered. "Maybe nothing. Maybe everything."

"We're simply trying to get a better idea of who Marty is," Milner cut in, softening the hard edge of his partner's bullish personality. "He was having trouble remembering things, so unfortunately we don't know much about him. We were hoping you could help us put together more pieces of the puzzle."

"He has amnesia?"

"Something like that."

"Because of the shooting?"

"We're not sure."

"He was shot, though, right? That part's true?"

Milner answered with a nod.

"But he's okay? He's expected to make a full recovery?"

"As far as we know, yes. But that was when he was in the hospital. He still needs medical attention."

"He left without being cleared by the doctors?"

"Correct. He walked out late last night." Milner left out the part about Marty being sequestered and under police surveillance, which meant his walking out was more of an escape than a voluntary discharge. But that information, though known by most hospital personnel, and Ally, had not yet been released to the general public ... and it wouldn't be, if they could help it. "So you can see why we're concerned," Milner went on. "There are health issues involved."

Charlie sighed and shook his head. "Poor Marty," he said. "I hope he's okay."

"He will be," said Rainer. "If we can find him."

"We want to find him and help him remember," said Detective Milner, continuing to display the hallmark traits of good intentions: the kind eyes, the calm demeanor, the sympathetic tone of voice. "Then he can get the medical treatment he needs and we can solve this crime."

"Anything you can tell us will help," added Rainer.

Charlie nodded solemnly and said, "Whatever I can do to help." And just like that he threw open the vault.

Without really knowing what his friend's standing in the investigation was, and without having to be cajoled or coerced, Charlie Bates told the two detectives everything he knew about his best friend, focusing primarily on the last six months, from the time Marty lost his job and caught his fiancée getting ramrodded by a greasy Neanderthal to the last time the two of them spoke. He went into detail about Marty's depression, his injuries from the fight, and his ever-increasing reliance on booze and pain killers. He told them everything he knew, thinking only about helping his friend.

The two cops barely had to question him, and when they were finished, they made the same request to Charlie as they had to Ally: they handed him their cards and told him that if he remembered anything else, anything at all, or if Marty tried to contact him, he needed to call them immediately.

"He needs help," said Milner, laying it on thick, taking full advantage of Charlie's naïveté and willingness to help.

"I understand," Charlie replied.

The two cops, now satisfied that they had closed off another avenue, got up and left Charlie's parents' house, taking with them an extra muffin each, because free muffins and cookies were part of the job. At the car, Milner looked over the roof at his partner and said, "So, where to now?"

"The Quick Stop on Hudson," Rainer replied. "I'm suddenly in the mood for one of those coffee dust cappuccinos. Then I was thinking we could drop in on Mister Holt, see what Hagerstown's preeminent crime boss knows."

Milner nodded, and got in the car. "My thoughts exactly," he said as his partner climbed into the passenger seat.

And they buckled their seat belts and went on their way.


Vaughn was tired of running around town, chasing leads, digging through the alleys and crack dens of north Hagerstown, talking to derelicts and junkies, searching for a man everyone seemed to know – "Oh, that guy. Yeah, I know that guy," they'd say after Vaughn gave his name and described him – but no one was able to finger.

He and Chauncey had been to the homeless shelter, twice, to Lou Franco's Pool Hall, a known hangout for vagrants with only a few coins in their pocket, and to the Pack House. They'd been to Jack's on the Tracks, the courts, and the outlets. They'd been everywhere, and Adam 'Scarecrow' Dubinsky was nowhere to be found.

Eventually, Vaughn and Chauncey returned to Teasers to see Holt. Chauncey had a shift to work, and Vaughn had a few late calls to make.

When they walked in, Amy, the girl behind the bar, told them that Holt was in back with the police, and Chauncey took that as a cue to get to work. "Can't bother a man for working," he told Vaughn as he was leaving.

Vaughn stayed at the bar, drank a beer, and talked to Amy. She was a sweet girl from somewhere in Virginia, but Vaughn didn't pay her much attention after she mentioned a boyfriend that she lived with. From that point on he concentrated on drinking his beer, smoking cigarettes, and, when occasion arose, making small talk with the dancers, one of whom he knew intimately. Caroline was her name, though on stage she went by Cece, and she told Vaughn with mock concern and a mannequin smile that she was sorry to hear about him and Ally breaking up, and if he ever wanted to talk about it, and by 'talk about it' she meant hang out, have a couple drinks, do some cocaine and each other, he should give her a call.

"Sounds good," he told her, rubbing her hand in a lewd, sexually-suggestive way. "Maybe later tonight."

"Yeah," she said, beaming now. "I'm done at one."

"I'll let you know. Got a few things to do first."

Vaughn had a couple deals to turn, but he was planning on stopping by Ally's before it got too late; and if he had his way, that would be his last stop of the night. But if she wasn't receptive, he thought to himself as he continued to rub Caroline's silky hand, Door #2 was unlocked.

It was then that Holt emerged from his office with two gentlemen in cheap, poorly-fitted suits. One was large and square-shouldered, the other short and pudgy. It was obvious they were cops, and Vaughn said to Caroline, "You know anything about that?"

She glanced over her shoulder. Holt was smiling and leading the two cops out of the back office, looking like a guilty politician who'd just bought his way out of a scandal. "Not really," she said. "Heard they were cops. But I don't know what they're doing here."

They were heading towards the bar now, towards Vaughn, and Caroline politely excused herself. "Call me," she said as she stood up, revealing a body meant to be seen naked. "Or just stop by. You remember where I live?"

Vaughn smiled at her, and nodded. She then she started off, just before Holt and the two cops reached the table.

"Vaughn," Holt said, taking the seat Caroline had just vacated, "these are Detectives Milner and Rainer." He made no distinction between them. "They had a few questions about that shooting at the A&P Mart, the one Ally was involved in."

"She's your ex-girlfriend, isn't she?" said Rainer.

"She's a girl I sometimes see," replied Vaughn coolly. "Might see her tonight."

"You know the name Martin Loomis?" Milner inquired.

Vaughn thought about it, and shook his head. "Why? Who is he?"

"He's the guy that took the bullet the other night. He was supposed to be in a secure room, but he left the hospital."

Vaughn shrugged as if that meant nothing to him.

"We went by Ally's place to make sure she was safe."

"You think he might be a threat?" Vaughn asked.

"Maybe. I know we need to find him."

"Well like I said, I'm supposed to stop by there later. I see anything, I'll let you know."

Rainer pulled out a card. Milner, too. They handed them over. Vaughn took them without looking at them and set them on the table.

"We'll be on our way now," Milner said to Holt. "Thank you for your assistance."

Holt stood and shook hands with them. A few comments were made, and there were a couple laughs, a couple slaps on the back. Holt was a smooth operator when it came to the police; he had a few of the local boys on the roll, buying their special badge favors with money and sex. These two, though, Milner and Rainer, they were detectives, and as far as Vaughn knew not under thumb.

Holt finished up by telling the two plain clothes coppers that if they ever felt like having a good time they should stop by. "A couple of the girls here really like cops," he said to them in his best snake oil tone.

"Whadda you know," replied Rainer. "We really like strippers."

Holt laughed, and Rainer and Milner laughed, and Vaughn watched it all with a petulant smile. When the cops were gone, Holt came back to the table and took a seat.

"Fancy cops," he said, and lit up a cigarette.

"What they want?" Vaughn asked.

"Wanted to talk about Ally. And you. Wanted to know if you knew this Loomis guy."

Vaughn shook his head. "Never heard of him."

"That's what I said. I don't think they know shit right now. That's why they came scratching round here. What'd you find out?"

Vaughn snorted. "Been all over," he said. "Can't find this Dubinsky kid anywhere. Everyone knows him, but no one's seen him. What about this Loomis guy? What's got the police so jacked they come here?"

"They were tight-lipped on the particulars. He escaped, and they're suspicious. They said things don't add up. You know cops."

"Too well," said Vaughn. "Too well."

"So, what's on the agenda tonight?" Holt asked. "You going to see Ally?"

"Gonna drop by there, yeah. After I make a couple runs. Gotta see Otis, then I'm running out to the Boro to catch up with Mixie."

"That fucker still owe me money?"

"Says he's got it. That's why I'm going."

"How much?" Holt asked.

"All of it. Six large."

"Nice. You get it, keep a grand for your troubles. Buy Ally something nice."

Vaughn liked the sound of that, and nodded his approval.

"And don't worry," Holt added, "I need anything tonight, I'll call on Dado or Chauncey. They're capable. You take the night off after your runs, spend it making up with that girl of yours. She's a keeper."

Vaughn liked the sound of that, too. He missed Ally's taut little body and beautiful face. He wanted to see her, and he wanted to have her. And if by chance she remained stubborn and sent him away without any, well, sweet Caroline was waiting wide open in the wings.

"Got a feeling it's gonna be a good night," he said to Holt.

As a buxom brunette worked the stage in nothing but a smile and heels, the small town kingpin laughed and said, "Most are around here, my friend. Most are."


Whitman realized that showers were amazing. Back when he was alive, he'd been treated to a few hot baths, and once, when he was fresh from the army, that bath had included soap and bubbles. But mostly he had cleaned himself up in the creek when it was warm, and when it was cold, he boiled water and washed indoors. His wife, when she was alive, took baths every now and again, but she was a plains' woman like Jeremiah was a plains' man, and usually she cleaned herself in the creek, too.

Whitman had seen modern day showers but he'd never experienced one before, and from the moment the steaming hot water smacked his naked skin he was totally absorbed. On top of that, Ally had tubes of fancy body soaps, creamy bath gels and moisturizers, and exotic shampoos and conditioners; they smelled like coconut and strawberry and lavender, and contained kiwi extract, whey protein, and microbial beads. Whitman tried all the soaps, experimentally, finally deciding on a pear-scented body wash that made his skin sing. He used the shampoo for his hair, and because it felt so good, and the instructions on the bottle said to lather, rinse, and, if necessary, repeat, he washed it twice. He stayed in the shower until his skin was red and wrinkled, and after he toweled off, he dressed in clothes that Vaughn had left behind – a pair of sweats, a t-shirt that Ally liked to wear to bed, and a thin sweatshirt. The clothes were big on Whitman, but they fit better than the rags Edmund had procured for him, and they were more comfortable and smelled better, too.

When he exited the bathroom, Ally was busy in the kitchen, chopping and dicing vegetables for a salad.

"My oh my," Whitman said to her, his moppish brown hair slicked back, giving him a more grown up look, "that was incredible."

"What?" said Ally. "The shower?"

"Yes. It was wonderful. I feel so *relaxed* and *comfortable*."

"A good shower will do that."

"It's been a while," said Whitman. He smelled cigarette smoke, and saw a fresh butt in an astray on the window sill.

Ally looked at him, she saw that he saw the ashtray and the cigarette, and when he looked at her, with a shade of disappointment in his eyes, she said, "I know, I know. But it's harder than you think."

Whitman had been a smoker when he was alive, back when tobacco was a big cash crop in Virginia and the Carolinas. He'd roll himself a smoke and ease back with it on the porch after dinner. He'd smoke, have a shot or two of rye, and let the hard work of the day fall off him. But that was a long time ago, back when tobacco was just tobacco, before they started tainting it with dangerous additives and chemicals, turning a fine, natural product into the scourge of the land.

"It's fine," he said, fighting the urge to judge and chastise her. "I understand."

Ally dumped a handful of cut tomatoes into a bowl and started on the onions. "Is there anything you can't eat?" she asked him as she sliced and diced.

Whitman shrugged and said, "I don't think so." Allergies had never been a big deal back in his day. Just more fallout from all the chemicals and preservatives.

It was then that Alina appeared, taking ghostly form next to Ally. She said, "Sorry, Whit. Got caught up with this teen girl who likes to steal her mom's prescriptions. Are you okay?"

Whitman slyly nodded to Alina, and then said to Ally, "Everything smells divine." He then excused himself, proclaiming he had to get something out of the bathroom. He left, and Alina met up with him there.

"I think I'm okay," he said to her after closing the door for privacy. "I've got my bearings now. I don't know how much I'll need you."

"And what if she asks for more examples of your psychic prowess?"

There was cynicism in Alina's tone, and the young, scruffy face of Martin Loomis returned her a look. "I don't think she will."

"Well, regardless, I'm going to be in and out all night, just in case."

Whitman said that was fine, but unnecessary. Then he said, "Have you ever had a really long shower before?"

Alina, who had died in 1973, at the tender age of twenty-four, had always lived in a house with indoor plumbing. "Of course," she said. "Why?"

"They're *amazing*. I feel so clean and warm and cozy."

"That's great. Really. Now, I feel I should warn you, Clay is on the warpath."

"Why?"

"Why do you think? He found out that you left the hospital."

Whitman was appalled. "How'd he find out?" he said. "Who told him?"

"We think it might have been Deirdre. Your doctor is one of

her clients. Or it may have been Will or Geoffrey. They watch over the two cops who are leading the investigation."

Whitman gave a pettish shake of his head. "Dammit," he grumbled under his breath, though loud enough for Alina to hear. She said nothing of it, though, being prone to cursing herself. "Though I suppose it couldn't be avoided forever."

"No. Too many people, too many variables. But I felt you should know that Clay's got everyone looking for you. The whole damn Garrison is out there walking through walls and turning over stones. And Edmund ... well ... " Alina cut that statement short, but it hung in the air nonetheless, like an unpleasant odor.

Whitman sighed dolefully. "Edmund," he said, and shook his head. "What did Clay do to him? Do I even want to know?"

"Nothing yet. Believe it or not, Eddie's holding his mud. He's denying that he knew anything about the escape, and Clay has no proof. Not yet, anyway."

"I haven't seen him since earlier."

"Clay interrogated him something fierce and now he's laying low. Doesn't want to lead them to you."

Whitman was impressed with young Edmund, and with a hint of pride he said, "I knew he had it in him."

"Well, it's not over yet. Clay's going to the Elders."

Hope, what little Whitman had, dashed away. "I suppose it was inevitable," he said. Then, trying to remain positive, "And who knows, maybe this'll snap them to action."

"That might not be a good thing, considering," replied Alina.

"They're the ones dragging their heels while I rot down here. They're the ones playing games. I'm just trying to survive."

Whitman's voice had risen a couple octaves, prompting Alina to put a finger to her lips and go, "Shhh. Keep it down. Remember, Ally thinks you're alone in here."

He nodded that he understood, and when he spoke again, it was in a soft, mannerly tone. "They left me here. This isn't my choice."

"Hey, I get it," said Alina. "I do. But that doesn't change the fact that you disobeyed a direct order. *And* you dragged Edmund into this mess."

"What? He wanted to help," Whitman replied, and though he

strived to keep guilt from his voice some bled through.

Not that Alina could be fooled. "*Right*," she said, heavy on the sarcasm. "You didn't have to twist his arm at all. Next you're going to tell me it was his idea, him being such a rebel."

Whitman thought about arguing, but quickly concluded it was pointless. Alina was a shrewd one, and he had not a leg to stand on. "That's not the issue," he said, switching gears. "They left me here. Alone. In human form. I don't know why they're doing it – punishment, a test of some kind – but I'm not about to stand idle and take it. Humans get freewill, and I'm human. Am I not?"

Alina had little patience for semantics; she also didn't care for lines drawn in the sand or bushes that needed beating. "I just wanted to warn you," she said. "They're looking for you, so stay sharp."

A moment of silence passed between them, and in that moment the considerable bulk of the situation dropped on Whitman like a safe from a ten-story building. "I don't know what I'm doing here," he moaned, giving into doubt, which had been whittling away at him for a while now. He sat down on the toilet, rested his elbows on his knees, his head in his hands. "What am I supposed to accomplish? What's the point? I'm out of my element. Best I can hope for is the Elders step in and put things back to normal. But given my insubordination, I'm guessing if I do go back, I'll be demoted. Or worse."

Alina thought about that and agreed. "You're probably right," she said.

"Then what am I doing? What am I *supposed* to do?"

"Your job," she replied, quickly and plainly. "Do your job."

This simple, brusquely-delivered statement brought Whitman out of his doldrums and lit within him a flicker of hope. He looked at Alina and said, "My job?"

"Damn right," she told him. "Do your job. You're Jeremiah Whitman, one of the finest Custodians the Spirit World has ever known. You've been a good man for a long time, and you're still in there. Don't go soft now. You do your job. You help people. You have an actual voice now. Use it.

"But what about the Elders? And fate?"

"If the Elders and Angels were so concerned about you

messing with fate they should've gotten you out of here already."

Emboldened by Alina's motivational speech, Whitman stood. The sad, weepy look on his face had been replaced by steel-jawed conviction and a burning glare in his eyes.

"You may look like a goofy kid," Alina went on, "but you're still Jeremiah Whitman, and you can do something that none of the rest of us can do. You can talk to them. You can look them in the eye and give them square advice."

"What about laying low?" Whitman inquired. "You just told me that the whole Garrison is looking for me."

Alina hesitated. She had gotten swept up in the moment and forgot that Whitman was living on borrowed time. The Garrison was looking for him, with orders to report back to Clay the moment they found him. Worse yet, Clay presently was consulting the Elders, which meant even greater scrutiny was about to fall on Whitman. It was only a matter of time before they found him.

Instead of lying about it, Alina, true to form, shot a straight arrow. "They're going to find you," she said, her voice strong and steady with the truth. "You know it, and I know it. They're going to find you. It's only a matter of time. But until they do, you can make a difference. You can do what you do best."

Whitman took in Alina's words, and he nodded confidently. They would find him, sure enough, and when they did there would be a reprimand. He would be punished, demoted, perhaps even sent back to Purgatory.

But until they found him ...

"Dammit! You're right," he said, once more feeling the buzz of determination. "I'm Jeremiah Whitman. I've seen almost everything there is to see, and I know the difference between right and wrong."

"Sure do!" Alina shouted.

"I can make a difference."

"You sure can."

"I can change things."

"That's the spirit."

Whitman was puffed up with confidence and ready to take on the world. Alina's little pep talk had worked, and he was anxious to strike a blow for Custodians everywhere, starting with the young woman currently cooking him dinner. Ally was a nice girl who'd made some bad choices, but now Whitman was in a position to change all that.

"With me talking to her, and you gently nudging her in the right direction," he said to Alina, "I know we can help Ally."

He got no response, and when he turned around, he discovered that Alina was no longer there. "Alina?" he said, wondering where she could have gone. He pulled the shower curtain back. "Alina?" He opened the closet door and checked in the hamper and the medicine cabinet. "Alina?"

She was gone.

He waited about ninety seconds for her to reappear, but she never did. He called her name, repeatedly, then he called for Edmund and Emilia. He received no reply from any of them, and the very tangible sensation of loneliness closed in on him, making the bathroom feel like a jail cell.

He went out and checked the hallway and living room, thinking Alina may have wandered out there, but she was nowhere to be found. It was like she had vanished into thin air, and though Whitman understood that was normal when it came to Custodians, he was perplexed by the timing.

"Hey. You okay?" It was Ally. She was standing in the open archway between the kitchen and the living room. Her hair was up, and she was wearing an apron and holding a breadknife. "You look lost?"

Whitman glanced around one last time, hoping to find Alina peeking out at him, smiling impishly, like a kid playing a game of hide and seek. But there was no sign of her, and though he told himself it was not a big deal, that she probably had somewhere else she needed to be, a bad feeling crawled into the pit of his gut and nested there.

"No. I'm fine," he said to Ally, a bit distractedly. "Just ... thinking."

"What about?"

He looked at her, and his eyes constricted with focus ... and, underlying that, interest. "Nothing. Everything."

"Okay," she replied in the tones of someone skeptically amused. Then she said, "I'm ready to put the steaks on if you're ready to eat."

Whitman nodded, and said that he was famished.

"Well you just sit right down and relax. We'll eat in about fifteen minutes."

Fifteen minutes later, dinner was served.


Alina didn't return during dinner, and neither did Edmund. Emilia was a no-show, too, which left Whitman alone in Ally's company, a fact he forgot about quickly after she placed a filet mignon topped with a bleu cheese tapenade and on his plate. A baked potato and asparagus spears followed. The smell alone was divine, and Whitman almost didn't want to spoil the moment by eating.

Then he took a bite. The flavor was intense and immediate, and his eyes shut automatically, allowing his sense of taste unfettered domain. The next eleven seconds his mouth was busy either chewing or making noises that brought to mind the sounds of intense sexual gratification.

"This is *delicious*," he told Ally after finishing his first bite, and she smiled sweetly at him and said, "Thank you."

"It's *incredible*," he told her after a few more bites, and she laughed and said, "I'm glad you're enjoying it."

Near the end of dinner, with his steak and potato gone and only a couple asparagus spears remaining, he said, "Where did you learn to cook like this?"

Ally had never been complimented on her culinary skills before, and truth be told this was the one recipe she relied on. She had seen it in a magazine, and it quickly had become Vaughn's favorite, though the most effusive he'd ever been with his praise was, "That was good, babe." Then he'd pull her close and make some remark about her being dessert.

"My mom was a good cook," Ally said. "Me, not so much."

"All evidence to the contrary," said Whitman as he stabbed the last asparagus spear. He popped it in his mouth and chewed, relishing the final taste of the best meal he'd ever had. "You should think about doing this for a career."

Ally snorted out a laugh. "Unlikely," she said. "I'm not that good. But thank you anyway."

Whitman wiped the corners of his mouth with a napkin and sighed appreciatively. "That was divine," he said. He then leaned back in his seat and sighed again.

"Wow," said Ally, basking in his delight. She still had some food left on her plate; she picked at her baked potato, dipped it in sour cream. "I take it you don't get too many home cooked meals," she said, and took the bite on her fork.

"Not lately," replied Whitman. "Unless you count the hospital."

"No," said Ally, chuckling. "I don't."

"Oh." Whitman took a drink of his coffee. "Then no."

"You're an odd guy," Ally said, not as an insult, just a general observation. "Not in a bad way," she was quick to add, not wanting to offend him. "Just ... different."

Now there's an understatement, thought Whitman. He wasn't just different, he was off the map, though in actuality he had forgotten how different he really was during dinner, when it was just him and Ally and a plate of food that very well might have come from heaven's galley. He hadn't felt much like a Custodian hopelessly trapped in a human body; he had felt like a human being, like Jeremiah Whitman, a man he hadn't been in more than two-hundred and fifty years.

"You're not like other guys," Ally went on, attempting to explain herself further. "That's all I meant. And that's a good thing."

"Good," Whitman replied. "Maybe it's the amnesia."

"Maybe. So, no progress with that yet?"

He shrugged and said he still didn't remember anything.

"Maybe I can help you remember," Ally said. "I don't know much about you, but we did talk a little when you came into the club."

Whitman winced at the mentioning of the strip club. He was embarrassed about being the kind of guy that went to a place like that, even though he wasn't that guy and he had never been to a place like that before. He also didn't like that Ally worked there. But, he mused, this could be the opening he needed to talk her into pursuing a better profession.

"The club?" he said. "I don't remember that."

"You were upset about your fiancée."

Whitman shrugged ambivalently. "If you say so."

"What about your apartment?" Ally inquired.

Whitman shook his head. "Don't remember it."

"You don't remember anything about your life?"

"No. Sorry. It's very frustrating."

"Yet you seem to know the most intimate details of my life."

Their eyes met, and Ally's smile caused Whitman's heart to stop. She was so beautiful, and thoughts decidedly un-Custodian-like bubbled up in his head. He went, "Ummm ... " and then, "Errrr ... " and then, "Uhhh ... "

Ally said, "Maybe you're dead, like something out of the movies."

Whitman, in thrall of Ally's unique beauty, had been on the verge of swallowing his tongue. The 'maybe you're dead' statement, spoken in jest, nearly made it happen. He choked on a breath, and proceeded to have a coughing jag.

When it went on for more than three seconds, Ally got up, hurried around the table, and clapped him on the back a couple times. The jag subsided, and Whitman found his breath. His face was red from exertion, his eyes watering, his throat raw and hot. All that disappeared though when the cognizant part of his brain realized that Ally was no longer slapping him on the back but gently rubbing his back, right between the shoulder blades, her hand going round and round in small, concentric circles.

The cognizant part of his brain evanesced into the soft, milky soup of delirium, and Whitman found that he rather enjoyed having his back rubbed by a beautiful woman. Then, by no fault of his own, while he was otherwise distracted, his brain rerouted a rush of blood to his groin area, and once more Jeremiah Whitman felt the stirrings of manhood.

"I'm okay, I'm okay," he called out, jerking away from Ally's kind touch, not because he wanted to, but because he felt he had to. "Sorry," he said, his red face now having more to do with embarrassment. "Don't know what that was."

"It's okay," Ally told him, taking no offense. "You just had surgery."

"I guess," he said, and reached for his coffee. He took a sip, and then another, and Ally returned to her seat. "I think I'm better now," he said, though there remained a little scratch to his voice. "Thank you."

"Good. Are you ready for dessert?" she asked him.

That got his attention. "Dessert? I get dessert, too?"

"Apple pie," Ally said. "I had one in the freezer. It'll be ready in ... " she paused to check the clock on the wall "... a couple minutes."

"Apple pie," Whitman said dreamily. "Sounds delicious."

It was then that the timer went off, and Ally said, "My bad. I guess it's ready now." She got up, and Whitman, unable to stop himself, followed her into the kitchen. He stood back and watched with wanton eyes as she slipped on oven mitts and carefully pulled out the fresh baked pie. The smell filled the kitchen, and Whitman felt himself swoon.

"We should give it five minutes or so to cool down," Ally said, and then she went to the trash, retrieved the box, flipped it over, and scanned the instructions. "Yes," she said. "Allow to cool for five minutes before cutting."

Whitman huffed disappointedly.

"How about some more coffee while we wait?" she offered.

"Sure," he said. "I'll get my cup."

A rather loud knock at the door interrupted them, and Ally remembered that Vaughn had yet to stop by and check on her. She looked at Whitman, in Vaughn's clothes, and determined his presence would not go over well.

"Your door," Whitman told her. "Someone's here."

"That's going to be my ex," said Ally. "Shit!"

"The drug dealer?" said Whitman, unable to stop himself.

Ally looked at him. "I swear I don't know how you know the things you know."

Whitman offered up a guilty shrug and made no further comment.

"You're going to have to hide," Ally told him.

"What?"

"Hide." She grabbed his hand and led him out of the kitchen with a fair amount of speed. "I'm coming," she called out, just as another set of knocks sounded in the apartment. Then, to Whitman, in the frantic, quiet tones of someone doing something they didn't want to get caught doing, "Come on. Hurry up."

"Why do I have to hide?" he said in his normal voice as Ally led him to the spare bedroom. "I don't understand."

"Because my ex can get a little crazy. And jealous." She opened the door, shoved Whitman inside. She put a finger to her lips and went, "Shhh. Just stay in here. I'll get rid of him as fast as I can." Then, before he could protest, she closed the door on him.

"Hey, baby girl, it's me. You all right in there?" Vaughn's voice was big and booming, and it blew through the apartment.

"I'm fine," Ally called back. "Hold on." She stopped at the hallway mirror to check her face; she looked a bit frazzled, but not bad. "Hold on," she called out again.

After running a hand through her hair, she unlatched the dead bolt, turned the lock, and opened the door. "Hey," she said, giving a friendly smile.

Vaughn eyed her with suspicion. "What took you so long?"

That's when she remembered the pie. "I was taking a pie out of the oven," she told him, holding strong at the door, not granting him access.

Vaughn looked over her, into the apartment. "A pie?" he said, his suspicion growing. "Since when you bake pies?"

"I had one in the freezer. It was getting close to its expiration date."

Vaughn's gaze narrowed. "You all right?" he said.

Ally nodded, her head going up and down in a quick, jerking motion. "Sure."

"You don't seem all right."

"I'm fine. Why? What's up?"

Vaughn hadn't been invited inside yet, but that never stopped him; he took a step, expecting Ally to move away and let him in. When she didn't, he took offense. "Girl, what's wrong with you?" he said to her. "You're acting crazy. You gonna let me in or what?"

"No," said Ally. "What do you want?"

"I want to talk to you, that's what I want. I told you I was coming by."

"You said you'd call first."

"So what. That don't mean nothing." He looked over her again, into the apartment. Then, thinking about what the cops had said about the guy who'd escaped the hospital, he leaned close to her and whispered. "Are you okay?"

Ally's brow bunched up. "Yeah. Why?" she said.

"Then why won't you let me in?"

"Because I ... "

That was as far as she got before Vaughn pushed open the door and bulled his way inside.

"Hey," she cried out as he stalked into the apartment, his head going this way and that way . "What are you doing?"

When Vaughn didn't see anyone, he turned to Ally and said, "Police stopped by the club tonight, said that guy from the shooting had escaped. They said he was dangerous, and that he might try to contact you."

"No one's here but me," said Ally.

Vaughn looked at her. "I came here to make sure you were all right."

"I'm fine. I was baking a pie."

Vaughn glanced around again, and he noticed, quite astutely, two place settings on the table: two coffee mugs, two dinner plates, two salad bowls, two sets of silverware. Ally picked up on this and immediately tried to get him to leave.

"Look, Vaughn," she said to him. "I'm fine. Really. I'm just in no mood for a visit, okay? I want to relax and have a quiet evening in."

He turned on her, anger swelling up inside him. "I'll bet," he said in his deep bass voice. "Who with is what I want to know."

"No one," said Ally, unconvincingly.

"I ain't stupid girl." He went over to the table. "Two plates. Two sets of silverware. Who'd you have dinner with?"

"Sheryl," Ally tried. "She just left."

"Bullshit!" Vaughn stalked into the kitchen like a bull. "Whoever's here better be ready to get an ass whoopin'!" he shouted, his voice echoing in the tiny apartment.

Whitman heard the threat and decided that now might be a good time to take a tour of the closet. He was not a violent man by nature, nor was he all that confident in his ability to move in the body he now occupied. That in mind, he quietly slid open the closet door, ducked inside, and quietly slid it shut.

Just in the nick of time, too. A moment later he heard the

bedroom door open and Vaughn barrel inside.

"I don't know who the fuck you are, but when I find you I'm going to beat you senseless!" Vaughn bellowed, while Ally followed after him, yipping at his heels, telling him that he was being ridiculous and that she wanted him to leave!

Then they were gone, and Whitman relaxed.

He listened as Vaughn tore through the rest of the house, shouting and cursing and threatening violence, with Ally yelling after him, demanding that he leave. His footsteps shook the floor. Doors were opened and slammed shut.

In the safety of the closet, Whitman offered up a silent plea. "Edmund," he said. "Where are you? I could really use your help right about now. There's a madman here, and I think he's going to kill me."

He got no response.

"Edmund!" he said again, quietly but intensely.

Again he received no response.

"Alina?" he tried. Then, when that didn't work, "Anyone?"

He was alone, it seemed, there was a maniac in the house looking to indulge violence, and caught in the middle was a young pregnant woman whom Whitman had grown quite fond of in the short amount of time he'd known her.

That's when he heard her shriek, loudly, and there was something in that desperate squelch of hers that sounded very much like fear. Suddenly Whitman felt compelled to act, and he burst out of the closet, and then out of the spare bedroom, his gangly, foreign body carried by a surge of courage and determination.

Ally was saying things like, "Stop!" and "I want you to leave!" when Whitman barreled into the living room like a linebacker and shouted, "Leave her alone!"

Vaughn was so shocked that he actually flinched and backed away. Ally cried out, "Marty! What are you doing?!" She knew her ex all too well, and Marty, besides the fact that he was only a few days removed from being shot and having heart surgery, didn't seem the type to throw his fists.

Ally jumped in front of him to protect him. Vaughn, meanwhile, had recovered from the initial shock of Whitman's entrance, and he dug in his heels, tightened his fists, and put a scowl on his face.

"Who the fuck is this?!" he woofed. His eyes narrowed to a point on the tall, gawky twenty-something with pale skin and moppish hair who was wearing his clothes and having dinner with his girl.

"Don't! Vaughn!" Ally cried out, using her svelte frame as a shield. "This is the guy that saved my life."

Vaughn, who was half a step from flinging Ally out of the way and beating the crap out of Whitman, stopped. "What?" he said, seeming confused by Ally's admission.

"He's the guy that saved my life?" she said again.

"And you shouldn't be yelling at a woman like that!" Whitman scolded Vaughn from behind the safety of Ally's protection. "What's wrong with you?! Didn't your mother teach you any better than that?!"

Vaughn's expression went as flat as a penny. He went, "Uhhh," mostly because he had no idea what to say. People usually didn't talk to him like that, and they certainly never mentioned his mother. Such impertinence was grounds for an ass-kicking.

He recovered quickly, though, and stabbed a threatening finger in Whitman's face. "I'll talk to her anyway I want to," he said, his voice shaking with anger. "And if you ever mention my mother again, I'll fucking kill you!"

"Vaughn!" Ally shouted, and swatted at his hand.

He grabbed her wrist, squeezed, and twisted. Ally yelped, more in surprise than pain, and Whitman saw red.


The fight lasted one punch. It took Vaughn longer to fall than it took him to lose consciousness. He was out cold before his limp body bounced off the side of the loveseat and crashed to the floor like a fallen redwood.

Ally was stunned.

Her emotions were split between concern for Vaughn, who'd gone out like a light, and shock at the idea that the skinny, amiable guy she knew as Marty, who only a couple days ago had been in a coma after emergency heart surgery, was the one who'd laid him out.

"How'd you do that?" she asked him as she cradled Vaughn's unconscious head in her lap and lightly stroked his cheek.

Whitman, who was even more surprised than Ally by his outburst of strength, didn't have a good answer. He looked at his fist, which didn't hurt at all, and shrugged. "I don't know," he said, amazed. "I just ... reacted. Sorry."

Ally wasn't happy about what Marty had done, but she wasn't a fool either. Given the chance, Vaughn would have done the same, and to say that he'd got what he deserved was an understatement.

"It's all right," she said as she continued to stroke Vaughn's cheek. "I was just surprised."

Me too, thought Whitman, who hadn't acted out violence in a quarter of a millennium, not since he was a young man with little sense and nothing to lose. Guilt wormed its way into his conscience and he began to feel bad about what he'd done.

"Is he all right?" he asked.

Ally tapped Vaughn's cheek and softly called out his name, and his eyes blinked opened. Then they closed. They opened again a couple seconds later, and gazed up at the beautiful face of Alison Armenti. There was no focus in his gaze, and his eyes looked as though they were made of glass. His jaw had already begun to swell.

"What ... " he began, and then he groaned.

"Are you all right?" Ally said to him with genuine concern. She looked over her shoulder at Whitman. "Get him some ice."

He nodded, rushed off to the kitchen. He returned a moment later with a tray of ice and a dishcloth. "Here," he said, handing them to Ally. Then he helped her get Vaughn seated upright against the loveseat.

"What happened?" Vaughn managed to ask after a few minutes. He kept looking at Whitman as if he knew him but couldn't remember from where. "Who's he?"

"That's Marty," Ally said. She chose not to answer his first question about what had happened, and in his clouded state of mind Vaughn didn't think to re-ask it. He didn't think to say anything at all for about two minutes; he just sat there, half slouched over, his entire world a scary blur of weird colors and constantly changing shapes. And Ally sat there with him, holding a makeshift ice pack to his jaw.

"Can I do anything?" Whitman asked. He felt guilty and out of place, and he wanted to be somewhere else.

"I think we're okay," Ally told him.

That's when Whitman caught a glimpse of a faded Edmund standing near the bathroom, frantically waving him over. Whitman gladly took the opportunity to excuse himself, and when he closed the bathroom door behind him, Edmund appeared in gossamer shades.

"Edmund?" Whitman said to him, straining his eyes to better see him.

"Sir, I have distressing news."

Whitman didn't like the sound of that. "What is it?" he asked.

"Things have taken a turn, sir. The Elders know, and everyone's looking for you."

"I know that already. Alina told me as much."

"Did she tell you that the Elders are cutting you off?"

"Cutting me off from what?" Whitman said. "I'm already cut off. I'm here." He flung his hands in gesture to his body. "In this."

"They're officially stranding you until you turn yourself in to the police."

That piece of news changed the entire complexion of Whitman's face. "They're stranding me?" he said in sullen tones.

Edmund nodded timidly. "Afraid so. Being cut off means we won't be able to contact you anymore. It's already started. Alina's been here numerous times tonight and she said you were unable see her or feel her presence."

"No," Whitman said, suddenly worried. "When was she here?"

"Off and on throughout dinner," replied Edmund. "She said you really laid out that guy in the living room. One punch, eh? Technically I can't condone violence, sir. You know that. But well done, you. If anyone deserved it."

"What am I supposed to do?" Whitman asked as the wavering visage of Edmund Van Roy faded a little more. He waved a hand through his friend's ghostlike form and said, "Edmund?"

"Sir!" Edmund squelched. "Kindly refrain. That felt really odd."

"Sorry."

Edmund shivered, and made an odd croaking sound.

"Sorry," Whitman said again. Then he said, "What about Emilia? Can I see Emilia?"

"Afraid not, sir. I'm having a hard time communicating with you myself and I'm your Custodian. From my understanding, your liminal abilities will begin to slowly diminish. Pretty soon you'll be purely human and entirely on your own."

"Unless I turn myself in?"

"That's the gist of it, yes."

"Sans Custodial assistance?"

"Precisely."

"And what happens then?" Whitman asked. "Do I get to go back? Are they going to make things right? Or are they going to leave me here to rot in an asylum?"

Edmund shrugged guiltily. Then he cleared his throat and said, "Don't know, sir. They don't tell me much."

"They're going to leave me here," Whitman said, certain of it. "Perhaps not forever, perhaps for only a few weeks or so, but I can guarantee you they're going to make an example of me. Again."

"Emilia believes that to be true, sir," replied Edmund. "Though she predicted a longer sentence. Six months, I believe." Then, after Whitman glared at him, he added, "Terribly unfair if you ask me."

"So what do I do? I can't stay here, can I?"

Edmund had discussed the situation with Emilia and Alina before making his visit, and they all were of the opinion that Whitman should turn himself over to the cops. There were bigger forces at play here, and the Elders were threatening to leave him in Marty Loomis's body until he surrendered. They all had agreed that conceding was the wisest, most logical course of action, only Edmund wasn't sure he wanted to voice that opinion. It was one thing to cast a vote, another to break the news.

"Edmund?" Whitman said to him desperately. "Any ideas?"

The shy British Custodian need not say a word; the answer was written all over his face, making him look a mess. "Sir?" he said.

"You think I should turn myself in? You think it's not worth it?"

Edmund nodded guiltily, and looked away.

"What about Emilia and Alina? What do they say?"

"They concur." Then, because he felt he needed to expound, "Grudgingly, of course."

Whitman's head sagged, and a soft moan seeped out of him. "Why?" he said.

It was a query meant for God, not Edmund, though it was Edmund, not God, who answered it. "Ineffability," he said. "I suppose." Then he scratched his head in puzzlement and added, "I wish I understood that more."

"As do I," replied Whitman. "As do I."

"They have all the power, sir. You're at their mercy."

"And what about Ally?"

"What about her?"

"What am I supposed to do about her?"

Edmund thought about this deeply, calling on his vast experience with women. Finally, he said, "Just be yourself, sir."

Whitman nodded as if this was good advice when in truth it had badly missed the center of the question. Not to mention, Whitman wasn't even sure who he was anymore, and his self-doubt went much deeper than the reflection staring back at him in the mirror. Not only was he flagrantly disobeying direct orders from the Elders, but he was swearing and raising his voice, and he was having really impure thoughts about Ally, and he had hit a man with the intention of ... well, he really wasn't sure what his intention had been, he had just attacked, like a wild dog.

"Sir? You still with me?" Edmund said. "Sir?!"

Whitman looked at him and saw that he was barely there; wisps of faded color and a broomstick figure were all that remained of Edmund. Even the plaintive slant of the prim Brit's intonation was dying.

"Edmund?" he said.

"Sir," Edmund called back in a frantic voice. "Remember, we're going ... "

It was then that what left of Edmund Van Roy disappeared for good, and Whitman found himself alone in

Ally's bathroom, in Hagerstown, Maryland, in a strange world that, though he had lived it in for seventy years and had been observing it for more than two hundred, he had very little understanding of.

They had pie, and coffee, and Ally and Whitman labored to explain to a foggy-headed Vaughn that the man the authorities knew as Martin Loomis wasn't a threat to anyone, least of all Ally. Throughout, Vaughn nodded a lot, and went, "Mmhmm," and "I get it," whenever a verbal response was called for.

By the time his head cleared, it was near morning, and while Ally slept, Whitman kept Vaughn company on the couch; they didn't want Vaughn driving in his impaired state, and Whitman wasn't about to leave him alone with Ally, especially after Vaughn had displayed such a violent temper.

The two men sat together on the couch like a couple of convicts in a holding cell: they didn't look much at each other, and they spoke only sparingly, and without friendliness. Whitman wanted to connect with Vaughn, but it had been a long time since he'd had an honest talk with someone, and he had never met anyone quite like Vaughn before. He felt like he needed an opening, and when Vaughn pulled out a pack of cigarettes, Whitman decided to take a chance.

"May I bum one of them?" he asked. The colloquialism sounded unnatural to him, but he wanted to be authentic.

Vaughn shot him a look.

"I have one now and again," Whitman added.

Vaughn lit his cigarette, and then handed the pack to Whitman. "Here," he said.

Whitman took one, lit up, and shortly after drawing his first hit in more than two hundred years he began to cough and hack.

"Whoa," said Vaughn. "Easy now."

By the time Whitman regained his composure, his eyes were watering and his face was red. He struggled through a couple deep breaths as the cigarette burned between his fingers. "Been a while," he managed in a hoarse voice.

"I see that," said Vaughn. Then he said, "So, you and Ally?

Anything there?"

The words were easy enough to understand, but Whitman tended to get lost in the slang of modern language. Contextually speaking it could be quite ambiguous, and Vaughn's question flummoxed him. Figuring it might not be a good idea to answer until he knew exactly what was meant, he asked, "How so?"

Vaughn cracked a sardonic smile. "You know what I mean," he said. "She's a pretty girl, and you're a guy."

Whitman's face went blank as his mind scrambled to come up with an acceptable response to those two obvious facts. He went, "Ummmm ... "

"I'm asking if you two are together," Vaughn went on, his words coming with a bite now. "I mean, here you are, in her apartment. Just had dinner. You're wearing my clothes. I know you know what I'm getting at."

Whitman believed he understood. "You mean ... *sexually?*" he said.

"Yes," Vaughn sneered back at him. "Sexually."

Whitman shook his head. "No," he said, and technically that wasn't a lie. He made no mention about how much he wanted to be with Ally, though, believing such a sensitive subject could further strain the already strained relationship he had with Vaughn. "She's helping me out," he explained. "I need a place to stay for a while."

"You escaped the hospital?"

"They were going to have me committed?"

"Why?"

"Because I can't remember who I am and they think that's suspicious."

"You don't know who you are?"

"They say I'm Martin Loomis, but I don't remember."

"The police talked to me today. They say you were dangerous." Vaughn unhinged his jaw, and the pain caused him wince. He could attest to that personally; the entire left side of his face was pounding, even after six ibuprofen tabs.

"I'm not dangerous," Whitman said to him. "I'm not. I'm just ... confused. And they were going to send me to the loony bin and attach electrodes to my brain and make me take all kinds of pills. I didn't want to do that."

"Don't blame you," said Vaughn. "But what you gonna do now? Police are looking for you. Can't stay here forever."

Whitman shrugged in a way that suggested he had no idea. He never thought this crazy situation would last as long as it had, and he was hoping, despite everything, that it would end soon. He knew what the first step was, but he wasn't sure he wanted to take it, not just yet, anyway. He was even less sure that that's what he was supposed to do. If the Elders had really wanted him back, he believed that they would have brought him back by now. Or perhaps there was no way to bring him back.

Whitman did not want to consider that possibility, not even for a moment. He had started to think that all of this had happened for a reason, but what that reason was and how it involved him remained a mystery. And apparently he would have to figure it out on his own, without the help of his friends.

"To be honest, I don't really have a plan," he said. He took a small hit, inhaled it deep in his lungs, and let it out. He felt like he might cough again, but the feeling passed and he continued. "I hope my memory comes back. Soon. I just want all this to be over with."

Vaughn nodded, took one last hit, and stamped his cigarette out in the ashtray. "So," he said, "you were there that night? What do you remember?"

Whitman looked at him. "You mean about the robbery?"

"Yeah. You remember anything about it?"

"Not really." Whitman drew in another hit. It had been a while since he'd had tobacco, and this stuff smelled and tasted drastically different than what he used to smoke; it was stronger, and harsher, and possessed a distinct chemical bite. Other than that, Whitman found himself enjoying an old habit. "I remember waking up at the hospital," he said. "All my memories start there."

"So you don't remember the guy who shot you?"

"No."

"What about Ally?"

"What about her?"

"You remember her from that night?"

"No. All I remember is that she came to see me at the

hospital and she brought me a cheeseburger. It was delicious."

"You don't remember her before that?"

Whitman shook his head. "Nope."

Neither one of them said anything for a while, but then, feeling as if he needed to make note of it, just in case Vaughn really was that stupid, Whitman said, "You know, she really is a great girl. Ally, I mean."

Vaughn grunted, and said that he agreed.

Then Whitman said, "So why do you treat her so badly?"

It was a question that would've gotten just about anyone else smacked upside the head. But Vaughn wasn't quite himself, and after what had happened he was a little leery of Whitman, not that he ever would admit that, not under the threat of death or even castration. And so his outrage was less rage and more offense.

"I don't!" he woofed. Then, with considerably less emphasis, "Not always. And she's no angel, okay? You might think that now, seeing how she's helping you out and all, but you don't know her yet. Not like I do. She ain't perfect. She's got her faults, too, and she likes to press my buttons."

"No one's perfect," replied Whitman. "But she deserves to be treated better."

Vaughn growled under his breath as his animal hindbrain thought about jumping this know-it-all neb-nose and seeing whether or not that punch had been lucky. He didn't, mostly because something told him that luck had had nothing to do with it; and even if it had, he reasoned, there had been nothing lucky about the force of the blow. His jaw was busted and swollen, and it felt like the whole left side of his face was on fire.

Still, he wasn't about to sit there and be talked down to. "Listen," he said, his voice coming out thick and coarse due to the pain and swelling in his jaw, "I don't need this shit from you. You don't know me, so don't act like it. Hell, you don't even know yourself."

"I didn't mean to upset you," said Whitman. "I was just trying to be honest."

"No. You were being a smart ass, because you think you can. And you only know one side of things, so nothing you say matters."

"Then tell me your side."

Whitman made the offer with sincerity, but Vaughn wasn't the type to open up or share his feelings. He preferred blunt refusals, threats, and fisticuffs. "Fuck you!" he spit back. "I don't know you, and I don't want to neither." He stood up, grabbed his coat from the back of the sofa. "I'm outta here."

As Vaughn made his way to the door, Whitman jumped up and went after him. "You're not going to tell anyone I'm here, are you?" he said.

A light bulb went on over Vaughn's head and he stopped. Going to the police was usually the last thing on his mind, but that didn't mean he wouldn't do it if he had to, especially if it benefited him. He didn't like Whitman, and he certainly didn't like the way that Ally looked at him. And, truth be told, it was never a bad idea to curry favor with the fuzz. Holt had taught him that.

"I mean her no harm," Whitman went on, desperate. "I just need some time. Please."

"I'm not making any promises," Vaughn said as he opened the door. He looked back over his shoulder at the moppish young man who'd knocked him out cold with one clean shot and gave him a cowboy sneer. "I got my own investigation going on," he said. "I find out anything I don't like about you, and the police will be the least of your worries." And then, because he understood how to make a point, he walked out the door and slammed it shut behind him.

Whitman stood there for a long time, worrying that Vaughn would call the cops and rat him out. He feared that within an hour a SWAT team would come busting through the door, like on Miami Vice or any of those other fascinating police shows that were all over television, and he'd be cuffed and carted off to the bin, where faceless men and women in white coats and bifocals would go about tinkering with his brain. He couldn't understand what was going on in his own head so he doubted how anyone else could. He remembered who he was, but he had started to remember other things, too, vague and mysterious things, things that had never happened to him. He kept seeing flashes of a woman's face, a pretty woman he had never seen before, yet somehow he knew her. He wondered if maybe she was the heartless lover who had driven Martin Loomis to suicide.

He checked the clock, saw that it was almost four in the morning. He hadn't gotten any sleep last night, and the effect of that was noticeable. He kept yawning, and it felt like some invisible force had made it its sole mission to pull his eyelids shut. He was worried about the cops stopping by, but something told him that Vaughn wasn't the type to involve the authorities, not unless it was absolutely necessary. So instead he decided to relax and get some much needed rest. All it took was him lying down on the couch, lying his head on a pillow, and shutting his eyes. Nature took care of the rest.

# Chapter Eleven

It took them long enough, but the police finally got a warrant to search the home of Martin Loomis. Rainer and Milner led the charge, and were forced to call in a forensic team after finding the bloody remnants of Martin Loomis's last act on earth splattered on the walls and caked on the carpet. They found a bullet wedged in the concrete block wall, and Milner asked the comely young forensic scientist collecting samples if there was any way that the person who'd been shot could have survived.

She gave him a look that told him that while that was not the stupidest question she'd ever heard, he really should have known better than to ask it. Then, not that she needed to, she answered him. "No. Not a chance."

"Large caliber," Milner noted.

She agreed. "My guess is a .45."

"He was sitting down?"

The young woman nodded while picking a jagged piece of skin off the wall with a pair of forceps. She carefully placed it in a clear plastic bag marked with an evidence tag, and then looked over her shoulder at the two cops. "That's what the angle of the bullet suggests."

"They shot him while he was sitting down?" said Rainer.

"No," said the forensic woman. "My guess is that it was suicide."

Milner and Rainer spoke at the same time, with near equal amount of skepticism and surprise: "Suicide?"

"That's what it looks like to me, and I've done enough of them to know. Did one like this a few weeks ago."

"If it's a suicide," said Milner, "where's the body? Not many suicides get up and walk away, from my experience."

"Might have a zombie on our hands," Rainer joked.

Milner didn't laugh.

The forensic girl said, "The gun was placed against the chest at a slight upward angle, at close range. Like this." She simulated the scene, holding a phantom gun out in front of her with both hands and using her thumbs to mimic pulling the trigger. "That's what the splatter pattern indicates, anyway."

Milner and Rainer were not convinced.

"And there's the note, of course," she went on.

The note. One cryptic line scratched out in an uneven hand. *Nothing left but this.* Hardly a definitive piece of evidence, especially since there was no body to go with it.

"That could have been forged," said Milner. "It's not even signed."

"But who moved the body? And why didn't anyone report it?" Rainer posited.

The young forensic woman knocked on the concrete block wall with a blue-gloved hand. "These suckers are pretty thick. As for who moved the body and why, sorry, I can't help you there. I do blood and gore."

"Could it have been a forced suicide?" Rainer wondered. He picked up one of the empty bottles of wine setting on the nightstand. "You know, someone got him hammered and forced him to do it? Then wrote a stupid note."

"Okay. But why move the body? If you're trying to make it look like a suicide, you wouldn't move the body. That'd be the last thing you'd want to do."

"Plus there're no signs that the body was moved," said the forensic tech. "There's no blood anywhere else but in the kill zone."

"They could have used a tarp," Rainer put it.

The forensic tech shook her head. "Not likely."

Milner looked around, taking in the mess. There were clothes, beer cans, wine bottles, and pill containers all over the place. And lingering beneath the very real stench of death was an odor of desperation and despair.

Rainer said, "This doesn't make any sense."

Milner nodded, and cleared his throat. "Not yet," he said. "But dammit, I knew he was hiding something."

"Who? Loomis?"

"Yep."

"You think maybe he had a partner?"

"Perhaps. But if it's a suicide."

Rainer scratched his head and went, "Hmm."

Low on facts, Milner decided to favor a bit of conjecture. "Stay with me here," he said. "What if Loomis and whoever this guy was were in cahoots? Maybe they were robbing the store together. Then this guy, for whatever reason, gets nervous and points the gun at the girl. That's not part of the plan, though, and Loomis reacts automatically, jumping in front of her just in time. So the one friend shoots the other friend and then runs off. And later, racked with guilt, this guy takes his own life."

Rainer took all that in and gave it some thought. Then he said, "But who moved the body? Couldn't have been Loomis."

"He could have slipped in."

"How? He was in the hospital."

Milner conceded with a nod. "Yeah," he said. "You're right." Then he said, "Maybe there was a third guy."

"A third?" Rainer was skeptical.

"Bates?" Milner posited.

"Charlie Bates? The kid who lives with his parents?"

Milner thought about it, thought about sweet, naïve Charlie Bates, and agreed with his partner. "Yeah, you're right. I can't see him being involved."

"And if Marty Loomis was robbing the store with the gunman, why wasn't he wearing a mask, too?"

Milner had a theory for that. "Simple," he said. "Loomis was a plant. He goes in, pretends to be a customer, and later, when he's questioned, he throws out misinformation. Happens all the time."

Rainer shrugged. "I suppose that's a possibility. But we're back to who moved the body and why."

"Had to be Loomis. He escaped, what? Thirty, thirty-two hours ago? That's plenty of time to come here, find the body, and get rid of it."

"Without us seeing?"

"We didn't have the place under surveillance."

"No. But patrols have been going by."

"He could've snuck in."

"But where'd he take the body? And how? That's his car out front. Looks like it hasn't moved in days. Not to mention, he just had heart surgery. He can't be lugging a two-hundred pound body around."

"Bates," Milner said. "Gotta be Bates."

Rainer shook his head. "Can't see it. That kid's a daisy."

"What about Loomis's connection to Vaughn and Ally?"

"What about it?"

"Maybe there's more to it than they're letting on."

That idea piqued Rainer's interest. "Perhaps," he said in the tones of someone thinking things through. "Vaughn's a dealer, everyone knows that, and if Loomis got in deep with drugs there's a chance they crossed paths. But how's the robbery slot in?"

Milner's brow creased as he attempted to work up an answer. Finally, after a handful of seconds, he said, "Don't know. Maybe it's nothing more than a coincidence."

"So we're back at square one?"

Milner sighed heavily. His shoulders slouched and his head lolled back. "Dammit!" he said. Then, after a brief pause, he said it again. "Dammit!"

Rainer was baffled and frustrated, too. Not many cases like this came through Hagerstown, and the Chief and the Mayor were on them to solve it quickly. They had a robbery, an attempted murder, and an apparent suicide all wrapped up in one confounding mystery that seemed to center on a young man named Martin Loomis. Only Martin Loomis had escaped custody and presently was on the lam.

Milner returned to the crux. "We have to find Loomis," he said. "He's the key. We find him, we get our answers."

"I agree," said Rainer. "Where do you want to start?"

"Where we've already been. We go back and see Bates, and Holt, and Ally."

"Won't mind seeing her again," said Rainer, a lewd grin crinkling his lips.

Below them, the forensic woman let out an audible groan.

"Aren't you done yet," Milner said to her.

"Just about," she told him.

"When do you think you'll have the results?"

She stopped, swiveled her head in his direction, and gave him a look. "Any minute now," she said. "Just like on CSI."

Both Milner and Rainer grunted disdainfully. They didn't particularly like forensic techs, and they certainly didn't like being on the receiving end of sarcasm.

"Just call us when they're in," Rainer said. "And leave the attitude at home."

"Yes, sir," said the forensic woman, and went back to picking bone and flesh off the wall.

Milner tapped his partner and said, "Come on, Rain, let's go get some breakfast. I suddenly got a hanker on for pancakes."

The forensic woman looked up at them and frowned.

They woke up around nine and had breakfast together, making small talk about the prior night as they enjoyed coffee and scrambled eggs with ham and cheese. Ally was still shocked that the rather skinny, non-threatening man she knew as Martin Loomis had laid out her badass ex with one clean shot, and she told him that perhaps he had missed his calling as a bouncer, or a boxer, or a CIA agent.

"Lucky punch, I guess," Whitman told her as they reconvened in the living room, sitting next to each other on the couch. He knew it was wrong, but he couldn't help but swell with pride. He had dropped Vaughn like an old sack of potatoes, and, despite his aversion to violence, it felt good and right when he thought about it.

"So, any plans today?" Ally asked him. "I have to work at noon. I'm pulling the lunch shift, which I don't really care for."

Whitman gave her a look. "At the club?"

He hadn't meant to be judgmental, but that's how it sounded.

"Yes," she said. "That is where I work. Why?"

"No reason. It's just that ... well ... "

"What?" Ally said. She didn't snap at him, but her voice was short and sharp. "Go on. Say it. You don't approve."

It was one thing to be a Custodian, to hide in the shadows of the spirit world and subtly nudge a person's reasoning this way or that way, not directly influencing them to make a specific decision, merely bringing to their attention the right one to make. The choice was theirs; it was always theirs, always had been theirs, from the moment that Eve ate the apple. All you could do was get them to think about it.

This was different, though. He was sitting in front of Ally; she could see him and talk to him, tell him to mind his own.

Regardless, he felt he needed to try.

"It's just that ... " he began, and then he didn't say anything else. He just sat there, dumbfounded, his face looking like a bad Halloween mask.

"Well?" Ally said at him. "It's just what? Let me guess – you don't approve of me working at the club. A bit hypocritical seeing that you went there, don'tcha think?"

Whitman was about to bluster at the accusation, but caught himself. No, he had never been to the strip club before, but the man whose body now belonged to him had been, which was, in the history of the world, the most solid case of guilt by association ever.

He quickly cast off the sanctimonious line he had planned to go with, a line that included the phrase, 'den of sin', and instead said, "I just think you could do so much better than that place." Then he struck another note. "In addition, I know it can't be the safest place for a young woman to work, especially considering your ... *special condition.*"

"My special condition?"

"You're ... " He hesitated, and his eyes drifted to her flat midsection. "You know," he went on. "You're ... You're *pregnant.*" He whispered that last word as if it was a secret that could not be allowed get out.

"That? I haven't decided what I'm going to do about that yet," Ally replied, and then she guiltily looked away.

Whitman's mouth gaped. "You don't mean ... " he said. He left it at that, unable or just plain unwilling to utter that sacrilegious word.

Ally picked up the thread. "Yes," she said. "I'm thinking about having an abortion. Tell me you don't approve of that, either."

"Noooooo!" Whitman cried out. "Not that. Please, anything but that."

Ally was startled by the volume and anguish in his voice, and it took her a moment to respond. When she did, she went with the ever popular, "It's my body, my decision."

"Your *decision* was to have sex," Whitman shot back at her. "That was your decision. And the result of that decision was a life."

"It's not that simple. I took precautions. I used birth control. It wasn't my fault."

"It's no one's *fault.* Things happen. But make no mistake, that's a life inside you."

It was very early in her pregnancy and Ally had done enough research to know that the fetus inside her was no bigger than a walnut; it didn't have a face, or bone structure, or even a central nervous system. It did have a heartbeat, however.

Ally put that thought out of her mind, not wanting to deal with it. It wasn't a baby inside her, she told herself. It was a ... It was a ...

She couldn't put a finger on the word she wanted to use. The one that popped in her head first was 'thing,' and that made her feel horrible. But that was it, wasn't it? That was how people got through it. It wasn't a baby; it didn't have a cute baby face, or little baby toes, or chubby baby cheeks. It was just this tiny 'thing,' this unformed blob that you wouldn't even know was there without the help of modern medicine.

An abortion was a safe and legal alternative for a consequence that Ally had taken precautions to avoid. It was hardly her fault, so why should she be burdened. Perhaps if Vaughn was a better man, she reasoned, things would be different. But he wasn't a good man, and he wasn't a good boyfriend, and as poor as he was at those two roles, from what Ally could tell he was even worse as a father.

It would be on her plate, and she wasn't ready.

Despite all that, the thought of having an abortion made her sick to her stomach. It might not be a baby right now, but the natural progression of life would undoubtedly bring it to that point. If you would have asked her a month ago if she was pro-life or pro-choice she would have said, emphatically and without hesitation, that she was pro-choice, that a woman had a right to choose what she did with her body. But now here she was with a choice to make; she knew what she wanted to do, and she knew what the logical thing to do was, she just couldn't seem to convince herself that it was the best decision.

Short term? Yes. But life, she reasoned, was a long journey, and what might be best one day may not be best for all the ones lined up behind it.

"I really don't know what I'm doing yet," she said, and there was a moan behind her words, a quiet, woeful moan that hinted at the great struggle she felt. "I'm still considering my options."

Whitman had his opening, but emotion, something he hadn't had to deal with in a couple centuries, seeped in and clouded his judgment. He wanted to tell her that abortion was wrong, that it was murder, that every life, from conception to death, was sacred. But seeing firsthand the doubt and misery she was suffering, those words fell away in favor of more sympathetic ones.

"I believe abortion is wrong," he said to her, "and I would advise against it. I know how hard it would be for you, being alone, not having anyone to depend on. And your job, and your recent lifestyle, with the drugs and the drinking, it's hard to ... "

"Are you trying to make a point," Ally cut in, not at all pleased at having her faults dragged out into the open ... especially by someone who seemed to have divined them.

"I'm sorry," said Whitman. "I'm not trying to judge. Really. That can be hard, you know. Not judging. We think we know what's right, but every shoe fits different. I just want you to really think about it, that's all."

"I have been," said Ally. "For two weeks now." She sniffed, and looked away. "That's all I've been doing," she added.

Whitman nodded supportively. He could see the pain on her face, and in an odd way he could feel it, too. She felt alone, and confused, and angry with herself. He wanted to assure her that everything was going to be okay, and that he would stand by her no matter what, but he had no idea what the future held and he didn't want to make promises he couldn't keep. So instead he said, "That's life. Decisions are often weighted with emotion, and a lot of times what we want to do seems like the best choice. But we know. You ever notice that?"

Ally looked at him with her big brown eyes.

"We know," Whitman went on. "We always know. No matter how confusing, no matter what the circumstances are, we know what the right decision is. We know what we're supposed to do. We don't always want to do it, and often it's the harder choice, but we know, and in the long run it usually works out."

Those big brown eyes of Ally's moistened with tears, and she nodded, and she leaned into Whitman, putting her head on his chest and her arm around his lower back. "I know," she said, her voice a whisper. "I know I should keep it. Or give it up for adoption. I just don't know how I can do it. Not by myself. Not now."

Whitman stroked her shoulder and said that he understood, and Ally put her free hand on his chest and nuzzled against him. Suddenly the shoe was on the other foot. Whitman knew that the right thing to do was to comfort Ally, to hold her close and tell her that everything was going to be all right. But emotion had him, and she was so warm and soft, and she smelled like spring flowers in the morning.

Emotion quickly devolved into want and Whitman began to feel uncomfortable. He felt hot, and nervous, and his heart was racing like he'd just got a shock from a live wire. He tried to relax, but that, he concluded, would be like trying to towel off during a shower.

"I'm sorry," Ally said to him quietly, her voice choked up. "I hardly know you and here I am laying all my problems on you."

"It's okay," Whitman replied. "I'm here for you."

"It's just that these last couple of years have been ... " She stopped, not wanting to refer to them as a 'waste,' even though that's exactly what they had been. "I don't have anyone," she said. "Not anyone I can depend on."

Whitman could barely take it. He might not last the day, or the next two hours, so who was he to tell her, in her most vulnerable state, that she could depend on him, that he would be there for her, through thick and thin, for support and encouragement, for friendship and whatever else she might need. Or want.

Whitman hadn't been human in a long time, but he knew that a man was only as good as his word. Ally was lonely and in need of a friend, someone to ease the burden of her cross, and Whitman, overcome, wanted to be the one to fill that role.

"I'm here for you," he whispered to her, against his better

judgment, and against the faint echo of his conscience, which was telling him, in a prim and proper British voice, to stop, to quit before he said something he couldn't take back. He firmly pushed that voice out of his head and exorcised his conscience with the warm caress and wonderful scent of Ally Armenti. He squeezed her tighter. "I'll do whatever I can to help."

Technically that wasn't a lie, he told himself; he *would* do whatever he could to help. But like most decisions based off-center from the truth, this one came with consequences, immediate in nature. Ally, consoled and comforted by this incredibly kind young man, a young man who had saved her life and whose presence seemed to be fate, pulled back from their embrace and gazed up at him, her big brown eyes beckoning.

Whitman didn't know much about women, especially modern women, but he knew he was in trouble. He heard his conscience screaming at him not to do it, to put a stop to things now before they raged out of control. Then, as Ally's gaze lingered, becoming something more, becoming an intimate moment dripping with emotion, he heard his conscience, again in a posh British voice, screaming at him to run, to flee, to hide in the bathroom.

But Whitman was locked into a gravitational pull much stronger than his moral will, and as Ally tilted her head towards him, her eyes closed, her rosebud lips pursed seductively, he found it impossible to stop himself.

And for the first time since his wife died of cholera two-hundred and sixty-eight years ago, Jeremiah Whitman kissed a woman.


It started off tender and sweet, but soon escalated, becoming more passionate and aggressive in nature. Kissing led to petting, which led to groping and fondling. The more experienced of the two, Ally took charge, and with her hands she explored the most intimate parts of Whitman's body. She eventually worked one of those hands down his pants, and shortly thereafter Whitman felt a primal surge take command of him. He quickly put a stop to things then, pushing himself way from her. He wanted her more than he had ever wanted anything, but he still thought of himself as a Custodian, and as a Custodian there were lines that could not be crossed. He also didn't want to ruin Vaughn's sweatpants.

Between heavy, panting breaths, his hair wild and mussed, his face quivering with lustful exhilaration, he told Ally that it probably wouldn't be right for them to sleep together, not with everything they were going through. And Ally, though she had a strong feeling that if she pressed the issue or even did something as simple as remove her top she could get him to change his mind, agreed.

She saw the nervous look in his eyes and told him that she understood, though she was just as turned on as he was and what she really wanted to do was throw him down, climb on top of him, and make him howl at the moon.

"No. Probably not a good idea," she said, a bit disappointedly.

Whitman, his face the color of a Valentine heart, nodded in agreement. Then he sat on the couch for no less than five minutes, with his legs crossed and his hands on his lap, waiting for his uncomfortably hard erection to subside.

Ally thought he was the cutest thing she'd ever seen, and having got a feel for what he had under the hood, she resigned herself to sleeping with him sooner or later ... although the sooner the better, she believed.

"So, what do we do now?" she asked him as he marshaled all his powers of concentration into looking as though he did not have a hard-on.

He stared at her helplessly, and said nothing.

"Marty?" she said. "Are you okay?"

The question hung out there for a couple seconds before Whitman nodded awkwardly, his head bobbing out of balance. "Yes," he managed. "I think so." Then he said, "I think I need some clothes. I can't wear these."

"Do you think you can go to your apartment?"

Whitman no longer had Custodial assistance to rely on, no invisible friends to advise him, to lead him down the right paths, or to misdirect others. That meant he would have to earn his own keep, and make his own way. Then he remembered something that Edmund had told him during one of their chat sessions in the hospital, and without thinking about it he said, "I have a friend. Charlie."

Ally looked at him strangely. "You remember him?" she said.

It occurred to Whitman that he had just blown his amnesia cover and he scrambled for an explanation. "Uhhh," he said. Then he said, "Ummm." He followed that up with "Errrr," and, "Mmmmm."

"You remember anything else?" Ally asked him as he continued to blush and make strange noises. "Well?"

"Not really," he said. "I ... The ..."

His guilty eyes and stammering uncertainty drew Ally's suspicion. "Marty? Are you not telling me something?"

Where was Edmund when he really needed him, Whitman wondered. And then the pure, terrifying inanity of that idea struck him and he realized just how much trouble he was in.

"Marty?" Ally said to him, and grabbed his hand. He looked at her, and like every other time he looked at her, he forgot who he was and where he was at. "What is it?" she asked him. "You can tell me."

He hesitated, unsure of what he should say. Then, because he had to say something and he wasn't comfortable lying, he told her that he had started to remember 'little things' about his life.

"That's great," replied Ally. "That means you're getting your memory back."

"I guess. But I still don't remember much. I don't even remember where I live."

"That's okay," she told him. She then began to softly stroke his hand, and once more Whitman felt himself rousing. "This is a good thing, Marty. Little by little, that's how it works. You went through a traumatic experience."

He nodded, and squeezed her hand. "Thank you," he said.

"Maybe you should call the police and tell them that you're starting to remember things."

"No!" Whitman blurted out, surprising Ally. Then, with a little more composure, he said, "Not yet. I'm still not sure of anything."

"Okay. What about this friend of yours? Charlie. Maybe you can call him. He might be able to help you put things in order."

Whitman nodded at the suggestion, but then a lie came to him and he switched lanes. "I would," he said, "but I don't remember his last name, and I don't know how to get in touch with him. I just remember the name Charlie." Whitman put his face in his hands and moaned. "This is so frustrating," he said, his voice somewhat muffled. "I just wish everything would go back to normal."

Ally told him that everything was going to be okay, and that he shouldn't rush things, and that he could stay with her as long as he needed to.

"Thank you. You're so nice," he told her.

"Please. You saved my life, Marty. And if I decide to have this baby, you saved its life, too."

"I hope you do," he said. "I think you'd make a good mother."

She looked at him. Her hand went to his face, and she tenderly stroked his cheek and chin. Whitman felt himself getting hot and hard and dizzy again; his muscles tensed, his vision blurred at the edges.

"Ally," he said to her, his voice a soft croak.

"What?"

"We can't," he said, not meaning it.

She nodded, told him that she knew that.

Then she kissed him anyway, and he kissed her back.

In the grand scheme, the bird that crashed through the window the next moment and stopped them before they tore at each other like dogs in heat was a prime example of the ineffable hand of fate.


Otto Williams was a junkie that had no problem singing so long as the song netted him a fix of something that would help him forget his life for a spell. He was an old junkie, well into his fifties, with a ratty beard, ratty clothes, and an odor that was hard to ignore. He was a well-known townie that usually made his scratch bumming coins and cigarettes, and the people who knew him best call him Rags.

Rags had information that was worth something. Word on the street was that Holt was looking for Adam Dubinsky, and it just so happened that Rags knew where Adam liked to hang his hat when he found himself on the street. That brought him anxiously to Teasers, where he told Dado, who was working the front door, that he was in possession of information the big boss wanted.

Dado took one look at the ratty bum and said, "I ain't letting you in here, old man. You'll clear the fucking place out."

Teasers' was far from the Taj Mahal, but there was a certain element not welcome. Otto was such an element. He was dirty and broke, and he smelled like bad tuna stuffed in sweaty socks.

"I know where that Dubinsky kid is," Otto said. "And I want my reward."

"You tell me, and I'll tell Holt," Dado said.

Otto started shaking his head like it was on fire. "Oh no. Oh no. I tell *him* only. I got the info, and I want the goods."

"What goods?"

"Word is five hundred dollars. Five hundred!"

Dado eyed the twitching, rail-thin junkie with suspicion. Rags might have been a real mess, but there was an unyielding look of determination on his face, born out of greed and want. It had been a long time since he had had five hundred dollars in his pocket, and his imagination was brimming with ideas.

"Wait out here," Dado told him. "I'll see what the boss says."

Rags waited at the door, and a couple minutes later Dado returned and told him that Holt would see him. He then escorted the spindly junkie around the backside of the club, to an unmarked door that led down a flight of stairs. There was a hallway, and then another door, and then a small block room that had little more than a table and a couple of chairs in it. Dado told Rags to have a seat and wait.

About a minute later, Holt and Vaughn came into the room, and Rags snapped to attention like a first class private. "Mr. Holt," he said, doffing his dirty cap as a show of respect. "How are you, sir?"

"I'm good," said Holt. "I hear you have information for me."

Rags nodded eagerly. "Surely do. Surely do. Solid info, too, if I do say so myself."

Holt had already detected the foul odor coming off of Rags and decided it might be best to speed things along. "All right," he said. "Let's have it. I'm a busy man."

But Rags had money on his mind. "Wait," he said. "I want to talk about payment first."

"Five hundred dollars if the lead pans out," Holt said. "That's the deal."

"It'll pan out," said Rags, certain of it. "You got my word."

"Need more than your word, I'm afraid."

Rags looked crestfallen. He thought about playing hardball, about withholding the information and negotiating a better deal, but it dawned on him that while he may have had information, he wasn't necessarily in a position of power. Holt, he knew, was no one to mess with, and neither was Vaughn, whom Rags had seen break a man's jaw with one clean shot. The cold, hard truth was that they could torture him for the information, kill him where he stood, and no one would know or care.

Still, he didn't like the arrangement.

"How about half up front, the other half when it pans out," he said.

Holt smiled, and chuckled some. Vaughn's expression remained implacable.

"What?" Rags said. "It's gonna work out. I know where he stays."

"A hundred up front," said Holt, and *five* hundred more if it pans out."

Rags did the math in his head and a smile cracked his scraggly, time-beaten face. "That's six hundred?" he said, making sure.

"Correct," said Holt. "So, where is he?"

Rags thought about it, and started to nod. But he still had one last request to make. "I was wondering," he said, shyly, his hat in hand. "Well, it's just that it's been a long time since I've had any ... female company."

A smile betrayed Holt, and Vaughn started to laugh. "You gotta be kidding me?" Vaughn said. "You want one of the girls."

Self-consciousness mangled the worn-out lines on Rags' face, making him look fearful and ashamed. "It's been a while," he said, his voice barely audible. "I was just thinking, you know, you have girls here."

"I don't think any of them would consent to that, I'm afraid," said Holt.

"Not for five hundred dollars," said Vaughn, still racked with amusement.

"I could shower and shave," Rags said. "I mean, it's been a while, and I'm not getting any younger. This could be my last chance."

Holt thought the idea was a riot, but he had to respect the guy for trying. That in mind, he made him an offer. "Okay, Rags, I'll leave it up to you. Door number one: fifty dollars cash up front and a room at the Wonder Lake Motel. You clean yourself up, shave, shower, cut your nails, put on some deodorant ... and then some more. And if the tip pans out, I'll send you over a girl and two hundred dollars cash. You'll get the girl for two hours. Door number two: a hundred dollars cash up front and six hundred more if the tip pans out."

Rags put his fractured, wanton mind to work and discovered that decision-making was not an easy task. "I get more without the girl," he said, though he wasn't sure how much more, or even if that was right.

"Not really," said Holt. "Our girls aren't cheap."

Rags forced his mind back to work, and his thoughts swung toward the perverse. "What's this girl look like?" he asked.

"Cute as a button. Twenty-two years old. Brunette."

"What about her tits?"

"She's got two of them."

Rags nodded as if that was very much acceptable. Then he said, "And this girl, she's all mine for two hours?"

"Yep. Two whole hours."

Vaughn looked at his boss, wondering who it was that he was planning on punishing so vilely. "Who you thinking about?" he whispered to him.

Holt grinned and said, "Felicity owes me how much money?"

Vaughn shrugged. "A grand, maybe."

"Well, I think she should jump at the opportunity to cut into that, don't you?"

Vaughn looked at the rat junkie Rags. "I don't know about that."

Rags didn't seem to hear them; he was too busy thinking about the spoils to come. "And this girl," he said, "I can ... you know, do whatever I want with her?"

"Well," said Holt, "I wouldn't want you to tie her up and

smear dog shit on her lady parts, or beat her with a bat, or punch holes in her with a Number 2 pencil. I think I'd take exception to that. Otherwise, have your fun."

Rags, not grasping the joke, seemed confused. "Why would I ... " he started, but he stopped when he heard Vaughn laughing.

"I'm only kidding," Holt said, and Rags, finally realizing it was meant to be funny, relaxed and let out a smile. "You can have sex with her, any way you like."

"So I can get a blowjob?" Rags inquired. It had been more than eleven years since he'd had one of those, and from what he could remember, it was a wonderful, mind-blowing experience worth having again ... and again ... and again.

"Of course, my friend. Your tip pans out, you can have whatever you like. No violence, though. Can't have my girls walking around with bruises and black eyes."

"No. Of course not," said Rags.

"So, door number one then?" Holt said.

Rags thought about it and nodded tentatively. "You think you could ... well, maybe add some ... " He hesitated, afraid to ask what he wanted to ask.

"Add some what?" said Vaughn bluntly. He didn't like junkies, especially old, deadbeat junkies angling for a free ride.

Rags looked at him, then at Holt. "I'm not trying to be greedy," he said. "Really. It's just that if I'm going to have a girl, well, I could use some ... well, some cocaine, too. You know, to get the old motor running."

Holt laughed. Vaughn laughed and shook his head.

Holt said, "All right, Rags. How's this deal strike you? Fifty in cash and a room at the Wonder Lake up front. If the tip pans out, you get a hundred more, the girl for two hours, and a sixteenth of coke. Is it a deal?"

Rags got back to thinking, and what he thought was that he really liked the offer on the table: a hundred and fifty dollars, a room for the night, a pert young woman who had to do what he said for a couple hours, and some of Holt's fine powder cocaine. It was a solid payout for the one measly sentence he had in his arsenal.

"But," Holt cut in, "the girl is contingent on the grounds that you clean yourself up. When they bring her over, you have to be showered, shaved, and smelling decent. Understand? You look and smell like you do now, and she's out."

Rags was fine with that caveat. He was actually looking forward to cleaning himself up some. It had been months since his last shower.

"Okay. Deal," he said, his mind humming with anticipation. Cocaine and showers and blowjobs – it was going to be a swell night indeed. He thought that he might spring for a decent bottle of wine, too; not a fancy one with a cork in it, but something he wouldn't be ashamed to take out of a brown paper bag.

Vaughn stepped forward and cleared his throat, rudely interrupting Rags' pleasant train of thought. "Okay," he said, bearing down on him with a severe look, "let's have it. Where can we find this Dubinsky guy?"


The results had come back a positive match for Martin Loomis.

"There's no doubt in my mind," the head of forensics told Rainer and Milner. "The blood and skin and bone fragments, they're a match for Martin Loomis."

That was a loop the two detectives hadn't been expecting. They had spent the majority of breakfast debating the possibility that Loomis was in cahoots with the shooter at the A&P Mart. The blood and gore at Loomis's apartment, they assumed, either belonged to the shooter, or a third, yet unidentified individual. Of course, the shooter was yet unidentified. The only person who had been identified was Martin Loomis, and he'd just been identified as dead. Not only that, but the head of forensics had said that the remains of Martin Loomis, the ones collected at his apartment, were at least three days old, putting the time of death right around the time of the robbery.

None of it made sense.

"Only one explanation," said Milner as he and his partner strolled through the front door at Stenson and Henson Tax Service, where Charlie Bates worked as a junior accountant. "Wormhole."

"Wormhole?" replied Rainer. "Seriously?"

"What else could it be?"

"I want to hear you tell the Captain that. I want to be there to see his face when you tell him that a wormhole's to blame."

"Some really smart people, scientists even, believe in wormholes," Milner said, defending his inane theory, which in no small part had occurred to him because he had watched something about wormholes on television a couple nights ago. "Who knows what's possible in this crazy universe."

Rainer shook his head. "Might as well say pod people?"

"Sure. Why not?"

"I'm being facetious. Do you have any logical thoughts on the case?"

Milner gave the question some thought, then said, "Forensics has to be wrong. Samples must've got mixed up. Either that, or the guy at the hospital was never Martin Loomis."

"But we have positive identification. Not just from Bates, but from three people in Loomis's building, too."

Milner didn't have a good answer for that, mostly because there wasn't one. "I don't know," he said. "None of it makes sense."

"And then there's the suicide note. Not to mention, the gun has Loomis's fingerprints on it. They're the only prints on it."

"Okay. So what do you think it is?"

Rainer shrugged his broad shoulders. "Twin brother?" he said, just as a guess.

"I don't know what to think," Milner admitted with a sigh. He also didn't know where to steer the investigation, other than to go back and revisit everyone they'd spoken to. They were starting with Charlie Bates because of all the people they'd met so far Charlie was the one closest to Marty.

The two detectives approached the front desk, where a portly older woman with bottle blonde hair sat tapping at a computer.

"Excuse me, Miss," said Milner. "We need to speak with Charles Bates."

She looked at them closely, and something told her that they weren't clients. "Ummm ... Is he expecting you?" she asked them.

Milner pulled out his badge. "No. But I think he'll see us."

The woman looked at the badge and went, "Oh. Of course." She got up from her seat with a grunt, and the chair let out a slow, soft whine of relief. "Follow me," she told the two detectives, and led them around a slight corner to the main office area, which was nothing more than one large room cordoned off by a maze of cubicle walls.

Charlie's cubicle was the third one on the left, and he was hard at work watching an internet video of cats singing and playing instruments to the tune of 'It's a Wonderful Life' by Louis Armstrong. The cat that was singing was a fat calico with one ear, and Charlie couldn't help but smile at the show.

Until Rainer interrupted him.

"Hard at work, I see," the surly detective said, and Charlie quickly whipped around, expecting to see his boss standing over him. Instead he was greeted by Milner and Rainer, and Sheila the receptionist.

"Charlie," she said. "These gentlemen are with the police. They want to talk to you."

Charlie went, "Uhhh."

"Sorry to bother you at work, Charlie," said Detective Rainer. "But we have a few more questions for you. Is there somewhere we can go?"

"Charlie went, "Uhhh," again, while his mind fought for a coherent answer. He was not good with surprises, and though he had nothing to hide, cops worried him.

"There's an empty conference room right there," said Sheila, pointing across the way. "You can use that if you want."

"That'll be perfect," said Milner. "Thank you."

Sheila beamed, and asked the officers if she could get them anything, some coffee or water, perhaps a fresh baked muffin. They thanked her kindly, and told her that they were fine. "Just some privacy," Rainer said to her. Then he looked at Charlie, hitched his head in the direction of the conference room, and said, "Come on. Let's talk."

Charlie nodded sheepishly, cleared the cat video from his computer screen, and followed the two detectives into the conference room. No sooner did the door shut before the office gossip started buzzing around the room like an angry swarm of bees. Charlie was a criminal and a deviant. "He's quiet, he never dates, and he lives with his parents," Caroline whispered to Doug and Dan and Sheila. "I'm telling you, he's a serial killer. Or a child molester."

The others were nodding along as if they had suspected this, too.

Meanwhile, in the conference room, Rainer got things started. "Charlie," he said, pulling from his shirt pocket the photo they had taken of Martin Loomis, "who is this?"

Charlie took the photo, looked at it. "That's Marty," he said, a bit perplexed. He had already gone over this with them.

"Martin Loomis?"

Charlie looked at Milner, then Rainer. "Yes," he said. "I told you that already. Why? What's this about?"

"Martin Loomis is dead," Milner blurted out, and Charlie's confusion fell to sorrow.

"What?" he gasped, pain and anguish distorting his pudgy face. "What do you mean he's dead? How can he ... I though he was ... " The idea that his best friend in the whole world was dead had him reeling. His bottom lip began to quiver. "How could he have ... " he started, but again failed.

"We were hoping you might be able to shed some light on things," said Rainer. "Because none of this makes sense."

Charlie pulled out a chair and dropped into it; two-hundred and ten pounds of dead weight landing hard. "I just ... " he said, his voice brittle and broken. "I can't ... I mean ... I can't believe he's dead. What happened?"

Milner decided to ignore Charlie's question, mostly because he had no idea how to answer it. He didn't even know if Martin Loomis was really dead. More than anything, he had wanted to see Charlie's reaction to the statement.

"We think your friend might have been involved in the robbery," he posited as Charlie sat there blank-faced and somber. "We think he may have known the shooter."

Charlie looked up at them. He shook his head. "No. Not Marty."

"You said you were worried that he'd gotten involved with drugs. Drugs make people do things they normally wouldn't do, like rob convenience stores."

Charlie shook his head again, adamantly. "No," he said. "Not

Charlie. You don't know him. He's not like that."

"I know this is hard for you, but we need you to tell us everything you know."

"I already told you everything I know."

"We need you to tell us again."

Charlie sniffed, and nodded his head. "Sure," he said as one tear fell, tracing down his pudgy cheek. "I will."

"Okay now," said Rainer, ready to play a wild hunch. "Let me ask you this: Did Marty have a twin brother?"

Charlie's sorrow returned to confusion. "Twin brother?" he said. Then, answering the question, "No. Why?"

"A regular brother?" Rainer tried.

"He was an only child."

His wild theory shot down, Rainer grumbled discontentedly.

Milner promptly stepped to the fore. "What say you tell us about that ex-girlfriend of his, the one that broke his heart. And the guy who broke his jaw, and shoulder, and ribs."

"You think they're involved?" Charlie inquired. His eyes were red and puffy now, his cheeks as pale as cream cheese.

"We're just trying to put the clues together," Milner said.

As yet, none of the clues fit.


Vaughn pulled into the lot of the old school and slowly drove up over the crest of the hill to the abandoned schoolhouse. There were no cars in the parking lot, and the playground, once alive with the sound of laughter and excitement, was empty and overrun with weeds and tall grass. The pine bushes around the school were thick and unruly, and the concrete in the lot was cracked and busted with potholes.

Vaughn had gone to school here, umpteen years ago; he had played on the jungle gym, had swung on the swings, had shot baskets on the court. The rims, he noticed, were bent now, and there were no nets hanging from them. He had kissed his first girlfriend, Tamara Wilkins, behind the maintenance shed.

The school had closed its doors six years ago, when North Elementary merged with Hagerstown Elementary. The two schools combined to form one, and all the students transferred to Hagerstown because the building was newer, bigger, and more centrally located. The first couple years after the switch there had been talk about transforming    North into a nursing home, or an outpatient medical center, even a homeless shelter, but those plans never came to fruition and now the building was too far gone to be easily renovated. The furnace no longer worked, the pipes and duct work were falling apart, and the floor was a mess. Crack addicts and heroin junkies had raped the interior, stealing copper pipes and copper wiring to fund their habits. A lot of the windows had been busted out, and eighteen months ago, during an uncommon Spring blizzard, part of the roof on the gymnasium had collapsed.

Until Adam started crashing there, no one had bothered to venture inside for years. It was a home for rats, and birds, and all kinds of bugs. It was dark, and cold, and damp, and it reeked of gross abandonment.

Vaughn veered around the front entrance and parked away from the main doors. He cut the engine, and for a lingering moment he stared at the crumbling edifice that was the first house of his meager education.

"Fuck," said Berto, who was riding shotgun on the mission. "This place is a fucking hole."

"Otto said he was here," Vaughn said. "We're gonna check it out."

"Fuck," Berto said again.

Berto had come because Holt had told him to. Chauncey and Dado were muscle, and they were good at being muscle, but they mainly worked at the club, taking care of drunks who thought they could mouth off and grab ass. They were tough, but they weren't Berto. Berto was the guy Holt called whenever he needed bad stuff done – bones broken, fingers dislocated, ears removed. Even Vaughn was afraid of him.

"Guy must be desperate to be here."

Vaughn agreed. He then opened his door and got out. Berto followed him.

Vaughn was mindful not to slam his door shut. If Adam was inside, Vaughn didn't want to alert him to their presence. Berto got the hint and closed his door quietly, too. "Junkies," he said, shaking his head. "Hiding in an abandoned school."

Vaughn started for the door. "Come on. Let's check it out."

The front door was locked, and there were rusted chains wrapped around the handles. Vaughn waved for Berto to follow him, and the two of them began a search for alternate points of entrance. The next door they came to was locked, too, but the window next to it was broken. Shards of glass jutted out from the frame, and Berto, a seriously big man, said, "I'm not crawling through that. This is a new shirt."

They didn't have to. The next set of windows they came to were busted out in full, and Vaughn carefully peeked his head through to take a look around. He didn't see anything but garbage and debris, the rotting residue of vagrants, junkies, and long-absent partygoers. "Here," he said, and lifted a leg over the sill. A moment later he was inside, squinting in the dim light, looking for signs of his quarry.

Berto wasn't as agile as Vaughn, and he grunted from the effort it took to climb through the window. He nearly fell when his back foot caught the edge of the frame, and he snorted out, "Fuck!" as he stumbled inside.

Vaughn looked at him and said, "Easy now. If this fucker's here, I want to get the drop on him. Remember, he's armed."

Berto nodded once, and pulled a nine millimeter from the inside pocket of his jacket. "So are we," he said. "Let's go."

They walked slowly and quietly, the murky light and scattered garbage keeping their pace down. Vaughn took the lead, and Berto kept on his heels. They were in the hallway for the lower grades, if Vaughn remembered correctly. Kindergarten through grade two. Down the way and to the left was the cafeteria; to the right, the classrooms for the higher grades and the gymnasium.

Vaughn went left. On the floor he saw torn pages from porn magazines, empty soda and water bottles, empty beer cans, crumpled bags of chips, and discarded pizza boxes. Graffiti marked the walls and lockers: sexual words and innuendo, people's names, the crude, spray-paint drawings of cocks and balls, breasts and pussies.

"You really think he's here?" Berto asked in a whisper.

"Don't know," Vaughn said without looking back.

"Can't trust a junkie's word."

"Maybe not. But when money's involved, it's amazing how

clear people get."

"I like Felicity," Berto said, changing the subject. "Can't believe Holt's gonna make her fuck that vagrant. I'll never go for her again."

Vaughn said, "She's down over a grand to him."

"Yeah. Still."

"Plus, Holt thinks she's a smart ass. She made a comment about him one night that he didn't like, about him having to take a little blue pill to keep up with young girls. He don't forget stuff like that."

"No, he don't."

As soon as they turned the corner, coming to the hallway that led to the offices and the cafeteria, the harsh sound of someone coughing echoed out. Vaughn stopped in his tracks, and Berto stepped back.

"Maybe the junkie was right," Vaughn said.

"Poor Felicity," said Berto. He wished he could save her the disgrace of having her cute little ass humped by a junkie bum. If anyone should get to disgrace her and hump her cute little ass, Berto believed it should be him. He would do it right.

"You think he's alone?" Vaughn asked with a whisper, interrupting Berto's ruminations on Felicity, which had become deviant in nature.

The massive hench shrugged heedlessly and said, "Only one way to find out."

They continued on, following the sporadic hacking and retching sounds that bounced off the walls and long-forgotten lockers of North Elementary.

The hallway opened up at the end, leading to what once had been the cafeteria. The mess and debris was far worse here, as was the graffiti. There were names and gang signs everywhere, scrawled in mostly red and black paint, and on the far wall, over where the food line once had been, someone had painted a rather artistic mural of zombies on the march, with piles of dead, mutilated bodies in their wake.

Berto's eyes widened, and he said, "Wow. Check it out."

But Vaughn was looking at something else. He tapped his partner on the shoulder and hitched his head in the direction of a body lying on an old, discarded mattress. The body was curled in the fetal position and facing the other way. Berto nodded to let Vaughn know that he understood what came next, and the two of them started that way.

Another coughing jag from the man on the mattress stopped them, but only for a moment. When he didn't move or shift positions, when his head remained hunched and hidden, Vaughn and Berto picked back up and closed range.

Finally, they reached him.

The man on the mattress was small in stature, and he was shaking and breathing heavily. His hair was a greasy mess, and around him lay a scatter of garbage: liquor and wine bottles, empty cans of raviolis, empty potato chip bags.

Vaughn didn't see a gun. Berto readied his just in case, leveling aim on the wasted, derelict pile of humanity that was Adam Dubinsky. The two of them exchanged a look, and Vaughn nodded once, a tacit sign that he was ready. Then he nudged the body with his foot, gently at first, then with more of a kick.

Adam Dubinsky felt something poking him in the lower back, around the kidney area, but he had so many aches and pains that he paid it little mind at first. Then he felt a kick, and the pain was more immediate, more tangible. He groaned, stirred, reached behind him and groped at his back. Not feeling anything, he uncurled and lifted his head. The sight of two men looming over him, one of them holding a gun, sent a surge of panic through him and he yelped and rolled away.

"Easy now," said Vaughn as Adam recklessly stumbled to his feet, nearly falling at first. He looked terrified and confused.

"Adam Dubinsky?" Berto said.

Adam edged away from them. His eyes were wide and unsteady, and they kept bouncing back and forth between Vaughn, whom he knew to be a major player in the Hagerstown drug game, and the gun gripped in Berto's hand.

"Whadda you want?" he gasped.

"We have a couple questions for you," Vaughn said.

Adam nodded frantically. "Sure, sure," he said, the terror he felt escalating. He knew Vaughn well enough to know that respect and agreeability were paramount when dealing with him. Vaughn worked for Holt, and Holt was the shot caller – not *a* shot caller, but *the* shot caller – in the Hagerstown area.

"You don't look so hot," Vaughn said as Adam stood there twitching and nervously looking around. "Looks like you're detoxing."

Adam let that statement hang for a moment, and then he started to nod. "I could use a hit of something, sure," he said, hoping a junkie's blind hope that Vaughn might take pity on him and dole out a rock or two of heroin.

"Maybe we can make a deal."

Adam liked the sound of that idea. "Sure. How?" he said.

"You answer a couple questions for us, we fix you up."

Adam couldn't see a downside to that arrangement, but he kept his distance nonetheless, remaining wary. "Okay," he said. "What questions?"

Vaughn shrewdly measured the skeletal young man before him. Adam was small, frail, weak, and scared; it looked as though he hadn't had a decent meal or a decent night's rest in more than a week. There were blood and vomit stains on his shirt, and he couldn't stop trembling. Some of that Vaughn attributed to fear, but most of it, he believed, had more to do with sickness, the dread sickness of a junkie going cold.

Vaughn smiled at him, but it was a smile that lacked any sort of compassion or care. It was the smile of a predator, showing its prey that it had teeth.

"I want to know why?" he said. "That's all. Why?"

Adam was confused. "Why what?"

"Why a shitbag junkie like you thought you could get away with it?"

Adam didn't know how Vaughn knew about the robbery, but it was obvious that he did, and Adam felt the walls close in on him. He had buried his gun outside as a precaution should the police happen to track him down, hiding it under one of the many pine thickets that guarded the west side of the school. He wished that he had that weapon now. Not that he could outdraw Berto, who already had the drop on him, but so his death would be quick. He got the feeling that as things stood, a quick death would be a win.

"I don't know what ... " he began, but his words became a high-pitched shriek when he saw Vaughn break down and charge him. He tried to run, tried to juke the angry drug dealer, but days of lying curled up on a mattress, sweating and detoxing, had stolen what little athleticism he had. He made it exactly two steps before Vaughn caught him and clamped a powerful forearm around his head. Adam fought to spin away, but he was no match for the bigger, stronger Vaughn, and in a blur he felt himself flying through the air. Then he felt himself falling. He hit the ground with a thud, and pain screamed out from his right hand. Though he was hurt, and scared, and dizzy, he tried to regain his feet. The last thing he remembered was looking up and seeing a fist coming at his face.

# Chapter Twelve

Edmund was endeavoring not to look directly at Brandon Coples as the young man fought and squirmed his way into a pair of silky black pantyhose. It was an ugly, distasteful display, one that never failed to make Edmund cringe. Brandon was short and fat, and he liked to dress in women's undergarments and masturbate. He was not gay, but he wasn't necessarily straight, either. He considered himself a solo-sexual; he liked to have sex with himself only, playing the part of both the man and the woman.

Edmund had been trying to persuade him to stop defiling himself in such perverted ways, but Edmund wasn't very good at his job, and as he'd learned some time ago, sexual sins were among the most difficult to prevent. Though Brandon wasn't hurting anyone, what he was doing was undoubtedly sinful, and there would be penance to pay in the next world. Sexual reparations were huge in Purgatory.

Presently, however, Edmund couldn't care less about Brandon's weird little habits; not with Whitman out there on his own, with no one to help him. Edmund had been trying to reach Whitman for the last eight hours with no success. He had called on Alina and Emilia for help, but they had been unable to contact him either. They could go to him, they could watch him, just like any other living human being, but they could no longer interact with him. He was flying blind, and in jeopardy.

Out came the baby oil, and Edmund jumped to action. "Please don't," he imparted to Brandon, his Custodial voice soundless in the sexual vacuum that currently possessed the young man's mind. Edmund might as well have been speaking Chinese to a monkey. Yet he continued to try. "Stop it!" he said, putting some spiritual oomph into it. "You're better than this." When that didn't work, he tried another approach. "There's a wholesome PG movie on the telly right now. A funny one, with a talking pig."

Brandon squirted baby oil into his hand and rubbed it in.

"Oh gees!" Edmund groaned. In a few seconds the party would commence, and Edmund would hurry off before Brandon started doing all the unseemly things he liked to do to himself. Edmund had caught the whole show once, back when he was green and eager to help. He would not be making that mistake again. There are some sins you can't stop, and, as he'd learned, there are some things you can't un-see.

So he left Brandon to his vices and floated off into the spiritual ether that surrounded the real world, ready to have another go at Whitman, or to check in with Emilia and Alina to see if they'd learned anything new. But *something* jerked him out of the spirit realm, and Edmund felt himself plummeting. A chill struck his bones, and his vision blurred at the edges, then altogether. His fall picked up momentum, and he began to scream. At first he only heard the sound in his head, but then he heard it all around him, his panicky voice bawling out one long, high-pitched note of fear. And then ...

He hit the ground with a mighty thud, and a blunt, vivid pain coursed through his entire body. It was real pain, too. Human pain.

Edmund groaned, and slowly rolled onto his back. His left arm ached, his left side ached, his ribs and chest ached. He tried to take a breath but couldn't, and that scared him. Then his mind came back and he remembered not only who and what he was, but that his body shouldn't feel pain or need air. That's when he noticed the sky above him, slate gray and bunched with fast-moving clouds. But he didn't put two and two together until after the first raindrop smacked him in the face. That's when he realized that, like Whitman before him, he was human again, and very much alive.

This terrifying prospect lifted him to his feet and had him patting himself down as if he was on fire. "Bloody hell!" he said. Then, realizing he had sworn, he slapped a hand over his mouth and whined regretfully.

"Under the circumstances, I'd say we can forgive that."

This voice, regal and strong, caused Edmund to squeal. The poor, off-kilter Brit spun on his heels, lost his balance at the unexpected sight of a tall man with white hair, and fell to the ground. "Dammit!" he cried out.

"Alright. Don't abuse the privilege," replied the man, as Edmund scurried away from him like a frightened crab. "Easy. I'm here to help you."

"Who ... Who ... Who are you?" Edmund muttered desperately. Then he said, "Who am I? And where am I? Am I human?"

Four questions fired off one after the other, and the regal man with the blinding white hair decided not to answer any of them. Instead, he said, "You know who I am, Edmund."

At first he didn't, but then the rigid features of the man's face slowly took shape in Edmund's memory. He had met this man once before, soon after passing the trials of Purgatory. This was one of the men who had inducted him into the Custodial tradition. "Tyrus?" he said.

"Correct."

Edmund's heart swelled with a mixture of confusion and joy. It was a great honor to get a personal visit from an Elder, but foremost on his mind was the fact that he once again could feel pain. Everything else, including Whitman's current travails, was now on the back burner.

"What is this?" Edmund said. "Tell me what's happening." Fear weighed on his words and turned his face into an ugly pale splotch. "First Whitman, and now me? Why is this happening?"

"We need you to help Whitman," said Tyrus, as the rain began to fall harder.

The feel of rain was both wonderful and terribly disconcerting to Edmund. And wet, of course. It had been decades since he'd felt anything other than concern and empathy; he hadn't felt hot or cold, tired or hungry; he hadn't felt desire or greed, anger or fear. Nothing like that since 1941, when he was alive, just before a concrete block fell on his head and killed him instantly. It was the result of an air raid by the Luftwaffe, and up to that day he had thought that avoiding World War II because of a severe kidney infection had been a stroke of luck. He learned the hard way that variables are incalculable, and there's no such thing as luck.

"Help him how?" he asked as the rain soaked him. "What am I supposed to do?"

"We lost touch with him," said Tyrus. "We can't reach him. And he needs help."

"What kind of help?"

"He needs to find Adam Dubinsky. Lives rest on his ability to save Adam's life."

Bewilderment washed over Edmund's face. "But I thought we weren't supposed to ... you know, *influence* life."

"Normally we're not. But if Whitman is unable to save Adam, chances are we're not going to be able to bring him back."

"How come? I don't understand any of this, sir."

"To be truthful, we're not too sure of things either. Whatever happened, however it happened, it's proven to be quite a dilemma. But we have to get Whitman back, and right now you're our only hope."

"Me?" That thought not only shocked Edmund, it scared the living daylights out of him. "Why me? I mean, I'm widely regarded as one of the worst Custodians in the district, perhaps the entire realm. And now I'm human."

"It has to be you because you're his Custodian. We assigned you to him, and now you're the only one who can help him."

"There's no one else? No one more qualified?"

"More qualified, yes. But it has to be you."

"But why am I human?"

"Because he can't see us anymore. He's losing touch with the spirit realm, and we fear he's losing touch with himself."

"I thought you were the ones who cut off contact with him, for his insubordination."

"No. We weren't happy about that, not at all, but we didn't cut him off."

"I don't understand what I'm supposed to do, though. I have no experience with this sort of thing. And how do you mean to get us back?"

"None of that matters right now," said Tyrus.

"It matters to me!" cried Edmund. "I'm not going to be stuck here, am I? Tell me you have an exit strategy? Please, sir, once around was enough. And I don't even want to think about Purgatory again."

"Edmund!" Tyrus snapped, and there was a sharpness to his voice which hadn't been there before, and a look in his eyes that said he really didn't care to hear any more questions or complaints. "Whitman needs our help and this is the only way to do it. Now are you willing or not?"

Edmund was reluctant, but his loyalty won out over his fear and he somberly nodded his slender, misshapen head. "Right-O," he said, choosing an old British phrase, which made his accent that much more noticeable. "You can count on me, sir. I'm your man. What would you have me do?"

"Listen close," Tyrus said. "We haven't a lot of time."


It felt strange to walk, to feel pavement beneath his feet, to feel the wind blow back his plush brown hair, to feel his muscles tighten and relax, to feel ... hungry.

There was a rumbling in his stomach, and this caused Edmund to think about his death. He didn't remember being crushed by the seventy pound shard of concrete that a German bomb shattered loose from the building he was walking past at the time; but he did remember that he was on his way to Hemlock's Gaff for some pork sausage and a pint of ale. He remembered being famished then, and he wondered if that's why his stomach was growling now. He made a mental note to ask Tyrus should he ever see him again.

Sight and sound, he quickly realized, were essentially the same, though substantially limited. Colors weren't as bright, sounds weren't as clear, but Edmund often thought that as a Custodian he saw and heard far too much. That idea made him think about Brandon, and he quickly pushed that thought out of his head lest it get stuck up there forever.

Two more blocks to go.

As he prepared to cross the street, he caught a glimpse of himself in the reflection of a car window, and he stopped in his tracks to have a better look. It had been decades since he'd last seen himself, and he was surprised by how quickly he remembered his own face. "Not a top drawer looker," he said as he gazed at his dim, murky reflection in the car window, "but not half bad neither." It was something he used to say to himself all the time when he looked in the mirror, and if he happened to be feeling particularly snappy, he'd add a wink and a shot from his finger-pistol.

Presently, such frivolity seemed inappropriate, and Edmund pulled himself away from his reflection, cut in between two parked cars, and hurried across the street. Whitman should have little problem recognizing him, he believed, seeing how his real self looked identical to his spiritual self. Whereas Whitman had accidentally inherited the body of a recently-deceased young man, Edmund had merely rematerialized as himself. It might take Whit a moment or two to process the idea, but there was no earthly way he could deny it. And Edmund couldn't wait to glimpse the look on his boss's odd young face whenever he first saw him. A part of him thought it might be fun to yell out 'Surprise!', but once more he had to consider the appropriateness of such an act.

A swirling gust of wind swooped down, and Edmund felt his hair whip back. It felt rather good, he mused, and he broke into a slow trot. It felt good to jog, too. It felt good to feel things again. Strange, but good. And he discovered that though he had not exerted real physical energy in more than fifty years, he did not become short of breath or tired. His muscles felt loose and relaxed. And strong.

He soon reached Ally's building, and he bounded up two flights of stairs and moved at a brisk pace down the hall. He couldn't wait to see his friend and mentor, couldn't wait to show him that he too was human again; perhaps they could have a chat over a cup of tea, or go have a pint somewhere ... should time permit. Edmund had always wanted to have a pint with Whitman.

He went to the fifth door on the left, composed himself, stood straight and tall, and put his knuckles to work. Three loud knocks echoed out, and a moment later he heard slow, heavy footsteps approaching. Then he heard the dead bolt being undone and the door latch being unlocked. Finally he saw the door knob turn.

The door swung open, and Edmund, unable to stop himself,

threw his hands up and called out, "Surprise!"

The hoary, slumping, eighty-year-old man who had opened the door stumbled back, his withered old eyes bursting with fear. He would have toppled over, but the wall stopped him.

Realizing his error, Edmund hurriedly reached out to lend the old man a hand. "Sorry," he said, helping to steady him. "My mistake. I didn't mean to frighten you."

"No? Then what for you shout at me like that?" the man replied in broken English. To Edmund, the accent sounded Eastern European, perhaps Czech or Romanian. "Dear goodness, boy. I'm an old man. What's wrong with you?!"

"Sorry," Edmund said once more. "I thought you were someone else."

"I nearly was. I was nearly the *late* Herman Louche."

Edmund made sure the old man had his balance back before saying that he thought a young woman named Ally lived here.

Herman Louche scratched his chin with a gnarled thumb. "You mean the colored girl?" he said. "Well, half-and-half, right?"

Edmund thought about gently correcting the good Mr. Louche by suggesting more appropriate terminology, but ultimately concluded it made little difference. The man had to be in his mid-eighties, and it wasn't like he was being purposefully insensitive. Besides, time was ticking and it wasn't about to stop for a lesson on political correctness.

"Yes," he said. "Then, just to put it out there, "She's bi-racial."

The old man's face soured, which deepened most of his wrinkles, making them look like jagged little scars. "I don't like her," he said. "All hours of night with the doors closing, the music playing, the people talking. She's got too many friends. I'm an old man."

Edmund nodded understandingly. "Right, sir. I'll tell her to keep it down. Only ... " he looked left and then right, " ... I'm not sure which door is hers."

Herman stuck his head out, lifted a wavering arm, pointed to the right. "Next one down," he said. "And tell her I'm an old man. Tell her no more parties. I don't like it. You don't see me having wild parties."

"I'll tell her, sir," said Edmund. "And thank you."

Herman grumbled petulantly under his breath, something that contained the phrase, " ... these damn kids today have no respect ... " but Edmund didn't stick around to hear it. He was on his way down the hall, to the next door on the right, to find his friend and give him Tyrus's all-important message.

Whitman wasn't expecting a visitor, and the first thought to cross his mind was that Vaughn had indeed called the cops and they were here to arrest him. He stood perfectly still for a few seconds, just staring at the door, not making a sound. Then came a second round of knocks, accompanied by a prim British voice: "Sir? Are you there? It's me. Edmund."

Whitman could hardly believe his ears, and he started for the door at the sound of the familiar voice. Then he stopped, thinking that it must be a trick of some kind. Custodians didn't knock on doors; they were spiritual beings who simply appeared out of thin air.

"Sir?" the voice called out again, that British tone undeniable.

Though apprehensive, Whitman inched forward, moving on his tip toes, keeping his breath in so as not to give himself away. When he reached the door, he craned his head forward, pinched one eye shut, and peered through the peephole. And what he saw caused that eye of his to open unnaturally wide. It was Edmund, but he looked different somehow; there was color in his normally pale cheeks, and his hair was badly mussed. Whitman wouldn't have wagered on it, but Edmund looked ... Alive. And, as usual, befuddled.

"Sir? Please, sir, if you're in there, open up."

Whitman was skeptical, but far more than that he was curious. And while he refused to unlock and open the door, he did offer his friend a greeting.

"Edmund?" he said. "That really you?"

Edmund's heart jumped with relief. "Yes, sir. It's me. Can you let me in?"

Whitman's hand was on the lock, but he wasn't going to turn it until he got a few answers. "Edmund?" he said. "What are you doing here?"

"I'm here to help you, sir."

"Why don't you just come in?"

"I can't, sir. I'm ... Well, I'm stuck out here. I'm like you."

"Like me?"

Edmund looked left, then right, making sure he was alone, that no one was eavesdropping on him. "I'm alive, sir," he said, mindful to keep his voice low. "I have a message from Tyrus."

"Tyrus?"

"Yes, sir. Can you please let me in. I'm not very comfortable out here."

Whitman felt he had enough information now, and he turned the lock and opened the door. Edmund rushed in like a gust of air, a worried look furrowing his fine English brow. "Sir?" he said. "Are you alright?"

"I'm fine," said Whitman, staring at his friend, hardly believing his eyes. Then, because he wanted to make certain, he reached out and touched Edmund's arm. "Holy crap," he said, feeling the unquestionable realness of Edmund's body. "You're corporeal."

"No more than you," Edmund replied.

"But ... How? When?"

"About twenty minutes ago. Tyrus unceremoniously yanked me out of the spiritual world. Against my will, mind you. I mean, I know he's the big boss and all, the head honcho, as they say, but there ought to be a law." Then, once more feeling the empty rumble in the pit of his stomach, he switched gears. "Say, you wouldn't happen to have any sausage here, would you?"

"No," said Whitman. "I don't think so."

"It's just that I haven't really eaten anything in ... well, decades, and I find that I'm rather peckish. I'm sure you can relate."

Whitman could relate, but presently he had more urgent concerns. "Edmund," he said. "What was Tyrus's message? And why did he have to animate you in order to give it to me? None of this makes sense."

"You're telling me, sir. One minute I'm watching Brandon Coples defile himself, the next I'm walking the streets of Hagerstown. It's not been a good day."

"But why did Tyrus make you corporeal?"

"He said that we'd lost touch with you and this was the only way to reach you?"

"He said that? This is the only way?"

"That's what he said."

Whitman kept silent while the thought sank in. Normally he would have believed it impossible, only recently the line between possible and impossible had become less of a line and more of crack. Quite unexpectedly he cried out, "What the hell is going on here?!" Though the question was rhetorical, the exasperation in his voice was clear. "First me, now you. This is ridiculous."

"Perhaps," said Edmund. "But it doesn't change anything."

"No," said Whitman, "I suppose it doesn't." He refocused. "What was Tyrus's message?"

"He told me to tell you that we need to save Adam Dubinsky. He's been kidnapped?"

"Kidnapped?"

"Yes. By Vaughn."

"But ... Adam was the one who shot me?"

"I know."

"And we're not supposed to intervene in daily life. Not directly. That's a rule. Are you sure it was Tyrus who told you this?"

Edmund nodded intently. "Yes, sir. It was Tyrus. Trust me, I was as shocked as you are. But this is real, and apparently we have to act."

"And do what? Save him? How are we supposed to do that?"

That simple query caused Edmund to hesitate. "I'm not rightly sure," he said. "Come to think of it, Tyrus never specified."

"Excuse me?" Whitman cried out. "What do you mean he never specified?!"

"He just said that we have to save him. I figured you'd know what he meant."

Whitman rubbed his forehead and sighed. "No," he said. "I have no idea how to save him. I don't even know where to find him."

"Teasers!" Edmund shouted out like a manic game show contestant. "The club where Ally works. Tyrus told me that much."

Whitman began to nod his head meaningfully. "Okay," he said. "That's a start. Do you know how to get there?"

"No. You?"

"No."

"I suppose we could ask directions."

"I suppose we'll have to."

"Tyrus also said that time was of the essence. He made note of that twice, sir."

Whitman gave a sarcastic snort. "Isn't it always?"

Edmund took a moment to think on that. He did this often with rhetorical questions. Finally, he said, "Yes."

"'Yes' what?" said Whitman.

"No?" Edmund tried.

Whitman did not understand. "What are you talking about?"

"Time being of the essence, sir," Edmund explained. "I agree with you." Then, slyly hedging his bet, "I think."

Whitman let loose a groan that expressed total frustration. "Not now, Edmund," he said. "We need to go."

"Yes, sir. Right away, sir."

"Give me a minute and I'll be ready."

Whitman went to change, and Edmund made a path to the refrigerator, hoping to find some of Ally's delectable food. Unfortunately, pickings were slim, and he had little choice but to settle on a brown-spotted banana.

Ninety-seven seconds later Whitman exited the bathroom wearing Vaughn's bulky sweatshirt and sweatpants, and the same clunky boots Edmund had procured for him at the hospital. He looked a right mess, especially next to Edmund, who was decked out in his funeral suit. It was gray tweed, and though the cut was old fashion, it fit him well and he looked rather dapper in it.

Whitman said, "All right then, let's go. No time to waste."

"Right on it, sir." Edmund replied, his words mumbled by mushy banana.

And away they went.


Delusional thoughts are part of the whole detox process, and Adam had had his share over the last few days. But freedom has a way of giving false hope, and no matter how depressed the sickness and heroin-hunger got him, Adam's fractured mind occasionally entertained scenarios where he not only avoided the law and prison but also managed to put his life back together. He told himself that once the heat died down he would go to rehab, clean up his act, make something of himself.

Against the odds he had managed to avoid the police, hiding at an abandoned school and venturing out only when necessity dictated. And it had been a few days since he'd had a fix so the worst of the symptoms had passed. He still got the shakes and the chills, and the suffocating despair of impending death hovered over him at all times, but those things had diminished over the last eighty hours.

Because so, he had actually allowed himself to think, in the most optimistic part of his mind, that he stood a chance, that somehow, someway, everything would work out. Then Vaughn and Berto had showed up and abruptly severed that thin thread of hope, dropping him into an abyss from which, Adam believed, there could be no escape.

He wished that the drugs would have gotten him, that detox would have stolen the last vestige of life from him and laid his bones to rest in the squalor of the abandoned school; or that he would have accidentally shot himself during the robbery; or that the police had found him first and gunned him down after a brief standoff.

Anything but this. Anything but Vaughn and Berto.

They had already given him a pretty good beating. Berto had pounded on him for a spell while Vaughn had interrogated him. Not one for pain, Adam held out less than two minutes before breaking down and admitting that he was the one who had pulled the robbery and shot John Doe. Not only that, he told Berto and Vaughn where they could find the gun he'd used. Vaughn went and dug it up while Berto prepared Adam for delivery.

Presently, Adam was in the trunk of Vaughn's car. The car was moving, and every time it hit a pothole, the cotter pin that secured the spare tire jabbed him in the back. The thick, heady smell of gasoline, along with the unpredictable motion of the car – turning, slowing, stopping, accelerating – was making him sick. He felt like he might throw up, which was unfortunate because he was bound and gagged.

They hadn't told him where he was going, but he had a good idea that he wasn't going to like it. "You're going where we take you," Vaughn had told him when he'd asked, and then Berto had slapped him upside the head, putting a ring in his ears that still remained. He hadn't asked anymore questions after that.

He felt the car slow down, felt it turn to the left, felt it pull to a stop. He felt the subtle thunk of the transmission sliding into Park; and though the engine continued to run, he heard car doors open and then slam shut. A moment later, a key was slid in the trunk's lock, there was a click, and then the trunk was thrown open and a flash of light came rushing in. Adam squinted against the sunlight, and he winced when he saw both Vaughn and Berto reach for him. He was pulled out of the trunk and quickly escorted down a flight of stairs, Vaughn carrying him on one side, Berto the other.

He was at Teasers, that much he knew; they'd taken him in the back way. He'd been behind the building a few times before and recognized the blonde brick façade and green chain-link fence surrounding the dumpster. Back when he first started using, he partied with a girl who worked at the club, Harriet Something, whose stage name was Coco. She did the job for smack, and as her habit grew, so too did her willingness.

She had beaten the monkey the hard way – she overdosed and died. They found her in an alley wearing a short skirt, no panties, and one high heel. Her last act before sticking a needle in her arm had been to orally pleasure a man for twenty-two dollars – a ten, a five, and seven ones for a back alley blowjob. Not her finest moment, but at the end Coco's life had become an essay on not-fine moments.

A door was opened, and Adam, as he remembered Coco and the sultry way she used to go, "Damn," whenever the heroin hit her, was shoved through. Down the hall he went, with Vaughn leading the way and Berto pushing up behind him. He felt like a prisoner being led to the electric chair, and though the thought was unnerving, he couldn't help but wonder if perhaps he was worse off than that.

Vaughn made a left and stopped at the first door he came to.

The door was marked Storage, and he opened it, reached inside, hit the light. Berto then shouldered Adam in, and Vaughn closed the door behind them.

It was the same room where Otis had given Adam's whereabouts to Holt and Vaughn for payment he currently was getting ready to enjoy. It was the confessional room, and Vaughn had every intention of making Adam confess his sins and apologize to Ally before passing final judgment on him.

"Sit down," Berto told Adam, and pushed him toward the chair.

Adam stumbled, but didn't fall. Berto pulled out his cigarettes.

A few seconds later there was a knock at the door, and then the door opened and Holt ducked inside. The small town crime boss glanced at Adam, then said to Vaughn, "This him?"

Vaughn nodded and said, "Yep."

"And he confessed?"

Vaughn nodded again, and from his coat pocket he produced the gun that Adam had used to rob the A&P Mart. "We *encouraged* him to turn over the weapon. He had it buried in the bushes outside the school."

"All right then." Holt clapped his hands once, then began to rub them together, a sign that he was ready to get to work.

Berto understood. He stuck his cigarette between his lips and, with his hands now free, worked to remove the gag from Adam's mouth. As he did, Holt made a speech. "We don't have to tell you not to scream, do we?" he began. "You scream, we get mad, really bad things happen to you. As it stands now, only mildly unpleasant things are going to happen to you. That can change, though. Quickly."

"You cooperate, do as we say," said Vaughn, "it won't be the worst day of your life. You get stubborn, play hard, and it will be. Understand?"

Though the gag had been removed, Adam nodded his response instead of speaking it. He felt sick to his stomach, and he didn't want to open his mouth lest he throw up all over himself, and all over Holt's floor.

"You robbed the A&P four nights ago," Vaughn said. "You shot someone."

"It was an accident," Adam sniveled.

"You almost shot my girl!"

"I didn't mean to. Honest. The gun just went off."

"Guns don't just go off. You got to pull the trigger!" Vaughn cocked the hammer on the .38 Special and pointed it at Adam's head. "Here, I'll show you."

"No!" Adam cried out. "Please don't!"

For raising his voice, Adam received a stinging backhand across the face from Berto. "No screaming," the massive hench commanded. Then, for good measure, he slammed a fist into Adam's junkie-thin midsection.

A horrible croak leaked out of Adam, and he doubled over in pain. "I'm ... sorry," he managed, choking on his words. "I'm ... I'm sorry."

Berto struck him again, this time slapping him on the back of the head, and Adam whelped liked a scared dog.

"Stop your fucking crying," said Vaughn. "This is nothing but the start."

Adam nodded to let them know he understood, but thin, delicate, whining sounds kept seeping out of him, like air out of a pinched balloon.

"Junkies like you," said Holt, "deserve no better."

"Robbing stores? Shooting people?" Vaughn said. "You're a rat, and the world will be a better place without you in it."

Adam coughed up some blood, and he grimaced at the pain it caused him.

"Stop your fucking blubbering!" snapped Berto, and once more he backhanded Adam across the face again.

"You're going to make things right," Vaughn said to Adam. "You're going to apologize for what you've done."

Adam was nodding, and sniveling, and weeping. "Yes. Of course," he said. "I'm sorry. I apologize."

"Not to us," said Holt. "To the girl you almost killed."

"Of course," said Adam. "I'll apologize to her. I'm sorry for what I did. Really."

"And then there's the matter of reparation."

Adam had no idea what Holt was getting at, but he truly believed, given where he was and who he was dealing with, that agreeability had its merit. "Of course," he said. "Anything you want. Just name it."

"That's good to hear," said Holt, and off to the side Berto laughed. "Because I'll be requiring financial restitution."

The first thought that went through Adam's mind was that Holt owned the A&P Mart and he wanted his money back. Adam had no idea how much he'd taken from the store, or from the girl whose purse he'd snatched, though he vaguely remembered having around two hundred dollars on him when he went to see Bobbo. Of that, he had thirty-some cents remaining. Not feeling confident enough to admit that, he said nothing.

"If you can't afford to pay me back," Holt went on, smiling deviously, "we'll need to settle on another arrangement. All sorts of ways to square things up these days. And business is business."

"Anything," Adam wailed, believing that he was pleading for his very life. "I want to make things right," he added. "I do."

"Good," said Holt, and patted Adam on the head like a housebroken mutt. "That's a good boy. I have something special in mind, actually. And it's something you're going to have to get used to, I imagine."

Knowing his boss's sinister plan, Berto laughed again. He was the type that relished other people's pain, and the plight of frail, young Adam was fuel to the fires of hell that burned inside him.

"I should probably get Ally," Vaughn said, and Holt agreed.

"Good idea. Time to get the ol' ball rolling. Berto and I will keep Mr. Dubinsky here company while you're gone."

"Don't hurt him too bad," Vaughn said, handing Adam's .38 Special to Holt. "Ally's got a soft heart." He then stepped out of the storage room and went on his way upstairs.

As soon as the door shut behind him, Berto laid into Adam with a crisp right hand that spun him to the whistling, whirling edges of unconsciousness.

"My heart ain't so soft," said Holt as Adam whimpered and bled. "Berto's neither."

"I don't know. I like puppies," Berto said, and laughed.

Holt laughed, too.

Adam was the only one who found no humor in the situation.

The mere sight of them was like something out of a bad stage play: the tall, gangly one, like a human stork, stepping around in a proper suit and tie, his head swiveling left and right, his wide eyes beholding everything with wonder; the shorter, stockier one wearing sweats and plodding along in big, clumpy boots. They were walking quickly, and everyone who saw them gave them more than just a passing glance.

"I didn't think I'd like it, sir," Edmund said as they hurried along Jefferson Avenue, on their way to Teasers, which, from what the clerk at the convenience store had told them, was more than three miles away.

"Perhaps we should hitchhike?" Edmund suggested. "Or hail a cab."

"I'm not hitchhiking," replied Whitman. "Too many crazy people."

"But it will take us two hours to walk," Edmund reasoned. "At least."

"Don't care. I've seen too many things happen to people who hitchhike."

Edmund half-agreed with a grunt, and tottered on, following half a step behind his boss, who was stomping around like a clumsy giant in a cabbage patch.

They rounded the block, saw the antique store that Bob the clerk had told them to look for, and veered to the left. They hustled across the street. Whitman nearly fell due to his cinderblock boots, and Edmund, always ready to lend a hand, reached out to steady him. "Careful, boss," he said.

Whitman found his balance and clomped away, and Edmund chased after him with high, knee-bending steps. They hurried down the next block and saw the Arby's that Bob had mentioned in his directions.

"Look," said Whitman, pointing at the fast food restaurant's inimitable sign. "Two blocks after the Arby's we make a right on County Line Road and take that all the way to the club."

Edmund saw the sign, but his eyes were drawn higher, up to the heavens, where thick, dark clouds had begun to clot. It had been raining all day, and more was imminent. He could feel the moisture in the air.

"You don't happen to have an umbrella, sir, do you?"

Whitman gave the clouds a passing glance and said, in a gratingly sarcastic tone, "Does it look like I have an umbrella? It's not like carrying a quarter in your pocket."

Edmund agreed, and hurried along. They walked in silence until they reached the Arby's parking lot, at which time Edmund was struck by a powerful hunger, thanks to all the posters in the windows depicting, in colorful, mouth-watering detail, beautiful roast beef sandwiches smothered in creamy melted cheddar cheese. The curly fries scattered around the sandwich like shrubbery looked pretty damn tasty, too.

"Sir," Edmund said, the strain of hesitation dragging that one word out.

Whitman glanced back at him. "What?"

"Well, sir, it's just that ... well ... "

"What is it, Edmund? Out with it."

"Well ... I was wondering if you have any money left."

"I believe I have thirty-six dollars. Why?"

"Good. May come in handy."

They were nearly across the parking lot and Whitman wasn't slowing down. Arby's and wonderful melty-cheese roast beef sandwiches would be in their rearview in a matter of seconds unless Edmund could summon the courage.

"Like now, for instance," he said, pulling to a stop.

Whitman looked back at him, and stopped, too. "What is it?" he said. "Something wrong?"

Edmund glanced over his shoulder at the Arby's. "It's just that I'm quite peckish, sir. That banana did little to stem my appetite."

Whitman gaped at him. "Seriously? Now? You're honestly thinking about food now?" Then he caught wind of the sweltering fried food smell coming from inside the Arby's and he realized that he was rather hungry himself. And out of the corner of his eye he saw a poster of a roast beef and melty-cheese behemoth with onion rings and a drink, and the image was enough to make him decide that a bite to eat would be a good idea.

"Perhaps some food would be appropriate," he said. "Got to

keep our strength up."

"My sentiments exactly," agreed Edmund. "I don't know about you, sir, but I think better on a full stomach. Used to take all my exams at university after a pork pie."

Five minutes later they had a tray of food that held four sandwiches, an order of curly fries and an order of onion rings, and two large sodas.

They sat at a booth near the window and barely spoke as they vigorously consumed their meal. Edmund ate quickly, though he was mindful to maintain proper manners, which was something he spoke on frequently about being one of the declines of civilization. His napkin was folded neatly across his lap, his elbows were off the table, and he carefully brought his food up to his mouth instead of attacking it like a hungry coyote.

"You can tell a lot about a person by the way they eat," he always said.

Whitman, a deep-rooted plainsman, was a bit less proper, but he chewed quietly and with his mouth closed, which Edmund appreciated. And he had offered up a prayer before eating, thanking God for the meal and asking for His blessings.

When they were finished, they went to the bathroom, washed their hands, and got on their way. Edmund, learning that refills were free, filled up his Dr. Pepper before leaving the Arby's for good, and Whitman had the girl up front top off his coffee.

"I was wondering, sir," Edmund said as they exited the building. "What's our plan?"

Whitman took the lead crossing the street. "Plan?" he said.

"Yes. We have to have a plan. Plans are very important."

Whitman was paying more attention to where he was going than to Edmund. He grunted something that wasn't a word, then said, "I just want to get there and talk to Ally. Maybe she'll know something."

Edmund accepted that as a reasonable strategy, and sipped at his soda. "This stuff is amazing," he said.

"Too sugary for me," replied Whitman. "Those sandwiches were pretty damn tasty, though. Roast beef and cheddar cheese."

"Oh yes, they were quite good, sir. The curly fries, too. I must say, I am enjoying this."

Whitman stopped, turned, looked at him. "Enjoying what exactly?"

"Being alive again. It's really quite invigorating."

Whitman thought to chastise Edmund, given where they had come from and all they had done to get there, but the words wouldn't come out. Instead he thought about Ally, and the food they had just eaten, and wind in his hair, and he said, "Can't think on enjoyment, Edmund. We have a job to do. Now let's go."

That's when a car on the street, a boring beige sedan with a dent in the front fender, came to a tire-screeching halt, and all the drivers behind it, each of them stopping just in the nick of time, began to lay on their horns and shout out curses. It was mayhem, and it drew everyone's attention.

A moment later, a young man's head popped out of the boring beige sedan's window. "Marty! Marty Loomis?!" the man called out.

Whitman gave no response, and offered no sign of recognition. It was Edmund that first understood what was going on, and he said to his boss, "Sir, I believe that young man is talking to you."

That's when Jeremiah Whitman realized that *he* was Marty Loomis, and the urge to flee struck him like a smack to the face.


Charlie Bates's emotions swung swiftly from confusion to relief, from relief to happiness, and then from happiness back to confusion. The cops had told him that his friend was dead, but obviously they had been mistaken because Marty was walking the streets of Hagerstown, very much alive and well. Well, very much alive, anyway.

As Charlie parked the car, Whitman panicked. "What do we do?" he implored Edmund. "What do I say to him?"

"He's your friend," said Edmund. "We went over all this at the hospital."

Whitman remembered the name Charlie Bates, but that was all he remembered. "What do you suppose he wants?"

"Probably wants to make sure you're all right."

Whitman nodded uneasily, and watched as Charlie Bates looked both ways before bounding across the street.

"You have to help me with him," Whitman told Edmund. "You know more about him than I do. You have to guide me."

"Perhaps he can give us a ride," Edmund suggested.

Whitman straightened up as Charlie approached, and he stuck out a hand to shake. But Charlie ignored the hand and went in for a hug, and he squeezed so tight that Whitman found it difficult to breathe.

"Marty! Oh Marty!" Charlie blubbered as he suffocated his friend on the street. "Thank God you're alive. They told me you were dead!"

"Who?" Whitman squelched. Then, in the same pinched voice, "Charlie, you're hurting me. I was shot in the chest."

"Oh, right," said Charlie, and let his friend go. He stepped back, wiped the tears from his eyes, and apologized. "It's just that I never thought I'd see you again. They told me that you were *dead.*" The catch in his voice betrayed deep-rooted emotions, and he had to pause to compose himself.

Whitman said, "Who told you that?"

"The police. There were two detectives."

Whitman snorted disdainfully. "Obviously they were mistaken."

Charlie's cheeks were bright pink, his eyes moist with tears. He turned away from Marty, to Edmund, and said, "Hello."

"Top of the day to you," Edmund said to him. "I'm Eddie."

Charlie stuck out his hand, and Edmund shook it.

"Charlie Bates," Charlie said. "You're English?"

"That I am. That I am. I was wondering, Charlie, we're in a bit of a pickle and could use a ride. Would you mind helping us out?"

Charlie turned to his friend again. "A ride? Where to?"

Whitman hesitated. He was not comfortable mentioning aloud the name of the strip club, deeming such an act improper and decidedly un-Custodian-like. He'd had the same issue when asking for directions. That task eventually had fallen to Edmund, and even then Whitman wouldn't let him ask until they found a suitable (male) clerk.

As Whitman floundered, Edmund once again stepped up. "Teasers," he said without a hint of shame. "It's a club that features naked girls dancing."

Charlie Bates nodded and smiled awkwardly. "Yes, I know," he said. He then looked down at his wrist watch. "You want to go there now?" It was two-thirty in the afternoon, not exactly high time for the titty bar.

"Yes. Right away, please."

Charlie looked at his friend, who presented rather good considering he'd been shot recently, and had, according to the authorities, died. In fact, he looked better than he had in months, since before the whole Amanda debacle.

"Why do you need a ride to Teasers?" he asked him.

Whitman shrugged guiltily. Once again, he looked to Edmund for help. "Eddie," he said to him. "Tell the man."

Edmund really didn't have a good answer for that, other than to say they wanted to drink adult beverages and watch naked women dance. He didn't want to say that in front of his boss, though. So instead he put on a smile and blurted out the first thing that came to his mind: "Scavenger hunt."

"Yes," Whitman cried out automatically. Then, realizing the pure insanity of the statement, he gaped at Edmund and said, "Scavenger hunt? Really?"

The look on Charlie's face – the flat brow, the crooked, frowning mouth, the eyes pinched close together – might best be described as befuddled, but he nodded nonetheless and said, "Sure, I can give you a ride."

"Thank you," Whitman said to him, relieved. "That'll really help us out."

"Truly," said Edmund.

Charlie pointed across the street to where he was parked. "My car's over there." He started that way, and Edmund and Whitman followed after him. At the car, Charlie said to his friend, "I don't understand. Why did the police think you were dead?"

Another difficult query, and Whitman couldn't help but wonder if getting a ride was going to be worth all the trouble. He was busy formulating an answer when Edmund jumped in with some more of his famous on-the-spot thinking.

"The police don't know from dead," he said. "Got to talk to doctors about that. They're the ones that know." And in his posh British accent the idea actually sounded sensible, and went a long way to satisfy Charlie's curiosity.

# Chapter Thirteen

Ally wasn't sure what Vaughn was up to, but she knew him well enough to know that he was up to something. He had come to the bar to get her, saying that he had a surprise for her downstairs, and when she asked him what that surprise was, he told her it was something that would make her happy. She had told him that she was busy and asked if it could wait, but he assured her that it was something she'd want to see now.

He then led her to the back of the club, past the velvet ropes, to the door that led to the infamous downstairs lounge where Holt shot his special movies. Ally didn't like it down there, and she said to Vaughn, "Do we have to go downstairs?"

"Yes," he said, leading the way. "Trust me, okay?"

It was then that Ally realized she didn't trust Vaughn, and that gave her something more to think about when it came to the baby in her belly.

"You know I don't like surprises," she said to him.

"And you know I like surprising you."

Ally shook her head as if to say she had no desire to play these little games, but she continued after Vaughn just the same. When he stopped at the door marked Storage Room, she said to him, "What are we doing here?"

"You'll see," was all he said, and then he knocked twice and opened the door.

He went in first, and held it open for Ally, who tentatively peeked inside before daring to step a foot in. She saw her boss, Holt, and she saw Berto, too, whom she knew to be a sadistic bastard. Vaughn used to call him Holt's 'Shark' because he handled the boss's wet work. Ally had always been afraid of him, and not just because Vaughn had told her some of the reprehensible things Berto had done under Holt's orders: taking a man's hand off with a machete; dislocating kneecaps and thumbs; severing a man's ear; having sex with a man's wife while the man was forced the watch. But it was more than that. There seemed to be something missing in him. Same as with Holt, though in a different way. When Ally looked at them, she got the distinct impression that they were as dead as stone inside. Ally knew that Vaughn was not a good man, but he wasn't Holt or Berto. Not yet, anyway.

Ally then saw the surprise intended for her. It was a bloody, beaten, slumped over surprise that had soft whimpering sounds coming out of it. Adam's head hung between his shoulders, there were blasts of blood on his shirt and pants, and he was laboring to breathe. Off to the left, Berto was rubbing his fist.

"Well," said Holt, gesturing for Ally to come in, "what are you waiting for?"

She looked at Holt, then at Vaughn. "Come on," Vaughn said to her. "This is for you."

Ally didn't so much walk through the door as she floated through. That's what it felt like to her, like an invisible force carried her inside; not against her will necessarily, but more or less involuntarily. She was outside the room, and then she was inside the room, and she couldn't remember making a move.

When the door closed behind her, she blinked, as if waking suddenly, and Adam's head lifted up. He looked at her, a beaten man with almost nothing left, and then his head sagged down between his shoulders again.

"Vaughn?" Ally said, looking for an explanation. It had yet to hit her that this was the man who had robbed the A&P Mart and nearly took her life.

"This is him," Vaughn said.

"Told you we'd find him," added Holt.

"Him?" said Ally vaguely. Then she said, "You mean the guy who ... " Her voice caught in her throat then, and a slew of emotions bubbled up inside her. She felt anger, and pity, and confusion. "How?" she asked.

"Simple. We put the word out," said Holt.

"Police are a fucking joke around here," said Berto. "They never would've found him."

Ally stared at the young man sitting on the chair; despite everything, her heart went out to him. Part of her wanted to slap him hard, just once, for what he'd done, but mostly she felt pity for him. It was like seeing the dog that had just taken a chunk out of your leg lying shmushed but half-alive on the side of the road after being hit by a car – yeah, you were upset about what it had done to you, but it was hard to call on that anger while it was clearly in agony and clutching hopelessly to life.

"He confessed," Vaughn said as Ally fought back tears.

"Got the gun right here," Holt said, holding up the hunk of steel that had been Adam's uncle's .38 Special. "And he's got something to say to you."

When Adam didn't immediately respond, Berto smacked him on the back of the head. "You got something to say to the girl, don't you?" he said to him.

Adam gazed at Ally with bleary eyes. "I'm sorry," he said to her, his voice choked with pain. "I didn't mean to shoot you."

"You shot my friend," Ally said. "Not me."

"I didn't mean to shoot him. I swear. I was … I needed the money is all. And I got nervous, and the gun just went off."

"He almost died," Ally said.

"He okay? I read that he's okay."

"He's going to live, yes."

"Not that that matters," said Holt. "You shoot people, there has to be consequences." He turned to Ally. "How much did he steal from you, dear?"

Ally was trying to remember how much had been in her purse that night when another thought jumped in her head. She said to Holt, "You're not going to kill him, are you? I don't want you to kill him. Look at him."

Adam was thankful for the compassion, but hardly hopeful.

Holt, Vaughn and Berto all laughed. "Told you she had a soft heart," Vaughn said, and Holt, shaking his head, added, "Women."

"Look at him," Ally said again. "Hasn't he been through enough?"

"We're not going to kill him," said Vaughn. "We wanted to make sure he understood what he'd done and let him know he better never do it again." He grabbed Adam by the hair, yanked his head back, said to him, "You're sorry for what you done, right?"

Adam's face was smeared with blood and tears. "Yeah, yeah," he cried out. "I'm sorry."

"And you're never going to do it again?"

"No. Never."

"See," Vaughn said to Ally. "That's all."

"We have the weapon," said Holt. "We can turn him over to the police now. We just wanted him to apologize to you first."

"That's what this is all about?" said Vaughn. "This is for you, girl. So people know."

The gift was one she could have done without, but at the same time Ally felt a sense of appreciation. It seemed to her that the cops had no leads, and the thought that her attacker might go free upset her. She believed that gun-toting junkies who robbed convenience stores to support their habit shouldn't be on the streets, and so she was glad that Vaughn and Holt had found him. That didn't mean she wanted him tortured and killed, though. To her, it looked as though he'd already suffered enough.

"I accept his apology," she said. Then, to put a stamp on it, she confronted Adam, making sure to catch and hold his bleary-eyed gaze. "I forgive you," she said to him.

"Thank you," he muttered. "I'm sorry."

Ally then turned to Vaughn. "Okay. Is that all?"

He seemed offended by her attitude, which he viewed as indifferent, and said to her, "No, it's not. A 'thank you' would be nice. You know this took some doing on our part, and Holt had to make a deal and front cash."

Ally felt little guilt for her reaction, or for her part in all this, but the need to apologize rose up inside her nonetheless. "You're right," she said. "I'm sorry." She addressed Holt first. "Thank you," she said to him. "I do appreciate it."

Holt seemed pleased enough with that, and he smiled, and he hugged her. "Anything for you, girl," he said. "You're family. Someone messes with you, they have to deal with the family."

She hugged him back, half-heartedly, and next went to Vaughn. "Thank you," she told him. "I'm sorry I was ... Well, I guess I was surprised. I didn't mean anything by it."

"It's okay, baby girl," he said to her, and hugged her tight. "You know you my girl and I'll always take care of you."

Ally wondered if he'd take care of their baby, too, but that was something she had no intention of bringing up. Not here. Not now. Not ever. She knew better, and besides, she already knew the answer; he undoubtedly would claim that he would do his duty, then she'd never hear from him again.

"Thank you," she told him again, and pulled away from his embrace. She then thanked Berto, who merely nodded back at her. "This was sweet, guys, really. I just don't want you to get in trouble over it. It's not worth it."

"What trouble?" said Holt brashly. "Cops don't know shit in this town. Besides, we're the good guys here. We're the ones who found him."

Ally nodded hesitantly, and said that she should probably get back to work now.

"I'll be up in a bit," Vaughn told her. "We'll talk."

"Vaughn?" she said. "Don't do anything stupid. It's not worth it." And though she tried to keep her voice flat and free of scorn, some slipped through.

"Relax. We're turning him over to the police," he told her. "You have my word."

Ally nodded, accepting his word, though she couldn't say she believed it, having known him to be a liar so many times. Before leaving, she threw poor Adam one last glance, and with genuine sympathy she wondered if she'd ever see him again. He looked like a man who had nothing left, a broken man waiting for the end to come. She hoped for his sake that that end would not come in Teasers' basement.

"Okay," she said, "I'll be upstairs."

She left, and Vaughn closed the door.

Holt smiled and said to Adam, "Too bad she's not the judge and jury, eh?"

Adam would have sobbed only he had no more tears left in him.


There was some confusion at the door. Whitman didn't understand why it should cost so much to get into a club, especially when they had no desire to partake in any of the merriment or nudity.

"We're only here to see Ally," he explained to Chauncey, the mountainous bouncer who was working the door.

"Don't care. You want through these doors," he hitched a thumb over his broad right shoulder, "you have to pay the toll. Ten dollars. Apiece."

"Do you think this is the World's Fair?" Whitman replied with sass.

"Finest naked women in this zip code are behind these doors," Chauncey explained. "You either want to see them or you don't. It's that simple."

"Let's just pay and go in, sir?" Edmund said to Whitman. "Remember, time is of the essence."

"Hold on now. I don't think I can let you in regardless," Chauncey said to Whitman. "We have a dress code here, and sweatpants don't make the cut. Gotta keep the riffraff out. Part of my job."

"I'm friends with Ally Armenti," Whitman said sharply, and both Edmund and Charlie cringed a little when they saw the look that took shape on Chauncey's hambone of a face. "And I need to speak with her. It's imperative."

"You're about to have an imperative conversation with my fist," Chauncey shot back, and for show he made a fist and shook it.

"Hopefully your fist has more wits than your brain," Whitman replied smoothly.

It was then that Charlie and Edmund recognized the possible catastrophic danger, and they quickly jumped in front of their friend. "Here," said Charlie, proffering a twenty dollar bill. "For me and my friend." He then nodded to Whitman and said, "He'll wait in the car."

Chauncey was going to send them away, but money was money, and he figured he could always have Dado help him throw them out if they caused trouble.

"Fine," he said, snatching the twenty from Charlie's hand. "You and you," he said, pointing at Charlie and Edmund. Then, to Whitman, "Not you."

Whitman snarled, but decided he should let well enough alone. Edmund and Charlie could go in and bring Ally out, which was good enough for him. He really didn't want to see naked women dancing, anyway. Well, not very much.

He pooled his concentration and centered it on Edmund. "Tell her you're a friend of mine, and that I'm in the parking lot. Tell her I need to speak to her. Tell her it's important."

Edmund nodded along. When Whitman finished, he cleared his throat and said, "I'll tell her, sir. Have no fear, I'm on the job."

Chauncey opened the door for them, and as they stepped inside Charlie Bates said, "Eddie, what does any of this have to do with a scavenger hunt?"

Edmund looked at Charlie Bates, shrugged, and then was struck quite hard by the un-ignorable ambient sensations of Teasers: the air thick with cigarette smoke, perfume, and fruited body sprays; the manic, cacophonous sound of hip-hop music blaring and echoing back on itself; the shiny, glittery, reflective panorama of strobe lights, disco balls, and mirrors. It was loud and insane ... and oddly titillating.

He stopped dead in his tracks at the sight of one of the dancers; she was on stage in nothing but high heels and a garter, and she was bending, and twisting, and flailing her breasts around. His mouth nearly hit the floor, and a sound like, "ehhhhhehhhhhheeeh," came oozing out of him. Then he saw another girl, this one working a private table, kicking her legs up and shimmying in a way that made that word seem so right.

Charlie bumped into Edmund, and said to him, "Dude? We going in or what?"

Edmund nodded, but didn't move. His eyes were locked on the blonde at the table, and he marveled at how high she could kick her legs ... and what he could plainly see whenever she did.

Charlie pointed across the room and said, "There's the bar."

Edmund nodded again, and again didn't move. "Very limber," he managed to say, and there was a croak in his voice that would've had most doctors reaching for their prescription pad.

Charlie took in an eyeful of the brunette on stage and agreed.

"I can see what the ten dollars is for," Edmund said. And the word 'bargain' jumped to mind.

Though this was not his first time at a strip club, it was his first time at a strip club as a human being. He'd been to plenty of places like this before; he'd even been to Teasers itself on numerous occasions. But being there as a Custodian was different than being there as a human. For one thing, Custodians lacked physical desire, whereas humans were slaves to it.

Edmund, like Whitman before him, was not entirely human. Technically he was liminal, though currently he would not have been able to say the word liminal with all the saliva pooled in his mouth.

"Edmund Von Roy!"

The snapping voice of Emilia rang out over the sound of the music and yanked Edmund from his drooling funk.

"Emilia?" he whelped with shame and surprise. He could see her through the seductive darkness of the club and she did not look pleased.

"I thought her name was Ally," Charlie said, not following.

"You have an important job to do," Emilia told Edmund. "Do it! And stop looking at that young woman. She's someone's daughter."

"Yes, ma'am. Sorry."

Charlie was baffled. "Sorry about what?"

"Wait!" Edmund cried out when he noticed Emilia fading away. But it was too late; she was already gone. "Son-of-a-bitch!" he said.

"What's wrong?" Charlie inquired. "Who's Emilia? And what are you sorry about?"

Not knowing what else to say, Edmund muttered, "No worries. Scavenger hunt business." And with some effort he pulled his eyes off the dancing girl and started for the bar, where temptation took on an even more attractive form.

Ally was a ten-bell knockout, and dressed in her skimpy uniform, with all the best bits of her squeezing out, Edmund found it difficult to work his tongue. He said to her, "Uhhhhhhh." Then he said, "Errrr."

Charlie stepped up. "Excuse me, Miss, is your name Allllll ... " It had been going quite good until she looked at him, and then he lost all feeling in his extremities and every thought in his head scattered like dandelion spores.

"I'm Ally," Ally said. "Can I get you something to drink?"

"Would love a gin-rickey," Edmund said, and then he smiled and burped out an uncomfortable laugh.

"Don't know what that is," Ally said. "I'm guessing it has gin in it."

Edmund nodded his head up and down like a happy mental patient. The smile on his face appeared to be spackled there.

Charlie Bates said, "Beer."

"Any particular kind."

"Beer," he said again.

"Okay then."

Ally sauntered off, preoccupied by what was going on downstairs and wondering what was in a gin-rickey. Edmund, meanwhile, sucked in a huge breath of air, not caring in the least that half of it was secondhand smoke. He had seen Ally before, many times, so he had no clue as to why he was having so much trouble talking to her. It had to be the nervous, anxious, self-loathing human part of him cropping up like a weed. Being human was such a nuisance, he surmised, though he had to admit the food was rather good.

Then he thought about Whitman; his boss's fate was riding on his ability to be, at the very least, competent, and Edmund, though uncomfortable and painfully out of his depth, was determined to be just that. He could be competent, he assured himself. He could be adequate, too, should the situation call for adequateness.

On the other side of the bar, Ally was consulting her phone on how to make a gin-rickey. After learning the ingredients, she got to work, while Charlie Bates alternated between leering at her and leering at the buxom dancer on stage. He wasn't the type to go to a strip club, just like he wasn't the type to score with women or pay for prostitutes. Given that, it had been more than two years since he'd last seen an actual woman naked and he was rather enjoying the sights.

Ally returned with their drinks and told them it would be twelve dollars – she was charging seven dollars for the gin-rickey and five for the light beer on tap – and Edmund looked at Charlie and said, "You have twelve dollars on you?"

Charlie nodded and reached for his wallet. While he found the money, Edmund consciously put the lustful human part of his mind in the corner and said to Ally, "We we're hoping to talk to you. We're friends with Whitman."

Ally's brow crinkled with doubt. "Whitman who?" she asked.

Then Charlie, with a fresh twenty dollar bill in hand, said to Edmund, "Yeah. Who's Whitman?"

It was then that Edmund realized his mistake and began to fluster. "Ummmm," he stammered. "Uhhhhhhh. I was ... " With both of them looking at him, waiting for an explanation, he reset himself and tried again. "Whitman," he said. "You know, Marty. I call him Whitman. That was his nickname back at university, on account of his love of the poet, Walt Whitman."

Charlie Bates had never heard that before and was skeptical, though Edmund's British accent made him seem above reproach. Ally, meanwhile, had no interest whatsoever in what may or may not have been Marty's nickname in college; she just wanted to know who these guys were and why they wanted to talk to her about Marty.

"You know him?" she asked Edmund. "How?"

"He's an old friend."

"I've known him all my life," added Charlie, and once he had Ally's attention, he handed her the twenty dollar bill.

She took it, but made no move to cash it in. "You know him well?" she asked.

They both said, "Very well," at nearly the same time. Then Edmund added, "He's here, out in the parking lot. The doorman wouldn't let him in."

"Why not?"

"Something about a dress code."

"He's outside now?"

Charlie nodded.

Edmund said, "He wants to talk to you."

Ally quickly took the twenty to the register, rang in the drinks, and returned with Charlie's change, which she put on the bar in front of him. Then she said, "Where's he at?"

"Right outside. He told us to come in here and get you."

Ally hurried from behind the bar, hurried across the club, and went straight out the front door, where she ran into Dado.

"Girl, what you doin' out here?" he said to her. "Something wrong?"

The air was damp and cold, and she realized immediately that she was in her uniform, which provided little coverage and even less warmth. She huddled into herself and said, "There's a guy out here you wouldn't let in. Something about a dress code."

Dado was about to answer her when from the left Whitman called out, "Ally. Thank goodness."

Ally turned to see him, and Dado said, "You know him?"

"Yes," she said. "He's my friend."

"Sorry. I didn't know."

Whitman was happy to see Ally, and, against every thread of common decency that he believed was his duty as a Custodian and a man, he instantly noticed just how much of her there was to see. He discovered that he was happy about that, too. Until now, Whitman had never understood the term 'hot' when it was applied to a woman who looked attractive; but when he saw Ally in her tight, skimpy outfit, 'hot' was the word that sprung to mind. It had to have something to do with temperature, he imagined, because he suddenly felt warm under the collar.

"Marty?" she said to him. "What are you doing here?"

"I had to see you," he told her. "I need to talk to you."

Ally thought about leading him into the club, but the club was Vaughn's domain and she didn't want any trouble. There was enough of that already, she believed.

Instead, she said, "Come on, my car's over here," and she started to the left. From over her shoulder she told Dado that she'd be right back.


Meanwhile, downstairs at Teasers, Holt was in the process of strong-arming Adam into appearing in one of his movies. Vaughn was standing at his boss's side, sneering, while Berto provided motivation.

Holt said, "You're dead to rights, kid. We got the gun, and they'll match that to the bullet that shot that guy. You're going down for a long time."

"I know, I know," Adam sobbed, his face a smeared mess of blood and dirt and tears. "But I needed the money."

"Money? Cost me money to find you," Holt went on. "Had to put the word out on the street. A local vagrant turned you in for some cocaine and a few hours with one of the dancers here. He's how we found you."

Adam gave no reply, other than to snivel and weep.

"That brings me to my offer. I have a venture I'm rather fond of. I make movies. Adult movies. Right here in the basement of the club. We have five different sets, and a lot of the girls who dance for me star in the films. I have a website where the movies can be viewed. Got sponsors and advertisers, too. Not surprisingly, I turn a tidy little profit, and it's a great deal of fun. I'm sure you can imagine." Holt stopped here, and stepped up on Adam. "I could be wrong," he said to him, "but you look like someone who watches pornography. Most guys do, some more than others. You look like one of them. Am I right?"

Holt waited for an answer. When one didn't come, he glanced at Berto, who immediately slapped Adam upside the head. "Boss is talking to you," he barked at him.

Adam whimpered and grimaced in pain, but he possessed enough wherewithal to form a reply. "Yes," he said. "I've seen it."

"Thought so," Holt said, and got back to the point of things. "Anyway, as I'm sure you know, girl-on-girl porn is quite popular these days. Lesbians are all the rage, and a lot of the girls here are into it. They've got their toys, and they know how to use them. Do you like watching girl-on-girl porn?"

This time Adam was on the mark. "Yes," he said. "I do."

"Of course you do, you're a guy. Am I right?" Holt pointed at Berto. "You know what I'm talking about, don't you?" he said to him. Then he nudged Vaughn. "You, too. We all do. Those girls are crazy."

"Love me some girl-on-girl action," said Berto. "Especially when they break out the toys."

"You know it," agreed Vaughn.

"It's the best!" Holt cried out happily. "And our girls love toys. Mostly, they bring their own. All sorts they have. And they love fucking each other. They like it more than getting fucked, I'd say. Some of them, anyway. There's one, Candace, she's this petite little blonde, might weigh a hundred pounds soaking wet. But when that little pixie gets going, I'd wager there aren't many guys that can lean into it like she can.

"She's one of my favorites. She was my first star, and has been in ten or twelve of my movies since then. And she always gives her best, no matter if she's getting or giving. She has this fantasy she told me about, which is where you come in."

Adam sniffed, and nodded hesitantly.

"She did this dominatrix scene with one of the other regulars here, Gina, and she railed on her like the end was nigh. One of the best scenes we've ever done. It got more hits on the website than any other video we posted, and it has the highest ranking, too. You should see it, it's incredible. And Gina, she's cute as a button. The two of them together, with sweet little Candace laying the pipe." Holt closed his eyes, shook his head appreciatively, and went, "Mmm, Mmm, Mmm. You want to talk about hot."

"I remember that scene," said Berto, and a lewd expression crept over his face. "It's burned in my head. I had to fuck Gina after that. What a piece."

"See," said Holt. "That's Candace for you. Unforgettable. And this fantasy of hers, well, I'd really like to make it happen. I owe her that much, after all she's done for me. And seeing how you owe me, I figured the pieces all fit together."

Adam had recently gone through near-death withdrawal symptoms; he'd also been knocked unconscious and rapped upside the head numerous times, to the point where there was a continuous ringing in his head. He was exhausted, dizzy, half-delirious, and in a great amount of pain. In spite of all that, he had enough sense to not like where this was heading, and the glum, fearful look he showed his captors was a perfect portrait of that.

It made Holt crack a big ol' smile. "Whatcha think, Adam?" he said, unable to lessen the width of that smile even a little. "You want to be a film star?"

Berto let out a chuckle, while Vaughn's sneer turned slightly upwards, becoming an evil grin. Adam pretended not to understand, and said, "You want me to fuck Candace?" It was a shot in the dark, hope against reason.

Holt laughed heartily. "No, no, dear boy," he said after he regained himself. "Candace is going to fuck you." And Adam's pasty face lost whatever delicate shade of color it had left, going pure white. "She's always wanted to fuck a guy, and as you can imagine, it's not so easy to talk a guy into something like that. Even when you offer to pay them. I was going to go to an escort service, but they have rules, and part of the fantasy is that the guy be straight and ... well, *reluctant* to be dominated. She's got it all planned out, from the outfits to what she wants to do and how. She's rather creative, and while I don't want to specialize in these sort of films, I do owe her this."

Adam began to shake his head. "No, I don't want to do it," he said. "Are you crazy?"

Holt laughed again, but this time his laugh had a snarling quality to it. "Me?" he said. "Am I crazy? I'm not the one who tried to rob a convenience store. I'm not the one who tried to hide out at an old school. I'm not the one who got addicted to drugs and lost all control of his life. That was you, and you ask me if *I'm* crazy?"

"I didn't mean it like that," Adam said. "I just meant that ... I mean, I'm not into that kinda stuff. That's all."

"Well, where you're going," said Berto, that deep bass voice of his booming in the small, block room, "you're going to have to get into it, whether you like it or not. You're going to be entertainment."

"Precisely," said Holt. "Call it a precursor for the next ten years of your life. I'm guessing that's what you'll end up serving, about ten years. You'll be what? Forty when you get out?"

"Thirty-six," Adam corrected him.

"Thirty-six then. Not old, but hardly young. I'm guessing you don't have a good lawyer?"

Adam didn't have any kind of lawyer. He'd managed to survive seven hard years as an addict without ever being arrested. That was about to change, though.

"I could get you a decent lawyer," Holt said. "Refer you to one, at least. A decent lawyer can be the difference between ten years and five."

Adam, who had a tenuous control over his emotions at best, was beginning to lose even that. He wasn't the sharpest knife in the drawer, but even he knew that he was being blackmailed. "No," he said, holding his ground.

Holt nodded as if he was disappointed but ultimately

understood. Then he reached into his pocket and pulled out a small vial of heroin. Adam's eyes went as wide as racquetballs and his mouth opened as if he was hungry and the heroin was chocolate cake.

"You know what this is?" Holt said, and put it on the table in front of him. The two lumps of dirt brown nirvana sung to Adam, and the song was beautiful. "Where you're going, they don't have this. Gonna be years before you get another taste, and this stuff is pure. Call it a going away party, if you like."

Adam's mouth was watering, and he realized that his left leg was bouncing up and down.

"You go in, you get clean, you never have to touch this rotten stuff again. But wouldn't it be nice to have one last go before that happens. One last party, one last night of fun, and all you have to do is let a girl fuck you with a rubber penis. Really, who cares about that? You're going to be gone. And like my friend noted earlier, it's something you're going to have to get used to, because in jail, you're going to be pretty popular, my friend. So why not ease your way into it, see how it goes."

Being sodomized scared Adam something awful. The threat of being raped in prison was one of the main reasons he'd always avoided committing crimes against the public. It terrified him to think about it, especially now that it seemed to be inevitable. If they turned him in, he would go to jail, most likely state or federal prison, and in those kinds of places, with those kinds of people, he would be lucky to last a night or two. That in mind, he decided to try and make a deal.

"How about this?" he said to Holt. "I'll be in your movie, but only if you don't turn me in. Throw the gun away, don't tell the police anything about me, and I'll do whatever you want. Deal?" He then held on with hopeful anticipation, pleading with God for Holt to take the bait.

But Holt wasn't one to bend to the will of a junkie. "Sorry," he said, slowly shaking his head back and forth. "What kind of citizen would I be if I knowingly aided a violent criminal escape justice? Why, I couldn't live with myself." It was hard to get all those words out without smiling, especially when he saw the big ol' cheese spread across Berto's face.

"They don't have to know," Adam pressed. "It can be our

secret."

Holt grabbed the vial of heroin from the table and put it back in his pocket.

"Wait!" Adam cried out. "No."

"What?"

"There's got to be something. Please."

"I'm not here to barter with you, kid. I made you an offer. A good offer, considering. Either take it or leave it. You're lucky I'm even doing this. You almost killed one of my girls. That's Vaughn's woman, and Vaughn's my right hand. Now, you either want the smack or you don't. You want it, you have to work for it. You don't, tell me, and we'll get the police here now."

"How long?" Adam asked.

"How long what?"

"How long can I ... you know, stay here before you call them? If I agree to it."

"Well, we won't call the police until tomorrow. You'll have all night to party and live it up like a wildman. But part of that is the movie, and that's nonnegotiable. That's for my girl Candace. So, you in or out?" And for added incentive, Holt again removed the vial of heroin from his pocket and placed it on the table in front of Adam.


"I have to find the guy who shot me," Whitman said. "It's imperative. And I received information that he was here."

Ally said, "Why do you have to find him? I don't understand."

"I don't know how to explain it," he said to her. "I just have to find him."

"Were you working with him?" Ally inquired. "That's what the police think."

"Working with him how? He shot me."

"I don't know. They said it was suspicious. I think that's why they had you sequestered at the hospital."

"I don't know what the cops are thinking," Whitman said. "But I certainly wasn't in cahoots with Adam Dubinsky."

"I don't know what ... " Ally began, but she stopped as soon as Whitman's words sank in. "Wait," she said. "How do you know his last name? You do know him, don't know? You *were* working with him."

"On my life, no!" Whitman insisted. "I've never even met the man. But I don't ... " He stopped, hung his head. He wasn't comfortable lying, but he realized that the truth was a dead end street. He couldn't tell Ally the truth without seeming out of his mind, and if she thought he was out of his mind, he couldn't help Adam Dubinsky.

It was a Catch 22.

"Okay," he said, and summoning all the resolve and audacity it took to lie, especially to someone he cared about, he locked eyes with her. "I can't explain it," he began. "Just like I can't explain the things I know about you. I woke up from this damn coma and everything's been a mess. I can barely remember myself, but I remember all sorts of other things. It's very frustrating."

"What about your friends?" Ally asked, not done grilling him yet. "You remember them?"

"No. Not really."

"So the two guys in the club ... What, you just happened to run into them today?"

"I needed a ride."

"And they came and picked you up?"

"Yes."

He said it in a calm, even tone, but his face wore a look of pure guilt. Ally had seen that look before, and she stared him down. "Something isn't right here," she said. "You're not telling me everything."

Whitman wanted to be glib and rejoin with confidence, assure her that he was on the up-and-up and she'd be wise to trust him, but the way Ally, in her tiny little outfit, had turned produced a rather distracting view, one that Whitman was unable to pull himself away from. Her breasts were small and perky, like ripe peaches, and seemed to be aimed right at him, and her shapely legs, bent and slightly open, made him think about ... Sex. He wanted to touch her, caress her, kiss her, make love to her.

"Ummmm," he said. Then he gulped down some air and added, "Ummmm."

"Marty," she said to him, and her voice was different now.

Gone was the snappish, accusatory tone she'd been throwing his way; it was replaced by something softer, gentler, and unquestionably feminine. "I don't know what's going on here, I just don't want any trouble."

"Me either," said Whitman. "I promise you that."

"What do you want with Adam? And tell me the truth."

Whitman took a deep breath, and sighed as he exhaled. "I don't know the truth," he said, lying to her. "I just have to see him, and talk to him."

"But why?"

He shrugged. "Because he's in trouble."

"No kidding. They're turning him over to the police."

"So he is here?"

Ally nodded, said, "Yes. Downstairs."

"I need to talk to him before they turn him in. Can you help me with that?"

She looked him in the eye, reached out and took hold of one of his hands. Her skin was so soft, so smooth, and Whitman felt himself heating up. "I want to trust you," she told him. "I do trust you. I just ... "

"You don't want any trouble," he finished for her.

"Exactly."

"I don't either."

"I don't want *you* to get in trouble," she told him, and as she told him that, she lovingly squeezed his hand.

Whitman looked at her, leaned in to kiss her. She leaned in to kiss him back.

And the damn broke.


Charlie Bates was having a hard time concentrating with all the scantily clad women breezing around, acting as though it was perfectly natural for them to be in public in underwear and see-through lingerie. There was a blonde with large breasts, a skinny brunette with small breasts, and a young Asian woman in a G-string and bra whose ass, Charlie Bates believed, should have been hanging in a museum.

Edmund, meanwhile, was looking at everything but the girls, terrified that Emilia was hiding in the shadows, watching him, and would report back to the Elders that while on duty he had spent a large portion of time ogling naked women. He wanted to ogle the naked women – he didn't want to be rude, after all; they were only doing their jobs – but he really didn't want to go through Purgatory again.

"Look at her," Charlie said, nodding in the direction of the Asian stripper. "I love Asian women. Something about them really gets me going."

Edmund clamped his eyes shut and glanced that way. He then nodded and said, "Oh yes, very lovely. I like Asian women myself." And though he was terrified of the possible consequences, he gave into temptation and peeked.

The young woman in question was not only beautiful, she was coming their way, and Edmund began to have a mild panic attack. He looked to the left, then to the right, then down at his feet, figuring that was probably safest.

From the corner of his mouth, Charlie said, "She's coming over here. What do we do?"

The first idea that jumped into Edmund's head was 'Hide', but he wisely stopped himself from saying that. Instead, he said, "Act natural. And don't stare at her breasts."

"I'm more of an ass man, myself," Charlie whispered back, and then the young woman was there, standing in front of them in a thong and bra, a smile as sweet as candy titivating her beautiful face.

"I'm Suzy," she said. "Would you two like a table dance?"

Edmund Von Roy mustered the courage to look up, and as he looked up, he saw a lot of flesh that looked really, really good: sleek legs, slim waist, flat stomach, small but firm breasts. He tried with all his will and might to say, 'No, we don't want a table dance', but the words got lost somewhere between his brain and his mouth, and he just sat there helplessly clicking his tongue.

It was then that Charlie Bates took it upon himself to be bold. "Sure," he said. "We'd love one, Suzy. I'm Charlie, and this here is Eddie."

"Nice to meet you," she replied, and as the song playing began to wind down, she told them that it cost ten dollars a song, or twenty-five for three.

Charlie nodded as if this was acceptable and reached for his wallet. But Edmund was confused. He said, in his prim British accent, "Terribly sorry, Suzy, perhaps you're unaware, but we paid the entertainment fee on the way in."

She looked puzzled at first, then amused. "No. That's just to get in the door, sweetie. If you want me to dance for you, it costs extra."

That seemed a bit much to Edmund, and he was about to tell Suzy just that when Charlie cried out, "Three songs, please," and excitedly handed over twenty-five dollars.

Suzy smiled, stuffed the money in her garter, and began to limber up.

Edmund's eyes darted around in search of Emilia or Alina, or one of the other Custodians in the Garrison, but as far as he could tell there was no one from that world in the club. His plan as Suzy began to seductively sway and move to the music was to politely excuse himself and go to the bathroom, where he could hide, but it seemed as though his legs, like his mouth, refused to respond to even the simplest neurological commands. Currently his groin was hogging every impulse he had, and most of the blood; sweat began to bead on his brow like raindrops on a windshield, and it felt as though his ears were on fire.

Then, in a fluid, well-practiced motion, Suzy's bra came off, revealing her wonderful little breasts, and Edmund felt as though the entire world jerked to a stop.

Suzy turned her focus on Charlie, who had paid for her time, and Edmund, flushed and flustered, wiped his suddenly sweaty palms on his tweed trousers and sucked in a couple deep breaths. He wondered where Whitman and Ally were at, and he hoped that they would return soon, before he did something stupid.

Charlie Bates had no such worries. Spiders could have been crawling on his head and he wouldn't have noticed. Or cared. He was completely enthralled with Suzy, and his eyes went wild and wide when she effortlessly lifted her left leg and placed her high-heeled foot on his shoulder, giving him a view of her that he was powerless to ignore. She smelled like ... Well, Charlie wasn't sure what she smelled like exactly – some kind of exotic fruit or flower – but he knew that she smelled really good, like women are supposed to smell, and he breathed in the scent of her.

Her leg came down, she whirled around, bent full at the waist, planted her lovely backside in Charlie's lap. She began to move it around with incredible control, and Charlie was no longer able to subdue his erection. It poked at Suzy's firm butt like a divining rod, and as soon as she felt it, she knew she had him. That's when she snapped upright and moved on to Edmund.

She went right to work, and in seconds her beauty and incredible gracefulness left him as helpless as a scarecrow in a tornado. She climbed on top of him, knelt on his lap, and slowly leaned in, arching her back and ever-so-slightly brushing her plum breasts against his cheeks. Then, as her jet-black hair cascaded down on him, she moaned softly in his ear. It was her signature move, and Edmund's erection very nearly tore through the thick wool weave of his trousers

It was about then that Ally led Whitman into the club.

Whitman didn't see his friends at first, not until Ally pointed them out. "There," she said. "Looks like they're enjoying themselves."

This is what Whitman saw when he looked: Charlie Bates was staring sidelong at a young woman performing some sort of erotic calisthenics on a chair. Then he noticed an extra pair of legs coming from the chair. Unlike the woman's legs, which were bare and lovely, this second pair was rather gangly and draped in wool suit pants. Then the young woman doing naked calisthenics changed positions and the embarrassed, dementedly-blissful face of Edmund Von Roy came into full view.

"What's the meaning of this?" Whitman cried out.

"Relax," said Ally. "Suzy's one of our most popular. She's beautiful, isn't she?"

"That's not the point."

"A couple fish like that," Ally said, "she'll pick their pockets 'til they're empty, have them running for the ATM three times."

"No. That's not going to happen," Whitman vowed, and started over that way.

Suzy didn't have to nuzzle her backside in Edmund's lap to affirm that he liked her; it was on his face, and in his eyes, and beyond that she could plainly see the outline of his manhood beneath his vintage wool trousers.

Got you, too, she thought to herself, but just as she was about to seal the deal by dropping her G-string and showing them all she had to show, Whitman came up behind her and shouted, "Edmund Von Roy!"

Suzy jumped back, while Edmund yelped and fell over in his chair, crashing to the floor.

"Holy shit!" Suzy exclaimed, putting a hand to her heart, slightly covering her left breast. "What's your problem?!"

"Sorry. He's with me," said Ally, coming up behind Whitman to explain. "Sorry, Suze. This is his first time here."

"Dear God," Suzy said. "You almost gave me a heart attack."

Edmund had managed to scramble to his feet, which was not an easy chore given the granite state of his penis. While the others spoke, he turned slightly to the side, reached a hand down his pants, and shifted things around. Then he said to Whitman, "Sorry, sir. Meant no harm. Was blending in is all. Wasn't really enjoying it."

"Yeah, right," said Suzy. "All evidence to the contrary."

"Marty?" Charlie said. "What's going on? Why are you acting so strange? And are you seriously on a scavenger hunt right now?"

Whitman had no time for Charlie Bates, friend or not, and he ignored his questions. "Edmund," he said, "I need your help. Ally's decided to ... " he stopped, glanced at Suzy, and then finished with a conspiratorial whisper, " ... let us see you know who."

Suzy looked at Ally. "You have some weirdo friends," she said to her, and Ally had no choice but to agree.

"What about me?" Charlie Bates asked.

"Well ... Can you stay for a while?" Whitman said to him. "We may need a ride home."

Charlie appeared to be offended at first – being treated like a jitney and not a friend made him feel second-rate – but then he remembered Suzy and the way she moved, and looked, and smelled, and suddenly he didn't much care.

"Sure," he said. "Go on. I'll be right here." Then he leaned back in his chair and said to the near-naked Asian goddess who'd been dancing swan-like for him, "We're still okay for a couple more songs, right?"

Oh yeah, she thought to herself with supreme satisfaction, he's hooked. She showed him a smile, leaned close to him, tickled his cheek with her silky fingers, and whispered something in his ear.

Charlie replied, "I don't think I have that much on me," to which Suzy said, "There's an ATM right over there," and she pointed to the prominently-displayed machine that had made her and so many of the other girls thousands of extra dollars over the years.

Ally nudged Whitman and said, "See," and he frowned at her, not finding it the least bit amusing. He then turned to Edmund and said, "Are you ready?"

"Yes, sir. Right away, sir. Right as the wind."

Ally, though suspicious – even more so after noting Edmund's reaction to Marty, the way he kept calling him 'Sir' – told them to follow her. And she led them across the club and through an ominous black door.

There's an old saying about best laid plans, but Adam didn't know the saying, and none of his plans worked out anyway. Nonetheless he had a plan, and he figured that given the alternatives, his plan was as good as any.

He didn't want to go to jail, and he didn't want to be bent over by a hundred pound dominatrix living out a fantasy. He just wanted to get high and be left alone. His fondest memories were of those days when his addiction was yet in its nascent stage and he'd secretly take his score – be it pills or powder heroin – lock himself in his room, and get wasted. He wouldn't do anything more than watch TV or listen to music, but outside his room the rest of the world ceased to exist and thus was perfect.

Those wonderful days were long gone, though, never to return. Adam knew that now. He knew that his life was over, one way or the other, and knowing that, believing that, he wanted to be the one who dropped the axe.

An 'accidental' overdose was all it would take, and he knew that what Holt had given him was more than enough to end his life forever. Cook a little too much, inject a little too much, and slide numbly into the great dark slumber of forever. No jail. No cowgirl pixie with a strap-on rubber penis. No Holt, no Vaughn, no Berto. And, beyond that, no more living like a rat in the sewers, scrounging for bits. One push, he mused, and it'd all be over, and a life wasted would finally be laid to waste.

But like all best laid plans, variables ensued. For one thing, Berto cooked the smack, and he kept the content low.

"You know, I can do more than that," Adam told him. "I have a pretty high tolerance. Been doing it for years."

"This stuff is pure," Berto replied. "Besides, boss doesn't want you whacked out of your skull. Just ... *loose*."

"But ... "

"Now, now, no arguing with the boss. Unless you want to renege on your deal?"

It wasn't as much a threat as it was scornful mocking, Berto knowing that a junkie like Adam could not go back on any deal while he was close enough to smell the wet, sour clay of pure heroin cooking. It was bubbling on a spoon, and Adam's eyes were locked on it, like Charlie Bates's eyes were locked on Suzy upstairs.

"I'm not arguing," Adam said. "I'm just saying I can handle more."

"Keep that thought in mind when Candace gets here." A sinister laugh echoed from Berto's chest like rumblings from a volcano.

Adam sagged in defeat. His eyes stayed with the heroin, though, the little bubbles forming and popping in the curve of the spoon.

"Almost done," Berto said, and he pulled the spoon from the flame and held it up to his nose. He took a whiff, and turned his head. "Nasty."

"I actually like the smell," Adam put in.

"Like Pavlov's dogs liked the song of the dinner bell."

Adam didn't bother with a reply. There was none to give, and besides, he was only moments away from getting high. Berto rested the spoon so that it was level and the heroin pooled evenly within; then he grabbed a syringe, opened the package it was in, removed it, removed the tip guard from the needle, and gave it an experimental push.

With Adam watching, salivating, thinking only of the high to come and not the inevitable lows sure to follow, Berto placed the needle in the heroin mix and pulled back on the plunger, filling the vial with dirty brown fluid. He filled it all the way, then eased the plunger forward, spraying some of Adam's high across the table.

"Okay," he said, "let's do this."

Adam's hands were still bound. Berto put the needle down, removed a knife from his back pocket, opened the blade, and went around the back of Adam's chair and cut his hands free. He closed the knife, put it back in his pocket, and returned to his seat.

Adam was already grabbing for the rubber strap to tie around his arm.

"Gees," Berto said. "Relax, man. You've got all night."

Part of Adam wanted to get stoned and enjoy it, while another part of him wanted the heroin to stop his heart and end his life. He had gone through a difficult detox and still wasn't very strong so the possibility of an overdose existed, even on an average amount of product. That in mind, he quickly tied off and told Berto he was ready.

"You do it," Berto told him. "I'm not your fucking doctor."

Adam nodded, grabbed the syringe, tapped the needle a couple times. He didn't shoot anymore out, though, figuring an air bubble, if he should be so lucky, would kill him just as well as an overdose. Then he tightened the strap around his arm, bit down on one end to secure it, and waited for a vein to pop.

There were faded track marks on his arm, little maroon bumps with black centers, like spider bites. The tracks had been there for years, forming and fading away in odd, closely-grouped patterns. He barely noticed them anymore, just like he barely noticed himself when he saw his reflection in a mirror. The sum of the whole is greater than its parts, and sometimes parts are all there are.

A vein showed itself, big and blue in the crook of his elbow, like a goldfish swimming to the surface at feeding time. And with ease and no forethought whatsoever, Adam sunk the needle into the vein and pushed down on the plunger, transferring the dirty brown nectar from the vial of the syringe to the blood of the junkie. Liftoff came ten seconds later, and Adam slouched in his chair like he'd been shot. His eyes closed, his body went limp, and a demented smile drooped on his face.

The knock at the door didn't startle Berto, but it was unexpected. Holt had told him to shoot up Adam with the smack while he and Vaughn discussed some business in the office. They'd be gone for twenty minutes or so, and then they'd get the dastardly plan rolling.

But only five minutes had passed since they'd left, and Berto called out, "Who is it?" like it might be the police.

"Ally," was the reply, and Berto recognized her voice right off.

"Hold on, girl," he said. He stood, unlatched the lock, and opened the door.

Ally came through first, and then Whitman and Edmund came in on her heels.

"Who the hell are they?" Berto asked.

"Friends," Ally replied.

"What's this about? Does Holt know you're here?"

"Yes," she told him, lying point blank, and quite convincingly. She then looked past Berto to Adam, who had sunk in his chair like gelatin in a mold. His head was down, and he showed no outward signs of life.

"You killed him!" she cried out. "You said you were going to turn him over to the police."

"We are," Berto said. He stepped in front of Ally, partially blocking her sightline. "Boss has a job for him first."

That's when Ally noticed the contraband on the table – the needle, the charred spoon, the lighter – and the rubber strap coiled loosely around Adam's arm. "You got him high!" she exclaimed. "Why on earth would you get him high?"

"Because that was part of the deal."

"What deal?"

"That's between Holt and Mister-Soon-to-be-a-Star here."

Ally didn't understand, and in her silence Berto took the opportunity to address the new people in the room. "Who are you guys?" he said to them, thinking the shorter one in sweats looked awfully familiar.

"They're friends of mine," Ally said before they had a chance to answer. "They're here to see Adam."

"Why?"

"Because Marty's the one who Adam shot the other night. The one who saved my life."

Berto looked at Edmund first, then at Whitman. And that's when it hit him, when the events of a day six or seven months gone came rushing back to him like a storm: the girl, Amanda Something, the freaky one who liked it dirty and rough, calling him up and saying she had a couple hours to kill; and the apartment, the second-story walkup done in girly colors and girly décor, lots of pink and pastel, lots of flowers and silly pictures. When he first walked in the place, Berto remembered thinking that the guy Amanda lived with must be a real Nancy-boy, a 'Yes, dear,' 'Right away, dear,' kind of fellow; and he remembered laying into her that day extra hard, railing her like a cheap whore. And then something crashed into him, knocking him to the floor.

He remembered it all so well; he remembered beating Marty senseless and then going back and finishing off the girl, the slutty Amanda, who resisted him at first but then gave in and enthusiastically took what he had. He left her sticky with his spunk, her cute little backside covered in hand-print welts; he left her to deal with the busted, bleeding, broken young man on the floor, a man she claimed to love though she never passed up an opportunity to play on the side.

It was definitely him, thought Berto. It was the same frail, feeble guy he'd pummeled in between defiling Amanda.

"It's you," he said to Whitman. "Marty, right?"

Whitman wasn't expecting recognition and figured the best course was to go with it. "Yes," he said. "It's me. Marty."

"Wait. You know him?" Ally asked Berto.

"In a manner of speaking."

When Ally looked at him, Whitman shrugged and said, "I don't know."

"Really?" said Berto, laughing. "Well, I suppose if you'd done to me what I'd done to you, I'd have trouble remembering, too."

Ally was confused, as was Edmund and Whitman. Adam, meanwhile, was lounging in a state of unrefined bliss, truly believing that he was watching some kind of strange reality television program. He couldn't have said where he was or what he was doing, and he couldn't have cared less.

"Is he all right?" Whitman asked Berto.

"This is a joke, right?" Berto replied. He looked at Ally. "What is this? Seriously?"

"I don't know what you're talking about," she said to him.

Whitman edged around Ally, moving closer to Adam, trying to get a better look at him. But Berto blocked his path, and even put a hand out to stop him. "We don't want a repeat, do we?" he said to him. "Because I went easy last time."

Whitman was confused. "What last time?" he said.

Berto sneered menacingly. "Last time when I beat your ass and fucked your girl," he said. "Amanda, right? You gonna tell me you don't remember?"

Now Ally was confused. She glanced back and forth between Whitman and Berto, searching their expressions for signs of truth.

Edmund said, "Sir, I have a feeling this is the man who ... well, you know."

Whitman did know, and his face hardened with a scowl. "You," he said to Berto, pointing a disapproving finger at him. "This all started with you."

"Say another fucking word and I'm going to end it now."

"No one's ending anything until I know what the hell is going on," Ally cried out.

"That's what I want to know," said Berto. "Why'd you bring this guy here?"

"I'm here to see Adam," said Whitman. "Now move out of my way."

He pushed out a forearm to nudge Berto aside, and the massive henchman took immediate exception. He grabbed Whitman's forearm with a powerful hand, lifted and twisted it, and shoved him away.

"Don't fuck with me, boy!" he threatened him. "Or else!"

Whitman was not a violent man, but his dander was up and he was feeling pretty confident after having knocked out Vaughn. So he put up his dukes like an old time fighter and said, "I warn you, I know how to box."

Berto started to laugh, until Whitman caught him with a jab. The punch was quick and crisp, and it knocked Berto back a step.

"Marty!" Ally cried out. "Don't."

Berto wiped at his nose with the back of his hand, smearing the blood Whitman had drawn across his upper lip. When he saw the blood, he grumbled out a laugh, said, "Wrong choice," and charged forward.

Fearing the worst, Ally screamed and jumped in front of Berto, and when he barreled into her like a freight train, she went flying and he lost his balance and stumbled to the floor. With his meat-chin teed up like a golf ball, Berto was a sitting duck. But Whitman didn't take the shot. He was more worried about Ally, and he rushed to her side.

Berto didn't stay down long. He rose up with vengeance in his heart and his fists clenched, ready to hammer Whitman into oblivion. And he would have done just that, only Edmund stepped up in the nick of time. Berto never saw the prim, gangly Brit coming, but he certainly felt the impact of the shoulder that struck him. He felt the sensation of flying, too, right before crashing into something hard and flat – the wall – then landing on something just as hard and flat – the floor. The ceiling spun above him like a fan with a broken blade, and he yelped and bewilderedly threw his hands in front of his face when he thought that the walls were caving in on him.

"Ally?" Whitman said, stroking her hair. "Ally? Are you okay?"

Her beautiful dark brown eyes were aimed up at him in a glassy stare. But she nodded and said, "I think so. What happened?"

"Just relax," Whitman said. "We're going to get you out of here." He then looked at Edmund, who was standing over them, all puffed up with pride and vigor, looking very much like a conquering hero.

"I had to do it, sir," he said in the solemn tones of someone who was sorry for their actions, though not all that sorry. "He was coming for you."

Whitman glanced at Berto, who was muttering incoherently and lolling on the floor like a helpless baby. "Not a problem," he said. "Get Adam. We have to get out of here."

Edmund turned to the junkie in the chair. Adam was barely awake, but seemed quite happy with life nonetheless. He was smiling, and drooling, and blinking a lot.

"He smells quite ripe, sir," Edmund said as he prepared to lift him up. Then he remembered how Suzy had smelled, how the intoxicating flowery scent of her body spray teased and enticed his olfactory sense, planting thoughts in his head of a decidedly lewd nature. And for the first time he believed he understood one of Whitman's favorite sayings: "Like a bunch of jigsaw puzzles spilled out together."

Whitman lifted Ally up like a groom carrying a bride across the threshold, while Edmund heaved Adam over his shoulder like a fireman saving a man from a burning building. Adam went, "Whoa," when Edmund turned around, and then mumbled, "Floor. There. What."

Ally, though dazed and barely conscious, draped her arms around Whitman's neck, and Whitman took the opportunity to breathe in the scent of her.

Edmund had a free hand so he leaned down some and opened the door. Standing there, ready to come in, were Holt and Vaughn.

"What's this?" Vaughn said.

"What is it?" said Whitman, who was standing partially behind the door and couldn't see.

"Who the hell are you and what are you doing with him?" Vaughn said as he edged his way into the room, forcing Edmund back a step. That's when he caught sight of Whitman on the periphery, holding Ally in his arms. "What the hell are you doing here?! he barked at him. Then he glimpsed Berto on the ground.

"Vaughn, this isn't what it looks like," Whitman said.

Holt had just come through the door, and he looked at Edmund first, then at Whitman, then at Vaughn. "What's going on here?" he said in general, leaving the question out there for anyone who wished to answer it. Then he saw Berto on the ground. "What happened to Berto? And Ally?"

"We came to see Adam," Whitman said as Edmund slid back another step, aligning himself with Whitman. Holt had aligned himself with Vaughn, giving the scene a standoff quality. "Ally let us in."

"What happened to her?" Vaughn said. Then he said, "Ally? Baby girl, you all right?"

Ally's head lifted off of Whitman's shoulder, and her glassy eyes fought for focus. "What?" she muttered. "Vaughn?"

"Berto knocked her over," Whitman said when he saw a fire light in Vaughn's eyes. "She's okay, but probably needs to lie down."

Berto was working himself to his feet with the help of the table and the wall, and Holt said to him, "Berto? You okay?"

"*Fine,*" he said, though he slurred the word and nearly fell over.

"Seems we have a problem here," Holt said to his guests. "This is my club, and you're not welcome here. I know I didn't invite you."

"We'll leave then," said Whitman, and started for the door.

"Not with her," said Vaughn. "She stays here."

"Him, too," said Holt, gesturing to Adam. "He's got a hot date later tonight."

"They're coming with us," said Whitman.

"The hell they are."

"You're leaving, they're staying," said Vaughn, putting some street in his tone, making it more of a threat than a statement.

"No," said Whitman, standing his ground. "Not going to happen."

"Yes it is," replied Holt evenly, and he pulled Adam's .38 Special from his belt. He aimed it at Edmund and said, "Put him down or I'll put you down."

Whitman's eyes went wide. "There's no need for a gun," he said.

The gun was pointed at Edmund, whose eyes were

considerably wider than Whitman's. But his eyes had been wide since Holt had walked in the room. "Sir," he said to Whitman. "Do you see it?"

Whitman looked at his friend. "See what?"

"*It*." Edmund said through clenched teeth, and he made a face that was meant to convey a very specific, very critical message. What that message was sailed over Whitman's head, though, and Edmund wasn't about to say anything aloud.

"You mean the gun," said Holt, showing it off, figuring that's what had the peculiar Brit so rankled. "It's not invisible, you know? I assume it shoots real bullets and everything. You're about to get a demonstration."

Already had one, thought Whitman, and with that exact gun. But he'd learned enough in his years to know that tempting fate was not unlike poking a bear with a stick: there really was no point in doing it.

Instead, he said, "She needs a couch to lie down on."

"She's out cold. She'll be just as comfortable on the floor," Holt said.

"Put her down here," said Vaughn, and he pulled out a chair for her.

"She can't sit there. She's ... "

Whitman had more to stay, but he found himself at a loss for words after seeing Edmund suddenly flail and collapse in front of him. Adam, who was slung over Edmund's shoulders, landed on top of him, driving him into the ground.

Holt started to laugh, as did Vaughn.

Berto, still a bit unsteady on his feet, said, "Wanna hit me? That's what you get." Then he grimaced and rubbed his hand, which had already started to thump with the flow of blood. "Bastard's got a jaw like a cinder block," he added.


Charlie Bates had money. He had always worked, he had always lived at home, and so he had accumulated quite a bank account. He would have been willing to give a chunk of that account to Suzy provided she continued to dance naked for him.

"You know," she whispered in his ear, mindful to brush her hair against his face and every-so-softly touch her lips to his cheek, "we could go backstage, to the private rooms. A hundred dollars for a half hour." Then, as added incentive, she traced her hand from his chest to his lap, gave him a good squeeze, and added, "It's worth it."

Charlie had been sporting an erection for twenty minutes now, pretty much since Suzy had started dancing for him, and the touch of her hand sent him over the edge. He jerked in his seat, then jerked again, struggling to stop himself from shooting off. He would have had better luck stopping a charging bull with a stern look. And so for the second time in his life, Charlie Bates came in his pants in a strip club.

Suzy felt the undeniable release – this was not the first time she had caused something like this to happen – but did not recoil. Instead, she tightened her grip and moved her hand up and down to help finish him off.

"Wow," she said to him as his face turned beet red with shame. "How about that."

"Sorry," he muttered, totally embarrassed. A large stain began to bleed through his pants. "I ... I was ... "

"It's all right," she told him. "Happens all the time. I take it as a compliment."

"Really?"

She smiled at him, knowing he needed reassurance more than anything else, and also knowing that with a little encouragement she could reel him in for a really big score. "Of course. Why wouldn't I? The question is, can I do it again."

"Do what again?"

"Whadda you think?"

Charlie Bates was horribly embarrassed, but also intrigued. It had been ages since he'd been with a real woman, and though he had always prided himself on the fact that he had never paid for it, he was beginning to wonder if that was something he should rethink.

Pride was a sin, anyway, whispered a little voice in his head, and Charlie agreed. Besides, not only had it been a really long time since he'd been with a woman, he had never been with a woman that looked like Suzy. Sure, she was a stripper, and technically they weren't together, but those points fell to the shadows in the glow of Suzy's nakedness. She was nice, and sweet, and what was he saving his money for anyway?

"A hundred dollars?" he asked her.

"A hundred dollars for half an hour."

"In private?"

"In our own booth," she said to him. "Just me and you."

"And ... " He was fishing, trying to find out what was included beyond the velvet ropes.

Suzy had played this game before, many times, and knew exactly what to say. "And I dance for you, naked. Uninhibited. You can't touch me, unless I ask you to, but I can touch you as much as I want, and any way I want."

"You ... " This time there was nothing shrewd about Charlie's incomplete sentence; the mere thought of Suzy dancing naked and touching him paralyzed his tongue and brought to a grinding halt the fragile clockwork of his mind.

"I touch you," she said, and she said it in an undeniably sensual way, not just saying it but telling him that she *was* going to touch him, touch him all over. Then she pulled back, traced a delicate finger around one of her nipples, and added, "It's worth it. Trust me." She leaned back into him again, pressed her lips to his ear. "Come on," she told him. "I want to see if I can get you to pop again. I want to feel it. Please."

There was a purr in her voice, and Charlie felt himself stirring again. It was at that very moment a familiar voice called out behind him. "Well, well, well, if it isn't Charles Bates," the voice said, and then another familiar voice, deeper in tone, added, "A more suspicious man might be suspicious seeing you here."

Suzy stopped her seduction and stared at the two men, thinking that they looked like cops. Charlie turned and looked over his shoulder, where he was greeted with a friendly wink and wave from Detective Rainer.

"Hello, Charlie," Detective Milner said. "What brings you here this fine day?"

"Uhhh. Nothing."

"Nothing?" Milner threw a glance Suzy's way, and through no fault of his own that glance lingered, becoming more of a leer. Finally, he said, "Looks like something to me."

Charlie had a sticky mess in his pants and a swirling vortex of unintelligible words in his head. The resulting expression on his face would have swayed any jury in America to come back with a guilty verdict.

Suzy bent down demurely and began picking up her lingerie, gathering it up like a little girl gathering flowers in a field.

"Don't get dressed on our account," Rainer told her. "You look just fine."

She fixed him with a coquettish smile and said, "Thank you."

"You're welcome."

Milner laid a hand on Charlie Bates's shoulder and said, "What do you say we have a little chat, Charlie. Got a couple questions for you."

Charlie nodded, said, "Of course. Have a seat."

"No, not here. At the bar."

"Excuse me," Suzy said. "I have a set coming up." She didn't have a set coming up, but she now believed that she had been right about Milner and Rainer being cops; they looked like cops, talked like cops, acted like cops, and she was in no way a fan of the police. Like most denizens of the seedy underbelly, Suzy avoided the law whenever possible, and with their attention focused solely on Charlie Bates she wasted little time dashing off and disappearing backstage.

"Sweet girl," Rainer noted as Charlie carefully got out of his seat. It was dark in the club so he didn't think the stain on his crotch would show, but he draped a hand down there all the same. He then followed detectives Rainer and Milner to the bar, walking somewhat crookedly.



Edmund leveraged Adam, who was still flying high on the wings of heroin, off of him and rolled over. He looked up at the towering beast that was Berto and said to him, in a voice full of surprise and disbelief, "You hit me." He rubbed his chin where Berto's fist had struck, then looked at his friend Whitman and said, in almost the exact same voice, "He hit me."

"I saw," Whitman replied. "Are you all right?"

Then something happened that had Berto, Vaughn and Holt shaking their heads. The gangly Brit in the vintage wool suit stood up, on steady legs, his eyes clear and focused, and brushed himself off. Berto was used to hitting people and having them lie at his feet for ten or twelve minutes, blood slowly leaking out of them; what he wasn't used to was a skinny Brit getting right up and giving him a questioning look. And dammit, he mused, his hand really, really hurt.

"You need to put her down," Vaughn said to Whitman after everything had settled. "Not going to tell you again."

Whitman did not want to put Ally down, not in this room, but the odds were three on two against them, and one of those three had a gun. Then Berto pulled a gun, too, and Whitman saw no other option.

"She should see a doctor," Whitman said, and the next words out of his mouth, had he not caught himself, would have been, 'She's pregnant.' But he did catch himself, just in time, and instead went with, "She took a nasty fall and might have a concussion."

"Noted," said Holt, boldly brandishing the .38 Special his guys had commandeered from Adam. "Now put her down."

Whitman made his way to the chair Vaughn had pulled out and very carefully set Ally on it, making certain she was secure. Then he tenderly ran a hand through her hair and in soft tones called for her attention. "Ally? Hey, can you hear me? Ally?"

It was then that Vaughn finally had enough. This was his domain – his work, his friends, his girl – and, by extension, his reputation on the line. It was one thing for this guy to come here and see Ally, it was another thing completely for him to stroke her hair and whisper to her like a lover. That he would not stand for.

And so with Whitman crouched at Ally's side in a vulnerable position, Vaughn bulked up and made a move. He grabbed Whitman roughly, one hand under his arm, the other around his throat, and ran him two or three steps. Then, using his momentum, he shoved him the rest of the way across the room. Whitman slammed into the wall and crumbled to the ground, and Edmund cried out, "Whit," and rushed to his aide.

Vaughn stabbed a finger in Whitman's direction and said, "That's my girl. Mine! You're lucky I don't break your fucking face open!"

"Gees," said Whitman as he worked himself to a seated position on the floor, Edmund kneeling at his side, doting over him like a nervous mother. "What's your problem?"

"My problem?! My problem?!" Vaughn was irate. The muscles in his neck stood out like cords of wire. "You're wearing my fucking clothes! You're holding my girl, talking to her like she's your girl! And you want to know what my problem is?!"

The umbrage in his tone was undeniable, and Whitman, morally speaking, had not a leg to stand on. Vaughn might have considered Ally his girl, but it was her and Whitman, not Vaughn, who had just made love out in the parking lot, going at each other with full-blooded passion that neither could hold back ... not even with Alina in Ally's head, screaming at her to stop. It had been amazing, for both of them, a volatile and beautiful mix of love and lust, and it had left Whitman a changed man.

"She's not your girl," he said defiantly, his voice strong and without doubt. "She's her own woman. And she's with me!"

"Excuse me?!" Vaughn replied. "Who the hell do you think you are?!"

Holt chuckled and said to Whitman, "Easy there, kid, he'll take you apart."

Whitman tried to stand, but Edmund subtly held him down. The gawky Brit then leaned in and whispered something in Whitman's ear, and Whitman immediately recoiled. He glanced at Holt, narrowed his eyes on him, then said to Edmund, "Are you sure?"

"Absolutely, sir."

"Well that certainly explains a few things."

"I know. Yet another unexpected wrinkle, sir."

"This just keeps getting more and more bizarre."

"My sentiments exactly."

"What are you two idiots babbling about?" Holt demanded, knowing full well they were talking about him.

"Nothing," said Edmund guiltily, and Whitman shook his head in agreement.

"What does it matter?" piped Vaughn. "They're leaving. Either on their own or with help."

Berto's massive chest and shoulders shook with a laugh. "Now we're talking. I vote that we help them. I like helping people leave."

"Me, too." Vaughn looked around the room and noticed a two-foot length of steel pipe on the shelf behind him. He went for it, and hefted it in a way that suggested he was more than comfortable swinging it.

"Ought oh," said Holt, a smirk cutting across his face. "You boys are in trouble now. Should've left when you had the chance."

Whitman sprung to his feet, and he and Edmund stood shoulder to shoulder against the far wall. Vaughn stepped forward, closing the distance on them, while Berto slid to the left, looking for a better angle of attack.

"Looks like things are about to get interesting," said Holt, he too edging closer, Adam's .38 Special leading the way.

Edmund glared at Holt, then, acting on a whim, he spoke to Whitman without saying a word. His prim British voice echoed in Whitman's head, and Whitman glanced his way and gave him a nod of recognition.

And that's when the lights went out.


The fight was on, and madness ensued in the uncertainty of the dark. Shot were fired, sparking off in the pitch black like bursts of fireworks. One shot from the left, then two from the right, then two more from the left. The noise was deafening in the small block room. The gun flashes showed glimpses of motion, but the flashes were so brief that it was impossible to tell who was moving or what they were doing.

Someone screamed, and then someone cried out, "Fuck!"

There was another round of gunshots – two, three, four in a row – followed by the sound of a body hitting the floor. And then there were no more gunshots.

"Stop! Stop! Stop!" Vaughn cried out. And for a moment the chaos came to a halt.

The lights came on, and Vaughn saw Edmund standing in front of him. Then he saw a blur, and just before everything went black he felt himself falling.

Edmund looked around the room at the carnage. Berto was laying face first on the floor, unconscious, blood oozing out of him. Vaughn was out cold, too, though he was lying flat on his back. Holt was awake but badly injured; he was whimpering and rocking back and forth, squeezing his hands around the gunshot wound he'd suffered to the knee.

Ally was curled up in a ball in the corner, and shielding her, either by accident or an act of genuine heroism, was Adam Dubinsky. Lastly, Edmund saw his boss, Whitman. He was sprawled out underneath the table, not far from Adam and Ally, his body twisted in an odd position. There was a thick pool of blood around him, and he was gasping for breath.

"Sir!" Edmund cried out, and rushed to his side.

Whitman looked up at him and grimaced. There was blood on his lips, blood in his teeth. "Edmund," he said, and his grimace morphed into a smile.

"Don't worry, sir, I'll get you help."

"No time for that, Edmund. There's work to be done. You have to do it."

"But, sir."

Whitman coughed and spit up blood. "I ... I'm going ... " Those were the last words he managed to say before death stole him, leaving behind the corpse of Martin Loomis.

"Sir?!" Edmund cried out frantically. "Sir? You can't die. Please, sir." He tapped his boss on the cheek a couple times, as if trying to rouse a passed out drunk. Whitman didn't respond, and when it was obvious that he was dead, Edmund hung his head and moaned.

"Hey! Hey! I think I need some help over here."

It was Adam, and he sounded desperate. Edmund looked over his shoulder and saw, through teary eyes, that Ally was unconscious and bleeding.

"I think she was shot," Adam said. There was blood on his shirt and on his hands. He was truly terrified, and hoping Edmund would know what to do.

The prim and proper Brit had never thrived under pressure before, not in his real life, not through the trials of Purgatory, and not during his time as a novice Custodian. But Whitman was dead and Ally was in dire need of help. Beyond that, he had a serious task to perform on Holt, one he could not ignore or forsake.

Lives hung in the balance, and he needed to act fast. With sudden determination, he hurried over to Ally to make sure she was still alive. From what he could tell she had been shot in the shoulder; the wound didn't appear life-threatening, but given that she was pregnant he wasn't about to assume anything.

"You need to get her out of here," Edmund told Adam. "She needs medical attention."

"Me?" Adam said. "How?"

"Carry her."

"But ... "

"You can do it. You have to do it."

"What about you?"

"There's something I need to do."

"What? What do you need to do?"

"Don't worry about it. Now come on. Here, let me help you."

Edmund helped Adam lift Ally's limp body from the floor, and though Adam was junkie thin, weak from detox, and still a little high from the heroin, he somehow found the strength to hold her weight and walk. Edmund told him to get her upstairs and call for help, and Adam nodded and staggered out of the room.

"What about me?" Holt gasped, his face wrenched in agony. "I need a doctor, too." His knee was destroyed, and he was bleeding from the arm. The .38 Special was lying at his side, the barrel still smoking. "I need help."

"I know," said Edmund, and made his way over there.

Being a Custodian, he possessed an intrinsic knowledge of not only life and death, but also the vast supernatural web that enveloped them and bound everything together. Thus he knew exactly what to say and what to do. Like all things untried, there was an element of doubt to contend with. But Edmund would not allow that doubt time to grow; he pushed it right out of his head and got to work.

He knelt at Holt's side. The small town vice lord gazed at him, his eyes moist with tears, his cheeks pale and gaunt, his lips quivering. "I need a doctor! I need to go to the hospital," Holt sobbed. "Please. I'm in agony."

"In a minute," replied Edmund calmly, and then he reared back and provided Holt with some instant relief ... by knocking him out cold.

Now that Holt was unconscious, Edmund need only to lay on hands and chant prayers, and as he did this, with one hand on Holt's head, the other on Holt's heart, his lips quietly whispering esoteric Aramaic phrases, something evil began to thrash inside the helpless carapace of Albert Holt. And it continued to thrash as Edmund continued to solemnly and faithfully practice the ancient art of exorcism, until that something rose ghost-like out of the body and with a primal demon shriek perished.

It was over, and Edmund, exhausted from the effort, collapsed.

# Epilogue

Marty's death (which actually was Whitman's death) taught Ally that life was to be cherished and every day was a blessing. She had always known that, of course, but it wasn't until she lost someone she truly cared about that she could say she understood what it meant. Marty's death inspired her not only to go back to school and better her life, but also to have her baby. Seven months after she was released from the hospital for a gunshot wound to the chest, she returned to give birth to a happy, healthy baby girl. She named her Martina, but mostly called her Marti, in homage to the man who had saved her life.

It wasn't an easy road for her – being a responsible single mother is as difficult a path to walk as there is – but Ally worked her tail off and never complained. She finished school, found a good job, and even met a decent guy.

Whitman was by her side throughout, and though she could not see him, or hear him, there were times when she would have sworn on a stack of bibles that she felt his presence. It was so real, and it gave her great comfort.

Whitman was glad to have his old life back – his old body, too – though there were times when he couldn't stop himself from wondering what it would have been like to stay behind. He thought of Ally often, and remembered with great fondness the short amount of time they had spent together. He did not feel guilty for what had happened, and he would not have cared if they had sent him to Purgatory as punishment.

Under the circumstances, the Elders granted him full amnesty.

They wanted him to resume his old post and lead the Garrison, but Whitman was a changed man who no longer cared about the numbers. He believed he could best serve humankind as a regular Custodian, and he recommended that Emilia be promoted to boss. The Elders agreed by a two-to-one vote, and

Clay, both angry and embarrassed, asked to be transferred to another group shortly thereafter.

As for the case, which included the robbery at the A&P, the crime/suicide scene at Martin Loomis's apartment, and the shooting at the club, it really couldn't have been any more confounding. The police breeched the room when backup arrived and found a fantastic tableau, like something from a far-fetched Hollywood action movie. Albert Holt was there, shaking, sweating, looking pale as a ghost. He was crying about his knee, crying that he needed a doctor, and complaining that he was freezing inside. Robert Foster, known around town as Berto, was pronounced dead at the scene. He'd been shot in the leg, the bullet severing the femoral artery, draining him of blood in less than two minutes. Vaughn was alive, but his injuries were also severe. He had suffered a fractured skull when Edmund knocked him out, his head losing the battle with the concrete floor. The ensuing hemorrhage in his brain caused a stroke and robbed him of all movement on the left side of his body. These days he could be found at St. Clair Village, a long-term care facility specializing in cases like his. He could speak, but he had trouble forming thoughts and he slurred most of his words, making it a struggle for him to communicate. He possessed average strength and dexterity on his right side, which allowed him to feed and clean himself, but mostly he was at the mercy of others. He remembered nothing about the shootout at the club, and he never would.

The police also discovered the body of Martin Loomis. He, too, was pronounced dead at the scene, killed by multiple gunshots from Robert Foster's 9mm. The police weren't sure how Marty fit into the picture, but they were thrilled to finally have a body to go with all the blood and speculation. They suspected Marty of suspicious activity, but *suspicious activity* is not, in itself, a crime. Besides, he was dead, for certain this time, which made prosecution infinitely more difficult.

Charles Maurice Bates, meanwhile, was questioned and cleared of any wrongdoing. However, three months later, while still mourning the loss of his best friend, he was served with a restraining order from one Su Chin Wang, who felt his interest in her had become somewhat troubling. Up to that point she had taken more than a thousand dollars from him, picking his pocket night by night, song by song, never failing to leave him with a smile and stained pants. For Charlie, it was the best relationship he'd ever had with a woman, and he swore he'd win her back someday.

As for Adam, Ally said nothing about him being the one who had robbed the A&P Mart. She couldn't say why she didn't say anything to the police, but something told her not to. Marty had mentioned that he needed to help Adam, and Ally felt she should respect that. For his part, Adam agreed to go to rehab. He got himself clean, and presently was working as a janitor at the local YMCA.

And then there was the mysterious British man, whom the police did not find in the room with the others. Adam had sworn he was in there, but Adam was a known junkie, and though Milner and Rainer didn't push the issue, they suspected he was high that day. He had that twitchy look, and he smelled street-ripe, as if he hadn't come in contact with water or soap for the better part of a month.

But others remembered seeing the British fellow as well, including Ally, though her memories of Edmund were foggy at best. Suzy remembered him, as did Charlie Bates, who referred to him as an intelligent, refined young man on some sort of scavenger hunt. "What he was hunting at the strip club, I do not know," he told Milner and Rainer. They had a pretty good idea, though.

How the British chap fit into the confounding puzzle that was the Loomis case, Detectives Milner and Rainer hadn't a clue. The deeper they dug, the more rocks they turned over, the stranger things got ... and, it seemed to them, the further they moved away from anything even resembling common sense.

An APB was put out on the British man, his name listed only as Edmund, his address unknown, his statistics estimated at six-foot-two and a hundred and ninety pounds. He was considered a person of interest, not a suspect, and the police asked anyone with information to call the hotline.

No one ever did.

With a dearth of contradictory clues at their disposal, the police were left with only a couple of leads. The brass was far more concerned with the gun battle at Teasers, that being the more sensational and newsworthy crime, and put all their eggs in that basket.

The most weight fell on Albert Holt's shoulders. Ballistics confirmed that Holt had shot and killed Robert Foster with a .38 Special; his prints were found on the gun, there was gunpowder residue on his hands, and both Adam and Ally testified that he had brandished the gun and threatened to use it. He was arrested and charged with second degree murder. He was also considered an accomplice in the A&P Robbery, along with Robert Foster and Vaughn Middling, due to the fact that all three of their prints were found on the gun that had shot and nearly killed the man identified as Martin Loomis.

As is often the case with those recently exorcised, Holt had very few memories of the things he'd done under demonic influence, leaving him with very few memories of what had happened in the storage room, and, for that matter, what had happened the last nine or ten years of his life. The demon had been inside him for more than a decade, digging down so deep and pulling the strings so subtly that no one would have ever suspected it, least of all him. But It had taken him over, almost completely, and Its influence had reached out and afflicted all those in his orbit.

"That's how they operate," Tyrus told Edmund, who'd been pulled back into the spirit world shortly after exorcising the demon that had inhabited Albert Holt for the better part of a decade. "They find an abandoned soul, crawl inside, and take control. Freewill is compromised, and the demon spirit has a vessel."

The white-haired Elder sighed and shook his head. "We whisper in their ears, and they possess them. Not exactly a level playing field."

"No," said Edmund, "I suppose not."

"Like freewill and life aren't hard enough already."

"Ineffability, sir. I find it's difficult to explain."

Tyrus chuckled, and agreed.

Edmund had proven himself beyond a shadow of a doubt, earning raves from his fellow Custodians, especially from Whitman, who couldn't have been more proud. Even the Elders sung his praises. And why not? He had come through when the chips were down. He had saved lives and exorcised a powerful demon.

"It's all part of a bigger picture, isn't it?" Edmund said to Tyrus, speaking in the pensive tones of someone who has just realized there's so much more beneath the surface. "Fate? Freewill? Cosmic glitches? Ineffability?" Then he dusted off one of Whitman's favorite sayings: "Like a bunch of jigsaw puzzles spilled out together."

"Or, if you prefer," replied Tyrus, "a Jackson Pollock painting."

The End